PRAISE FOR BRIANNA LABUSKES

What Can't Be Seen

"The book's well-constructed plot matches its three-dimensional characters. Psychological-thriller fans will be eager for more."

—*Publishers Weekly*

A Familiar Sight

"A horrific brew for readers willing to immerse themselves in it."

—*Kirkus Reviews*

"A strong plot and unforgettable characters make this a winner. Labuskes is on a roll."

—*Publishers Weekly*

"*A Familiar Sight* has everything I crave in a thriller: a shocking, addictive female lead; unexpected twists that snapped off the page; and an ending that made me gasp out loud. I never saw it coming, but it was perfectly in sync with the razor-sharp balance between creepy and compelling that Labuskes carries throughout the novel. This is a one-sitting read."

—Jess Lourey, Amazon Charts bestselling author

Her Final Words

"Labuskes skillfully ratchets up the suspense. Readers will eagerly await her next."

—*Publishers Weekly*

"Labuskes offers an intense mystery with an excellent character in Lucy, who methodically uncovers layers of deceit while trusting no one."

—*Library Journal*

Girls of Glass

"Excellent . . . Readers who enjoy having their expectations upset will be richly rewarded."

—*Publishers Weekly* (starred review)

It Ends with Her

"Once in a while a character comes along who gets under your skin and refuses to let go. This is the case with Brianna Labuskes's Clarke Sinclair—a cantankerous, rebellious, and somehow endearingly likable FBI agent with a troubled past. I was immediately pulled into Clarke's broken, shadow-filled world and her quest for justice and redemption. A stunning thriller, *It Ends with Her* is not to be missed."

—Heather Gudenkauf, *New York Times* bestselling author

"*It Ends with Her* is a gritty, riveting roller-coaster ride of a book. Brianna Labuskes has created a layered, gripping story around a cast of characters that readers will cheer for. Her crisp prose and quick plot kept me reading with my heart in my throat. Highly recommended for fans of smart thrillers with captivating heroines."

—Nicole Baart, author of *Little Broken Things*

"An engrossing psychological thriller filled with twists and turns. I couldn't put it down! The characters were filled with emotional depth. An impressive debut!"

—Elizabeth Blackwell, author of *In the Shadow of Lakecrest*

THE

LIES

YOU

WROTE

OTHER TITLES BY BRIANNA LABUSKES

Dr. Gretchen White Novels

See It End

What Can't Be Seen

A Familiar Sight

Stand-Alone Novels

Her Final Words

Black Rock Bay

Girls of Glass

It Ends with Her

THE
LIES
YOU
WROTE

BRIANNA LABUSKES

Text copyright © 2023 by Brianna Labuskes

Published by Thomas & Mercer, Seattle

www.apub.com

Amazon, the Amazon logo, and Thomas & Mercer are trademarks of Amazon.com, Inc., or its affiliates.

ISBN-13: 9781662511363 (paperback)
ISBN-13: 9781662511356 (digital)

Cover design by Damon Freeman
Cover image: © Sahana M S / ArcAngel; © Cosmic_Design / Shutterstock

Printed in the United States of America

To all the linguists out there,
from an author who has a new and deep respect for how
hard your job is

CHAPTER ONE

RAISA

FBI forensic linguist Raisa Susanto tucked the twenties into her bra strap as the men gathered around her. They were eager for a show, and she would give them one.

She hopped off the desk where she'd been sitting cross-legged and walked over to the glass board that spanned most of the wall of the Seattle FBI field office's main room.

There was one sentence written there.

"The quick brown fox jumps over the lazy dog." Raisa grinned as she turned back to the group. Six G-men stood in a half circle around her, all of them watching this play out with varying levels of smugness and doubt.

As a forensic linguist, she was used to skepticism. These field agents didn't exactly like people they deemed paper pushers, let alone someone who promised she could name a suspect on a sentence or two alone.

Raisa didn't have any allies in the bureau who would go to bat for her, either. Because of how specialized her field was, the FBI lent her out to cases rather than stationing her in one region. Making friends— or even cultivating some friendly colleagues—required spending more than one investigation with the same people.

But Raisa had found ways to earn respect and earn it quickly. What she was about to do amounted to a parlor game that she would never have agreed to perform had there been another linguist in the room. She did have some shame, after all. While it might be a cheap ploy, though, it had about a hundred percent success rate in impressing laypeople.

Most of the time, she saved this particular trick for when she was working with a team and needed them to trust her without question. She wasn't working with these guys. In fact, she'd only stopped by the field office to wrap up some paperwork. But one of them had made some snide under-his-breath comment about her being a waste of space and Raisa wasn't one to back down from a chance to put him in his place.

She cracked her neck, scanning the group. The ability to read people quickly had been a survival mechanism back in foster care. After losing her parents to a car crash at the tender age of ten, Raisa had been dumped in enough broken homes to be able to tell in a single glance who posed a threat.

These men gathered around her now were as easy to understand as the sentence on the board.

There were six of them. Three wanted to be convinced; one was along for the ride; one was skeptical but wasn't going to be rude about it. And then there was the cocky one, who was staring at her with such contempt she started to wonder if he'd had a bad run-in with a linguist in his life.

She didn't even need to look at the board to know he was the one who'd written the sentence.

But what fun was a magic show without a little pizzazz?

"This was written by a male, of course," she started to a few snorts since that was the only option. Raisa was amused that none of them seemed to realize the real joke was that out of seven FBI agents, only one of them was a woman—and she was being forced to prove her own expertise to win their respect. "In his mid to late forties, educated at a

2

small, non-Ivy, liberal arts college. Northeast, probably, by both birth and schooling."

"Please, that could describe half the bureau," the cocky one said. Andrew Cabot, if she remembered correctly. Sometimes she longed for the days when she'd been a scrappy kid, able to simply throw hands at someone who had such an obvious problem with her.

"He majored in statistics or political science," Raisa continued, without acknowledging the interruption. "Not English. His coworkers might admire his work ethic, but he has few actual friends in the department."

That was her grown-up, professional-FBI-person version of a right hook. It was *nearly* as satisfying.

There were a few coughs at that and darting eyes, though, notably, no one looked at Cabot.

"How did you get all that?" one of the men asked, the one along for the ride.

"This is a common pangram, the one most people know if they know any," Raisa said, tapping the board. "A pangram is a sentence that uses all the letters in the alphabet. This one was popularized with the rise of computers, as it was often used as dummy text in code. But I don't think as many young people recognize it, which gave me his age. There's no period at the end, which an English major who was trying to show me up would have certainly included. Because I know he's an FBI agent, that left two probable majors. I suppose it could have been history as well, but I'm guessing it was poli-sci."

"And how do you know he wasn't Ivy League?"

"Because he would have used something esoteric rather than the most common pangram," Raisa said with a little shrug that she knew would annoy Cabot. "It might seem obscure to anyone who hasn't studied language, but it's pretty basic for us word nerds."

"Would you have been able to tell the gender if you didn't know it was one of us?"

"It's hard to guess what I would have been able to do." That got an approving nod from one of the guys. "But I would say yes. I asked that one of you write down whatever came to mind, and from that I'd be able to narrow down a pool of people to build a profile." She tapped the board again. "This was meant to trick me because the person thought it would give none of himself away. The same as using *lorem ipsum* as filler text. But every time we engage with words, we make choices. It was a *choice* to try to give nothing away."

"How does that tell you about the gender?"

"When I ask women to do this, they tend to write something that would test me, not humiliate me in front of a group of colleagues," Raisa said, direct but not rude. As was her brand. "Everything comes with context. If I had picked up a piece of paper out on the street with just this pangram, I wouldn't be able to tell much about the writer at all. But I didn't pick it up on the street. And in investigations, we usually have evidence to work with.

"That's where you all would come in. You give me the context." She shot them an over-innocent smile. "Isn't teamwork beautiful?"

When none of the men said anything, she clapped. "Okay, stakes have been laid. Who was it?"

The man next to Cabot nudged his shoulder, and the other men shuffled a bit awkwardly.

Raisa turned to one of the younger agents, who now stared at her with just a hint of awe. "How accurate was I?"

"Spot on," he said with an eager little lilt, then coughed and slid a glance toward Cabot.

"Bucknell, political science major," Cabot finally admitted to some good-natured slaps on the back. "Forty-seven years old."

"And the friends in the department?" Raisa asked sweetly. When the man next to Cabot grimaced, she plucked the twenties back out of her bra strap. "I'll take that as a yes. And I'll take these winnings, as well."

She slipped the cash into the back pocket of her jeans and then caught movement out of the corner of her eye.

FBI forensic psychologist Callum Kilkenny leaned in the doorway watching them all, wearing a tailored suit with a matching tie and belt and shoes. His dark hair was swept back, silver at the temples to give him a distinguished air.

Raisa hid both her surprise and a wince.

Like her, Kilkenny got farmed out to investigations across the country. He also had a troubling tendency to come across her in her more cringeworthy moments. This one wasn't particularly bad—not like the time he'd witnessed her actually crying after a sniper case had gone south. But Kilkenny would never bet on a parlor trick just to convince some G-men that he could do his job.

All of a sudden, she felt young and foolish, like she was a class clown who had been caught out by the school's cool principal.

She lifted a hand in an awkward hello as the men behind her dispersed.

Kilkenny tipped his head to the hallway, and Raisa followed. He didn't stop there, though, just kept walking until they got to a little auditorium with movie theater–esque rows where the Seattle agents held larger debriefings. It was empty, and they took two fold-out seats toward the back, one apart so that Raisa could face him, her leg drawn up under her.

"You're scaring me," she said without preamble. It was a weird greeting. They hadn't worked together in four months, though she'd seen him in passing at an airport in Wisconsin in June. They weren't friends and they weren't partners, but they were the odd ones out when it came to any task force they were lent to. When they got a case together, they tended to pair up.

He looked serious now, but she could never really tell with him. No matter how good anyone was at reading people, no one could read Callum Kilkenny. He was one of the best forensic psychologists working in the bureau, and he had walls that were several layers thick, made of pure concrete. They had been hard-earned.

"I heard you were here," he said.

"We just wrapped up a case down near the border of Oregon," Raisa said, even though she had no reason to explain herself to him. "A kidnapping."

"You got your man." It wasn't a question.

She had, of course. A family friend who had been close enough to be called "uncle" had kidnapped a seven-year-old girl, demanding a ridiculous sum for her safe return. He'd given them fourteen hours. Raisa had needed only ten. She'd been able to parse through past emails and texts the man had sent and match up three unusual misspellings. It had been enough to get a judge to sign a warrant to search his place.

At another time she might have humblebragged a bit, as agents did when trading war stories. But that *you got your man* grated on raw nerves so soon after the Scottsdale incident. Kilkenny must have heard about it, everyone in the bureau had—or so it seemed. Where Raisa had always had a hard time fitting in with all her new teams, in the two months since the botched case in Arizona, she'd started seeing more and more outright doubt.

It was probably what had prompted her to do the parlor trick, even more than Cabot's smug face.

Raisa had always been the girl with something to prove, but now it seemed crucial for her career that she could.

"Yeah, we did," was all Raisa ended up saying.

"Do you have any assignments next?" he asked.

"Paperwork," Raisa said. She was about seven cases behind in filing her reports to her boss. The overachiever in her, the one who had got her from poor foster kid to doctoral candidate, cringed at the thought. But she was one of two linguists who worked full time for the entire FBI. As long as the paperwork wasn't urgent for court cases, her boss tended to grant her some leniency.

"Can I show you something?" Kilkenny asked, but he was already pulling out his phone. He tapped at the screen a few times and then looked up. "I should warn you. It's graphic."

Raisa nearly rolled her eyes. She waved to the ceiling as if to encompass the building they were in. She might be a word nerd, but she was also an FBI agent—and, Scottsdale aside, a pretty good one. "I'm not exactly expecting a picture of a cute puppy here."

"Right," he said, with a half smile before handing over the phone. "It was filmed by the killer themselves."

"Jeez," she breathed out. Then she pressed play.

Two bodies lay on a bed, a man and woman, their hands nearly touching.

The video zoomed in on the *plink* of blood dripping from the oversaturated mattress onto the wooden floors. A fly buzzed into frame, landed on the man's hand. He was older, maybe in his sixties, with a paunch. He was still wearing his shoes, a distant part of her cataloged.

The woman was still wearing her heels as well, which meant they hadn't been asleep. The killer had likely set them up like this, dolls to stage instead of bodies landing where they fell.

Raisa swallowed against the sour taste in her mouth. She hadn't been lying—she was used to violent images. Despite the fact that she saw more hostage notes and death threats than victims, there were still times an investigation went sideways and she had to witness the cleanup. But watching this footage was different. This was a predator's gaze lingering lovingly on its downed prey.

The killer walked away from the bed, into an en suite bathroom, making sure to keep out of the mirror. No rookie mistakes here.

A blood-flecked straight razor sat in an otherwise empty tub.

Why the bathtub?

The question shook loose something that had been waiting in the wings of her memory. But before she could grab hold of it, the camera panned to a white wall with a black square painted dead center.

7

Then the video cut off.

Raisa exhaled and handed the phone back, as if the evil could soak into her skin if she held it too long.

"A content moderator at Flik named Delaney Moore pulled this video from the app about four hours ago," he said, repocketing his phone.

Flik. That was the latest, most popular social media app for teens— if her annual FBI handbook was to be believed.

"It's been authenticated?" She had to ask.

"Yes," Kilkenny said. "They found the bodies. The crime scene is about an hour drive from here. A small town near the Cascades."

With that, the memory shook fully loose.

Why the bathtub?

"Everly," Raisa murmured, closing her eyes. "It was in Everly."

Hello, tin-hatters, skeptics, and everyone just here for a distraction while you do your dishes. Welcome back to *Below the Surface*, the podcast that digs deeper than anyone else is willing to go on scandalous murders where not everything might be as it first appears. I'm your host, Jenna Shaw, and I'll be your captain on this good ship *Conspiracy Theory*. As a reminder, this season we're traveling all the way back to 1998, when a murder-suicide rocked the tiny rural town of Everly, Washington, on one sleepy evening in August. The victims: Timothy and Rebecca "Becks" Parker, two beloved professors at the local college. The killer, according to the sheriff: Alex Parker, their teenage son.

Last week we talked about how, on the surface, this story seems straightforward, if tragic. Alex Parker was a troubled boy. Though he was popular, a star football player, and a math genius—yes, an unusual combination—his temper was legendary. During his sophomore season, a game had to be stopped because he'd started a brawl on the field. What's more, he apparently used his position to corner cheerleaders after hours in the locker rooms. Not a great guy, our Alex.

But does he deserve to be remembered as a vicious killer? The jury is still out. Well, our jury is still out. Alex never actually got his day in court because of that oh-so-convenient suicide letter that doubled as a confession. His last words that doomed him to history books as a murderer.

This season, we're going to start plucking at the Parkers' secrets to find out if Alex really was the killer or if, as some suspect, he was the third victim all along.

Go ahead and subscribe, my friends, to make sure you don't miss any of the scandalous details.

CHAPTER TWO

RAISA

"A copycat of the Parker murder-suicide?" Raisa asked as she checked her phone to confirm what she suspected.

August 27. The twenty-fifth anniversary of the killings. She whistled, low and soft.

"So you do know the case," Kilkenny said.

"Every linguist worth their salt does," Raisa said, because that's why she thought he was here. But just in case he got the wrong impression, she quickly added, "Though not well, not every detail. Just the letter."

"Alex's letter."

It wasn't a question, but she nodded.

Two weeks before he'd killed his parents and then himself, Alex had written a graphic short story for his English class about a cannibalistic serial killer—in which he'd slipped a few times and used his own first name instead of the character's. It had been disturbing enough that the teacher had notified the school's counselor, Nora Williams, who had notified the principal and Child Protective Services.

Alex Parker had also left a last letter—a suicide-note-slash-confession.

To have two samples of writing from a violent offender created so close together was rare and interesting. Most students going through forensic linguist classes picked up a passing knowledge of the case just through how much it was referenced when talking about authorship. Raisa included it in her own guest lectures at universities and local police departments.

"But you don't know much else about the case?" Kilkenny asked.

"No. I remember . . . there were three sisters who were left alive?" Raisa said, though she couldn't swear that was correct.

"Isabel, Lana, and Larissa Parker, ages fifteen, twelve, and three," Kilkenny confirmed.

"I don't think I'd have been able to come up with those names with a gun to my head," Raisa admitted. "I'm not going to be much help to you, if my knowledge about the investigation is why you're here."

"No, I'm here for your expertise," Kilkenny said, and Raisa couldn't ignore the warmth blooming in her chest. It felt good to be trusted again. "We found some online posts that suggest there are more victims to come."

"So, not a one-and-done copycat?" she asked.

"I don't know," Kilkenny said, his brows pinched. "To me, the scene reads like a message instead of just a reproduction."

"A message saying . . . what?"

"I have no idea," Kilkenny said, with a slight laugh that didn't have any humor in it. "There's a task force being assembled. I'd like you on it."

Raisa chewed on one of her knuckles. It wasn't as if she were going to say no. If they could prevent another scene like the one on the video he'd just shown her, Raisa would put up with anything. That wasn't the problem. She tried to figure out a way to phrase the question she needed to ask without revealing how much the answer meant to her.

"Who's the agent in charge?"

If he thought the question odd, he didn't show it. "Oliver Sand."

Raisa relaxed. After Scottsdale, she'd had an AIC or two put up a fuss about her presence on a task force. She didn't want to be booted off the Everly one in front of Kilkenny.

But Sand had always been respectful and fair, and he often called her in before shit hit the fan instead of when it was too late, as other AICs did.

"He's already approved you."

She made a face. She clearly had not been as smooth or subtle as she'd hoped. Or maybe Kilkenny was really that good.

"If you're not already committed somewhere else," he said, as if he didn't have enough power to get her reassigned anyway.

"I have at least a week, maybe more." That would be enough, even if the investigation went longer. She liked getting a feel for what was going on at the site itself, but after that, she could work from her computer anywhere. "Are we headed out now? I have a go bag in my trunk." She paused. "Actually, we can take my car."

He hesitated, and she could see the memory of the one time they'd ever driven together flashing before his eyes. It had been during that serial-sniper investigation down in Georgia, and Raisa might have had a few close calls with other cars' bumpers. But anyone could seem like a bad driver in Atlanta traffic.

"You can come with me," he said.

Raisa groaned in faked despair. "I'm never living that down, am I?"

"I have no idea what you're talking about," he said, ever the diplomat. "I simply have more room in my SUV than your little sedan." He slid her a look. "And you can pay for gas with your winnings from that little show-and-tell with the field agents."

Instead of burying her face in her hands like she wanted to—she'd kind of hoped he would do her the kindness of pretending not to have witnessed that—she shot him a sly smile. *Fake it until you make it.*

"I was going to splurge on a nice bottle of Four Roses Small Batch Select," she said, as they headed toward the elevator. "What better way to get misogyny to work in my favor?"

"Do you do that often?"

"Only when I get a particular vibe from the guys," Raisa said, ignoring his wince at the word *vibe*. She got a very proper *vibe* from him and guessed he wasn't into modern lingo. They'd only ever texted about logistics, but he'd never used slang in either his writing or his conversation. He probably considered himself ancient. But while the silver in his dark hair and the wrinkles by his eyes told of a life lived, he couldn't be more than a year or two over forty.

She guessed.

They didn't often chat casually, their conversation mostly revolving around whatever case they were on.

The only personal detail she knew about him was the one thing the rest of the world did, and people only talked about that in whispers, if they dared mention it at all.

About a decade ago, Kilkenny had been hunting a serial killer in what had turned into a real cat-and-mouse cliché over the course of several years. In the end, the Alphabet Man had ended up targeting Kilkenny's wife, Shay. She'd disappeared one night, only for her body to be found four days later in the same manner as all the rest of the serial killer's victims.

It was *the* nightmare scenario for any FBI agent who worked on dangerous investigations, and Kilkenny had nearly destroyed himself catching the man after that. And, of course, he'd done it. Kilkenny gave off the impression that he could do anything, no matter how superhuman the feat. The conclusion of the hunt had become legendary around the bureau.

Kilkenny still wore his wedding ring, even now, ten years later.

Shamelessly, Raisa had looked up the details on Shay's case after the first time she and Kilkenny had worked together, but after only a few pages, it had felt like a violation of privacy, like she was craning her neck at a car wreck, so she'd put it away.

He never spoke about his wife or the serial killer, but she imagined that's why he never fully smiled.

When they got to the garage level, they stopped by the trunk of her beat-up sedan. Eight years ago, while still in school, she'd scraped up enough money to buy the hunk of junk, and she'd been unreasonably proud of it ever since. Just like she'd been proud of finishing high school and going to college despite the fact that the social workers in her life had told her she was dreaming too big.

Even as dusty and broken-down as it looked, her car was a reminder: she was Raisa Susanto, and she got shit done.

Raisa glanced at Kilkenny. Usually she could tell what people thought of her in an instant. But Kilkenny seemed too professional to let anything beyond collegial respect slip through. "Does everyone in your life think you're analyzing them constantly?"

Kilkenny was startled into a half smile. "Yes."

"Are you?"

"Most of the time," he admitted, humor laced into his voice. "Not all psychologists do. Most don't, probably. But I'm a profiler more than a psychologist."

"What's the difference?"

"The big picture for psychologists is healing," Kilkenny said. "Mine is predicting." He studied her for a second. "Do you see yourself as different than the academic linguists?"

"In more ways than one," Raisa said, hefting her bag over her shoulder. She looked down at her beat-up jeans and the T-shirt she wore under her blazer. "I was never the type to dress in tweed."

"No," he said softly. "I wouldn't think you would be. I also guess you have a bit more flexibility in your thinking than the average linguist."

"Nailed it, Doc," Raisa said, dumping her bag into the back of his SUV. "I always drove professors crazy. They said I wasn't rigid enough in my analyses. Paraphrasing, of course. But language is a movable feast, is it not?"

"I thought that was Paris."

"Paris, language, tomato, tamahto," Raisa said as she climbed into his passenger seat. "What do we know about the victims?"

A hint of a smile showed in the crinkles of his eyes. She narrowed her own. "What?"

"Most people I work with ask what we know about the killer first."

"That's what makes us special," she said, propping her feet on the dash. He shot her a look but didn't say anything. "Considering the significance of the rest of the scene, I'd imagine the victims were chosen as more than proxies for the Parkers."

"Proxies," he repeated approvingly, and she grinned.

"I listen to you sometimes. I even read your memos," she said. "Some serial killers pick their victims for their similarities to a particular person—most commonly in the looks department. So they act as a stand-in. But the couple in the video had to be twenty years older than the Parkers when they were murdered. And they didn't resemble them at all."

"Bob and Gina Balducci," he said. "Bob was a history teacher and the football coach for the past few decades. He retired in June at sixty-five. The team never had much of a record—they barely had enough players together any given year—but it gave the boys in town something to do after school and kept them out of trouble. Bob hosted a pancake breakfast twice a year, and the players made the food and served. He and Gina put on a party for the Fourth of July that everyone in town went to. That kind of couple."

"The wife was . . ."

"A bank teller at the tiny local branch of a family-owned, Washington-based bank," Kilkenny said. "She just turned sixty-four and moved to part-time recently. The local paper did a little write-up on the couple when Bob retired. They were going to do more traveling. Both went to school there, and neither had ever lived outside of Everly."

"Would they have crossed paths with the Parkers at college?"

"The Balduccis would have been just a little older than the Parkers at school," Kilkenny said. "But it was a small town."

"Right. They probably knew each other, in passing if not well." Raisa had only ever lived in cities, but she'd worked plenty of cases in places like Everly. Everyone knew each other's business, and no one could go to the grocery store without being stopped by at least three neighbors in the aisles.

The Fourth of July party tidbit was interesting, too. Had the Balduccis been putting it on for at least twenty-five years? Had the Parkers attended before they were killed? Was there some kind of connection between the couples beyond the obvious?

Paths like that were dangerous, and she always tried to keep herself from going down them. In a contained community like Everly, links and patterns were inevitable. The threat of confirmation bias in these types of cases was always looming, especially when it was at least copycat adjacent.

"Okay, so those are the victims," she said. "Thoughts on the killer?"

"The scene was deliberately shocking," Kilkenny said, as they headed north out of the city. It was mid–Sunday morning, so traffic wasn't as bad as it could be, but that was a low bar for Seattle's highways. "Something interesting to note, though, was that for all the blood involved, there's no sign of overkill. A slit throat was the only wound. No torture or sadism, from what I can tell from the video."

Raisa cocked her head. "I'd always thought of the Parker killings as brutal, but really it was the same with those, too, I think? It was all more visually shocking than anything else."

"Then there's another pattern," he said. "The tech team out there says the scene is clean. The killer was careful not to leave any evidence, and they felt confident enough to film a video after committing the crime."

"What do you make of that?"

"That this isn't their first kill," Kilkenny said, with grim certainty. "Even for someone who meticulously planned it all out, even for a psychopath, killing . . . it's different actually doing it. And the cold calculation you see in the Flik post, the fact that they felt comfortable spending that much time in the house without worrying about getting caught? It just doesn't look like a first-time killer to me."

"Maybe that means we'll be able to find their metaphorical fingerprints on another homicide case," Raisa suggested. "One where they were sloppier."

"We can hope," Kilkenny said. After a long pause, he added, "It's strange to me that an experienced killer would switch to copycat murders. There are different psychological drives going on there."

"Than with . . ." Raisa trailed off, not sure how to describe what she meant. Then she tried, "Original killings?"

Kilkenny tilted his head in agreement. "Copycat killers are all about putting distance between themselves and the murder. They can don a persona or a mask. They tend to be people who have hovered on the edge of violence, but could never cross over it as themselves. Copycat killings allow their brain to pretend it's not really them doing it."

"And you don't see that here."

"Not if I'm right and the person has killed before," Kilkenny said, not arrogant but confident. "They wouldn't need to hide behind a mask."

"Or they're a copycat fanatic," Raisa suggested. "They want to be a serial killer, but they can't shed that last vestige of their humanity, so they cross the country imitating famous murders."

"Except wouldn't we have heard about the victims by now?" Kilkenny asked. "I can't think of a single notable copycat killing in the past year or two, can you?"

"I can't say I pay attention to them," Raisa said. "But no, you're right. We probably would have been sent a memo if there was a copycat serial killer out there."

Kilkenny huffed out an amused breath. The FBI did like their memos.

Raisa ran through the video in her head, mentally fast-forwarding through the moments the camera had lingered on the victims. "The box on the wall. What was that?"

"Maybe a signature of some sort?" Kilkenny said. "There's still so much we don't know yet."

"Just that more victims are planned."

"And . . ." Kilkenny started, but then trailed off.

"And what?" Raisa asked, and when he hesitated again, she gave him a look. "You know I'm not going to drop it."

His mouth quirked up. "Well, this isn't official."

"Oh, wait, let me report you," Raisa teased.

"I tend to categorize serial killers into different personality groups," he said slowly. "This one has what I call the puppet-master personality. They want everyone to dance to their tune, to be in control at all times. It's a strength because they tend to be smart, the kind of person playing four-dimensional chess while the rest of us are trying to win at checkers. But it can also be used against them."

"What makes you think our killer is one of these puppet-master types?"

"The video," Kilkenny said simply. "He posted it to Flik for the sole reason of bringing in the FBI. He uploaded it under the 'murder' hashtag—which automatically flags the video for review. If he wanted the attention of the public, he wouldn't have announced the contents so blatantly."

"It could have easily gone viral if it had slipped through the moderators' filters," Raisa said.

"And if the video hadn't been on Flik, the content moderator—"

"Delaney Moore," Raisa interrupted, mostly just to cement the name in her memory.

"Right. Delaney wouldn't have traced the username back to message board posts that let us know there will be more victims coming," Kilkenny pointed out. "The Everly Sheriff Department would have had jurisdiction and the FBI would never have seen the case."

"They wanted the FBI there," Raisa realized. "Specifically the FBI."

Kilkenny tapped his wedding ring against the steering wheel, a reminder that he had plenty of experience with puppet-master-type serial killers. "Maybe not just the FBI in general."

Raisa finished his thought. "Maybe one of us in particular."

CHAPTER THREE

DELANEY

The Whidbey Island Rapist was the first unsub Delaney Moore ever identified, long before she knew what that portmanteau meant.

She'd just turned fifteen, and the internet had been in its infancy—or at least toddlerhood—back then, populated with basic message boards, forums, and chat rooms.

For Delaney, they'd opened up a whole new world.

She'd learned quickly what words older men used when they preyed on younger girls, what phrases they trotted out when trying to pretend to be cool college-aged bad boys rather than the sad fiftysomethings they were in real life. *Can you keep a secret?* they asked her, time and again.

But she'd also learned slang, learned how it could sound lead-heavy in the wrong voice, clunky and obvious. She learned she could tell the age of a person from their pop culture references or punctuation use, the location of a person by what they called a water fountain or soda. The gender of a person by how they talked about women.

She learned how to find the patterns. She began to read sentences as if they were fingerprints, the construction of each as distinct as the whorls on skin.

One phrase might not tell her too much, but post after post, long chat messages, a history of writing and writing and writing for anyone out there to read, that all created an identifiable voice she could pick out in a crowd. Even when she heard it out of context.

With that first tip, she hadn't realized she should stay anonymous. She'd walked to the police station after school. The nice lady at the desk in the lobby had given her two Oreos and lukewarm water-based hot chocolate that Delaney hadn't been able to make herself drink. She'd dumped it into the fake plastic plant near her chair and started on her homework for the one hour and fifteen minutes the detectives had kept her waiting.

Delaney had gone to the library the day before to print off the messages from the forum she'd gotten herself invited into pretending to be a man named Joseph Ferguson, age forty-two, with a penchant for girls who'd just hit puberty. She had the language to use, after all, phrases in a tool kit that was ever expanding.

One thing she'd discovered in that forum was how small the deviants' world was. It had been almost comically easy as Joseph Ferguson to find the man who said his ex-cellmate had bragged about sleeping with one of the Whidbey Island Rapist's victims.

That's how these predators signaled who they were. They never said they'd actually done it. Not the smart ones. But they attached themselves to the periphery of the crime.

The two detectives had humored Delaney at first.

And then she'd given them a name. Seth Buckley, of Anacortes. He'd worked in construction, but had been laid off six months earlier. It was why he had escalated to a victim a week, where before it had been only one every month or so.

That's when more men had come into the room, looming over Delaney, asking for her full name, a contact number for her parents, asking for her internet history.

Did she know this man? Did she have contact with him? Was she his girlfriend-slash-accomplice who had gotten cold feet? How could she, a fifteen-year-old-kid, have solved a mystery that had stumped the FBI task force?

She didn't think they'd appreciated her answer, which had leaned heavily on the implication that maybe they were all too dumb to navigate their way out of a paper bag, let alone catch a rapist. But finding patterns had always been a lot easier for her than getting people to like her.

Delaney had received her lowest grade ever on her history paper the next day because she hadn't had time to study that night. Her parents had also made sure to install some sort of locking and monitoring system on their family PC.

From then on, Delaney kept her tips anonymous.

The truth was, she wasn't seeking out crimes, not really. That came with the territory of plundering the internet's darkest corners.

It wasn't a *what* that she was looking for with these searches.

It was a *who*.

CHAPTER FOUR

Raisa

"There's a file in the back," Kilkenny said, as he took the exit toward Everly. They still had a good half hour before they got to the remote town, but the rest of the drive would be rural roads. "On the Parker murder-suicide."

Raisa twisted to find his briefcase tucked neatly behind his seat, and it didn't take long to dig out the folder. "Thin."

"The sheriff closed the case after twenty-four hours," Kilkenny said, a grim set to his mouth.

"Samantha Mason," Raisa read.

"She's still there," Kilkenny said. "She's our local lead on this investigation."

Mason would have been relatively young at the time, and a woman to boot. "She must have had strong local support."

"Close friends with the Parkers, who seemed to have been Everly's version of royalty." He jerked his chin toward the folder. "I haven't gotten a chance to go through the file thoroughly. Can you read it out loud?"

"On the evening of August 27, 1998, Alex Parker drugged and then killed his parents," Raisa summarized the first few paragraphs of the report. "Time of death, between 6:30 and 7:15 p.m." She paused, looked up. "Our copycat changed the timing."

"Logistics?" Kilkenny suggested. "It was when they could manage the killings?"

"Yeah, maybe," she said. "That's a narrow window for TOD on the Parker case."

"Because the girls came home."

"Isabel, Lana, and Larissa," she said, trying to imagine stumbling onto that scene as a fifteen-year-old. As a twelve-year-old. At least the toddler had probably been spared the trauma. "Why didn't Alex kill them, too? What's that called again? When they kill them all? I'm blanking."

"Family annihilation," Kilkenny filled in.

"And in those cases it's usually the dad who does it, right?" Raisa asked.

"Yeah, and Tim Parker fits the mold," Kilkenny said. "In ninety-five percent of cases, the annihilator is what you would call 'head of the household.' He's a middle-aged man, a good provider who is looked at by neighbors as a loving father and husband. Their killings can be the result of mental illness—and Tim was showing signs of schizophrenia."

"But you can't cut your own throat," Raisa said, stating the obvious. "So, what about teenagers killing their families?"

"Alex Parker fits pretty closely with what you would expect to see in those types of cases, too," Kilkenny said. "They're usually male, have a history of friction with their parents, and about fifty percent of them signal ahead of time what they're going to do. That's rarely the case with the adult annihilators."

"Alex's story."

"Yeah," Kilkenny said. "But he deviates in some specific ways that are interesting. About seventy-five percent are shootings, most kill all of the family members instead of just the parents. And . . ."

"And?" Raisa prompted.

"The big one," Kilkenny said. "None of the cases I've seen in research have ended in suicide."

"What?"

"Adult annihilators almost always kill themselves, but the teenagers almost never do," he said.

She blew out a breath. "What do you think that means?"

"Anomalies exist," Kilkenny said. "What else could it mean?"

Raisa didn't answer, because what she thought that could mean wasn't possible. She wasn't living out some conspiracy theory—Alex Parker was the one who had killed his parents. Dozens of linguists over the past twenty-five years had proved that without a doubt.

So she focused on more important things. "The girls were at a friend of the family's house. They got home at a quarter past seven and immediately called the sheriff on their home line."

"And there's a record of that?"

"Yup," Raisa said. "Christine Keller, the family friend, said the girls left around seven, two hours after they got to her house."

"It's strange he didn't lie in wait for them," Kilkenny said. "He could have just drugged them all if he was worried about controlling so many people."

He was right, of course.

"Both Tim and Becks had about a hundred milligrams of Ambien in their system," she said. "That's nowhere near lethal, but the standard dose is five to ten milligrams. So he could have used some of that on the girls, who would have required far less to become malleable."

"Now that we're talking about it, the drugging does strike me as strange," he pointed out.

"Yeah, it doesn't look like a kid with homicidal intent snapping," Raisa agreed. "But you said teenage family annihilators plan it."

"Family annihilators are only annihilators when they kill their whole families," Kilkenny said. "Alex Parker is just a murderer."

"A murderer whose kills were premeditated," Raisa said. For some reason, she'd always pictured the scene as incendiary—Tim or Becks saying something that pissed Alex off, Alex grabbing a knife. But now that she really focused and thought about it, of course that didn't make sense. Tim and Becks were even posed on the bed.

Kilkenny made a thoughtful sound. "Maybe he had originally planned on killing the girls when they got home, but after actually going through with murdering his parents, he couldn't do it. Were the girls interviewed?"

"Only Isabel gave a statement," Raisa said. "Lana Parker didn't say anything, and the baby—"

"Couldn't," Kilkenny said, a hint of amusement in his voice. "Fair enough. Anything of interest from Isabel?"

"Just recounting what we already know," Raisa said after skimming the short transcript. "There are only two other interviews in here. One from Christine Keller, and one from Shawn Dallinger, the oldest daughter's boyfriend."

"Two interviews? For the whole case?"

Raisa raised her brows. She didn't like to Monday morning quarterback other law enforcement officers' cases, but that seemed strange at best. "I guess she thought it was all wrapped up? Like a school shooting?"

"You'd still do the investigation, though."

"You're not getting an argument out of me," Raisa said. "It's strange. Maybe she was trying to protect the girls? They must have been fairly traumatized as it was."

Raisa spared a moment to hope the girls had ended up in good situations. But she knew better than anyone how the foster system in the country worked. At least she'd had ten happy years with her parents before they'd died. She wasn't sure yet she could say the same for the Parker sisters.

"Where'd they end up?" Kilkenny asked, all but reading her thoughts.

"I don't actually know," Raisa said. "I do think they were separated, but the records are sealed. Sand probably already has a request in to a judge."

"I wonder if we'll get the warrant in time to be helpful," Kilkenny said. "It's a weekend, and you know how hard papers like that are to get."

"Debbie Downer," Raisa joked.

He squinted over at her suspiciously. "How'd you know my middle name?"

The deadpan delivery surprised a laugh out of Raisa. "It's on my birth certificate, too."

Kilkenny half smirked, and Raisa turned her attention to the photos in the file.

They were gruesome but, as she'd thought earlier, nothing compared to watching a video of a killer lingering over his downed victims. These were stark, cold, and thus more palatable. At least slightly.

The crime scenes were strikingly similar. That didn't necessarily raise any alarm bells, though. This case was famous and old enough that she was fairly certain a motivated copycat killer could get their hands on these pictures. Still, the person had an eye for details.

The Parkers' shoes were still on. The bodies were positioned the same as with the new killings.

Raisa turned the page and inhaled sharply.

Kilkenny shot her a look. "What?"

"They tracked down where Alex Parker got the Ambien for that night," she said, staring at one of the last photos. It was a prescription bottle, the name on it highlighted.

"Let me guess," Kilkenny said, clearly reading the answer in her shocked expression. "The Balduccis' medicine cabinet."

She held up the file, Gina Balducci's name in dark, damning letters. "Got it in one."

EXCERPT FROM BECKS PARKER'S DIARY

August 1, 1998

Tim was back to his old self tonight. I nearly wept with relief, but we had a house full of party guests and I had no interest in reapplying my mascara. There was a bit of mania in his voice as he walked everyone through the proof that was the cause for celebration, but who can blame him? This objectively and without doubt proves he's the better mathematician out of the two of us. I think that's all he's ever wanted in life.

Was it why he married me in the first place? Why he gave me not one but four children to keep me distracted? I was working with two hands tied behind my back, while he got to stretch and flex that brilliant brain, unencumbered by the demands of domesticity.

That's neither here nor there, though. I've long ago made peace with the fact that I love a man that is flawed because of a mind that I had thought was perfection itself.

I started this journal when I first noticed the signs, the ones we'd seen with his mother. Back then, they called it genius and let her be. Writing all this down, recording Tim's moods for each day, well, it makes me more attuned to everyone else around me. To our children, that I'm starting to fear we've neglected, too often paying attention to their intellectual gifts and not them as whole, fully realized people.

Isabel and Lana are growing up to be beautiful girls. Isabel hardly talks to me anymore, but she was always her father's child more than mine. And at fifteen, she's firmly in her terrible teenage rebellion stage. I try to leave her be, though I'm not sure that's the right path. Lana is on the cusp of all that. At twelve, she's still my sweet girl, my little mini-me, but her tantrums these days are less of the childish variety and more of the hormonal kind. There are a lot of slamming doors in our house, and it's no longer just Tim making the noise.

At three years old, Larissa is starting to develop a personality, finally. I never liked the baby-blob stage, though, of course, I pretended to. I glowed with each of my four infants as if they weren't just strange creatures I was suddenly tasked with keeping alive. Tim had never been any help in that stage. He only liked them when they started showing hints of genius, as both Isabel and Alex had done by age four.

And Alex, oh, my Alex. My only boy, who used to move frogs out of the path so they didn't get crunched by bicycles. My Alex.

I started this journal to track the signs of schizophrenia for Tim. I love that it has made me notice my children once again. I hate that it has made me notice my children once again.

Because I can see a monster prowling behind Alex's eyes now. Alex hides him well, with a careful mask, but I have always been good at seeing monsters.

If I mentioned my concerns to Tim, he would just brush me off. Alex is his pride and joy, the boy who will carry on the Parker name into math textbooks even when the world forgets the two of us.

Tim would say Alex was just being a normal, moody sixteen-year-old boy. He would say I'm the paranoid one.

Maybe I am wrong.

I hope I am wrong.

CHAPTER FIVE

RAISA

Washington's flat coastline extended inward for fifty miles before the earth rose up, sudden and jagged, toward the sky. That's where Everly sat, at the mouth of North Cascades National Park, one of the more remote destinations in the country. Though it still drew plenty of tourists, it boasted only one hotel—a stout building with single-room cabins in the back of the property facing undeveloped woods. The Skagit River curved a lazy arc around the town, its turquoise water eerily beautiful.

Everly itself was tiny, with a main street that included one gas station, one BBQ-restaurant-slash-bar, one corner store, and a handful of knickknack shops. American flags hung limply off the streetlamps, and Raisa wondered if they were leftovers from the Fourth last month or if they served as decoration all year long. The sheriff's department was at the end of the block, forming a tee with the road, and had a large mural painted on the side of smiling children holding hands.

"Do you think our copycat killer is using the case file as a victims list?" Raisa asked Kilkenny as they drove by the one-story building.

"Maybe just anyone connected to the Parkers," he said. "Which apparently the Balduccis were."

"Although we don't know they were connected. Maybe Alex just saw an opportunity at some point," Raisa pointed out. "What if at that big Fourth of July party the Balduccis hadn't locked up their medicine cabinet? Maybe she had a bunch of Ambien kicking around."

"Why kill them now then?" Kilkenny asked.

Neither of them had an answer.

"Tell me about the letter," he said after a beat of silence.

"It was a fairly standard suicide-slash-confession note," Raisa said, back in her element. While she certainly couldn't recite the thing word for word, she had used it as an anchor to a grad paper she'd written about the authorship of suicide letters. "The reason it's semifamous— for us linguist nerds, at least—was that only two weeks earlier, he'd turned in a short story that was several thousand words long. That kind of sample, so close together, for someone so young, makes it a standout case in our field."

"That's how the authorship was confirmed?"

"Yeah," Raisa said. "There were little things throughout to look for, but it provides a pretty textbook example."

"Little things like what?" he asked.

"Like he used contractions in his negative language, and not in his positive language," Raisa said, throwing out just one of the examples. "What that means is he would write 'don't' instead of 'do not,' but never 'I'm' for 'I am.' He also used ironic repetition."

"Should I know what that is?" Kilkenny asked, the self-deprecation laced liberally into his voice.

Raisa laughed. "No, sorry, I'm getting technical. Ironic repetition is when someone uses the same verb in concurrent sentences, but its meaning drastically changes. You see it in Shakespeare a bit: 'Yet she must die, else she'll betray more men. Put out the light, and then put out the light.'"

"*Othello*?" he guessed.

"Points to you." Raisa doffed an imaginary hat. "And with Alex's letter, it was: 'Don't grow anxious, you will be growing daisies soon.'"

"More poetic than I was expecting."

"Yeah, he had some interesting turns of phrase," Raisa admitted. "His grammar wasn't great, but he was a high school kid who was better at math and football, from all accounts. Anyway, all of that was enough to form an impression of his idiolect."

"That's something like a dialect, right?"

"Yeah." Raisa had a tendency to start lecturing once she got started, and she hoped he'd stop her when it was no longer interesting. "But more specific to each person. Even if you're not conscious of it, you use certain patterns in your writing, and you'll do it as consistently as someone calls a fizzy drink 'soda' or 'pop.' There was a case that was solved because the unsub used the phrase 'devil's strip' to mean the grass between the sidewalk and the street. They only do that in a small part of Ohio, and one of the suspects was from that same place."

"That's a lucky break."

"Isn't it?" Few of the cases she worked on were so obvious. Like Kilkenny and his profiles, her authorship analyses often had caveats attached. Sometimes everything came together just right, though. "Writing, specifically, gives us this voice that becomes more and more distinct with each sample you have. People dangle modifiers or embed clauses in strange places; they misspell the same word over and over, sometimes on purpose."

"Why would they do that?"

"To camouflage their intelligence level," Raisa said as they parked on the grass outside the hotel's entrance, the little lot already full of black SUVs. "So someone might spell 'can' with a *k* instead of a *c*. But it's hard to mimic a lower education level in writing consistently. You probably aren't going to misspell 'can' and then spell 'can't' correctly in the next sentence, you know?"

They grabbed their bags and headed toward the building.

"When we look at confessions to see if they were coerced—or even written by the police themselves—we look for cop speak as a big red flag," Raisa said. "Words that have become a natural part of a cop's idiolect, but would be weird to be used by normal people. It can be as subtle as 'at an unknown time.' But I've also seen 'confessions' where a teenager 'said' something like, 'traveling South on Main Street by foot.'"

Kilkenny grimaced.

"Right—no one actually talks that way in real life. But cops have such a distinct vocabulary and such an insular community that it becomes second nature," she said. "Anyway, like I said, it's all little things. You can track if a person uses 'that' as an extra word: 'I told my mom we were going to his house,' versus 'I told my mom that we were going to his house.' If you're comparing two samples and one uses 'that' frequently and one doesn't, you can reasonably assume they're two different writers. I mean . . . it's more complicated, but that's the gist."

Raisa took a breath after she realized she'd been speaking mostly interrupted for a significant stretch of time. She could all but see him remembering the scene he'd walked in on a couple of hours ago, her holding court in front of that whiteboard. She wondered if he was thinking about Scottsdale.

"You don't have to prove your worth to me," Kilkenny said gently, in a way that made her esophagus burn with something close to shame. They both stopped just inside the hotel, and Raisa could see two agents over at check-in. She hoped Kilkenny would let it go. "Is there any doubt that Alex Parker was the one who penned his last letter?"

"There's always doubt," Raisa said, with a shrug. "You know that, as a profiler. You can never be certain in our line of work. It's why those field agents are always suspicious of us."

"I'm not the press or a jury," Kilkenny said. "What do you actually think?"

"Then no. His letter is linguistically consistent with the short story he turned in that got CPS called on his family," Raisa said. "I think the murder-suicide was exactly what it looked like."

"Is that usual, to call in CPS over a fictional story?"

"He slipped and used his name instead of the main character's a few times. Same with the girls' names," Raisa said. "Maybe somewhere else it would have been overlooked, but I think he was exhibiting other red flags as well."

Before she could say anything more, the hotel receptionist waved them forward. There were two single cabins left, and they both opted for those instead of anything in the main building. Some agents liked to be as close as possible to whatever war room the FBI commandeered, but Raisa liked a little space to be able to think.

After dropping their bags in their cabins, they found the hotel's conference room, which was packed with FBI agents. Raisa scanned their faces, but they kind of blended together for her—all middle-aged dudes in black suits with close-cut hair. One or two looked vaguely familiar, but there wasn't anyone she knew by name.

The story of her life.

Raisa's attention snagged on the woman near the head of the table.

She wore her long brown hair in twin braids, and even sitting down, she seemed lanky, slim and tall. In a roomful of people wearing black, she was almost too colorful to look at, her sunflower-yellow dress paired with a turquoise vest. She wore a ring on every finger and several layers of necklaces.

All in all, she seemed like she'd wandered into the FBI war room after getting lost on her way to a crystals store and decided this was an interesting place to hang out.

"Delaney Moore," Kilkenny whispered from behind her. "The Flik content moderator who pulled the video."

"What's she doing here?" Raisa asked beneath her breath. Usually, once a moderator flagged a video for law enforcement, they would simply go back to their jobs.

"Sand brought her in as a consultant," Kilkenny said. "And Flik agreed to let her work for us for a few days. She has her own custom program that trawls through the dark web for usernames and IP addresses—digital footprints that could give us more information about the killer's online presence. Apparently, it's more effective than anything we have."

"Hmm. That's useful." And convenient for someone who wanted to get themselves on a task force.

As if she'd heard them talking about her, Delaney glanced up directly at Raisa. Her eyes were the same eerie blue color of the Skagit River, and Raisa had to look away, all the while ignoring the shiver of unease that raced along her skin.

Raisa turned her attention back to Agent in Charge Oliver Sand, who was going over the basics of the video.

"What's with the box on the wall?" one of the agents called out when Sand paused.

Delaney Moore's fingers flexed at the question. "It's called a tombstone," she said, and the room dropped silent. "It's a mathematical symbol, signifying the end of a proof."

"Couldn't it just be a box?" the agent asked.

Delaney stared at him for a long minute. "It could be."

"Except that the murders are staged to replicate those of two world-renowned mathematicians," Kilkenny offered.

"There is that," Delaney said neutrally.

"Has it been run through the databases?" Raisa asked. The one Raisa used the most was the FBI's Communicated Threat Assessment Database that legend Jim Fitzgerald had started.

"No previous known uses," Sand said.

Despite the fact that psychology wasn't her lane, Raisa couldn't deny that everything about this was, for lack of a better word, bizarre. Regardless of what modern media might portray, the FBI generally had a good sense of the serial killers operating in the US, even if they didn't actually know their names. There were usually fewer than one hundred active killers at any given time. One who had a signature? One who seemed to have a high level of expertise but for some reason was now concentrating their attention on a twenty-five-year-old murder-suicide? This wouldn't have just come out of the blue. They would have seen signs of him before.

She couldn't make sense of it. And judging by Kilkenny's slightly pinched brow—the most confusion he would ever show in public—she didn't think he was doing much better.

Raisa's attention slipped back to Delaney Moore. It was curious that she'd recognized the tombstone. Raisa wouldn't go so far as putting money on it, but she'd guess that none of the agents on the task force could have come up with that answer.

It wasn't . . . damning. Not even close. But that combined with the fact that Delaney had flagged the video in the first place and then made herself an invaluable asset to the task force? Raisa shied away from *suspicious* and settled back on the word *curious*.

"Agent Susanto?" Sand said in a way that made it clear he'd called her name more than once.

Raisa tried not to flush as everyone stared at her. "Yes?"

"You'll be working with Ms. Moore on the Infinity9 posts that she believes were written by the killer," he said. "You can identify linguistic patterns for her to run through her program. That should let us find any other usernames associated with the killer."

It would be almost like tracking down aliases, Raisa realized, just ones that were rooted online. That was a helpful little tool Delaney Moore had created.

Sand clapped his hands in his typical way of dismissing the room.

Kilkenny leaned in slightly. "Should I know what Infinity9 is?"

Raisa shifted to face him. "It's a message board that doesn't have any rules. It's a cesspool where serial rapists brag about their victims and pedophiles share porn, all under the guise of free speech. There are a lot of innocuous threads, but people go there so they're not constrained by the restrictions other sites have in place."

He seemed like he was about to say something, but then his gaze flicked over her shoulder. Raisa turned to find Delaney Moore standing too close to her, staring directly into her eyes. "I'm not a killer."

Raisa took a deliberate step back. "Okay."

"I know that's what you're wondering," Delaney continued.

It had just been a fleeting thought, really. But Raisa straightened her shoulders.

"You're a civilian insinuating yourself onto a task force investigating a crime you reported in the first place," Raisa said. From ten years old on, she'd essentially been raised on the streets. She didn't back down when confronted. "And you're the only one in this room who recognized the killer's signature. I'd be a poor agent if it didn't at least cross my mind."

Delaney's thick brows rose. "True."

Then she turned and walked back to get her things.

"Making friends," Kilkenny murmured.

"That was weird, right?" Raisa asked. She had a feeling that would become the go-to phrase this investigation. "I think I looked at her twice. How would she have come to the conclusion I thought she was a killer?"

"Did you?"

Raisa sputtered. "That's neither here nor there."

Kilkenny laughed softly. "You're not the hardest book to read."

"I'd like to think I can hide 'I think you're a serial killer' at the very least," Raisa said, only half joking.

"She seems oddly perceptive about some things," Kilkenny said, serious now, clearly reading Raisa's concern. Okay, so maybe she *was* too much of an open book. "And not others."

"That sounds like you've worked with her before," Raisa said, her attention sharpening.

He wore that indecipherable expression of his for a long time as he watched Delaney shove files into her leather messenger bag. Part of

Raisa wanted to take a crowbar to him, to crack him open and see all the thoughts he so carefully monitored. Part of her had her own carefully guarded secrets she would hate to have revealed.

"Your points are valid," he finally said. "About why you shouldn't trust her."

She heard the *but* there, so she nudged him. He looked down at her. She was pint-size—something she didn't like to admit when she spent so much time and energy trying to take up space—and he was on the taller side, so there was a long way to go between them.

"That was an odd choice for someone trying to fly below the radar," he said. "Approaching you, that is. Calling you out on your suspicions. If she were actually guilty, I'd have expected her to ingratiate herself with you, not confront it head on. And then she simply walked away as if it didn't matter. So, maybe the killer, maybe not."

"Probably not," Raisa said, and Kilkenny lifted a shoulder in agreement. Still, she joked, "But if she turns out to be the copycat killer, you're buying me that Four Roses."

CHAPTER SIX

DELANEY

Delaney met Noah Webb when she turned sixteen and started taking classes at the community college in Tacoma. Her parents had wanted her to enroll directly into Stanford when she finished all her high school requirements, but Delaney wasn't all that interested in their plan for her.

She had her own to consider.

And that mainly involved staying in the Pacific Northwest for as long as she could.

Delaney was still legally a child, though, so executing her own plan came at the price of compromise with her parents. If they let her graduate at eighteen—instead of early—she promised she would enroll in a college-level calculus class to develop her unused potential.

Potential. That was all her life had ever been about, her potential and all the ways she was wasting it.

It was important to her parents, though, so Delaney had done it. She needed a roof over her head until she was eighteen, after all.

Professor Noah Webb may as well have stepped out of one of the soap operas Delaney pretended were trash but actually loved. His golden hair fell into green eyes, his button-down strained over broad shoulders, his facial features perfectly aligned with the golden ratio. Mathematically, he was gorgeous.

Delaney blushed that first day, ducking her head even as she felt his attention on her. Unlike him, she was not mathematically gorgeous, her face and limbs all too long and too often likened to a string bean. Her hair was a dark brown that lightened strangely over the summer to end up some in-between color that was the worst of both worlds. She didn't have any of the traditional markers of femininity or fertility—no hips or breasts to speak of—and yet still he watched her.

By that point, she was familiar with predators. She knew the type of men who gravitated toward young women, age making up for a whole host of other characteristics that would be turnoffs once their targets hit their twenties.

Professor Noah Webb called her Ms. Moore like she was an adult and asked her to stay after class. A few of the other girls shot her looks as they funneled out of the room; a few of them actually seemed worried for her. Delaney tried to give those ones a small smile, but Professor Webb had already grabbed her elbow, directing her toward his desk.

He backed her up against it until her thighs hit the edge, invading her space like it was his right. His thumb rested against the pulse point on her wrist, as if it were acceptable to touch a stranger with such intimacy.

To touch a student with such intimacy.

"I understand you're still in high school," he said, ducking a little so that their eyes could lock. Delaney stared into his, let herself get a little lost in them. Her body swayed, unbidden, toward his warmth, and she could see how easily all this could happen.

All she needed to do was give in.

"If you need any extra support, or need help with anything," he continued. "*Anything.* You'll let me know?"

She'd nodded shyly.

It went on like that for weeks. Delaney didn't encourage or discourage him, simply let him dig himself deeper. That was, until he gave her an F on one of her assignments. That, she couldn't let stand.

She visited him during his office hours to point out all the ways he'd been blatantly wrong in his grading. When he shut and locked the door behind her, she realized what was happening. It was almost embarrassing that it had taken her so long, but she'd been so indignant about the red all over her paper.

"I'm sure we can figure something out so that one assignment doesn't wreck your grade," Professor Webb said, his hand on his belt suggestively. As if she couldn't understand what he wanted without him literally pointing at his crotch.

Delaney took the F.

Three days later, Professor Noah Webb was found in his office, lying in a pool of his own vomit. An overdose. A suicide. The note found tucked beneath his elbow confessed to just how many girls he'd backed up against his desk.

No one really thought anything about the tiny black box beside his signature.

After all, who on the police force would know what it was?

Who would know it was called a tombstone?

CHAPTER SEVEN

RAISA

"Shall we go to your room?"

Raisa whirled, hand over her heart. Delaney stood there, again too close, her bag slung over her shoulder, her expression expectant.

"We have to get you some bells," Raisa muttered.

"You know, I tried that once, but people were actually *more* annoyed by that," Delaney said, and Raisa couldn't tell if she was trying to be funny.

Kilkenny made some interested sound, and she bet he was very much enjoying these awkward interactions, from a professional standpoint.

"Okay." Raisa waved a hand toward the door. "Lead the way."

When Delaney turned on her heel and marched from the room, Raisa said as an aside to Kilkenny, "I don't want to expose my back to her."

Kilkenny shook his head, then quietly said, "Send a flare if she brings out a straight razor."

"Oh, he's got jokes." Raisa pointed finger-guns at him because she was very cool and professional. "Won't be funny when you're trying to profile my murderer."

"Eh, it'll be the easiest job I've had in a while."

Raisa offered an obviously fake laugh as she walked away but made sure to toss a real smile over her shoulder as she left the room. It wasn't that Raisa had never had friends. After her parents had died, she'd been shuffled around more than a deck of cards, but she'd eventually landed in DC and built up a loyal crew with the other misfits. At college she'd been working three jobs, but she'd still managed to hit the bars despite the fact that she'd finished her undergrad in three years.

But since then, it had gotten difficult. She had been on an accelerated path for grad school, which had consumed every part of her, and then the bureau had sucked out what was left. Her nights off mostly involved gas station food eaten in hotel rooms or something from the stash of ready-made meals she kept in her freezer. Her hottest plans these days usually involved streaming the latest popular show and drinking exactly half of one IPA before falling asleep.

She couldn't remember the last time she'd laughed with someone who wasn't on a screen.

Kilkenny might be an odd choice for an ally. He didn't exactly give off friend *vibes*. But she was starting to wonder if somewhere along the way they'd become something close to it without her realizing.

He was also . . . safe. As frustrating as it was, she knew a lot of the men she worked with viewed her as potential dating material. Kilkenny, though, was famously devoted to the memory of his wife. Raisa thought it might have more to do with guilt than everlasting love, but she wasn't the psychologist. Not that it took a professional to know that Kilkenny probably didn't want to risk putting another loved one in the same position as Shay.

She thought Kilkenny might feel the same way about her—that she was someone he could get close to without leading her on romantically. He was good enough at his job to know she wouldn't risk her reputation on a relationship or even a secret fling.

As Raisa headed out the back door of the hotel, she made a mental note to ask him to dinner the next time they were in the same town and not hunting a vicious serial killer.

Each of the dozen or so cabins had been taken by someone on the task force, and Raisa wondered whether Delaney had chosen one of them for herself or opted for the main building. They were set up in a semicircle facing the back of the hotel, which Raisa had at first found odd until she'd realized they had elaborate decks that looked into the forest. The angle of each cabin also gave some semblance of privacy.

Delaney was already waiting by Raisa's door.

"How did you know this was mine?" Raisa asked. Jokes aside, Raisa hadn't truly harbored suspicions about Delaney more than what she would think about any civilian inserting themselves into an investigation. But she didn't like that Delaney seemed to know so much.

"I guessed."

Raisa crossed her arms. "Try again."

"There were two open cabins after I picked mine," Delaney said. "And then. I guessed."

She said that last part with deliberate emphasis. Not a pushover then. Raisa nodded once. "I'll get supplies. Meet me around back."

Without a doubt, she was being paranoid, but she didn't want Delaney Moore in her space if it could be helped.

They set up at the tiny café table, without even considering the more comfortable Adirondack chairs. The porch was screened—a blessing in August, when any exposed flesh became an all-you-can-eat buffet for hordes of black flies.

Raisa shrugged out of her blazer. She had been expecting cooler temperatures this close to the mountains, but the sun was baking the earth and reflecting the heat back at them in painful waves.

"We're actually at fairly low altitude," Delaney said as she pulled her laptop out of her bag. "It's a strange sensation considering the

Alp-like peaks right over there. But that's why you're perspiring with such volume."

She nodded toward Raisa's sweat-stained shirt.

Raisa booted up her own computer. "In case no one's ever told you before, there's really no need to comment on someone else's sweat."

"It's a perfectly natural bodily function."

"Even still," Raisa said. "Unless someone is in medical distress—which I can assure you, I'm not—pit stains can go in the can't-fix-so-don't-mention bucket."

Delaney blinked at her, all big eyes. "What's that?"

"If someone can't fix something about themselves in five minutes, you shouldn't mention the thing," Raisa said, finally really focusing on Delaney. It was possible she was messing with Raisa, but her expression was open and curious. "Lettuce in the teeth, yes. A snaggletooth? No. I'm not going to magically make it not a million degrees outside, and there's no air-conditioning in the entire state of Washington. So. Sweat stains are here to stay."

"If it was a million degrees, we would disintegrate into a loose cluster of atoms," Delaney said primly.

Raisa opened her mouth and then closed it when she realized Delaney was joking.

"What posts did you find?" she asked, unsure of what to make of this woman.

"There were three in total," Delaney said. "All on Infinity9's 'Alex is Innocent' thread."

"What's that?"

Delaney made some disgruntled sound. "There's a small contingent of people out there on the internet that thinks Alex Parker wasn't the killer back in '98. They're convinced he was a victim instead."

"Yeah, I'm going to need more than that," Raisa said, sitting back. "What do you mean, they don't think he was the killer?"

"They think Alex was framed," Delaney said. "And the real killer is still out there."

"Why on earth do they think that?"

Delaney shrugged. "Everyone wants to make things a conspiracy. It is worth mentioning that the group has been growing now because Jenna Shaw decided to do the second season of her podcast on the Parkers."

"Who is Jenna Shaw?" Raisa asked, feeling even more lost.

"She has one of those true-crime podcasts," Delaney said. "Her program is interesting. She debunks conspiracy theories about famous murders. Except she starts each season as if she believes there really might be something more than the police reported. Last season she did Brittany Murphy's death."

"The actress?" Raisa asked and Delaney nodded. "So Jenna isn't a true believer?"

"No, but that's what makes her so good at it," Delaney said. "The best way to get anyone to change their mind is not to lecture them from a place of superiority, but to become a part of their in-group and then alter their opinions from the inside."

Raisa wasn't sure if she should be insulted that she, an FBI agent, was being lectured on a well-known aspect of social psychology. Delaney had a particular kind of personality Raisa had seen before—different from the mansplainers or *well, actually* types. Instead, it was someone who was just used to being the smartest person in the room. They genuinely wanted to inform people but also lacked a strong grasp of what could be considered common knowledge in any conversation.

"How can you tell she's not a conspiracy theorist?" Raisa asked, shaking off the irritation.

"What can you tell me about a hostage note that talks about dropping a bag of money by a 'green big bin'?"

Raisa didn't want to answer, but she couldn't *not*. That wasn't how she was wired.

"I'd say it was written by a non-native English speaker who grew up in a British-colonized country."

Delaney's expression went smug, as if she were the one who had just won the point. "How do you know that?"

"That was a softball," Raisa pointed out, but Delaney just waited her out. "There are unwritten rules that native speakers inherently follow without thinking about it, and the order of descriptors is one of them. They have to go opinion, size, age, shape, color, origin, material, purpose. So you can say you have a lovely little old rectangular green French silver whittling knife and an English speaker will be able to follow along easily. Put those words in any other order and it sounds like nails on a chalkboard. A native English speaker would never write 'green big bin.' They wouldn't even think about it; they would write—"

"Big green bin," Delaney said. "And British-colonized?"

"'Bin' instead of 'can,'" Raisa said with a shrug. "Imperfect. Either could be faked, or someone could have had a British parent. It's a start, though, and can help you narrow down a list of suspects."

"I can tell the same kind of thing with conspiracy theorists," Delaney said, having proved her point. "I've watched a lot of Flik videos. Eight hours a day, five days a week, thirty seconds per video, you do the math. There's just a certain way of talking, dog whistles and lingo and such. Jenna copies it well—she's probably watched many of the same posts. But she isn't a diehard."

"Okay, well." Raisa blew out a breath, trying to figure out how to unpack all this. "Who do people think was the killer if not Alex?"

"Lots of options—the Parkers weren't exactly squeaky clean," Delaney said. "I think for the podcast, Jenna Shaw is going to focus on the oldest daughter's boyfriend. His name is Shawn Dallinger, and he's already been brought up a few times in just the first episode. You can kind of tell what direction she wants to steer people in."

"Why him?"

"He was poor and allegedly cheating on the daughter—Isabel—with Becks," Delaney said, and Raisa coughed in surprise. "The most popular theory with this particular group was that it was a robbery gone wrong. Shawn cozied up to the family to gain access to their house, then brought in his friends, they say. Some think maybe Alex tried to stop them and it escalated from there. Some think Shawn was a psychopath just waiting for a chance to kill. Some say the Parkers surprised the group, and so they had to silence them."

"That feels like three thousand jumps in logic," Raisa said. "If the Parkers walked in on a robbery in process, Dallinger would have had to go from a thief to a killer in a matter of a few minutes. That's not . . . easy to do. Also, they were drugged and staged in bed, which doesn't really fit. And what about the letter? They must know it matches Alex's idiolect."

"They think it was forged," Delaney said.

"But it matches the idiolect from the short story."

"It was typed, though," Delaney said. "His letter. So it is possible someone else wrote it, right?"

"Sure, but that would mean Shawn Dallinger somehow found the short story, which was in the possession of CPS at the time, and matched the writing voice perfectly. All this while trying to clean up a robbery gone bad?"

"Not everyone thinks it was Shawn, though," Delaney said. "They think the real killer either used the story to re-create Alex's voice or wrote both themselves and put Alex's name on it."

Raisa blinked. She'd learned long ago never to rule anything out, but . . . "That seems like a lot of work if someone just wanted to frame Alex. They could have just written 'I did it,' and no one stumbling onto that scene would question it."

"Don't hurt yourself overthinking this. Honestly, it seems the wilder the scheme, the better for some people," Delaney said, a bit of bitterness there, though she quickly shook it off. "The father was also exhibiting some signs of schizophrenia, and people, of course, have pounced on that. Mental illness is always a scapegoat."

"It's nearly impossible to slit your own throat," Raisa said, for the second time that day. She wondered what world she'd stumbled into that she had to remind people of this fact, although Delaney showed no signs of actually buying into any of this convoluted thinking. "And there would have been hesitation marks."

There were other reasons, of course, that the theory was a non-starter, but that was the one that did it for Raisa. It wasn't even worth considering. Neither Becks nor Tim could have been the killer in that particular murder-suicide.

Delaney shrugged. "You could bring them a video tape of the murder and they would say it was faked. It's a self-sealing loop. Any evidence against their belief is *a part* of the conspiracy theory. But only a few think it was the father, anyway."

"Who else has made their suspect lists?" Raisa asked.

"The TA the father was sleeping with, the sheriff, the neighbor. Christine Keller is the woman who was watching the girls at the time. They think she somehow left them and her own daughter at her house and went to kill the Parkers before coming back and telling the girls to go home." Delaney's mouth twisted into an unpleasant grimace. "It's a barbaric theory. But if there's any single person who lived in this town twenty-five years ago, there's someone out there in the world who thinks they're guilty instead of Alex."

"What about the Parker sisters?" Raisa had to ask. "Do they get any theories?"

"Sometimes they get looped in on the Christine theory—that they're covering for her absence for some reason. But in terms of them actually doing the killing, it seems like the tight timing has worked in their favor," Delaney said. "People have generally accepted it would have been incredibly difficult for that to have worked. I mean, some fringe people probably have pointed a finger at even the baby, but you know, that's how it goes."

Raisa nodded. Though it wasn't her job to do so, she still wanted to find the sisters. Just because they'd been innocents back then, that didn't mean they still were. Any one of them could be the current killer.

"How credible is the theory against the sheriff?" Raisa asked.

Delaney held up one finger as she tapped something out on her tablet before laying it in the middle of the table.

A cheery voice—presumably that of Jenna Shaw—played through the little speaker.

"It's that time, tin-hatters, the one I know many of you have been waiting for. We're going to talk about the sheriff. Samantha Mason was one of the youngest people to ever hold that position in Skagit County. Now here's where the fun begins—Samantha and Tim Parker were high-school sweethearts. You heard that right . . . the first law enforcement officer on the scene of the Parker murder-suicide was none other than Tim's ex. Who, from what I've heard, still carried a torch for the man."

Another voice came on.

"There were rumors that Alex had a few accusations lobbied at him over the years. Including from a freshman girl who had taken Tim's class."

"That's David Welch, a grad student who had Tim as a professor," Jenna told listeners.

"But the campus police deferred to the Everly Sheriff Department," David went on. "Tim Parker brought in too much money for any of the administration to actually take action against his son, and Sheriff Mason always took the statements. Then they disappeared into the trash."

"Was this a well-known practice?" Jenna asked.

"No," David said. "Tim and Becks kept it real hushed up. They viewed Alex as their little golden child. Sometimes I don't think they even believed the girls."

A new voice. "Samantha only ever had eyes for Tim."

"That's Kim Robbins, Samantha Mason's friend from high school," Jenna once again filled in the audience.

"I always tried to get her to date," Kim said. "But she only ever went through the motions to shut us all up. Samantha wanted to be part of that family. She wanted the children to be hers, but she was also obsessed with Tim and Becks. Loved them."

"Did she love them too much?" Jenna asked.

A crackle of silence followed. And then: "I think so."

Jenna signed off, urging listeners to subscribe so as not to miss a single salacious detail.

Raisa wrinkled her nose. The clip was everything they all hated about true-crime entertainment. She didn't have anything against the new trend in general—she actually thought it might be helping to draw attention to cold cases that, in another era, would have sat in dusty archive rooms for all eternity. But there was media that was done well, and then there was tacky hunger for sensationalism and trauma and pain.

If Delaney hadn't told them about Jenna Shaw's shtick, Raisa would have absolutely pegged her as one of the worst kinds of hosts.

"That sounds like a lot of smoke without any fire," Raisa said.

"I told you. She's trying to make a straightforward, solved case interesting," Delaney said. "But she's making money off people who think there's a conspiracy to cover up the fact that someone other than Alex Parker is the real killer."

It was a common enough tactic these days. Raisa wasn't sure she'd ever get numb to it, though.

Delaney tapped her tablet once more. "Now. Are you ready to meet the true believers?"

SAMPLE OF MESSAGES POSTED ON THE "ALEX IS INNOCENT" INFINITY9 THREAD

> **ALEXFAN:** Cant believe Jenna Shaw is doing the Alex case. That's exciting.

> **PENNYPARKER:** Hack

> **NOT-UR-TINHATTER:** Oh comeeeee on Alexfan . . . get ur head out of ur ass . . . JS thinks were all crazy . . . don't buy her act . . . final ep will just be like haha Alex did it 😏

> **ALEXFAN:** pls, attention to Alex's case is ALWAYS good. You see how many newbies we get everytime it gets talked about?

> **WHATYOUCANTSEE:** *raises hand* newbie here. I don't care what Jenna concludes, anyone with eyes can tell there is something super fishy about all this. Like what is even Shawn Dallinger doing these days? Isn't he a cop haha?

> **ALEXFAN:** Welcome to the other side @ WHATYOUCANTSEE. AND RIGHT?! Dallinger is a deputy sheriff in the same bumble-fuck town . . . probably to make sure the evidence doesn't get out. Who knows what they're hiding in that department . . . I've made the trip to Everly a couple of

times now and they never let me get past the lobby. Superrrrr fishy

ALWAYSALEX: Or it could be cuz you're a crazy stalker stan whose lost touch with reality. Go touch grass and then die. Please ☺

ALEXFAN: Ignore Benny, everyone, he's just bitchy because he wanted to do the podcast and JS beat him to it. Jealousy is a disease. Maybe I'm not the one who should go touch grass.

PENNYPARKER: Anywayyyyyy, next ep is on Mark the TA who Tim was screwing around with. Do we think . . . ?

ALEXFAN: Nah Mark has like a hard core alibi JS is using him to get listeners but it's a dead end . . . might not even listen to the ep, not here for queerbaiting

WHATYOUCANTSEE: soz I'm still catching up. @AlexFan who do you think did it?

SILVERFOXFORALEX: hahahahahhahahaha @ALEXFAN is all talk, newbie. He won't ever put his money where his mouth is—he says he wants everyone to 'do their own research' because this is 'not a cult' but he's just a dumbass who doesn't know anything

ALEXFAN: Fuck off Benny, I know you keep creating new usernames to harass us. @

WHATYOUCANTSEE here's a link to a master-
post on all the evidence we've collected over the
years . . . You can see for yourself

SILVERFOXFORALEX: elle oh ellle. Told ya.

CHAPTER EIGHT

RAISA

Raisa skimmed a few pages of the "Alex is Innocent" thread.

There was a whole subfield of study in linguistics these days about writing via new technology—on blogs and text messages and social media. Raisa had found that, in many ways, authorship was even more distinct online than it was through traditional writing, where there were some expectations for grammar and structure.

It was going to play a bigger and bigger role in all their investigations. Texts, especially, when comparing threatening messages, kidnapping letters, or suicide notes.

"Which ones have you identified as the killer?" Raisa asked Delaney.

"None of those recent messages," Delaney said. "I just wanted you to get a sense of the community first."

Community. In her dive into the internet linguistics sphere, Raisa had come to realize how important that aspect was to any online space. Especially with groups that rooted their identities in specific conspiracy theories. A sense of community was what first drew people in and then kept them from leaving.

"I actually tracked the killer back about three months," Delaney said. "Well, I say 'tracked,' but really I just searched for their username. It was nothing special."

"So the killer wanted us to find these messages," Raisa said, more to herself than to Delaney.

But Delaney nodded. "I wouldn't even call this bread crumbs, they left behind the whole dang loaf."

Raisa held back a snort of laughter. "Show me."

Delaney handed over the tablet once more.

The first thing Raisa noticed was that the posts weren't in internet speak. The second was that there were enough unique phrases to start building a profile of the killer's idiolect.

> **GALAHAD:** Thank you all for your wonderous work here. I am so glad I found like-minded individuals such as yourselves. I know some of you are worn with toil and tired of life, but we must continue to fight for Alex. I am certain that he would be proud of you. Someday soon there will be peace on earth, and silence in the sky.

> **GALAHAD:** I am not an imposter. I have never claimed inside information. I was appalled and felt sick when I saw some of you say I sounded as if I was trying to come off as an insider. I don't work at the sheriff's department, nor do I have connections with Alex's family. All I want is to clear his dear name. And we have miles to go before we sleep, my friends. Miles to go before we sleep.

> **GALAHAD:** I know who really killed the Parkers. Soon everyone will know who killed the Parkers. I can't tell you much, but I can tell you this: Alex is Innocent. First there will be two and then there will

be more. You'll know what I mean when it happens.
Keep up the good work, my lovely people.

On autopilot, Raisa opened the software she used to deconstruct sentences. Linguistics was an art to her, but in court it was a science. Her work needed to stand up to scrutiny from judges and juries, and so she had to document each step of her process with rigorous perfection. She had heard horror stories of months of effort dismissed as "whimsical" by old-school judges.

Delaney stood up and walked around the little café table to stare over her shoulder, and Raisa fought the urge to cover her screen.

"What are you doing?" Delaney asked.

"Every word in this message is a choice the writer made, whether consciously or not." Raisa tapped the tablet's screen to zoom in on the first one. "The killer actually has the same contraction patterns as Alex. That might be coincidence, or it might mean something."

"Contraction patterns?"

"The person uses 'can't' and 'don't,' but 'I am,'" Raisa supplied absently, reading the sentences over again. There were phrases that jumped out at her, but she wasn't quite sure why yet. Her brain worked that way sometimes—almost highlighting sections subconsciously for her to pay attention to. Only later, when she ran a full analysis on them, would she understand why. But she'd learned to trust herself.

In her spreadsheet she quickly typed out:

- *Wonderous work (spelling)*
- *Like-minded individuals*
- *Such as / sounded as*
- *I know that*
- *My lovely people*
- *Was appalled and felt sick*
- *Dear name*

- *Worn with toil and tired of life*
- *Peace on earth, and silence in the sky*
- *Miles to go before we sleep*
- *My friends*
- *Alex is Innocent (capitalization)*

"Everyone on the thread refers to it as 'Alex is Innocent,'" Delaney said, clearly reading along with Raisa's notes. "So that might not be important."

Raisa glanced at her. Her face was still too close, invading Raisa's personal space without thought. "Hey, Delaney?"

"Yes?"

"How about this?" Raisa offered. "If I need something explained, I'll ask for clarification. Otherwise, you can assume I know baseline information. Okay?"

Delaney pursed her lips as if digesting the request. And then nodded once. "That would save me some time."

Raisa couldn't help but laugh. "Ditto. Here's the thing, you have to look at linguistic work like a puzzle of the sky. Each piece is mostly unremarkable and looks pretty similar to the other pieces. But each one not only has a specific place in the puzzle, it's also important. If it's not there, the puzzle can't be completed."

"That was an apt metaphor. Well done."

"Thank you," Raisa said solemnly. She didn't want to start liking Delaney, but there was something about her earnest yet dry delivery that was appealing. "There are oftentimes phrases that seem commonplace to you but really aren't. Take the Unabomber case. Linguists identified twelve words that were used by Ted Kaczynski in a writing sample they found at his cabin, and looking at the list, none of them really stood out. They were things like 'presumably' and 'at any rate' and 'clearly.' But when the FBI ran a search on all twelve words, they got about seventy hits. On the entire internet." Raisa shifted to look at Delaney. "And all seventy were instances of the Unabomber's manifesto."

"How can that be?"

"Idiolects can be more unique than fingerprints," Raisa said. It wasn't always true. But in some instances, they got lucky. And already, with just these three messages from the killer, she could tell they had a wealth of information.

"Anyway," Raisa continued, "it's not just googling, which can be helpful, don't get me wrong. There's something called corpuses, which are essentially official databases of different types of speech, compiled through newspapers, TV, movies, sound clips, et cetera. That's why I'm picking apart unique words or word combinations. I can run the phrases through the sites and see how common they are in typical human speech and writing. The rarer the better, obviously, and then that gets a weighted signifier in my spreadsheet. It kind of becomes statistics after that, which is where most people's eyes start to glaze over."

Delaney hummed, and Raisa threw her a look. "What?"

"It's just . . ." Delaney paused. "I sometimes think I'm an expert with patterns and language. But I've never seen it as mathematical as you're describing. Certain words jump out at me, or it's a feeling I get."

The admission surprised Raisa. Delaney Moore was so literal, so logical, that Raisa would have said she'd never had a gut feeling in her life.

"That's where we all start," Raisa said. "My job can sometimes feel like looking at a Monet and trying to identify what brand of brush he used and the color code of each separate tube of paint—deconstructing something beautiful and human into inert parts. But if you go and tell a jury that you just get the *sense* that the authorship is confirmed, then you're going to get booted pretty quickly from the court."

She tapped the username in the screenshots. Galahad. "Any idea what this means?"

"Like the knight?" Delaney suggested.

"I guess," Raisa said, and then read through her list once more. She stilled.

"You've recognized something," Delaney observed, but Raisa heard the question from a distance, swatting it away as unimportant.

She hadn't let herself think too hard about any of the phrases when she'd been writing them. From experience, she'd learned she'd be able to see only the trees and not the forest if she didn't do everything in her precise order. So she'd trained herself to finish her spreadsheet before she really let herself absorb anything of note.

Raisa pulled up a basic Google search just to be sure. In the little box, she typed, "Was appalled and felt sick."

As she expected, the results were for an investigation in Britain. Four men had been charged with killing a thirteen-year-old newspaper delivery boy. The convictions had been made on the strength of a written confession from one of the men. It was later proved that the police had coerced the written statement and then faked a transcript from a nonexistent interview. They had simply cut and pasted sections of the coerced written statement to make it look like they'd actually talked to him.

One of the phrases that had stood out as awkward was the one included in this copycat killer's messages.

"When did you say the unsub posted these?" Raisa asked, her brain working too fast for her to keep up with it.

"Three months ago," Delaney said, watching her with that strange detached curiosity. "You found something important."

Again, it wasn't a question.

Raisa licked her lips. Maybe she was jumping to conclusions here. But the phrase was unique, unique enough that the only hits were from that British case or from linguistic research papers about it.

She quickly scanned the rest of the list in her spreadsheet. A hand-ful of phrases there were so odd that they must have one-source hits on the internet. That wasn't . . . rare, per se. But combined with the head nod to the British newspaper boy case, which was only famous in linguist circles, it was something she couldn't ignore.

"I think," Raisa said slowly, aware of Delaney's eerie eyes on her, "that the killer is talking to me."

CHAPTER NINE

DELANEY

At eighteen, Delaney decided to stop looking.

She still frequented message boards to flush out predators when she could, but it had turned into a hobby rather than an obsession. Even though she hadn't gone to Stanford like her parents wanted, she'd still landed at a prestigious—and thus, demanding—school, and that took time. She wasn't a cop or an FBI agent; finding criminals wasn't her job.

While all that was true, Delaney could admit that the main reason she'd decided to stop was that she didn't want to live in the darkness anymore.

All she really wanted was a friend. A single friend, something she'd never had before. Her parents had been older, so they didn't hang out with anyone who had kids her age to play with, and later she had been focused on school and her search.

College opened up a new door for her, though. There were a lot of people there, including ones who didn't know Delaney as the odd duckling with weird style and a stretched-out body that got her called Gumby more often than not.

There were people who were just as strange as she was. But Delaney didn't want to find the other misfits, who would cling to anyone who gave them attention. She wanted to prove that she could make a friend.

That's when she met Maura—bright and shining, tan and blonde Maura.

Maura was the type to always be walking somewhere with someone. She wore low-riding skirts that showed off her pubic bones and crop tops that revealed a winking cubic zirconium at her belly. She always had a boyfriend and an invite to the coolest party on campus.

She probably hadn't been lonely a day in her life.

She was also in Delaney's public speaking class. It was one of the few introductory courses Delaney had been forced to take.

Usually Maura flounced in two minutes late with an entourage, which meant Delaney never had an opening to talk to her.

But one day, Maura was early, and somehow—miraculously—the spot next to her was empty.

Delaney crawled her way over the boy whose limbs were spilling into the aisle to get to Maura, who didn't even glance up when Delaney dropped into the empty seat next to her.

This was her chance. Her one chance.

Yet every time she opened her mouth, nothing but hot, garlic-tinged air came out. The problem was that Delaney had never tried to be likable before, and she was fairly sure she was incapable of becoming likable just randomly in that moment. It had always seemed like an impossible paradox—to be able to make friends, she needed to talk to people, but to know how to talk to people, she needed practice with friends.

Trying to connect with Maura also had the feeling of skipping the bunny slopes for the double-diamond chutes on her first time skiing.

Delaney had always liked a challenge, though. What good was making a friend if it wasn't the best friend out there?

So she started small. That first day when Delaney sat next to her, Maura broke her pencil, and Delaney offered one of her own. That got her a nod on the next day of class. And when Maura missed a class the next week, Delaney offered up her own notes. Then Maura asked if she could practice her speech on Delaney sometime.

It didn't take long to realize that Maura was actually wicked smart—she just didn't like anyone to know it. Her speeches were always sharp, funny, and engaging, her knowledge of obscure topics surprisingly deep.

What Delaney liked most about Maura, though, was her eye for people. She knew how to collect them—someone to buy her coffee, someone to procure her fake IDs, someone to get her alcohol. The manipulation never came off as tacky or obvious. Maura helped people realize their potential through helping her and making them feel good for doing it.

Delaney knew Maura saw something useful about her, too, but she hadn't yet been able to identify what that was. That had been a fear lurking in the creases of Delaney's plan—that Maura would pretend to be her friend but really only want to use her for coursework help. Delaney wasn't averse to that, she simply wasn't good enough at public speaking herself to be of any use beyond as a proofreader.

They mostly talked only in class. Sometimes, Maura would wave to her in acknowledgment if they passed in the student center, but even halfway through the semester, Delaney hadn't felt like she could officially check "make a friend" off her to-do list.

Then Maura plopped down next to her one day on campus. Delaney had a favorite tree on the quad, the roots twisting just right to provide back support. She'd been working on a gnarly proof for one of her advanced math classes when Maura pulled her out of her own head.

"There's a party tonight," Maura said in lieu of a greeting.

Delaney didn't want to make assumptions.

"That sounds fun," she lied.

Maura's mouth quirked up at the corners like she'd clocked Delaney's fib but wasn't going to call her on it. "We could go together. We can go shopping now to get you something to wear."

Delaney agreed almost before the suggestion was even out. If she had learned anything from the spate of high school movies playing at the local theater, it was that a shopping montage was crucial to building friendships.

And to Delaney's delight, it wasn't just a shopping montage. It was also a makeover—which cemented friendships even further, if those movies were accurate.

After they picked out the perfect outfit, which showed more skin than Delaney ever had in her life, Maura cut Delaney's hair into a shaggy bob that made her pale-blue eyes stand out against her dark eyebrows. Maura swiped blush onto Delaney's cheekbones and taught her how to wrangle an eyelash curler that looked more like a torture device than a beauty tool.

When they arrived at the party, Maura introduced her to Chad and then Jensen and then Sam. Maura handed her a cup full of something that left sugar in her teeth, and when she'd drunk it, Maura handed her another. The room blurred at the edges and Delaney swayed into whichever boy she was currently talking to. She couldn't keep it straight.

"You seem tired," he panted in her ear, and Delaney thought she might have nodded.

Then she was in a bed.

From there, the memories became snapshots—the smell of old socks and corn chips; Destiny's Child's "Survivor" playing through the wall; rough fingers and a clumsy tongue.

After the boy whose name she didn't remember fell asleep, Delaney looked over to the doorway to find Maura, with someone standing at her shoulder. Delaney could have sworn the boy had closed the door, but the thought was fleeting when she noticed Maura receiving a small wad of money from her companion.

"How much was I worth?" Delaney asked the darkness.

"A tank of gas," Maura whispered back.

Curiously, she didn't feel betrayed. This was just like all those high school movies, too, a tradition hearkening all the way back to *Carrie*.

She hated Maura a little bit for finding the way Delaney could be useful. It proved Maura was just so much better at that one specific thing than Delaney would be at anything. Even math.

Chad or Jensen or Sam, whichever it was, emerged from the night unscathed. He hadn't been the one to get Delaney drunk; he'd just taken advantage of it.

Meanwhile, Maura Schmidt was found in front of the emergency room three days later, diagnosed with alcohol poisoning. Two days later, her organs shut down. Seven days later, Delaney attended the memorial service.

When Delaney went home afterward, she opened her journal and checked "make a friend" off her to-do list.

One thing Delaney had learned in her life was that the outcome didn't matter as much as the fact that it had happened at all.

CHAPTER TEN

RAISA

The stars were bright so far away from Seattle's lights.

Raisa took a swallow of her beer as she stared at the sky from the Adirondack chair helpfully placed by her cabin's back porch. The black flies had retired for the night, but the mosquitoes were out in force. Despite the fact that she'd doused herself in DEET, a big mama was currently feasting on her ankle blood.

"Any forward momentum?" Kilkenny asked, emerging from the shadows dragging his own plastic Adirondack chair toward her. Raisa wasn't sure she wanted him to join her, but she also didn't think she had enough brain space tonight to care either way.

"Our killer knows enough about forensic linguistics to plant messages to me as early as three months ago," Raisa said, picking at the IPA's label.

There was a beat of silence, and she glanced over. "What?"

"To you?" he asked, his voice neutral, but she heard the doubt there.

"Okay, maybe not to me specifically," she conceded. "But they inserted some head nods to famous linguistics cases. They were unique references, too. Why else would they be in there if not to talk to the FBI's linguist?"

"Huh."

"Enlightening," she teased, and he sent her his trademark half smile.

"It's just . . . Alex's letter is well-known in your field, too, right?" he asked, and she just waited because it seemed rhetorical. "And now they're referencing other investigations that used forensic linguistics? Maybe they aren't talking to a linguist . . . maybe they *are* a linguist."

"It's not really a big field," Raisa said. She wasn't shooting down the idea, but a conference of linguists in the country could pretty much fit in one hotel.

"Someone who fancies themselves an expert, then?" He lifted one shoulder.

"The messages are practically begging for expert analysis," Raisa said slowly. "Deliberately so. You're right, they could be playing linguist as part of the game."

"To see if they could match wits with an FBI agent," Kilkenny said, and she couldn't help the way her eyes slid to his wedding ring. "It wouldn't be the first time something like that has happened."

"A mathematician who longs to be a linguist," Raisa mused.

"You say that because of the tombstone?" Kilkenny asked, neatly following her train of thought.

Raisa hummed in agreement. "It's interesting the way math and language are intertwining on this case. It's very linguistic-y."

"The official word." But it was gentle, teasing.

She shot him a grin and then went back to contemplating the stars. "Most people think it's just language. But once you get past a certain level, it's all math."

"Psychology deals way more with statistics than I had anticipated when I picked it as a major," he said. "I was a dumb kid."

"Weren't we all," she said, toasting him.

"Was there anything else remarkable about the messages?"

"Yes," she said. "Some unique turns of phrases that were only used by certain eighteenth- and nineteenth-century poets."

"A poetry enthusiast, as well?"

"I think there's something more there," Raisa said, testing her theory out loud to see if it sounded unhinged. "If we go on your assumption that they like linguistics . . . there's another message buried in there, I just can't see it yet."

"That makes sense."

"There's also . . ." she started and broke off, trying to figure out the best way to ask what she wanted. Apart from the postings themselves, they couldn't ignore the fact that the killer identified himself with a community that believed Alex Parker was the third victim rather than the killer. "Is there any chance that the killer's motive could just be to bring attention to the idea that Alex wasn't guilty?"

"Without a doubt," Kilkenny said so quickly she knew he must have been thinking about it, too. "Do you remember anything about John Hinckley Jr.'s case?"

Raisa squinted one eye, trying to call up the specifics. "He was obsessed with Jodie Foster, right? He wanted to get her attention."

Kilkenny nodded. "He was actually obsessed with the movie she was in—*Taxi Driver*. Robert De Niro's character assassinated three guys to save Jodie's character. You see where this is going?"

"He wore the *Taxi Driver* character as a mask," Raisa said. "A different kind of copycat."

"Exactly. Not imitating a real-life killer but a fictional one. The psychology is the same, though," Kilkenny said. "And when he was asked about why he tried to assassinate Reagan, you know what he said?"

"I have a feeling you're going to tell me."

His lips twitched. "Something to the extent that it didn't matter if Jodie Foster outwardly ignored him for the rest of her life. He'd made her one of the most famous actresses in the world, and so he saw his mission as having been successful."

"So a person who thinks Alex was falsely accused could be trying to get someone to pay attention to the theories through any means necessary?" Raisa asked. "That would line up with the idea of them posting that video with the murder hashtag."

"There was no chance that wouldn't be flagged," Kilkenny said.

"Maybe one of those 'Alex is Innocent' members fixated on this case," Raisa said. "It would explain how they knew about the Balducci connection. They already have way more eyes on the Parker folder than there ever was before."

She thought about that one poster who had shown up at the Everly Sheriff Department multiple times looking for more information. "Does that make sense? It sounds extreme as I say it, but . . ."

"Absolutely, that could be the motive we're looking at," Kilkenny said. "It fits with a basic profile I'm building—all centered around attention and messages to law enforcement. It doesn't even matter much how they got onto that thread. The overlying cause—to make Jodie Foster famous, to clear Alex's name—is never as important as the psychology going on beneath all that. Someone prone to that kind of violence hyperfixates on an issue, but the issue itself isn't that important."

"They would find something that triggers them no matter what, is what you're saying," Raisa summed up.

"Exactly," Kilkenny said. "If it's not Jodie Foster and Alex Parker, it's a bad call in Dungeons and Dragons or the latest Instagram influencer. Obsessed people can't change their nature, but what they're focused on might adjust to their circumstances or surroundings."

"What you're saying is that it's believable that one of the 'Alex is Innocent' groupies snapped," Raisa said.

She was met with silence, one that was starting to feel familiar. "You don't think that's what's going on here."

"It's believable, but it doesn't feel right," he said, almost apologetically. "And I'll have to kill you if you tell anyone I just said that without any actual evidence to support me."

Raisa laughed. "Why the feeling, though? There must be something making your Spidey-senses tingle."

He made the same face he'd made when she'd said *vibe*. Then, slowly, he said, "Hinckley was erratic. A lot of copycats are. You just don't usually see the same methodical care as with organized serial killers."

"But this crime scene was impeccable," Raisa said, following his train of thought. Their techs had confirmed the original report that the place had been clean of DNA. They still had to go over the rest of the house, but the bedroom and bathroom had been sanitized of *all* fingerprints and hairs. They weren't even able to pull anything out of the drain.

"Everything with this has been so careful and planned," Kilkenny said in agreement. "This killer started seeding messages three months ago on an obscure internet site. He cleaned up the scene, left no physical evidence behind, and then stuck around to film it. Nothing about any of this screams 'erratic.'"

"That goes back to your theory that this isn't their first rodeo," Raisa said, then took a deep swallow of her IPA. Kilkenny wasn't drinking, and she wondered if he ever did. Something about the way he always had nearly perfect control of himself and his expression suggested he wasn't the type who would be eager to lose his inhibitions. Raisa threw out a wild theory because it was dark and she was starting to feel the buzz from the alcohol. "Hired assassin?"

Kilkenny didn't immediately dismiss the idea, as ridiculous as it sounded coming out of her mouth. "That at least fits better with the behavior we've seen, which has been cold and unemotional despite the gore. Look at this kind of murder, you'd expect to see boiling rage beneath, some kind of anger. But everything was so clinically handled."

"It doesn't seem personal, huh?"

"Right." Kilkenny pointed at her. "It must be, it has to be. Unless there really is some assassin running around town. But this wasn't a rage killing. I'm not even sure it was revenge. It was just . . . a message. Two lives, gone. To tell us something we can't even understand yet."

Raisa thought again of a puzzle of the sky. With each piece of the investigation, they'd be forming a more complete picture. It sounded so cold when she put it that way. She wondered if she was cold. If she came across as logical and detached as Delaney Moore did. As their killer did.

"Don't forget the signature. Tombstone," Raisa said. "From the Greek *tymbos*, meaning 'burial mound.' But some people argue it came before then, since several cultures use variations of it to mean 'grave.'"

"Why did you decide to go into linguistics?" Kilkenny asked, and Raisa's brain stuttered over the sudden shift.

She was surprised that he would ask a personal question; after all, it was Kilkenny who had always maintained the careful distance between them. Him a perfect senior agent; her a mess of a rookie even three years in.

Maybe it was the beer that made her answer. Or maybe it was the fact that he'd never once, in the cases they'd worked together, made her feel like she had to justify herself. This was curiosity, plain and simple and human. And she could appreciate that.

"It felt like a secret no one else knew," Raisa admitted. "The patterns of language. Even if you'd never come across a word before, you could deconstruct it to its basic parts and usually get the gist. Do you know what 'bailiwick' means?"

"No idea."

"The first part gives us the most information," Raisa said. "'Baili'— which would come from 'bailiff.' It's a fairly unique combination of letters. Meanwhile, 'wic,' or in this case 'wick,' means 'village.'"

"The village's bailiff?"

"Well, here's where it becomes fun," Raisa said. "Obviously that's its literal origin, but figuratively, how did the word evolve? A bailiff's village is his sphere of influence. So a bailiwick is essentially a person's area of knowledge, their skill set or where they have authority."

"That's all interesting. But how did you get there in the first place?" Kilkenny, ever the renowned psychologist, asked. He knew enough of her background to know that a kid like her wouldn't have been exactly pushed in the direction of linguistics. She'd fought her way up several broken ladders to even get into college.

Raisa picked at her peeling label, debating. She'd never been one for vulnerability. But that was how to get people to connect with you, and she liked the idea of Kilkenny as an ally.

Another cold calculation.

"My parents died when I was ten," Raisa finally said. "In a car crash."

"That must have been hard," he said, instead of the *I'm sorry* she'd been braced for. She liked him more for not saying it.

"I stopped talking," she said.

"That's a common—"

"For four years."

"Ah," Kilkenny murmured. "Language became the thing that you could control in an out-of-control life."

"Why am I not surprised that you got it in one?" Raisa said with a disbelieving laugh. So many therapists had missed that point. "Everything was so busy, after it happened. Social workers and psychologists and police officers all asking me to talk, all of the time. And what I wanted to do was build a little fortress where none of them could get to me. So I did. And everyone eventually got the hint."

"I take it that it didn't go over well with any foster parents."

"The ones who told themselves it wouldn't matter were the worst," Raisa said, then shook her head, stopping the word vomit before it could begin. She wasn't about to cut herself open that deeply. "Anyway. I began to view language differently at that point. Kids don't really know how powerful a tool it can be. But I did, and so I wanted to understand it more."

"What was the first thing you said?" he asked. "When you talked again."

Raisa laughed, because of course he'd homed in on the most important question. "At fourteen I was spending more time on the streets than in any of the revolving homes they tried to put me in. My family ended up essentially being the other kids that were out there, too. One of the girls had gotten beat up pretty bad by her boyfriend. I was the only one around, but I was small." She shot him a grin, an acknowledgment of her tiny frame. "I couldn't carry her. So I ran out to the street. I tried to get people to come with me, but they wouldn't, you know? They don't really like following a little mute girl with wild eyes, covered in grime and blood."

"So you spoke."

"So I spoke," Raisa repeated softly. "I found an ambulance just parked on the street. The EMTs were on dinner break, eating subs in the front seat. It smelled like pickles, I still remember that. I asked them if they could help me. Turns out that's pretty powerful, too."

The shadows had collected in the valleys of Kilkenny's face, but somehow she could tell she had his complete attention. "You put the two together. You help people by using language."

"I try to, at least." She wasn't always successful, and that ate at her. Scottsdale ate at her. But she did what she could with what she was good at. "After my parents died, there were all these people who said they wanted to help me. The social workers and the foster parents and the doctors and teachers. They all just talked at me, though. They told me I was strong, then they told me I was dumb, then—surprise!—they told me I was a genius. They told me they could be trusted. And they told me I was traumatized. Through all of that, no one ever tried to actually listen. Until the EMTs, who followed a dirty, nearly homeless girl back into an alley to save another girl who worked the corners most nights. I told myself to always be like those EMTs. To always listen."

She swallowed the last of her beer as Kilkenny watched her in silence, and she laughed when she figured out what he was doing. He was trying to listen rather than speak over her. He was quick, she would give him that. But she wasn't ten any longer. She didn't have the same scars as she did back then. Or, of course she had them, but they were faded. "What are you doing next for the case?"

"It's going to sound a little out there," he said, going with the change of topic beautifully, as most people familiar with trauma themselves often did. It's why she tended to gravitate toward those with shadows in their eyes—they were more likely to be respectful of hers.

Raisa leaned forward, gleeful. She liked "out there" ideas. "Lay it on me."

"I'd like to talk to Jenna Shaw," he said, a tiny bit of a wince in his expression. "She already announced she was coming here."

"Ohh," Raisa said, sitting back again, thinking about it.

"I told you it's outside the box."

"No," she said slowly. "She posted an episode today about the Balducci connection. If she's done her research—which it seems like she has—she might know more details than we do." Raisa paused. "But Sand might not love the idea."

"I'm not sure he cares too much about what I'm doing at the moment," he said, that self-deprecation back. He did it well, keeping far away from self-pity. "But I already cleared it with him anyway. He wants to know how big of a problem she's going to be for us."

That was absolutely a concern. Journalists were one thing—they tended to have ethical lines they drew and were used to working with investigators so as not to give certain things away to a press-savvy killer.

Podcasters, on the other hand, were wild cards. There were plenty of great ones out there, but at worst, it didn't require any degree or training. Just the right equipment.

If Jenna got to their witnesses before them, she could wreak havoc. And she clearly had no qualms about posting in real time. Keeping her occupied talking to Kilkenny might be a pretty strategic move on Sand's part.

And . . . Raisa thought about the message board. Kilkenny might not feel like it was the right theory, but it would be good to talk to someone more familiar with everyone on that thread. "She might know more about the big players on the 'Alex is Innocent' board. They certainly know about her."

"I could use someone else there," he said, brows raised. "She's getting into town late tonight, apparently. We're getting breakfast in the morning. Tag along?"

"Yeah, I think I might be able to squeeze that in," she said after pretending to think about it.

After all, if anyone was going to know who the killer's next target was, it was the woman who wanted to profit off the story.

TRANSCRIPT FROM JENNA SHAW'S *BELOW THE SURFACE*
PODCAST, EPISODE 4

I'm interrupting my normal schedule to bring you some breaking news. Now, I'm doing this on the fly, so please excuse any errors. I was just finishing off the editing on one of the episodes for later in the season when I got a Google alert for Everly. There's been two homicides reported there this morning—the first ones in that remote town since the Parkers were killed twenty-five years ago.

The details are sparse, but from what I can tell from the police language in the article, the victims weren't shot. Perhaps their throats were cut with a straight razor? That's simply speculation, simply speculation. What's not speculation is that the male victim has ties to the Parker family.

That's right. Bob Balducci was Alex Parker's beloved football coach at Everly High School. Reportedly, Bob acted as something like a mentor to Alex in the months before the teenager allegedly killed his parents.

I'll let you decide if that is a coincidence. Meanwhile, I'm packing my bags as we speak. I'll be on the ground for you guys, and don't worry—I won't stop asking questions until I get some real answers.

That means my publishing schedule might be thrown to shit, but I promise you it will be worth it in the end.

Don't forget to subscribe to figure out what happens next. In the meantime, enjoy this prerecorded interview with local high school teacher Pam Stevens. I was going to save it for a later episode, but you'll see why it needs to air now.

———

PAM STEVENS: You want to think things like that don't happen in Everly.

JENNA SHAW: That's Pam Stevens, the biology teacher at Alex's high school. You would think she's talking about the murder-suicide, but, folks, she's not.

STEVENS: I tried to do something about the allegations, especially when that nice girl came forward.

SHAW: What nice girl?

STEVENS: Hmm, I'm forgetting her name at the moment. Clara? Cara. Something like that. She was a quiet, studious girl. Wanted to be a marine biologist.

SHAW: Don't we all go through that phase?

STEVENS: Perhaps, perhaps. But she had a real gift for the field of study.

SHAW: You're talking in the past tense.

STEVENS: I'm not sure what happened to her after she left town, but I know that the business with Alex derailed her schoolwork. She graduated at the bottom of her class.

SHAW: What's the business with Alex?

STEVENS: She came forward with allegations that he, well, that he sexually assaulted her, is the language we use today.

SHAW: He never had a police record, though.

STEVENS: Ha. The report would never have made it past Sam Mason's desk. But it barely even got that far.

SHAW: The sheriff? She covered for Alex?

STEVENS: She would have if Bob and Gina Balducci hadn't stepped in. They gave him an alibi, told Sam that he was at their place all evening, and then Bob said he walked Alex all the way to the door of his house. It became a he said, she said, and when the football star and coach are involved in that, you know who comes out the winner.

SHAW: Pam was up front about the fact that she didn't have any hard proof against Alex. But she's adamant she believes the girl who spoke out.

STEVENS: You know, it was terribly hard in those days to say anything; she was very brave. I wish I could have done more for her, but the town tore her apart after that. Well, for the two months in between her accusations and the murders. I hope she's a little vindicated now.

SHAW: Vindicated indeed. Sound off in the comments, my dear tin-hatters. Alex was no prince, but does this change your opinion on whether he killed his parents? Subscribe to find out what happens next.

CHAPTER ELEVEN

RAISA

Jenna Shaw had bright-pink hair with bangs worn in that shorn-short style that reminded Raisa of when she'd taken scissors to her Barbie dolls. Jenna had about eight rings in her eyebrows, another two dozen spread out over both ears, and another in her lip; a constellation had been tattooed near the corner of her eye; and she wore bright-red lipstick that contrasted against her pale skin and clashed with her neon bob spectacularly.

They were at a Denny's close to campus, and at this time on a Monday morning, the restaurant was filled with sleepy college kids in sweatpants and sloppy buns. It was the perfect place to talk without worrying about being overheard or interrupted, but if Jenna was hoping to tape the interview, she'd be out of luck.

That made Raisa wonder if it had been Kilkenny who had picked this particular location.

"Agent Kilkenny," Jenna said brightly, holding out a hand. "It's a pleasure. I've been looking into cases you worked, obviously the Alphabet Man but also—"

Kilkenny held up his free palm, cutting her off, and Raisa studied her with more interest. Jenna was either incredibly dense in bringing up the serial killer who had murdered Kilkenny's wife or incredibly clever. What better way to throw off this particular FBI agent than to mention that particular case? Maybe he would be so shocked he would divulge more information than he would have otherwise.

"Right, ugh." Jenna smacked herself in the forehead. "I'm such an idiot. I'm sorry, my stupid mouth."

And that sealed it for Raisa. Kilkenny hadn't actually conveyed any distress, yet Jenna had immediately known what she'd done was wrong.

The mention of the Alphabet Man had likely been deliberate.

And now that Raisa was looking for it, she could see a feral kind of hunger lurking beneath Jenna's placid demeanor. It stank like desperation. Jenna saw the Parker murder-suicide as her big break, and that made her dangerous.

Raisa took the seat that put her back to the wall. Kilkenny's neutral mask hadn't flickered once, but somehow she could tell he was more alert than he had been only a few minutes ago.

"This is my colleague, Agent Raisa Susanto," Kilkenny said, and Jenna's attention shifted to her. Raisa had the sensation of a butterfly pinned to a display case.

Jenna nodded in acknowledgment.

"Do you mind if I record this?" she asked, already digging in her bag, head down.

"I'd prefer this conversation to be off the record," Kilkenny said, and Jenna paused, clearly doing the quick calculation—getting into Kilkenny's good favor would far outweigh one conversation on tape that would be too noisy to actually use. She dropped her bag and smiled widely.

"Of course, of course, it's, like, habit, you know?" Jenna said, as if it didn't matter, even though it clearly did.

They all ordered, though Jenna got only a black coffee, her turquoise fingernails tapping out a rhythm on the white ceramic mug, her eyes darting to each booth around them, lingering for a heartbeat and then moving on. Raisa was reminded of a hummingbird. On coke.

"As you know, this is an active investigation," Kilkenny started, and Jenna's full attention snapped back to him.

"I'm allowed to be here."

He smiled gently. "That is true. But you can imagine how delicate the situation is right now."

"An active copycat killer roaming the streets of Everly, yeah I can imagine, Agent Kilkenny," Jenna said, almost sweetly. Too sweetly. "The thing is, you're meeting with me on one of your first days in town. Which means one of two things. Either you need me or you want to threaten me to stay out of your way. Maybe a combination of both."

Raisa took a long swallow of her water to hide her expression. Jenna didn't beat around the bush, that was for sure.

"Maybe a combination of both," Kilkenny admitted. Wisely, Raisa thought. They were all putting their cards on the table, and it helped that no one was trying to play another game while they were at it.

Jenna blew out a breath. "Okay, how can I help?"

"Just like that?" Kilkenny asked.

"I'm not promising anything," Jenna said. For once, she seemed . . . normal. Raisa hesitated to think that, but before Jenna had been so amped up. Now she just seemed like someone off the street, having breakfast with them. "I've researched this case, though, and quite honestly I don't really like when people die. Because of me or not. So. How can I help?"

"Who are you planning on interviewing?" Kilkenny asked.

"Of course you have to ask a good question," Jenna said, but Raisa could hear the slight amusement there. "Mason. I'd love to get my hands on her. But I'm guessing she's a little busy right now. The girls' babysitter also works at the sheriff's station now. Weird coincidence. Or maybe just small-town life. But sometimes it's people like that who know more than they realize. You just have to ask the right questions."

"Which are?"

"Trade secrets," Jenna said, with a charming grin that somehow also conveyed a *back off* message. They'd found her line in the sand. "And anyway, I'm sure they can't compare with yours."

Raisa decided to jump in. "In your research have you found anything to suggest that Alex wasn't the killer in the Parker murder-suicide?"

Jenna stared at her hard, finished her coffee, and then pushed her mug to the end of the table for a refill she probably didn't need.

"I'm not going to bullshit you here—I'm sure you can smell that a mile away," she finally said. "Nothing I've found in, like, three months of researching makes me doubt the murder-suicide played out exactly as the report says. Alex Parker was a screwed-up kid with parents who didn't exactly do anything to help him not be a screwed-up kid. He slipped them pills that came from the house of his coach, where he'd just been the hour prior to the murders. On top of all that, his father was in the early stages of a schizophrenia diagnosis. None of this is actually complicated or scandalous." She did jazz hands. "But people like a little flourish with their storytelling."

Delaney was right, then. Jenna wasn't a true believer. This approach seemed dangerous, though. She was playing with fire she thought she could control. Except that's how entire forests burned to the ground.

"Why did you make it seem like the sheriff was covering something up?" Raisa asked, because there had been plenty of innuendo in that clip about Mason.

"Flourish," Jenna said. "At the time I recorded that, I needed to make it seem like there was something shady going on here to keep everyone's attention for the whole season." She paused. "Plus, come on." She drew that word out, leaning heavy on the *n*. "Samantha Mason is covering *something* up. I don't know what, but she's shady as—"

"Okay," Kilkenny cut in. "Who else do you have on your docket?"

"Christine Keller," Jenna said without missing a beat. "I'm sure you've all talked to her. She was Becks's good friend. When Mason interviewed her, she concentrated on the night of the killings. But Christine Keller must have a wealth of information about the Parkers. A wealth."

Jenna didn't have an accent Raisa could place, but she spoke as if she were on the air at all times, emphasizing words like a late-night infomercial host.

Raisa itched to get a hold of Jenna's writing. Her speech, like her dress, bent young in a very specific way.

"Look," Jenna said, tugging at one of the bars in her eyebrow. "I'm not here to get in your way, I promise. But, like I said, I can maybe help you?"

"Okay," Raisa said, not sure she really believed that. "Has anyone in this 'Alex is Innocent' community ever hinted at—"

"Murder?" Jenna cut in and then laughed in disbelief. "I mean, yeah? Every day? But not anything serious. It's just, you know, hyperbole. How people talk on the internet. None of the big names in the group have demonstrated any truly violent tendencies."

"Have you talked to any of them off the public thread?" Raisa asked.

Jenna didn't hesitate. "A few. They're all . . . well meaning."

"What do you mean by that?"

"I mean one of the most active posters is a stay-at-home dad who is bored out of his mind and looking for something to occupy all the hours the kids are at school. Everyone on a message board seems dangerous until you ask them literally one question about their personal lives."

Raisa thought about the messages she'd read on the thread yesterday. "They don't seem to like you."

"Who likes someone who might challenge your worldview? Who likes someone who comes in and says, 'Hey, all those hours you wasted looking into that conspiracy theory were . . . wasted'?"

"But you do it anyway," Raisa said. "Why?"

Jenna squinted at Raisa. Now she was ignoring Kilkenny. It was odd the way she seemed to be able to focus her full attention on only one of them at a time. It revealed more about her thought process than Raisa guessed she would want. "I got sucked into a conspiracy theory a few years ago. A true-crime one, too. It was . . . not pretty. I ended up hurting people. Emotionally, obvs. Ha." She rolled her eyes at herself. "Everyone thinks they're above falling down rabbit holes, too. But harmful obsession is like a hop, skip, and a jump away from a harmless hyperfixation, you know? We're kind of hardwired for seeing patterns.

"I kind of started this project as a way to see if I could convert, you know, diehards," Jenna continued. "A lot of conspiracy theories overlap or at least touch borders. So, like, theorists who follow 'Alex is Innocent' also think Kurt Cobain was murdered and that there were more people involved in the Oklahoma City bombing. Stuff like that."

Jenna looked away, watching their waitress buzz around to other tables. "When you're in the thick of it, you don't really see the harm you're doing. Like . . . it feels like a fictional mystery to solve. And not like actual people who died. I didn't like the part I'd played before, so I figured, this was kind of my way of making up for it."

Penance.

That's what this was, Raisa realized. Jenna had gotten out of whatever tight-knit conspiracy community she'd been in, and now she wanted to show others that it could be done. Of course, her podcast was also for profit and fame, that was undeniable. But even if those were bigger motivators, this part felt true, at least.

"The 'Alex is Innocent' group just keeps growing by the week," Jenna continued. "It seemed like the perfect case to pick for season two. That maybe I could help people who were doubting already make the final break."

"And lucky you," Raisa murmured. "To have chosen such a timely investigation."

"I'm not Mother Teresa, Agent Susanto," Jenna said, a bit of a bite in her tone. "I'm neither a nun nor a martyr, and I have to pay my bills. Why not do it in a way that I find personally satisfying as well?"

"Fair enough," Kilkenny murmured, but Raisa didn't know how she felt. She liked that Jenna was up front about her biases and motivations, both pure and capitalistic. But for some reason, she felt like she should be repulsed.

Jenna was using a brutal, traumatic crime for her own gain. No matter how she dressed it up in pretty ribbons, her podcast could never be altruistic.

And yet Raisa hadn't expected to walk away from this breakfast with a kind of respect for the woman.

"May I ask you a difficult question?" Kilkenny said.

"Of course." Jenna leaned forward, chin propped on her hand, eager.

"From what you know of this case," Kilkenny said, "who would you predict is the next victim?"

Raisa tried to hide her surprise with another long gulp of water. This was Kilkenny trying to get into Jenna's head, but it came off as an FBI agent unsure of where to go next. It was a risk, but she could see it paying off.

Jenna all but preened at being asked such a substantial question. "Of the copycat killer? That's what this is, isn't it? I knew there was no way for the Balduccis to be involved and *not* be connected to Alex."

Jenna didn't wait for an answer, just started digging in her bag. She pulled out a Lisa Frank binder, bright and colorful and covered in unicorn and cat stickers. Raisa thought she might have had one just like it in first grade. Back when she'd been able to have nice things.

"I mean, if I get this wrong, am I sending someone to their death?" Jenna asked with a nervous glance between them.

"No," Kilkenny said. "Any information will be helpful, I promise."

"If we're looking at close links to the family and the investigation . . ." Jenna said, a bit absently as she flipped through her folder. She landed decisively on one page and looked up at them. "And at the official timeline, I'd say Terri Harden."

Raisa flipped through her mental Rolodex. "The social worker from CPS?"

"She had an official visit to the Parkers in the two weeks before everything transpired," Jenna said, slamming her folder shut once more and shoving it away. "If you're working backward from the Balducci medicine cabinet, and things that went wrong, then she seems like the next target."

Psychology wasn't Raisa's forte. She wanted to ask Kilkenny straight-out if that made sense, but didn't dare do so in front of Jenna Shaw and her phone that may or may not be recording them. Jenna wouldn't be able to post anything from the meeting without consequences, but that didn't stop her from getting the raw conversation anyway.

"Why Terri over Samantha Mason?" Raisa asked, and in that moment, she realized how persuasive Jenna's storytelling abilities were. Raisa had been sold that the sheriff was shady by a few minutes and some deep innuendo.

Everyone thinks they're above falling down rabbit holes.

Raisa thought she was. She couldn't imagine getting pulled into a conspiracy theory considering what she did for work. But she couldn't deny the slight tug of her primate brain that said, *Ask about Samantha Mason.*

"Well, the Balduccis were some kind of statement, right? Samantha Mason doesn't actually represent anything in Alex's case," Jenna said, after a moment, almost like she'd surprised herself by not thinking of Mason. "She was the sheriff, she would have been there no matter what. And not to sound harsh, but, like, she could be killed for any number of reasons? I'm sure in her thirty years here, she's made more than a few enemies. Someone might write off her death as separate from whatever the killer is doing.

"Bottom line?" Jenna looked between them. "The Parker family was hella messy, and messiness is like fertilizer to conspiracy theories, you know? But you have to learn to ignore the mess and find the bones."

"What are the bones?" Raisa couldn't help but ask.

"Human error," Jenna said, with a shrug that seemed just as much a part of her vocabulary as *like* and *you know*. "Like most so-called conspiracy theories. Do you know how much I see 'well this just doesn't make sense' on those groups? But humans don't really make sense. Some people think Bob Balducci had this big plot against the Parker family, like he was in love with Becks or something. But, really, he was just a guy who didn't lock up his medicine cabinet, even when a troubled teenager stopped by his house. Not everything has a thousand layers to it. Some things are just mistakes."

She shot them a half grin and then stood, hefting her bag onto her shoulder. "Now, you'll understand, I've got to run to an interview. You have my number."

Jenna was already three steps away from the table when Kilkenny called out to her. "Any guess on who our copycat is?"

Of course Jenna stopped. She lived for the dramatics.

"No idea," she said after a weighted moment. "And to be honest? I don't care. It's going to be an interesting story no matter how it ends."

CHAPTER TWELVE

DELANEY

Delaney didn't like or dislike cops. They fell into her neutral category until she interacted with them. Some were grateful for her help, some distrustful, some contemptuous.

Some were charming.

Her first and only boyfriend had been a cop. His name was Lincoln Miller, and he had a military buzz cut, an upper lip that was fuller than his bottom lip, and a generous sense of humor that softened the edges of all her oddities.

They met at a bar on Delaney's twenty-first birthday.

"I should card you," he said even though he was in civilian wear— old jeans that didn't quite fit right and a hoodie that smelled of Tide and weed. She found out later it was his roommate's, and he wasn't actually into illegal substances.

"Please do," Delaney said, eagerly turning for her purse.

"Ah." He laughed and signaled the bartender. "It's your birthday, huh?"

He ordered them two shots of something green and sugary that burned so good on the way down.

"You're a cop," Delaney guessed before darting her tongue out to chase the residue on the rim.

"So obvious, then?"

"Don't worry, I'm special—I can always spot the cops." She closed her eyes, enjoying the swooshy feeling in her head. Delaney was fairly certain that if she stood, the floor would sway beneath her. Like a ship. She liked ships, how simple and yet effective they were.

"Oh boy, I think you need some water," the cop said, and Delaney blinked at him.

"No, I'm fine."

"You were talking about ships there for about seven minutes," the cop said.

"Oh, I think I need some water."

He laughed, long and hard, and then got her into a taxi that he paid for. He left his name in her phone as Lincoln (The Cop From the Bar).

"Is your dad a cop?" Lincoln asked four days later, on their first date. Mini golfing. He picked a pink ball and gestured toward the rainbow one for her.

"Oh, um, no."

"Sorry, mom?" he corrected, sinking a shot through an alligator's mouth.

"No, not that, either." Delaney toyed with the end of one of her braids, debating. She wasn't actually worried about him finding out anything. She was far too careful for that. Nothing could get her secrets out of her, not even a dozen of those sugary green shots. But she didn't want to shut down that gentle humor, that kind smile he wore whenever she made an observation about absurd mini-golf rules and the fact that alligators and polar bears certainly would never be found in the same environment. "I find patterns."

"Okay," Lincoln said. "I'm going to need more than that to follow along."

"Do you have to?" Delaney asked, turning to take her hit, to hide her face.

Silence followed her question. It was so long that Delaney finally broke and glanced over at him. He was watching her carefully, though he seemed thoughtful rather than annoyed.

"Only if you want me to," Lincoln finally said, and Delaney bit her lip to keep herself from smiling.

It took her six months of dating to finally explain her hobby. In typical Lincoln fashion, he thought it was "badass" of her. He asked literally—she counted—one hundred and twenty-three questions.

"Do you want to go into law enforcement?" he asked as his one hundred and twenty-second question.

She laughed harder than she had in as long as she could remember. "I can't see myself in a uniform."

He wiggled his eyebrows. "I can."

Delaney blushed as he gently tackled her onto the couch. They'd had sex on their third date exactly—Delaney liked rules such as those—and she'd been delighted to discover that doing the deed with someone more than once made it so much better.

A half hour later, after, his one hundred and twenty-third question had been, "Will you ever stop?"

She thought about the last case in which she'd sent an anonymous tip. She had been tracking a user on one of the message boards she'd frequented. Like many of the angry men who populated those spaces, he'd raged at all the ways the universe had treated him poorly. Nothing that had gone wrong in his life was ever his fault. There was always someone else to blame.

Delaney always paid careful attention to those men—they tended to be the ticking time bombs. She'd been right. When he finally posted about an actual target he had in mind, a way to take out his frustration, and himself, in one glorious spectacle that would "show them all," Delaney had texted one of the FBI agents she had in her contacts. He didn't know her name—she'd almost called herself Deep Throat, but that had been too silly and would have revealed too much personality.

He trusted her, though. It had taken a while, but she'd been right enough times that eventually he'd asked for a way to contact her through an encrypted app.

The FBI found the angry man on his way to his target, his vehicle loaded down with enough weapons to put him away for a long time.

"No," she finally said. "I won't ever stop."

On their first anniversary, they decided to rent an apartment together. A few weeks later, as they lay on their air mattress, Lincoln traced the freckles on the inside of her elbow.

"You don't talk about your past," he said, and she could tell by his tone that he'd been wanting to bring the topic up for a while now. That's how he sounded when he was serious and worried.

"Is that a question?" she tried to tease.

"Dell," he murmured, his lips at her temple, and she tried not to cry. He wasn't always the most observant person in the room, but he was smart and he was curious. If he started digging . . .

He wouldn't find anything. But that didn't mean she could risk staying with him when she knew he was looking.

Three more months, she asked the universe.

It gave her six.

They were almost in the exact same position, though they had a real bed now. Delaney had hesitated on that purchase, not sure how long she would use it. But he'd stopped asking about her family and her high school days. He knew all her classes, what she wanted to do after graduation, the fact that she wanted to stay in the Pacific Northwest. He knew how she drank her coffee, and the way she was obsessed with eating toast for lunch, and that she always forgot to change her oil until the warning light came on. How she laughed at movies that she knew people thought she would think were dumb. How she could get through a romance novel in a day and how she needed that after the time she spent on the dark web.

He *knew* her.

And she'd thought that had been enough.

"Would you ever . . ."

She didn't rush to fill in the rest of the question. She wanted him to ask it.

"Do you ever think it's justified," he said after a few minutes, "to kill someone?"

"Yes," she whispered.

Delaney waited until he fell asleep and then snuck out of bed. She left the Pacific Northwest for the first time in her life that night, buying a ticket to Arizona because it was the next bus departing the station.

Four years later, she finally worked up the courage to google him.

He had married two years after she'd left. His wife was pregnant.

Delaney let herself cry for exactly one hour.

A relationship built on borrowed time would never have lasted.

Delaney wasn't made for love.

She was made for death.

CHAPTER THIRTEEN

RAISA

Raisa wasn't sure what she thought of Jenna Shaw, but Kilkenny had enough faith in the woman's background knowledge of the case to call in the warning about the CPS worker as soon as Jenna walked out of the restaurant.

"Another cup?" the waitress asked, hefting her coffeepot in the air.

"Please," Raisa said, a little desperate. She'd had only the one beer last night, but she hadn't slept almost at all.

Kilkenny took a refill as well. She spotted bags under his eyes that told their own story.

"It's so hot here," Kilkenny said, as if he could read her mind. Maybe he could. "The nights don't even cool down."

It might have been why they were lingering in the Denny's. Despite what she'd said to Delaney, the restaurant had AC, and for the first time in twelve hours, Raisa didn't feel like her core was melting.

"Did you profile Jenna?" Raisa asked, as she toyed with the remnants of her pancakes.

"Mmm. She's good at reading people," Kilkenny said. "Like you are. What did you think?"

"Yeah, she figured out what approach would appeal to us pretty quickly," Raisa said.

"Most importantly, I don't think she'll be a problem with the investigation."

"Really?" Podcasters could be gadflies of the worst degree. Plus, Jenna was smart and invested in this case.

"Her insights were . . . limited," Kilkenny said. "She mentioned the obvious people you would interview for a case like this. I think she'll buzz around, but be more irritant than problem. I'll let Sand know."

"I guess we can put to rest the idea that Alex might be innocent," Raisa said.

Kilkenny raised his brows. "Were you entertaining the idea that he wasn't?"

"No. I mean, I've compared the two writing samples myself and they match." She paused, and then admitted, "I just skimmed through that message board last night. All those people, they're so convinced. The letter was typed; so was the school assignment."

"Do you really think someone was thinking so far ahead as to forge both?"

"No," Raisa said, with a little laugh. "Do you?"

"I'm not the linguist here, but it seems far-fetched," he said. "A note wasn't necessary to prove that he'd done it. Anyone coming upon that scene could see what had occurred."

"Right," Raisa said. "But when it's three a.m. and you've read enough of their theories, they start making sense."

A corner of his mouth twitched up. "When it's three a.m., faked moon landing stories start making sense."

She laughed. "Exactly."

On their way out, Kilkenny's phone rang. The exchange was short and terse. When he hung up, he ran toward his SUV. Raisa didn't bother shouting questions at his back; she just followed, sliding into the passenger seat as he flipped on the sirens.

"They just sent a team over to Terri Harden's apartment."

"The social worker," Raisa murmured, cursing softly. "Dead?"

Kilkenny's grim expression gave her the answer she didn't actually need.

That uneasy, off-balance feeling returned, as she quickly ran through a scenario where Jenna Shaw had killed Terri Harden and then calmly met them for breakfast.

Raisa knew killers that cold-blooded existed. She hadn't picked up on *psychopath* from Jenna. At the end of the day, though, it didn't matter: Jenna hadn't been in town in time to kill the Balduccis.

"Does she live on campus?" Raisa asked as she realized they were heading away from town.

"No. Sand wants us to detain Jenna for further questioning, and she's staying at an Airbnb near Everly College," he said. "Can you text her to meet us close to wherever she is now? Be vague about it."

Raisa dug out her phone and then checked his for Jenna's number. "They think she has something to do with the homicide?"

"Doesn't seem like it," Kilkenny said, confirming her own thinking. He slid into the oncoming lane to go around a Honda that was crawling at five below the speed limit, then cut back into the correct lane just in time to avoid a logging truck blaring its horn at them. "That was one lucky guess, though."

That was true, but Raisa didn't find it as suspicious as she might if someone else had offered up the name. "She knows the case."

Raisa's phone lit up with a message from Jenna.

Miss me already?

A second one followed almost immediately.

I'm in the South parking lot near the college's library. Look for a bright blue Toyota with a huge dent in the left side.

"She's not avoiding us," Raisa said, after she read the text out loud to Kilkenny.

He shot her a look, reading her face quickly, before turning his attention back to the road. He drove recklessly with confidence.

"You like her." Kilkenny was silent for a moment and then said, "Atonement."

Raisa pretended not to hear him.

"That part resonated with you," Kilkenny said, and it wasn't a question. "She's doing this podcast because she wants to make up for something." He didn't look at her this time, just drummed a beat on the steering wheel, humming thoughtfully. "But why do you connect with that?"

Raisa usually liked perceptive people, but she was starting to remember why she'd kept her distance from Kilkenny. He saw too much.

I ended up hurting people.

"Ah," he said softly, and she knew he was thinking about Scottsdale. She would let him think that. It was the safer option. "Yeah."

Everly College's campus gates saved her from having to answer further, but she didn't think Kilkenny would forget the observation. He couldn't press her too hard about history, though, not with his own gaping wound just sitting there waiting to be salted. Raisa didn't like playing dirty, but she knew how to do it well.

She'd had plenty of practice.

Raisa navigated them toward the south parking lot, where they found Jenna Shaw sitting on the hood of her Toyota, which did indeed have a large dent in the left side. She took one look at their faces and hopped off onto the pavement.

"I hate being right," she said in greeting. "The social worker? Terri Harden."

"We'd like to bring you in to ask you a few more questions," Kilkenny said.

"Shit," Jenna breathed out, her teeth working at the tiny silver ring near the corner of her mouth. "That was so quick. What was it? A twenty-four-hour cooling-off period? At most."

Raisa hadn't even made it there in her thought process, but Jenna wasn't wrong.

"Is that enough to qualify them as a spree killer? It might be. Twenty-four hours, does that even count as a cooling-off . . . ?" Jenna rambled, now seemingly talking to herself. She was digging in her massive bag once more, for who knew what.

"Ms. Shaw?" Kilkenny interrupted her.

Her eyes darted to him, then to Raisa. "Am I under arrest?"

"No," Kilkenny said without hesitating, though he wasn't rushing to comfort her, either. "But you can see—"

"How me guessing the next victim is sus, yes," Jenna said. Raisa noticed she had a pen shoved behind each ear to join the other metal crowding into the space. "Obvs."

"Sus?"

Raisa clued Kilkenny in. "Suspicious, it's internet speak. And obvs—"

"I got that one," Kilkenny said, with a tiny smile.

Jenna rolled her eyes, but Raisa got the impression it was at herself. "Besties, I have to stay hip to what the cool kids say."

It certainly went along with the rest of the youthful persona she wore like a slightly ill-fitting coat. But where Raisa had thought she was earnest about it before, Jenna's self-mocking tone seemed to signal she was aware of how it came across. How it all just made her actually seem older than she was.

"Are the cool kids your demographic?" Raisa asked.

"No, actually, it's adults age twenty-eight to forty," Jenna said, and started toward the SUV on her own. "But people who want to be hip are."

"The kind of people who say 'hip'?"

Jenna pointed at Raisa. "You're a smart one, don't let anyone tell you different."

As soon as she climbed into the vehicle, Jenna scooted into the middle of the back seat bench and leaned forward, an elbow on each of the front shoulder rests. "I wonder how the social worker was killed."

"This isn't a game of Clue," Kilkenny said. In Kilkenny tone variations, that was the closest to snapping that Raisa had ever heard.

Jenna raised her palms, placating. Raisa guessed she was familiar with backpedaling. Her tactic seemed to be to lob grenades and then act like it was a mistake that she'd pulled the pin.

"Who do you think is next?" Raisa asked as Kilkenny, once again, tore out of the parking lot.

"No clue," Jenna said, leaning heavily on the word. She was a bit of a brat, which could explain why Raisa—not quite but almost—liked her. Raisa had always preferred spice to sugary sweetness. "No, for real, I don't know. Bob was a gimme and so was Terri—anyone paying attention could have guessed those two."

Raisa shifted in her seat to get a better look at Jenna. "What about the wife? Gina."

Jenna actually looked thoughtful at the question, her teeth playing with her lip ring once more.

"She was home?" was what she finally offered, and Raisa exhaled, not sure what she'd been expecting. Possibly some brilliant insight into the mind of their copycat, but Jenna Shaw wasn't a psychic. She was just read-in on the case.

"Maybe," Raisa murmured, but she didn't think so. The wife worked a part-time job; there were guaranteed times for her to be out of the house. And their copycat killer—for lack of a better description—seemed to be fairly meticulous. Raisa didn't think they would kill someone because of logistics. Not when those homicides had been their opening salvo.

"Who would have thought we would have to be guessing at the *next* victim already?" Jenna said, almost to herself, as she sat back against the seat, apparently deciding Kilkenny and Raisa weren't going to be chatting carelessly in front of her. "That's not a lot of time to figure anything out."

Raisa could admit she'd been taken aback by the fresh homicide as well. She'd assumed they would have a few days to get their feet under them. It wasn't that the task force hadn't moved quickly, but there had been a general lack of urgency. They had all been too complacent, and Terri Harden had paid the price.

Terri Harden.

A shadow slipped along the far edges of her mind. A thought, a memory, a ringing bell from far away telling Raisa she was missing something important about that name.

When she reached out to grab it, though, the feeling dissolved, and all she could see was Jenna's small, satisfied smile in the rearview mirror.

This was going to do wonders for her show.

EXCERPTS FROM TERRI HARDEN'S CASE REPORT ON ALEX PARKER

TERRI HARDEN: Alex, can you tell me what inspired you to write the short story for your English class?

ALEX PARKER: It's me secretly wanting to kill my whole family, right? Isn't that what everyone thinks?

HARDEN: It doesn't matter what everyone thinks. I want to know what you think.

PARKER: I think my parents are stuck-up dweebs, but I don't want to kill them.

HARDEN: Can you tell me more about the short story, Alex?

PARKER: What if I said I didn't write it? What would you do then?

HARDEN: You're not in trouble, Alex. We just want to help.

PARKER: No one ever just wants to help.

———

HARDEN: Can you state for the record who you are?

MEENA AUSTIN: The school psychologist for Everly High.

HARDEN: Can you tell me what your assessment of Alex Parker's story is?

AUSTIN: I'm not concerned about it. I wish Eric had come to me first. Teenagers often develop what might seem like an unhealthy obsession with death but is really just part of the maturation process.

HARDEN: Alex seems overwhelmed by the attention he's getting from all this.

AUSTIN: I'm not surprised. Boys his age think things like that short story are funny until everyone gets really serious about it. I think with the allegations that he's faced over the summer, he's in an extremely vulnerable place.

HARDEN: You're talking about the charges filed by Cara James?

AUSTIN: The false allegations, yes.

HARDEN: You believe they're false?

AUSTIN: The charges were dropped because Alex had an alibi for the time the young woman said she was raped.

HARDEN: Have you noticed a change in Alex's behavior since then?

AUSTIN: Beyond all this fuss? No. Poor kid is just trying to keep his head above water. Some girls just want attention, I'm sorry to say.

HARDEN: What about the Parker sisters? Have any teachers ever come to you with concerns they were being abused?

AUSTIN: No, none. They're bright and inquisitive, active in their classes and hobbies with healthy friend groups. There are rumors that fly around, but in my opinion, there's only smoke there, no fire.

—

A SNIPPET OF THE STORY IN QUESTION

Fast girls and fast cars. High hemlines and higher heels. That's what New York City was all about these days. Alan Park used to let his head be turned by both, but he had more disapline now, now that he knew just how satesfying it could feel to sink a blade into the soft give of someone's belly, to let the voices in his head sink beneath the waves of satesfaction. Why bother with the flappers at the club when he could feel like a God out here in the darkness.

Alan turned up his collar against the cold as he huddled in the shadows of the Harlem firesescape, watching his trails of smoke disappear into the dark crushed-velvet sky and hearing the sirens wail in the distance as he imagined the mother across the street wailing for her daughters to run, run from the monster in there home. There were four children in all, sitting around the table so perfectly framed by the window as if it was a gift to Alex himself.

God, how he wanted to bite into the oldest girl, feel the skin give beneath canines sharpined by his insatiable hunger. Blood would taste like copper, he knew, from cutting his own thighs open just to see what it felt like. He wanted . . . wanted . . . always wanted more. The only time he didn't want more was when he stared into his prey's eyes and watched the light snuff out of them from one moment to the next.

———

CONCLUSION: I have no reason to believe Alex Parker is a danger to himself or others. As to not waste state resources any further, I'll be closing this case.

Signed, Terri Harden, LMSW
August 25, 1998

CHAPTER FOURTEEN

RAISA

Raisa wasn't allowed in the sheriff department's interrogation room, but she was allowed to huddle around the video feed with the rest of the agents on-site.

Though *interrogation room* was perhaps a generous phrase for what Everly had to offer. It looked more like a spare closet that someone had shoved a plastic table into along with two seats, one of which looked suspiciously like a camping chair.

Kilkenny had been invited into the room, and Raisa tried not to be annoyed over being excluded. There was no reason for her to join, she knew that. Still, she'd been part of the team bringing Jenna in; she deserved a spot at the table.

Sheriff Mason and Agent Sand were over at the crime scene at Terri Harden's place, so Jenna was being interviewed by a deputy who Raisa hadn't been introduced to yet.

Jenna seemed thrilled with this turn of events. She was obviously trying to hide her excitement so as not to come off as the actual killer, but every so often she had to tamp down a smile. The subscribers she knew she would net off this had to be making her giddy.

"Look, if someone is trying to draw attention to the Parker case, they're going to kill the people mentioned in the report," Jenna said over the crackly video feed, her tone suggesting that she couldn't believe she was having to explain something so simple. "The caseworker was an obvious one. The others probably aren't. I *might* suggest checking out the teacher who Alex turned that short story in to, but that's just a wild guess."

"The story where he fantasized about killing his whole family?" the deputy asked.

"Yup," Jenna said. She didn't seem to respect the man, though Raisa didn't necessarily blame her. There was visible sweat on his brow and his hands were shaking. "The one where he talked about eating a family."

Raisa didn't like the tendency people had to conflate fiction with the author's morals or personality. Writing dark stories about cannibalistic serial killers didn't make someone a cannibalistic serial killer—in fact, psychologists had long ruled out the idea that fantasies were precursors to real-life action. But looking back, it did seem to signal that not all was right in the world of Alex Parker.

The short story had been set in the *Great Gatsby* universe, written from the perspective of a young serial killer who had been targeting other families as practice for his own. In the story, the main character had killed his three sisters—who just happened to be the same ages as Isabel, Lana, and Larissa—alongside the parents.

In the piece, Alex had liberally used ironic repetition in the same way it had been used in the confession note. It was one of the things Raisa always mentioned in her lectures.

And . . . *shit.* The feeling that had been bothering all her morning finally clicked into something real, and when it did, she couldn't believe she'd missed it.

Raisa slipped through the crowded office that had become a viewing room for the interview. If Jenna said anything more of interest, Kilkenny would report back.

The rest of the sheriff's department was quiet, everyone either at Terri Harden's house or watching Jenna.

All but one person.

A man sat at one of the far desks, interrupting Raisa's single-minded determination to get to a computer. For a paranoid second, Raisa thought about the person on the message board who had traveled to Everly to try to get information out of the sheriff's department. This man wasn't in uniform, and he was packing things into some kind of messenger bag. It seemed far-fetched, but . . . what if it was a conspiracy theorist trying to take advantage of the chaos and snoop around? Or even just a journalist trying to get inside details?

"Can I help you?" Raisa asked, deciding to intervene just in case.

The man glanced up, raising a brow at her tone. "I think that's my line."

Raisa flashed her badge. "FBI Agent Raisa Susanto."

"Yeah, I figured," he said and went back to ignoring her. She crossed the room, catching sight of the nameplate on the desk.

Shawn Dallinger.

It rang a bell. Raisa quickly flipped through her mental Rolodex of the case and rocked back on her heels when she remembered who this could be. The oldest daughter's boyfriend, the one who had been supposedly sleeping with Becks. He'd even gotten a mention on the message board—something about him being a cop now.

She felt fairly confident in guessing, "Deputy Dallinger?"

He grunted something that she took as an affirmative. She studied him while his head was still down.

He was short, a brawler type, replete with a nose that had been broken a time or two dozen and knuckles that had white scars crisscrossing the bone. He had a shock of red hair and freckles that had been doled out with a generous hand. The slight paunch signaling middle age hung over his waistband.

"Sorry," she said. "There are civilians out there who would like nothing more than to riffle through a desk at the Everly Sheriff Department."

"I'm aware."

All right. Raisa had worked with her fair share of dismissive men. But she wasn't about to let this opportunity slip away, either.

"You're not watching the interview?"

He laughed, but it wasn't with any humor. His attention was still on the desk as he shoved a framed photo into his bag. "You think I have a choice in the matter?"

"You've been kicked off the case?"

"You G-men really are a notch above, aren't you?" he said, the eye roll in his voice evident. "How would we poor bumbling cops ever match your observational skills?"

He was pissed, which Raisa didn't care about. He was an asshole, which Raisa cared even less about.

"I'd say it's less about anyone's competence, and more about resources," Raisa said evenly, the line she always doled out when she got pushback from the local departments.

"You the spokeslady?" Shawn asked, finally looking at her. He leered as he did, his eyes dragging along her body, and Raisa struggled to picture Becks Parker finding this man attractive. He would have been young at the time, too, maybe seventeen or eighteen. Perhaps Becks had liked the rough type.

If the rumors had been true, that was.

"No," Raisa said, without offering any other information. Shawn had been barred from the investigation, and whether that had been Sheriff Mason's decision or Agent Sand's, it had clearly been the right one. "You want to answer a few questions about the Parkers?"

Shawn huffed out a disbelieving breath. "Sure, if you show me your subpoena."

"Okay." Raisa drew out the word in a pacifying manner, backing away. "Never mind."

"I knew that family was going to screw me over one day," Shawn muttered.

"What was that?"

He slung the bag he'd been packing over his shoulder. "I said go fuck yourself."

And with that he stormed out of the room, an exit that would have been more impressive had literally anyone but Raisa been around to witness it.

She stared at his desk—it was completely cleared off. His reaction had seemed overblown for having to make himself scarce for a few days, and she'd chalked it up to a man with poor control of his temper. Now she understood what had happened. This wasn't Shawn Dallinger off the case; this was Shawn Dallinger off the payroll. Raisa wondered if he'd thrown a tantrum and bought himself forced unemployment instead of forced vacation.

The outside door slammed against brick wall, Shawn making his displeasure known, probably. It was enough to get her moving again.

Raisa glanced around. She could just sit at Shawn's desk, but the sheriff's door stood ajar, tempting her.

Obviously, she shouldn't go in there to work. But the sheriff was at Terri's place, and the three other deputies had their hands full with Jenna—this being the most action they'd probably seen in years.

Raisa wasn't good at following rules when she could get away with breaking them.

The office was small, like the rest of the place. Three of the walls were completely bare white, but the fourth was covered in pictures, in that same way as restaurants that attracted famous patrons. Raisa did the quick math to figure out that Samantha Mason had been sheriff for more than thirty years. That passing of time was marked through the photographs, though they didn't seem to be in any chronological order.

Raisa scanned each face for the Parkers, and found Tim, smiling wide, his arm thrown around Samantha. But there was something . . . wrong about the photo.

She got closer, angling her head, and . . . right. A quarter of the photo had been cut off. It was too small in the frame, and the edge wasn't as straight as a print-off should be.

And now that Raisa knew a portion had been removed, she realized Samantha was looking in the direction of the missing piece, a wide smile on her face.

It was an odd choice—to hang this one.

Raisa spared a moment to wonder if Kilkenny could magic up some psychological reason that Samantha had picked a photo with the man she'd been allegedly in love with when she wasn't even looking at him.

Who had been cut out?

Becks Parker?

Raisa pulled out her phone and took a picture of the picture. She didn't really know why, but she'd learned long ago to listen to her instincts.

Then she turned to Samantha's desk. The sheriff was a neat freak, or at least one at work. There was no clutter, just a computer and two mesh bins containing equal stacks of files.

From her bag, Raisa dug out the tablet that she always kept synced to her laptop. The Excel spreadsheet could be pulled up on both of them.

She scanned it again, that feeling from back in the interrogation room returning to the forefront. Because, there . . .

We have miles to go before we sleep.

"Sneaky bastard," Raisa murmured. It wasn't the most famous example of ironic repetition out there, but if anyone googled antanaclasis—the literary device's official name—the poem always came up in the search results. In the final two lines of "Stopping by Woods on a Snowy

Evening," Robert Frost used "miles to go before we sleep" both literally and figuratively, the latter being an allusion to death.

Although the use of ironic repetition was what had jogged Raisa's memory, it wasn't why she had pulled up the spreadsheet.

She skimmed the list again and then opened up a browser to confirm what her subconscious had been trying to tell her.

First, she googled the phrase "peace on earth, and silence in the sky." The results led her to the source of the phrase: a Thomas Hardy poem called "And There Was a Great Calm." Her pulse kicked up, and she toggled to her spreadsheet to check the other strange phrase that had stuck out like a sore thumb. Navigating back to the web page, she typed in "worn with toil and tired of life." This one had two pages of results. But they all were of the same source—an old poem by a woman named Rose Terry Cooke.

Terry. Hardy.

Terri Harden.

Raisa sat back against the chair, blowing out a breath.

Three months ago, the killer had left a clue about who the third victim would be.

"Motherf—" Raisa's softly muttered curse was cut off before it could fully fall out because she was interrupted by a knock on the still-open door.

Delaney Moore.

Raisa wondered how long she'd been there and fought a shiver of unease even as she kept her expression calm beneath those cool, assessing eyes.

"You should see this," Delaney finally said. "The killer posted again."

CHAPTER FIFTEEN

RAISA

Delaney leaned over Raisa's shoulder as she opened the "Alex is Innocent" thread.

"I heard Jenna Shaw is here," Delaney said as they waited for the page to load. The wireless wasn't always the most reliable this close to the mountains.

"You didn't go see for yourself?" Delaney seemed like the type to want to insert herself into every part of the investigation.

"No. I wanted to find you."

Raisa didn't ask how Delaney had known she was in the sheriff's office. "The killer only posted this message and not another Flik video of the murder scene, correct?"

"Correct," Delaney said. "From what I can tell, of course. There are millions of videos uploaded per hour on Flik. But since they wanted us to find the previous one, I've been watching their account and the murder tag. Nothing has popped up there. And anything as graphic as Terri Harden's body would have gone viral if it wasn't pulled."

Once again, Raisa was struck by a singular thought—the killer wasn't trying to communicate with the public. If they'd wanted media attention, they clearly could have gotten it. They knew how to work social media and internet boards, a skill set missing for most killers the FBI had dealt with before. Raisa still worked cases where the perpetrator sent VHS tapes to their local news affiliate.

So it didn't seem like too much of a stretch—or worse, confirmation bias—to assume the killer wanted to exclusively communicate with law enforcement.

But why?

She returned to the idea that someone might be trying to bring law enforcement attention to the case. That would fit with the unsub setting up a messaging system with the FBI.

Delaney tapped the screen. "There it is."

"Thanks," Raisa said dryly. As if she would forget the killer's username.

> **GALAHAD:** Now you see it has begun, my friends, and everyone here will have satesfaction soon, because Alex's time has come now, now that the FBI agents can see see how wrong they are in there belief that we are all crazy here and there aren't any alternative suspects to Alex. I want you to know that I have appreciated all the support that you have shown for Alex and how that support is felt by anyone whose been wrongly accused of a crime. I am sure there will be more here soon who have turned up against injustice.

Raisa huffed out a breath. "They're imitating Alex's voice."

"That was a fast assessment," Delaney said. "Though I did think it sounded different than their other messages."

"Mm-hmm. Some of the idiolect is copied verbatim from Alex's short story," Raisa said, tapping on the *now, now* configuration and the misspellings and grammar mistakes. "But one of the things that always stands out in Alex's writing are the run-on sentences. They're common in internet speak, but the killer hadn't been using that before."

After reading it three more times, Raisa sighed. "They've studied the research surrounding Alex's letter. Which makes my job harder."

"Why do you say that? Couldn't they have just picked out obvious things?"

"They did," Raisa said. "But they also included something little. Here." She used Delaney's tablet pen to underline *turned up against*. "One of the phrases I include in my lecture is 'turned up his collar against the cold.' It's a somewhat unique order of the words. On Google, if you search 'turned up his collar,' you get just under eight thousand results. If you search 'turned his collar up,' you get closer to thirty thousand. That's a notable difference in preferences."

"Eight thousand still sounds like quite a lot," Delaney pointed out.

"Yes, but when you start building an idiolectic profile, it becomes one more—"

"Puzzle piece, right," Delaney cut in.

"This instance might not mean anything, but considering how awkwardly constructed the sentence is, it feels deliberate," Raisa said, adding the phrase into her spreadsheet for the killer.

Delaney didn't say anything, and when Raisa looked up, the woman had circled the desk. She lowered herself into one of the visitor chairs, pursing her lips like she was holding back a thought.

"What?" Raisa prompted, annoyed that she was curious enough to ask.

"It seems like a waste of a message, doesn't it?" Delaney said. "Just to show us they could fake Alex's writing style. That seems obvious. Anyone could fake his writing style if they had the internet. It's everywhere. It doesn't matter that they can fake it now, it matters that someone wouldn't have been able to fake it back then."

Delaney was right—there was enough research out there on Alex's style that anyone with enough time on their hands could do a decent job at replicating it, even with new concepts.

"Some people would have," Raisa said slowly, thinking through the implications of what Delaney had just pointed out. "Been able to mimic it back then, that is."

"The English teacher."

Who, incidentally, was Jenna's guess on the next victim.

"Family and friends," Raisa said.

"How difficult is it to mimic someone's idiolect?" Delaney asked. "Is it possible a stranger wandered into the house and Alex's short story was just lying around?"

"Nothing is impossible," Raisa said, a common refrain for her. People in her field liked caveats. "But it would have been difficult. You can feel the imitation in this. I mean, apart from some of the awkward sentence construction." She zoomed in on the post. "See, Alex had a distinct misspelling of words that had a vowel in one of the later syllables that sounded like another vowel. Think 'remembrance.' It sounds like there should be an *i* where the *a* is. But here, the killer spells 'alternatives' correctly. I would have expected an *i* instead."

"Puzzle pieces," Delaney repeated.

"They don't mean much by themselves, but put together . . ."

"The sky," Delaney said.

A throat cleared.

Sheriff Samantha Mason stood in the doorway, her hand resting on the butt of her holstered gun. "Can I help you ladies?"

Raisa didn't startle. She'd lost her jump reflex somewhere between stealing mac and cheese at the corner store when she was eleven so that she didn't starve at night and catching terrorists with bombs in their cars on the way to blow up a school.

Delaney didn't jolt or look guilty, either, but Raisa had begun to expect that kind of detachment from her.

The sheriff, meanwhile, seemed shaken at the sight of them behind her desk. Raisa took quick stock of the files in the basket, but none were labeled. What could Mason have back here that she didn't want them to find? Raisa might not follow rules all the time, but she would never have snooped in the drawers.

By the time Raisa looked back at the sheriff, she had hidden any distress.

Samantha Mason was about the same height as her, but whereas Raisa was petite, the sheriff had the stocky, chest-heavy build of a bull-dog. Her blonde hair clearly came from a bottle and was cut into a short, spiky style. She wore her years in the leathery, tan skin that carried valleys in the lines by her mouth and eyes.

"Oh, perfect," Agent Sand said, interrupting the tense moment when he popped his head in. "I need all three of you. We're doing a debriefing out there now."

Raisa watched Samantha to see if she would protest or essentially tattle on Raisa and Delaney for being in her office. But she just nodded and followed Sand toward the gaggle of G-men.

"I think I would have yelled more," Delaney mused, and Raisa couldn't help but laugh as she stood and restowed her tablet.

"Uh, yeah," Raisa agreed. "At the very least."

The main room was packed too full. Everly had three deputy sheriffs—sans Shawn Dallinger. The task force had nine field agents, plus Sand, Kilkenny, and Raisa, and the crime scene techs. Raisa found herself in the back, squeezed in between Delaney and one of the deputies, whose name she'd already forgotten.

"Teresa Harden's TOD is around six this morning," Sand said once everyone had settled down to listen. "Her throat was cut with a straight razor, just in case there was any doubt on if these three killings are connected."

"Was there a tombstone?" Kilkenny asked.

"There was, yes, painted above her bed." Sand checked his watch. "It is currently eleven thirty a.m. Depending on if the killer is escalating, we might have less than nineteen hours—at best—to stop the next homicide. You all have about thirty seconds to tell me who is doing what to make sure we don't have four dead bodies on our hands."

"I don't think the killer is escalating," Kilkenny said, not bothering to raise his voice to be heard. Everyone listened when Kilkenny spoke.

"Why's that?" Sand asked, arms folded over his chest.

"These first two attacks happened almost exactly twenty-four hours apart, yes?"

Sand nodded, once.

"I'm guessing the third one will be tomorrow at six a.m.," Kilkenny said. "Everything about these two scenes and about the killer's online activity has been organized and deliberate. We're not dealing with someone who is out of control with bloodlust. We're dealing with someone who has planned this for a long time. I think we have the full eighteen and a half hours."

"You're willing to bet someone's life on that?"

"Yes," Kilkenny said, without a single tremor in his voice.

Raisa pressed her lips together, impressed and jealous. Whenever she gave her opinion, she had to qualify it with a hundred caveats. She couldn't imagine looking Sand in the eye and staking her entire reputation—staking someone's *life*—on her own expertise.

"All right, you heard the man. That still gives us less than a day to catch this son of a bitch," Sand said. He didn't swear often, so when he did, it landed. Everyone around Raisa straightened. Two of the agents closest to Sand volunteered to go check on the English teacher, who apparently was retired and lived in a cabin close to the border of Canada.

Brianna Labuskes

Raisa stepped forward. "The killer just posted on the 'Alex is Innocent' thread."

"Anything notable?" Sand barked out.

"Not at first read," Raisa said. "But the killer gave us hints to Terri's name in the messages they posted before the first killings. I'm going to comb through the posts we have and match it up to the police report from the murder-suicide. We don't know what we could be missing." She paused and then added, "I'd also like to do a breakdown on the idiolects of the users who've posted on the 'Alex is Innocent' thread."

Sand nodded. "If it's someone who wants to call attention to the case, there's a good chance it's one of them."

Raisa didn't mention how it was more likely the person was a lurker. If they knew enough about linguistics to post messages about it, they probably would have avoided leaving their fingerprints—so to speak—in a place so obvious. But it was worth doing the work to cross those active posters off their suspect list.

"Great, take Ms. Moore with you," Sand directed. Raisa knew how to follow an order, and turned to leave the room. Except it wasn't just Delaney who followed her.

She met Kilkenny's serious eyes and lifted her brows in question.

"I think I'll be most helpful with you," he said. "Going over the Parker case, especially. There has to be something there that can give us more information on our current killer."

Delaney hovered between them. "I'll keep working on your spreadsheet, running it through my program. It should be able to tell us if the killer has ever posted under any other name on different sites. Or at least give us some places to start."

Raisa looked between them. Somehow, they'd formed their own little trio on this case. She wasn't sure how she felt about that.

"Go team," Raisa said weakly.

As they left the building, Raisa noticed Jenna Shaw lingering by the door, her tape recorder in one hand, three pens in the other.

120

"Any chance you three want to fill me in on what's going down in there?" Jenna called over to them.

Only Raisa glanced over, and that was just to shoot her an incredulous look.

Jenna simply grinned back. "You can't blame a girl for trying."

"Did she have anything else interesting to say?" Raisa asked Kilkenny quietly.

"It was what she didn't say that I found more notable," he said. "She never mentioned the boyfriend."

"Shawn Dallinger," Raisa said, not mentioning her own interaction with the man. "The one she's obviously going to center the podcast around. Or at least the one she was going to until all this happened."

"The deputy sheriff," Delaney added. "His eyes are too small for the rest of his face, and he smells of garlic. I don't think he's our killer, though."

"Right," Kilkenny said slowly. "But if I was being interrogated by police and had been asked to provide a guess for the next victim, I would immediately think of him."

"But Jenna didn't?"

"No," Kilkenny said. "And I'm not sure what that means." He paused, his mouth doing that almost smile thing. "I don't like not being sure."

"It had to happen sometime," Raisa teased, but she was thinking of Shawn, his angry eyes, his contempt even though she was a stranger to him. He had the body and the knuckles of a fighter, and that's how she pictured him killing, too. Bloodlust hot in his veins. She couldn't see him referencing a Robert Frost poem just to communicate with the FBI's forensic linguist. "Probably she wants him to herself."

Kilkenny's expression cleared. "Good point. Just because she told us she was cooperating fully doesn't mean she will."

"I don't think she thinks he's next, though," Raisa said, giving Jenna the benefit of the doubt.

"No, me neither."

"This is part of the game, isn't it?" Raisa realized. "To keep us so busy figuring out who the next victim is we can't devote proper resources to finding the killer."

"We're always going to prioritize saving someone if we can," Kilkenny agreed.

Delaney shook her head, her twin braids sliding over her shoulders. "And that's why they'll always win."

CHAPTER SIXTEEN

DELANEY

The men Delaney hunted always asked one thing: *Can you keep a secret?*

At thirty-five, Delaney had seen it so many times, she was almost surprised when she didn't get that lobbed in her direction.

Never in all the years she'd been sifting through the darkest garbage on the internet had she received the question that had just popped up in her chat box.

Do you want to be my friend?

Delaney's fingers hovered over the keys, then she withdrew her hands, resting them in her lap. She chewed on her lip as she looked over her shoulder, as if someone would be there watching her.

No one was, of course. She was in the tiny apartment she was renting in Eugene, Oregon. She'd left Arizona two years ago and returned to the Pacific Northwest because she couldn't stay away. Eugene wasn't Washington, but it was close enough.

And as an added bonus, Delaney actually felt like she fit in here in a way she hadn't anywhere else in her life. Eugene was a funky college town with hippie co-ops and used bookshops and kind people who remembered her coffee order and gave her treats to feed the store's dog.

The houses here were too much, too big, too overwhelming, though. She'd thought she was going to have to move on to a different town until she came across a listing for the basement suite in a tiny English-style cottage rented by a tiny Englishwoman named Lydia King. Every garden in Eugene was beautiful, but Lydia's was Delaney's favorite thing in the whole world. The older woman had embraced chaos, and what came out was a riotous mix of wildflowers and roses, of vines and ferns and weeds.

It was the functionality of the little suite, though, that had sold her. Delaney had her own entrance from the outside, and the only other entry point was a door that led into Lydia's kitchen. Delaney had added a dead bolt to that the night she'd moved in; Lydia had never tried to come down, anyway.

There were no windows.

There was no one here except for her.

Delaney turned away from the shadows and back to her screens. She had taken a boring job editing user manuals for everything from blenders to Jeep Wranglers. Her parents would roll in their graves if they saw all her *wasted potential* piling up in the compost behind Lydia's house. But the position paid well enough for Delaney to afford new computers when she needed them and to buy the coffee at the place with the dog. That was pretty much all she had ever needed in life.

Except, no. She'd always needed a friend.

The woman she was talking to called herself Kylie, but online Delaney called herself Hannah, so she didn't exactly trust Kylie was telling the truth. They'd connected on an Infinity9 thread for romance readers. Kylie had posted some pictures of old-school Johanna Lindsey covers, and Delaney had broken the one rule she'd made for herself while interacting with her hobbies online.

For the past three weeks, they'd been chatting back and forth publicly. Not too much, but enough that Delaney thought maybe the most basic demographic facts that Kylie had offered about herself were somewhat accurate. She seemed about Delaney's age, a woman, and from the United States, though where exactly Delaney couldn't pinpoint.

All this assumed, though, that Kylie wasn't trying to mask her identity. Delaney had no reason to believe she was being played, but she had learned quite a few lessons in the darkest corners of the internet. You could never be sure of anyone.

Still . . . Delaney had made certain she hadn't given anything about herself away. Even if Kylie had ill intent, she wouldn't ever be able to find Delaney. Not unless Delaney wanted to be found.

Delaney rested the tips of her fingers against her keyboard. She exhaled and then typed.

Yes.

CHAPTER SEVENTEEN

RAISA

Despite the fact that Raisa knew they were playing the killer's game, she was as helpless as the rest of them. They had to figure out who the next victim was. To do that, Raisa needed a list of names. She couldn't search for hidden messages without having something to compare the results to.

Raisa took one of the little café seats at the table on her cabin's back porch and pulled out her tablet to access the Parker file. She could tell Kilkenny and Delaney were doing the same. Delaney had taken the other seat at the table, leaving Kilkenny trying to look professional in the Adirondack chair.

Somehow the ridiculously flawless bastard still accomplished it.

The key to finding something fresh was to return to what she knew best. The words.

Alex's short story and his last letter.

In the fiction piece, Alex's fantasies had revolved around the girls, not the parents. The story was at its most graphic when he wrote about killing the sisters, but he hadn't hurt his own.

Isabel, Lana, and Larissa had been safe. Because they'd been with Christine Keller at the time of the murders.

Raisa found her interview in the Parker file.

"Becks called me at five or so, asked if I could watch the girls for two hours," Christine said back in '98. *"No, she didn't sound upset. Not more than usual."*

The sheriff asked her to clarify that.

"You know—you saw it, too. She'd been worrying a lot in the months before . . . well. Before. The thing with Tim. And then that girl accusing Alex."

The thing with Tim.

What the hell did that mean? Samantha hadn't asked her to clarify, so she must have known what Christine was talking about. Was it just his mental state? Or was there something more?

"And the girls were growing up so fast. Isabel had a boyfriend, Lana was turning into a preteen brat. I think baby Larissa was the only calm thing in Becks's life this past summer. Anyway, Becks called me up and I was, ha, I was a little peeved. You know, it's just me, and I have a kid of my own. Becks always sent the girls over to my house, though, instead of asking me to send Tiffany to her. Becks was . . . She didn't always see things that didn't involve her family. I'm not . . . I loved her. But she was very focused. She had her career and her family and . . ."

The sheriff had let Christine babble on. At points, the woman seemed to feel guilty over complaining about her dear friend who had just been murdered; at others the interview read like a bloodletting. Like resentment had been building up for so long that there was no choice but for it to come pouring out when given the chance.

When she looked up, she found Kilkenny watching her.

"Christine Keller," she answered his unasked question. "She said Becks was having a rough summer before everything happened." She jerked her chin toward his tablet. "Anything?"

"Yeah, I'm reading up on Shawn Dallinger. He was brought in for an interview," Kilkenny said. "But it seems like it was perfunctory. He didn't have a strong alibi, just one buddy who swore they'd gone driving around that night to get high."

"And Samantha didn't follow up after that," Raisa said. She'd skimmed that section of the Parker file, but she knew Kilkenny had hoped there would be some small detail that suddenly answered a bunch of their questions.

Raisa didn't buy into the theory that the killings had been a robbery gone wrong. But if Shawn had been sleeping with both Becks and Isabel, he would have had plenty of access to the house. It wouldn't take a huge leap in logic to say Shawn had noticed Alex had stolen some sleeping pills and capitalized on the moment.

Raisa could almost see it—Shawn as a teenager with those same angry eyes. A rage bubbled beneath his skin, pouring out over anyone it touched.

"Mason seems like a decent detective, but not on this case," Kilkenny said, sounding frustrated.

"She was young?" Raisa suggested. "A big murder case involving her close friends. She probably hadn't seen anything like it before."

"That's the generous assessment," he said.

"I feel like we just reversed roles," Raisa said. "I'm supposed to be the suspicious, mistrustful one."

His lips twitched into an almost smile. "I don't mind wearing the hat every once in a while."

"Anything about his affair with Becks?"

"No, but that rumor has always struck me as odd," Kilkenny said, crossing one long leg over his knee. "If it was such an open secret, what was Isabel still doing with him?"

"What fifteen-year-old girls know versus what the rest of the adults know are two very different things," Raisa pointed out.

"Right," Kilkenny acknowledged with a little head tip.

"It sounds like there's something you're not saying."

He squinted off into the distance. "It's not just this rumor. There's a lot of them floating around this family—you can see that from what people post on the Alex thread. What Jenna talks about, and how her guests speak of the Parkers. Everything is brimming with innuendo about their scandalous lives. The sheriff was in love with Tim, he was a lothario on campus—the very place his wife worked. Alex the cliché of a sleazy high school football player."

"Almost like a soap opera," Raisa said, catching on. "Too much to be true."

"Maybe it is all factual. Where there's smoke, there's certainly usually fire, but it does feel a bit excessive." Kilkenny shrugged. "People clearly liked talking about the Parkers. And in a small town like this, where that's the entertainment . . ."

"The rumors start snowballing," Raisa said, mixing the metaphor. "I wonder if the TA is still in town. The one Tim was allegedly seeing." She checked in her file for the name. "Mark Theroux."

Even as she asked the question, she did a quick Google search. One of those professional development social media sites popped up informing her that Mark Theroux was a professor at Everly College. She shot Kilkenny a questioning look.

He, in turn, glanced at Delaney, who shook her head. "Nothing from me yet. Maybe in another hour or two. The internet is big."

Raisa huffed out a laugh, beginning to recognize Delaney's humor. Then she pushed to her feet and Kilkenny followed.

"Let's go see how hot the fire was."

———

Professor Mark Theroux was a friendly man with an easy smile and easier charm.

He was tall with a thick red beard and long hair that he pulled back into a sloppy bun. In another century he could have been a Viking. In this one, he looked like he was worried about breaking the chair he was sitting in.

"I am uncertain what I can tell you," he said, stroking the ends of his beard. "That was so long ago, so long ago."

"If you feel comfortable," Kilkenny started gently. "Could you confirm if you had a relationship with Tim Parker?"

"Ah." Pink bloomed along the ridges of Mark's cheekbones. "No, no. That was a ludicrous rumor going around. He was so talented, I can't deny I had a tendre and he probably enjoyed my adoration. He basked in the spotlight. But, alas, no. Nothing improper or unseemly was happening."

Raisa nearly smiled at Mark's idiolect, his penchant for ten-dollar words and overly formal phrasing—charming to her instead of pretentious mostly because of how much it contrasted with his rugged aesthetic. She hadn't come into this interview thinking he was involved in this case, but after listening to him for only a few minutes, she could confidently say none of their writing samples belonged to him.

"Were there similar rumors back then?" Kilkenny asked.

"We're a small college in a small town." Mark shrugged and smiled at the desk, as if lost in the memory. "I basked a little myself in the fame that came with being associated—even in such a tawdry way—with the Parkers. But Mrs. Parker never seemed bitter about the prittle-prattle."

"You knew Becks Parker?"

"Indeed, I did," he said. "As did most people in town. She was Everly royalty. And she had a charming sense of humor about the insinuations." He grinned. "She said we should have an orgy and she would bring her daughter's boyfriend." He hastened to add, "That was another rumor that clung to them like a bad fish odor."

"Was there also talk about Tim seeing his students?"

"I'm sad to say there was." Mark dipped his head. "I can't promise there wasn't anything untoward going on. I was too starstruck and too oblivious at the time and lacked the moral fortitude it would have taken to act upon any such claims. This was long before Me Too as well." His eyes flicked to Raisa. "I'm more educated now, but back then, some flirtations were simply not unusual. I do hope it wasn't more than that, because to me, it seemed like it was all gossip. And since I featured as a supporting character in those fictitious stories . . . well."

"You assumed everything else was exaggerated as well," Raisa said, still enjoying how very much his idiolect was his and his alone. She itched for a sample of his writing for no other reason than the fun of mapping out his idiosyncrasies.

"Also . . ." Mark hesitated, his blush deepening. "Not to be indelicate, but Tim wasn't interested in pursuing a tawdry fling. He was consumed by his work, especially in the last year. He stayed late, but not to conduct any liaisons. He was running equations the whole time."

Kilkenny was quiet, and she knew there was something going on in that brain of his. Finally, he asked, "Did anyone on campus have it out for Tim? Or the Parkers?"

Mark drummed his meaty fingers on his desk, his face relaxed until it wasn't. "Well, there was one young lady."

Both Kilkenny and Raisa straightened. It was Raisa who asked, "A young lady?"

"I don't remember her name, I apologize," Mark said, tugging at the end of his beard. "She was a former student of Tim's. She thought he'd stolen work from her. She was pestering him those last few weeks before he died. Such a shame, that."

"Were her claims credible?" Kilkenny asked.

"I never saw anything that convinced me," Mark said. "It happens sometimes. Someone does something spectacular, spectacular enough to bring national recognition, and vultures come out of the woodwork. It can be hard to prove originality when you're working on similar proofs with classes full of students."

"And she disappeared after Tim died?"

Mark sat back at that. "Yes, that's accurate. The article about his proof was never retracted, so I assumed she wrote the whole affair off as a lost cause."

How hard would it be to figure out who the former student was? Was it worth it?

"Oh." Mark snapped his fingers. "I nearly forgot. There was the gossip columnist as well. She definitely had it out for the Parkers."

"Gossip columnist?" Raisa asked, still mostly thinking about the young woman.

"Everly—the town, not the college—has a newspaper that runs weekly. It's . . . glorified ad space most of the time. But that summer they ran a gossip column called Everly Ears. It published anonymously," Mark said, and Raisa winced, already seeing where this was going. Social media alone hadn't made people cruel to each other—it just made it easier. "If you're asking about rumors, well, I think that was the origin of all the innuendo about them. Becks tried to bribe the editor to stop running the damned thing or at least stop mentioning their family. But it printed every week, up until their death. I believe it was what was selling the paper, to be perfectly honest."

"And then that disappeared, too?"

"I suppose it did," Mark said, stroking his beard. "I thought at the time it was a guilty conscience." He seemed to read something on their faces, because he rushed to add, "Not that they were involved, but it cannot be good in terms of the karmic balance of the universe to have been spreading spurious stories about two people who were then killed by their own son."

They all sat with that for a minute before Kilkenny charged gamely on. "How was Tim's mental state that final few weeks?"

"*Those* rumors were true, unfortunately," Mark said, grief sliding into his expression. "I was doing much of his work for the college by the very end. His paranoia was the worst part of it all. He kept accusing me of stealing his proof."

"His proof?"

"The one the young lady was harassing him over," Mark said. "Strange that he then pointed his finger in my direction." He looked between them. "Ah. I forget that laymen don't know about Tim's masterpiece. A couple weeks before he died, he solved a proof. It was so revolutionary in the math world, and yet all he's remembered for is, well," Mark said. Everyone tangentially involved who talked about the murder-suicide did so in awkward tones, as if it were embarrassing the Parkers had aired their dirty laundry in so gruesome a fashion. "The Parkers hosted a party for Tim, and most of the town attended. They held it just a few weeks before they died."

"You said his paranoia was the worst of his symptoms," Kilkenny said. "Were there other concerning behaviors that you noticed?"

"His mood was mercurial." Mark sighed heavily. "His work was drivel at that point. Once, he was lecturing—this is difficult to explain—but he might as well have written the alphabet when he was trying to describe the Declaration of Independence. And he had no awareness of the fact that he had done that."

"But he still had a proof published," Raisa pointed out.

"That's a long and arduous process that was mostly done before he started to slip," Mark said. Then his voice went a bit dreamy. "It *was* revolutionary, though."

"Did you ever interact with Alex Parker?" Kilkenny asked.

Mark dipped his head again. "He would stop by in the afternoons. Mrs. Parker and Tim both thought he was showing a high aptitude in math, but, honestly, he wasn't. Not to speak ill, but everything about him was fairly average. He was always more interested in talking to the coeds." He paused, and leaned forward. "Now rumors about him? I would believe."

There had to be a psychological effect for thinking you could tell a monster apart from anyone on the street after they'd proved they were a monster. The cliché interview, where the neighbor said they never suspected anything, was actually rarer than the opposite. People liked to say, *Oh, I always knew that one was a bad apple,* even when they thought nothing about the person before they'd shown their true colors.

It seemed to center around a need to feel control in the midst of horror. If you could spot the wolves in sheep's clothing, you might not get eaten yourself.

When Raisa and Kilkenny made it back to the car, Raisa shifted in the passenger seat so that she was facing him. "You're thinking about something."

Kilkenny made a maybe-so face, and Raisa poked him in the shoulder. She didn't know what had possessed her to do it, though he didn't seem shocked.

"It feels like I might be on a wild-goose chase."

"You know, that term actually came from a form of horse racing," Raisa said, because that's how her brain worked sometimes. "The back horses would have to try to follow a lead horse on an unpredictable course. From above, they looked like how geese do when they fly in formation. Shakespeare—of course—was the first to use it as an idiom. In *Romeo and Juliet.*"

She could swear he was smiling behind his neutral expression.

"Well, I'm certainly the back horse in this scenario," Kilkenny said. "I'm not surprised that Mark said the rumors weren't true."

"He could be lying," she said to play devil's advocate.

"Fair, but he didn't seem to be," Kilkenny said. "He could also be misremembering, and painting himself in a kinder light. But he remembered Becks's joke about the orgy."

"That's something that sticks with you."

Kilkenny tipped his head in agreement. "What I think is that someone was spreading gossip about them. It seems like everything from innocuous rumors to more serious charges. But I don't know why. And if that has anything to do with their murder."

Raisa heard something layered beneath the musings. "You're wondering if Alex is innocent."

He made a face that was almost a denial but not quite. "No, like you've said, the note would have been hard to forge. And the timeline is clear. Alex went to Bob Balducci's place, got the pills, came home, probably threw some sort of teenage temper tantrum, and the parents decided they wanted the girls out of the house to deal with him. Becks sent them to Christine Keller's house. I'm guessing the parents sat down to dinner with Alex to try to talk things through. Alex drugged them and then killed them. The girls came home, found them, called the sheriff. Nothing seems extraordinary about any of that."

"So why the horse race?" Raisa asked.

Kilkenny rubbed at his wedding ring with his thumb, and Raisa tried not to stare at it. "Once upon a time, I ignored my gut. I wasn't thorough, and I paid for it. It's hard for me to look away now when something catches my attention."

They locked eyes long enough for him to see the understanding on her face.

She had the ridiculous urge to tell him her secret, the one she hadn't told anyone else.

The words sat on her tongue, eager to fall into the space between them.

And then her phone rang.

EXCERPT FROM EVERLY EARS GOSSIP COLUMN

July 7, 1998

Everyone in Everly is abuzz like little bees. Usually we only have one big summer blowout party to look forward to, but this year is granting us two. Invitations just went out for a celebration at the Parker house for Professor Parker's big accomplishment. This writer has been wondering for quite some time when the Parkers would figure out a way to steal back the limelight from the Balduccis. What better way than to host a get-together in August so that no one will be talking about the one on the Fourth?

Speaking of, a bashful birdie told me that Bob Balducci had a little too much fun at his own shindig. He ended up sleeping in Gina's prized rosebushes and had to be dragged in at dawn by the couple's embarrassed son, Greg. Rumor has it that Greg wasn't in much better shape—in fact, not only was he hungover while underage, he was sporting a black eye from the night before. No one knows how it started, but Greg and Alex Parker ended up coming to blows right there in the Balduccis' backyard. This writer heard that the entire football team intervened, taking sides. Greg is off at college now, but that doesn't mean his reputation hasn't garnered him some loyal supporters. He's the one who took us to states, after all.

Either way, it will be hard to top the wild Fourth party, but if anyone can do it, it's the Parkers. Maybe there will be a repeat fight between Greg and Alex. I doubt their feud was resolved with just a punch or two. What on earth could have been the cause? Was Greg defending some poor maiden's honor? Did he malign Alex's mother, who we all know has some low-hanging fruit any bully could pick? Either way, you'll want to grab your popcorn, folks. That's all for now. Kisses.

Everly Ears

CHAPTER EIGHTEEN

RAISA

Raisa's phone rang a second time, and Kilkenny looked like he wanted to tell her to ignore it. As if he'd known she'd been about to spill out some dark secret she'd never told anyone else.

But he was a consummate professional and they were in the middle of a serial killer case, so he just sat there in the driver's seat quietly as she murmured, "Delaney," and then answered.

"I think I know who the next victim is going to be," Delaney said without preamble.

Raisa immediately put her cell on speakerphone. "Who?"

"I was looking at the timeline, and, well, did I tell you? I'm good with patterns. And logic. Patterns and logic," Delaney babbled. "Sometimes things just click for me and I know that you're looking at tubes of paint and the material each brush is made of and that was a really good metaphor, did I tell you you're quite good at those? Because you are, with the sky, too. But anyway I see the lilies, you know? The bridge and the lilies, the full painting if you get what—"

"Delaney."

"Right. I was looking at the timeline. No. I was looking at the two deaths. Bob Balducci and Terri Harden," Delaney said.

"And Gina," Raisa couldn't help but add. She had a feeling people thought of the wife as collateral damage, but Raisa wasn't so sure.

"Not statistically relevant yet," Delaney said, almost as an aside. Raisa once again thought of the type of person it would take to moderate the videos that were uploaded onto Flik. Delaney must have seen her fair share of horror. Maybe the only way to deal with it was through detachment. "If we take Bob Balducci and Terri Harden, we start to get a pattern. And if I look at all of this through that pattern, the English teacher does not fit."

Raisa tried to parse through words for what Delaney was really saying. "Okay. So what's the pattern?"

"Neglect."

The word crawled along Raisa's nerve endings.

"The English teacher was the opposite of neglectful," Raisa said, realizing what Delaney had already figured out. "He flagged Alex's short story to the counselor, who called the authorities."

"If I'm correct, which I would say I am eighty-seven percent of the time, which is pretty good, considering most people are right about—"

"Delaney."

"Sorry, sorry, I get this kind of buzz when I figure things out," Delaney said, a bit sheepishly. "Okay, but if I'm right, the counselor and the English teacher are probably safe from our current killer. If they're still alive, that is. I suppose if they're not, they would still be safe. Can corpses be safe? There *are* grave robbers—"

"Delaney."

"Right," she said, and Raisa was almost amused. Even Kilkenny's mouth twitched. "So, I was going through the timeline, looking for neglect in particular. And I came across Stewart Young."

Raisa thought she knew all the players in the case by now, but the name didn't sound at all familiar. She glanced at Kilkenny, who shook his head slightly.

"Completely understandable if you don't know who that is," Delaney said, reading their silence for what it was. "He was an Everly deputy sheriff for six weeks in the summer of 1998, but he quit right before the Parker murder-suicide. He's now the only dentist in town—quite the life change, if you ask me. So I got to wondering what his come-to-Jesus moment was, and I found, well. Brace yourselves. I found Alex."

"Okay."

"Remember how the Balduccis threw a Fourth of July party every year? From what I can tell, the whole town went, and it was one of those things that everyone talked about for weeks afterward."

"Sure, yup," Raisa said, to get Delaney rolling.

"So at the one in 1998, Greg Balducci, one of Gina and Bob's sons, got into a fight with Alex. Apparently, it was bad enough that the deputy sheriff, who drew the short straw of being on duty that night, was called in. That deputy was Stewart Young."

"Do we know who instigated the fight?" Raisa asked.

"Police report suggests Greg, but the boys shut up once Young arrived on the scene," Delaney said.

"I'm not seeing the neglect yet," Raisa admitted. It was a fact of life that teenagers were little id-driven machines whose frontal cortices hadn't developed yet. They got in stupid fights and said stupid things to each other. Especially when at least one of them had homicidal tendencies that would emerge less than two months later.

"Right," Delaney said again. "I still found it strange that Young left the sheriff's department so abruptly after that incident. So I called him."

Raisa choked on her own spit. "You just decided to call Stewart Young out of the blue?"

"Yes."

"Well, okay." So apparently there were some benefits to a civilian being a part of the task force. They didn't worry about proper procedure.

"He said that Alex was on something that night," Delaney continued. "And that Young wanted to take him into the station. But the sheriff intervened."

Kilkenny cursed softly, and Raisa wanted to echo it. Why were all roads leading back to the sheriff?

"Right, Samantha Mason was at the party. She stepped in and told Young to let both boys off with a warning. She said that a little skirmish wasn't worth going on their permanent record," Delaney said. "So, I thought, oh, maybe he was just so committed to following the law that he quit on the spot. But no. Young said that part didn't bother him. He just realized in that moment he didn't want to take orders from a woman." She paused. "Not in so many words, of course, but his reasoning was fairly clear. Anyway, that's how we got Hermey."

Raisa wasn't sure she'd heard right. "What?"

It was Kilkenny who answered, though. "Hermey was the elf who wanted to be a dentist. It's in that old Rudolph Christmas special. You know, with the Island of Misfit Toys."

The tips of his ears turned red and Raisa had to just stare at him for a moment, stunned: one, that he knew the reference; two, that he was embarrassed about it; and three, that unshakable, poised FBI forensic psychologist Callum Kilkenny blushed in his ears.

"Anyway, whether he sees it or not, the fact that he listened to Samantha instead of hauling Alex in could be viewed as neglectful," Delaney said. "If the month before he killed his parents, Alex'd had to face official consequences for his behavior? Well, we don't know what would have happened." Delaney carried on without needing their response, as was her wont. "I have to admit, I haven't yet warned him of the danger he might be in."

That pulled Raisa back to the present and the fact that Delaney Moore had just magicked up a victim who seemed to fit the bill of exactly what they were looking for. Raisa should be thrilled—the task force would be.

"Okay, thanks," she finally said. "I'll call this into Sand, and report back."

"Aye, aye," Delaney said before hanging up.

"I understand Jenna Shaw's lucky guess," Raisa said. "It made sense—send a message by targeting people in the police report. But what kind of mind gets to Stewart Young in only an hour of studying the case?"

"Maybe one used to looking for patterns," Kilkenny pointed out, but there was a tightness about his mouth and in the way his fingers curled around the steering wheel. "And she could be wrong."

"Right," Raisa said as she typed out a quick message to Sand.

Stewart Young, Everly dentist. Possible next victim.

She got back a thumbs-up emoji.

Raisa wasn't sure what to think of Delaney's guess, but the unease from yesterday had crept back in. Stewart Young had never once been mentioned in the Parker file. Delaney's reasoning in identifying Young as the next possible victim seemed plausible, but . . . it was one more *curious* thing, and they were starting to add up to suspicious.

"Logistically, I think it would be difficult for Delaney to be the killer," Raisa thought out loud.

"Agreed. Delaney was on the third shift when the Balduccis were murdered," Kilkenny said. "Which runs from midnight to eight a.m."

"Omph," Raisa grunted. "That's a rough life to be living by choice."

It made her wonder about Delaney, who seemed wickedly smart. Smart enough to design her own algorithm to trawl the internet for speech patterns. Raisa would never disparage the work done by content moderators, but to not only choose a job at Flik but stick with it through the third shift was interesting, at least.

"Could she have been online remotely?"

"I don't know. It would be the perfect alibi if she couldn't," Kilkenny admitted. "Or near perfect."

"Or she's an accomplice," Raisa added what she'd been thinking for a while. Delaney didn't strike her as a killer, but she *did* strike her as someone who could be persuaded to think a certain way. What if she'd delved further into the "Alex is Innocent" thread than she'd led them to believe? Maybe she'd been convinced by someone that this was a cause to fight for. Maybe that someone was now using her to keep tabs on the FBI investigation.

"Delaney didn't sound nervous at all," Raisa observed. "Like, a little hyper. But not nervous. If she's involved, then she's ice-cold."

"Which fits the psychological profile," Kilkenny admitted. "But I don't think she is. Ice-cold."

Raisa studied him. "You like her."

He cleared his throat. "I trust her."

Again, it sounded like he knew Delaney better than he was letting on.

"You worked with her before," she said, realizing only in this moment that he'd never answered that question.

He didn't say anything.

"You're not going to tell me, are you?" she asked.

"I'm sorry," he said.

With just that apology, her sense of a budding partnership with Kilkenny was snuffed out. He was keeping secrets, and they involved Delaney Moore. Raisa felt foolish and small that she had believed she might be working her way into his inner circle of trust. "Will you tell me if it becomes relevant?"

"It's already relevant," Kilkenny admitted, though he didn't sound ashamed about it. Not a romantic relationship, then. "I'll tell you if it becomes dangerous."

Raisa nodded slowly, but she hated that they were now on shaky ground. Five minutes ago, she would have followed Kilkenny without a single question, but now she wasn't sure if she could trust him. The taste of that disappointment sat sour on her tongue. She had always loved the newness of being shipped around the country; everything was always exciting and different. But she'd also longed for this easy give-and-take, the brainstorming sessions over beers and fries, the sense of camaraderie that she could never quite get when she was defending her very existence on the payroll. She'd wanted it so much, she'd clung to the hints of it Kilkenny had offered, only to be splashed with this bucket of cold water.

They weren't partners. They certainly weren't friends. They were nothing but two people pushed together because of circumstance.

She wouldn't forget that again.

"But will you know?" Raisa asked softly. "If it becomes dangerous?"

Kilkenny didn't answer, but his thumb rubbed over his wedding ring. A clear sign that, no, he wasn't sure that he would.

CHAPTER NINETEEN

DELANEY

Delaney knew it was wrong to keep talking to a friend she'd met on a message board where they were both probably using fake names.

Or maybe Kylie had told her the truth. Not everyone was like Delaney. Not everyone realized how dark and terrifying the web could get. They saw it as a place to share recipes and chat about newly released books or swap parenting tips.

For Delaney, the dredges of humanity ruined the rest of it for her. So she knew it was foolish to have said yes to being Kylie's friend—which was more than just a symbolic gesture. Being each other's "friend" on the board gave them a different level of access to each other's interests, activity, and connections.

It was stupid; it was foolish. And yet Delaney couldn't regret the decision. For the first time in her life, she felt like she had met a kindred spirit.

She had loved Lincoln, but he hadn't been her *friend*. She'd kept so much of herself from him.

Delaney kept herself from Kylie as well, but in a different way. All the personal information Delaney had given Kylie had been fabricated, of course. Her age, her location, her job, her childhood. But she didn't lie in her reactions or conversations.

With Lincoln, Delaney had always found herself trying to give him the response he wanted rather than the one that came naturally. There had been times she'd hit just left of the mark, and then there were times when she hit far left of the mark. But most often, she'd been pretty spot on in donning the persona he'd expected of her.

She hadn't faked her way through their whole relationship, of course. That would be rewriting history in her own mind, which she tried not to do. If he asked if she liked a certain movie or band, she didn't try to guess what he wanted to hear. But on important topics, the big questions in life, she always guessed.

Until that last time.

"Do you ever think it's justified," he'd said, *"to kill someone?"*

"Yes," she'd whispered.

In that moment she'd given him the truth, and in that moment she'd realized she needed to run away from him.

It hadn't taken her and Kylie long to move past the basic chit-chat of strangers. Within a month of talking online, Kylie confessed that her boyfriend was stealing money from her. Or, she thought he was.

Delaney helped her come up with a plan to catch him in the act, and when Kylie had been proved right, a plan on how to dump him.

Kylie talked about her demanding boss and flighty friends and the diet she could never stick to, all the while accepting Delaney's advice like it meant something. Delaney fabricated her own problems, but, again, that didn't feel like she was being dishonest. Because she was being her truest self when she talked to Kylie in every other way.

She was waiting for Kylie to sign on now. Everything that Kylie had dropped into conversation so far seemed to have confirmed that she lived in the Tampa area. She worked as a hairstylist, and so her work hours were outside the typical nine-to-five. Since Delaney worked whenever she was awake—which sometimes could be four in the morning, Oregon time—she didn't mind the odd hours.

So I have a trip booked to New York City, Kylie typed as her hello.

That's where Delaney had told her she lived. If Kylie took a chance of googling the name Delaney had given her, about three thousand Hannah Smiths would populate in the results of a city as big as Manhattan.

Awesome, Delaney typed. She didn't panic in situations like this. She wanted to maintain Kylie's friendship, but there was no actual danger here. At the very worst, Delaney would just delete her username and start fresh. When for?

Next month.

That was vague. Do you want to meet up?

She had been thinking about it as a logistical question, but as she stared at the words in the chat box, Delaney's heart kicked up a notch. She had assumed that's what Kylie was hinting at. But putting it out there, being the first one to suggest it, was terrifying.

An alert came, but it wasn't from Kylie.

Delaney switched her attention to the encrypted app she used to text the FBI man. She had picked him because he lived in the Northwest, though he seemed to travel out to other regions frequently, if his airline logs were anything to go by. What had really sold it for her, though, was that he had a tragedy in his past. She always trusted traumatized people more, though she wasn't sure why.

On it, was all his text said. She'd forwarded a credible brag-post about a serial rapist who seemed to be stopping at college campuses all up and down the coast. The latest attack had been in Eugene, and for a split second, she'd wondered if she should keep the information to herself. She didn't want him getting any ideas about who she was or where she lived.

Once he started wondering about her, he might also start to wonder about what had happened to the tips that he hadn't followed up on.

What had happened to those monsters, the ones the FBI didn't listen to her about.

And Delaney wasn't ready for that.

Not quite yet.

A ping came in from Kylie.

Absolutely.

CHAPTER TWENTY

RAISA

The tiny video camera found in Stewart Young's bedroom was perhaps the most damning evidence that Delaney had been correct. But then, so was the fact that his fancy security system had been disabled.

"There was a technician," Stewart mumbled to the FBI agent assigned to take his statement. "I don't know, a week ago? Brown hair, medium build, a mole on his left jaw. He said he was from the internet company. My wife let him in."

As if Stewart wouldn't have. Raisa turned away from him, her eyes going back to the fire alarm that was now hanging by its innards from the ceiling. That's where the killer had hidden their gear.

"Delaney shouldn't have been able to guess this," Raisa said as softly as she could to Kilkenny. He stood next to her, arms crossed. His expression, per usual, gave little away.

"She still doesn't fit the profile," Kilkenny said, but it didn't actually sound like an argument. "And she has an alibi."

And a connection to Kilkenny, apparently. Raisa no longer trusted Kilkenny's take on the situation.

"I need samples of her writing," Raisa said.

"You really think—" Kilkenny cut himself off, pressing his lips together, clearly having been about to say something along the lines of, *you really think that'll prove anything?*

It was a rare slip, and she could already see him silently beating himself up over it.

Had it been anyone else, Raisa would have squared up, looked him in the eye, and dared him to finish that thought. But Kilkenny had never before made her feel small about what she did.

It hurt all the more for it. Especially coming on the heels of realizing he didn't trust *her* enough. Otherwise, he would tell her why he was defending Delaney Moore.

"That was my careless way of saying that Delaney might have been able to fake a different voice if she was posting as the killer," Kilkenny said after a weighted silence where Raisa tried to fight her instinct to slink off and lick her wounds. "Would that small of a sample size really help you?"

Raisa had seen worse saves than that, but still she turned away when she answered, as if she were interested in surveying the room. "Because I would be comparing a questioned sample—a.k.a. the posts from the killer—and a known sample from Delaney, it's easier. I don't have to narrow down the field from literally everyone. The more of Delaney's writing I could get, the better, of course, so that I can more confidently match her idiolect to that of the killer's." Part of her wanted to scratch at him, just to feel the flesh give beneath her fingernails, metaphorically speaking. The Raisa of her alley cat days would have. But she was a goddamn professional now. "I'm going to get a ride back to the cabins. I'm not needed here."

"Agent Susanto," Kilkenny said, but she pretended not to hear him.

Okay, so mostly a goddamn professional.

He didn't chase after her, and she hadn't expected him to. They had different roles to play here, and it was just one more reminder that they weren't a team. They were distant colleagues, at best.

The shadow of Scottsdale lurked behind her confident facade, a little voice at the back of her head saying that maybe Kilkenny would have trusted her if that incident hadn't happened.

It had started out as a fairly normal kidnapping. Raisa hated that she could think of a crime that way, but those were the facts of her life.

Sarah Stone had been taken in broad daylight. People thought these kinds of crimes happened under the cover of darkness, but it was so, so much easier to snatch a kid on a busy street than to sneak into their homes at night. The case had caught national attention, in that way some investigations just took off for reasons that never became clear.

A week after the disappearance, the task force got an email from a person claiming to be the kidnapper.

And that was when Raisa had been called in.

She was tasked with matching the idiolect to a list of suspects the parents had provided. Raisa had easily narrowed it down to a daycare teacher who had shown a particular interest in the little girl. On Raisa's say-so, the task force had devoted their entire attention to the woman. It hadn't taken long to secure a warrant.

Only, the girl hadn't been at the teacher's apartment. Nor at the apartment of the teacher's boyfriend.

The girl had been in a warehouse across town. By the time the task force realized that, she had been killed. The man who had kidnapped her had blown his brains out. Both corpses were found after neighbors reported the gunshots.

The man had been the girl's swim coach.

Raisa had barely made it to the bathroom to throw up when she'd heard the news, remnants of the bile catching behind her molars.

No one had made her go to the warehouse to see the consequences of her mistake.

They should have made her go to the warehouse.

When she'd been brought in front of an internal review board, she'd been able to defend herself. She'd always been meticulous about her research—jurors who were raised on *Law & Order* episodes demanded it. On that case, the rigorous documenting had paid off. The similarities between the daycare teacher's writing and the email to the parents were uncanny. The forensic-linguistic evidence had been sound, and going over it in front of a terrifying panel of suits hadn't made it any less so.

Raisa hadn't suggested it, afraid it would hurt her credibility even more, but she couldn't shake the feeling that someone had interfered with the case. They'd found a sample of the daycare teacher's writing and contacted the FBI to send them in the wrong direction.

She knew how the argument sounded, though—paranoid, defensive, self-pitying. So Raisa had kept quiet about it and taken her slap on the wrist.

In the end, she'd walked away from the whole thing with a note in her file and an entire bureau that distrusted her research.

It was a minor miracle she'd even been called onto this case.

But she had. And if she was here, she had work to do.

Raisa bummed a ride off a junior agent who swore she was going back to the hotel anyway, and wasn't just doing a favor for a superior.

When Raisa got back to her cabin, it was to find Delaney still there, bent over the café table, just where they'd left her. Raisa took a moment to study the woman.

Something about Raisa's own logic wasn't squaring right.

Why would Delaney have led them straight to the next victim if she was the killer's accomplice? Was it because she'd been talked into it and, after seeing both the Harden and Balducci crime scenes, had gotten cold feet? Was this her way of stopping someone she hadn't been able to by herself?

Or was the tip her attempt at building credibility and goodwill with the task force? Had Stewart Young been a sacrifice by the killer—and Delaney—for later gains? Young couldn't have been considered a high-value target by the killer. His connection to Alex Parker was fleeting at best. And if someone had taken umbrage over him letting Alex off with a warning, their frustration really should be directed at the sheriff.

If someone deserved the blame for letting Alex off that night, it was her.

But Samantha had yet to voice any concern about her own safety. Maybe she was old-school; maybe she thought she had to play tough in front of the FBI agents. Maybe she really wasn't thinking about herself as a potential target.

She was so intertwined with this case, though, Raisa couldn't see how she wouldn't be.

The only reason Raisa could think Samantha wouldn't be worried that she was the killer's next target was if she was the killer. What if she was exacting revenge on the people who had led to the deaths of a family people said she loved?

Or was that just a rumor like all the rest?

Delaney looked up, then, directly into Raisa's eyes, as if she'd heard the question.

Raisa wondered if anyone had let Delaney know she had been correct in her guess about Stewart being the next victim. Everything had moved quickly after her phone call with Raisa, Sand circling the wagons with the rest of the task force.

But Delaney didn't ask what had happened or if she'd been right.

Instead, she said, "Shall we figure out who is next?"

———

Raisa had been recruited by the FBI straight out of her grad school program. Her eyes were still blurry from years of endless research when she stumbled into the first FBI training seminar at Quantico a week after successfully defending her dissertation.

She'd sat next to a kid who looked like he'd been stretched on a taffy rack. He'd worn a bow tie and trendy glasses, and Raisa had hoped he didn't have to face down any of the jocks who were training to be field agents.

Of course they had. Raisa held her own against them because she was scrappy and tougher than she looked. For sparring, she was paired with a burly dude with bulging neck muscles and had him on the mat in less than two minutes flat.

On the other hand, Topher Sullivan—her fellow paper pusher—got his ass kicked. As an extra humiliation, his sparring partner had broken his glasses in one of the more middle-school moves Raisa had witnessed at the bureau.

In retaliation, Raisa had volunteered to take the Roid Machine on next. She'd handed him his ass in less time than she'd taken with her first opponent.

Afterward, Topher had stuck to her like a little duckling.

"How did you do that?" he'd asked, eating his lunch at her table even though she hadn't invited him to join her.

"You have to use their expectations against them," Raisa had said. *"And know your own weaknesses. That's the only way you can win against brute strength."*

Now, years later, they still talked every once in a while, offering their opinions on any cases that crossed into the other's specialty. Topher was a genius at research. Not online, like Delaney, but classic research. Plenty of agents thought you didn't need people like Topher these days, with Google and a thousand other searchable databases, but Topher made it into an art.

Raisa stepped into the cabin's bathroom, away from Delaney's prying ears, and pulled up his contact.

"I need a favor," she said quietly when Topher picked up. "If you're not slammed."

"I'm always slammed, darling," Topher said. "But for you, I can try to fit something in."

"Could you build me a dossier on a woman named Delaney Moore?" Raisa asked. "Off the record."

"Delaney Moore," Topher said, absently, like he was writing it down. "Any other helpful info on this mysterious Delaney?"

"I think she lives in the Seattle area," Raisa offered. "Works as a content moderator for Flik."

"Ooph," Topher muttered.

"My reaction exactly," Raisa said. And then, without really thinking about it, she added, "You would like her, actually."

A beat of silence. "Then why the cloak and daggers?"

Raisa squeezed one eye shut. "She might be a killer."

"Ahh. Well, you know me—famously gets along with vicious murderers," Topher said, teasingly. "I'm guessing this is urgent?"

"If possible," Raisa said. "Just . . . any red flags. I don't need to know her high school math teacher's name."

"You just want to know if there are any dead bodies in her wake," Topher said. "I gotchu."

"Thanks, I owe you one."

"You owe me about a hundred," Topher said, though they probably ran about even in terms of favors. "Talk soon, peaches."

Raisa exhaled a shaky breath as she held her phone to her chest and stared into the splotchy bathroom mirror. "What are you doing?" she asked her reflection.

She didn't need to be making waves. Kilkenny and Sand both trusted Delaney for undoubtedly good reasons. Delaney had been odd and pleasant and almost fun to work with—the way she thought just differently enough from Raisa for them to play off each other nicely.

But that had been an impossible prediction Delaney had made.

What would it hurt to just check?

Raisa exhaled, slapped some color into her cheeks, and then stepped out of the bathroom.

Delaney stood in the middle of the room, just staring, her twin braids hanging down her back, her eyes nothing more than shadows in the afternoon light.

Her hands hung loosely at her sides. No weapon, Raisa's hindbrain was quick to note.

"Delaney?" Raisa asked softly, with the same voice she would use with someone who was sleepwalking. Or a cornered animal.

But Delaney flinched like Raisa had slapped her.

"I'm not a monster," Delaney finally whispered, and it sounded gutted, hollow, and broken.

Shit. "I never said you were."

"You didn't have to," Delaney said, and then turned and left the cabin.

Raisa closed her eyes and cursed again, this time out loud.

Maybe all the people who now doubted her were right. Once upon a time, she would have trusted her instincts implicitly. Now listening to them just seemed to be causing her trouble.

Still . . .

"I'm not a monster."

Even if Delaney had heard Raisa request a background search, what made her leap to that level of defensiveness?

Only someone who already thought of themselves as a monster came into a confrontation braced for that accusation.

CHAPTER TWENTY-ONE

DELANEY

As someone who had been combing through the darkest corners of the web since she was fifteen, Delaney thought she knew what hell looked like. But she'd been naive, or in an upper circle of Hades.

Hell was the list of tags that Flik had provided on her first day as a content moderator. When she'd seen the job posting, she'd thought it was a message from the universe. This was what she had been doing in her free time. At least she'd get paid for it now.

Her boss was named Brian. He was a nice young man in his twenties who wore Patagonia zip-up fleeces and called her champ. When she got out of orientation with HR, he told her that the entire team was on high alert: a scandal had just broken where moms who had been posting videos of their toddlers by the hundreds suddenly realized that they were being saved with alarming frequency by accounts run by older men.

"Just look at the saved numbers," Brian said in a chipper voice that added a dystopian flair to what he was telling her. "If they cross the threshold of icky, flag it to me or your shift supervisor. We're on a real kick these days to be a safe platform. Otherwise, here's your list of hashtags you'll monitor every day."

An hour in, Delaney wanted to pour bleach into her eyeballs. There was something about videos that made all the garbage seem more real. Words could be faked. Video could, too, she supposed, but the ones she'd watched were authentic. And terrifying.

Already thinking about quitting, she texted Kylie on the same encrypted app she used for the FBI man. She'd managed to avoid Kylie's trip to NYC by being "out of town" on a big interview for a new job. She hadn't been lying about the interview, just about when it had happened. And she'd fudged the details of the new job to Kylie enough that it wouldn't be easy to figure out.

Oh, the wonderous world of the grind, Kylie sent back with a winky emoji.

Four days in, Delaney found her first apex predator. He wore the mask of a lower-level offender, the kind she was used to seeing in droves, the ones she flagged if they violated some Flik rule but who weren't worth her time otherwise.

They weren't truly dangerous.

This one, though. This one was supplying rich assholes with their choice of evening entertainment on the daily. The video that got him flagged wasn't even from his account. It was a girl who could have reasonably passed for seventeen with the amount of makeup that hid the baby-fat softness of her face. A quick look at her real—Delaney cringed—profile, though, showed she was much younger. Her most recent Flik, the one that came through as flagged, had been only about seven seconds long. The video showed a yacht and then panned down to an expensive watchband. The girl had tagged it "all-inclusive incall," with an ironic angel halo emoji, not even trying to hide the reason she was on the boat. Anyone with a basic knowledge of slang would be able to decode what the girl was doing.

So Delaney went hunting. It wasn't technically in her job description to flush out the pimps, so she did it in her own time. Nights had never been her friend, anyway. At most, she tended to get three to four hours of uninterrupted sleep. The rest she spent on her hobby.

It didn't take long to figure out this predator was operating a ring out of Seattle. He didn't just specialize in teenage girls, either. For a price, he was willing to supply even rarer wares.

Delaney fantasized about tying him down, about cutting off his scrotum with gardening shears.

Instead, she was a good girl and sent a message to her FBI man.

Will pass along.

He wasn't in the right division, of course, but she'd gained his trust a long time ago, and she knew he'd pass along her information to the correct person.

Two months later, another video cropped up, this time from a younger girl.

Delaney opened the thread to her FBI man once more. **Any progress?**

The reply came in quick. **Sorry, not enough evidence to move on him yet. We're watching, though, don't worry.**

She didn't say anything back, just tossed her phone on her desk and then took an Uber out to Alki Point Lighthouse to stare at the endless stretch of the Pacific. It was one of those nights where you couldn't tell the water from the sky, and the wind sliced its way past her useless, fashionable scarf. Delaney sometimes believed she'd left her past behind. Most days—most years, really—she didn't think of Noah Webb or Maura from college or the handful of nameless predators on the internet who happened to have had fatal accidents not long after she'd discovered their true faces.

She liked her life. Eugene and now Seattle. She'd managed to make a friend, even, without giving away any of her secrets.

Delaney sucked on her front teeth and considered.

Doing anything about this particular predator would be risky since she'd already told the FBI man about her suspicions. She was confident that he didn't know who she was, that he wouldn't be able to track her even if he thought it worth the resources to do so. Delaney had become an expert at all this.

Still, she didn't want to invite questions. Avoiding them was how she'd maintained all this for so long. It was why she'd left the only relationship she'd ever had, sneaking out like a thief in the night.

There was, of course, something else to consider—right and wrong.

Delaney knew her morals didn't exactly align with the bell curve average. She tended toward unemotional, hyperrational thinking. In the trolley experiment, she would—of course and without hesitation—pull the lever to kill one person instead of four, even if it was someone she knew she was dooming to death. She'd never even understood how it was a test.

She also didn't believe in an afterlife. Her sins weren't being tallied somewhere and held up against everything she'd done right. In all honesty, if she'd bought into that kind of thing, she probably had consigned her soul to the pit long ago.

Just because she was a logical atheist, though, didn't mean she didn't feel guilt over her actions. She wasn't a sociopath. She just thought there were some pros to the time when it was socially acceptable to slay monsters and emerge as the beloved knight. Now it was considered barbaric to take matters into your own hands.

She wouldn't feel bad about Benton Davenport the Third, though. She had to believe that if there were some creator out there, if there was some mystical scoreboard, than putting down this rabid predator would be a mark in the *good* category.

What would happen to his victims? Some were forced to do this, of course, but some of them were in that life for a reason. They had siblings to support or rent to pay. Likely, they would be scooped up by the next apex predator waiting in the wings.

The thing was, Delaney was there waiting, too.

Always.

EXCERPT FROM LANA PARKER'S DIARY

July 6, 1998

Today was an attic day. Isabel woke me up with a hand over my mouth. She pulled me out of bed. I asked if I could bring my art book to draw in. Attic days were long. But she shook her head. She looked scared. But Isabel always looked scared. Most scared on attic days, though.

We got up to the attic the way we always do— Isabel dragged Larissa's bathroom-sink step stool under the trapdoor in the hallway's ceiling.

Larissa clapped her chubby baby hands and giggled when the steps came down, and I could tell Isabel wanted to slap a hand over her mouth just like she had with mine. But she wouldn't ever hurt the baby.

It was okay. No one came, anyway. Isabel always came in to wake us before Alex got up. Especially on attic days, when Mom and Dad spent the mornings on campus. Isabel didn't trust Alex not to hurt us when they were gone.

I climbed the stairs first. That was my job. Always to go first. Then Isabel helped Larissa follow, a hand on her butt as Larissa made a game of the stairs. I found our corner in the dark. We never turned on a light in case Alex figured out where we went on attic days. He never checked up here, though, I don't know why.

Maybe we were just really, really good at hiding.

I sneezed at the dust and then pulled Larissa into my lap. She was the hardest to keep entertained, but Isabel usually thought of something. Now, she pulled apples from the deep pocket of her skirt. That was nice that she'd remembered to bring them this time.

I buried my face in Larissa's soft curls and wished attic days weren't so long.

CHAPTER TWENTY-TWO

RAISA

Raisa needed more samples. Right now, she was a forensic linguist playing at a psychologist waiting for a computer to spit out answers for her.

She had studied the most recent message from the killer, trying to find a hidden layer that would point to the next victim, but hadn't come out of it with any brilliant clues.

What she wanted her hands on was some actual writing from the people involved in the Parker case. And that meant the sheriff's department.

It was going on dinnertime, which Raisa thought should mean some relief from the sun, but the weather in Everly was extreme and relentless. She wondered how it had been back in the summer of '98. This kind of heat triggered rage, even in people who didn't have violent tendencies. What would it do to the control of a teenage boy who everyone described as walking on the edge of a conduct disorder diagnosis?

Raisa swapped her sweat-soaked shirt for a clean tee before cutting through the wooded path toward Main Street, which was only a ten-minute walk if she took this particular route.

The sheriff's department was empty save for the receptionist, who gave Raisa a friendly wave. Her name was Amanda, or so Raisa thought. But she didn't have enough confidence in that to actually use it.

"Everyone's split between Terri's house and Stewart's," Amanda said, as Raisa leaned on her desk. "If you're looking for anyone in particular."

"Actually, I was wondering if you all keep your archives on-site." Some smaller departments just didn't have the space.

"Yeah, we have a back room," Amanda said, pushing to her feet and grabbing a set of keys. "Not too many cases that require more than a folder's worth of paperwork, to be honest."

Raisa followed her down the hallway. She wasn't sure how old Amanda was, and if she'd said anywhere between thirty and fifty, Raisa wouldn't have been surprised.

"Have you lived in Everly long?"

"Born and raised," Amanda said proudly. "Knew the Parkers, too, if that's what you're about to ask. I know you G-men don't ever make idle chitchat." She winked over her shoulder. "'Scuse me. G-women."

"I'm sure you've gotten that question now a hundred times."

"Try a hundred thousand," Amanda said, but she seemed cheery about it. She liked being involved in the investigation. "I don't mind, though. I babysat for the girls. Larissa mostly, of course, since she was the baby."

That was small towns for you—everyone entangled in each other's lives. It didn't necessarily mean anything. Still, what a gift to be handed.

"Isabel and Lana didn't need much tending," Amanda continued. "And obviously I stayed far away from Alex."

"He was really the bad seed everyone says?"

"He was a horndog was what he was," Amanda said with an overloud laugh. "Never struck me as a psycho-killer stabby man. He was more interested in talking girls into his bed. But that shows you how much you can tell about a person."

Psycho-killer stabby man. Sometimes there was a phrase that just made Raisa fall in love with language all over again—unique and true and filled with personality. She filed the descriptor away. "There were rumors he was sexually assaulting some of the girls in school."

"Yeah, one accusation that almost went somewhere," Amanda said, with a sigh. "Cara. She was a sweetheart."

That was a name that kept coming up. "You knew her?"

"Not well. She was in Isabel's year," Amanda said, the keys jangling against her thigh. "But I was one of the few who believed her, poor thing."

"What do you mean?"

"She actually went to Samantha," Amanda said, glancing over her shoulder. "Tried to file a report and everything. At the time . . . I know you're probably not small town like we are, but at the time it might as well have been an earthquake. To say anything bad against the Parkers . . . beyond rumors, that is."

"What happened?"

"Bob and Gina Balducci—God rest their souls—said he was at their house all night," Amanda said, and Raisa just blinked at her swinging ponytail. Not just Bob but Gina, too. Raisa didn't let herself jump to any conclusions, but this was the first time they had a motive for the wife's death along with the husband's.

"Do you know what happened to Cara?"

"Nope, she got out of town as soon as she could, never looked back," Amanda said, with a careless shrug. "Can't say I blame her."

"No," Raisa murmured, wondering if they could track her down. She was fairly certain she'd seen the girl's name somewhere in some file, but she couldn't quite recall it. "Do you remember her last name?"

"James," Amanda said, without missing a beat. "Her file's in there, too. Not that there's much to look at. It was a different time back then. Anyway, Alex tried to talk himself into my pants every dang day, and he didn't really like hearing the word 'no.' So it wasn't hard to believe

Cara. I started carrying bear spray with me if I was heading over to their house."

"Smart," Raisa murmured. "What about the father?"

"Tim? Nah, he was a sweetheart, only had eyes for math. And maybe Becks."

"And was Becks . . . ?" Raisa trailed off, letting Amanda fill in whatever she thought would be relevant. It was a tactic Raisa liked to use.

"Having an affair? You mean all that nonsense about Shawn?" Amanda rolled her eyes hard. "I think he started those rumors to be cool. No, Becks was . . . hmm."

Amanda's eyes narrowed, lips pursing, something dark flickering in and out of her expression. She hadn't liked the woman.

"Becks was Becks. Anyway, here you go," Amanda said, nudging the door to the archives open, cheery once more. "Just keep a log of anything you check out. I'll let the sheriff know you're down here, of course."

The last part seemed to be as much of a threat as Raisa was going to get. She tried not to be astounded that she was being granted free rein in the department's archive room—or at least not show it on her face.

She pulled out her phone and started a voice memo. While digging around in evidence, Raisa liked to talk through what she was doing. It helped when she had to explain her process in court later on, and kept everything aboveboard. Raisa had standards she had to uphold, even if the place she was working didn't.

So when things like what happened in Scottsdale went down, she was reprimanded instead of fired.

A dusty box of latex gloves sat near one of the evidence boxes, and she blew air into two of them absently before tugging them on. She stared at the closed door, thinking about Amanda. She had babysat for the Parkers, which was already interesting. But she also had an idiolect similar to the Everly Ears gossip columns. It was a more mature version, but it was chatty and leaned into the juiciness of small-town scandal.

And she hadn't liked Becks. Was she the author?

It didn't take Raisa long to locate the entire shelf devoted to the Parker murder-suicide, and soon she was hefting boxes onto the wobbly plastic table that seemed to have been shoved into the room as an afterthought.

She spared a moment to wonder how this particular sheriff's department would have handled the Balducci murders had the FBI not been pulled in. Would they have even connected it to the Parkers?

Or would Samantha Mason have closed the case in less than twenty-four hours as she'd done all those years ago?

It took Raisa three boxes to hit the jackpot. For the benefit of the audio recording, she said, "Diaries."

There were three in total: one each from Becks, Isabel, and Lana. They were the same make and model—had they been Christmas presents for the whole family? They had varying degrees of blank pages, with Becks's almost filled to the end. Isabel's came next, and Lana's was almost empty. The twelve-year-old probably had to be prompted to write in it.

Raisa flipped a few pages in and skimmed one of the last entries.

Attic days.

She read it out loud, the words rancid in her mouth. This was what it had been like to share a house with Alex Parker.

There'd been a boy in Raisa's third foster home who had been just like Alex. He'd had mean, beady eyes, and he'd watched the girls too closely. Anytime he was reprimanded, he lashed out to younger, more vulnerable children, unable to handle any criticism, no matter how benign.

Her foster parents had ignored the problem. So Raisa had handled it.

The next time the social worker came for an in-home visit, Raisa had quietly provoked the boy into throwing scalding-hot coffee at her in front of a government witness. She still had a scar on her upper arm, a flat piece of dead skin that always reminded her of her own power.

For too long, it had also reminded her that adults wouldn't just ride in to save the day. No one was going to help you if it even slightly inconvenienced them.

You had to take care of things yourself.

She moved on to the next boxes, narrating her actions, audibly documenting each piece of evidence she found.

When she got to the seventh, her hands paused, midair.

She had thought she'd hit the jackpot before, but this last box was filled with paper. There were school essays from Alex, notes passed between the girls, Tim's proof workbook. And at the very bottom were two opened envelopes. Carefully, so as not to damage the twenty-five-year-old paper, Raisa placed each one on the table and then removed the letters from inside.

They were perfectly folded into thirds, the words slipping into the crevices.

Though she was far from a handwriting expert, Raisa had taken a few classes to pad out her résumé. She could say with some amount of confidence that the author had been a woman.

She skimmed them quickly on the first pass to get the gist. They were addressed to Tim Parker. The first was hesitant and a little gushy. By the time Raisa got to the end of it, she realized who the writer was. The former student, the one Mark the TA had told them about. The one who believed Tim had plagiarized from her.

In the message, she said she'd heard that Tim was working on a proof she had talked about in one of her papers for the class. She mentioned she was including a copy of the paper to jog his memory, but that must have been thrown away at some point. The girl suggested that all this had been an oversight on Tim's part, and would he like her to come work with him over the summer?

The signature had been completely blacked out by a Sharpie. Probably Tim's doing, since it was different from the pen used to write the letter.

Raisa moved on to the second message.

The tone was drastically different. It looked like it had been written after Tim had published the proof and was being lauded for his work. The writer threatened legal action and warned that Tim had messed with the wrong person. The style was a little over the top, but nothing about the warning felt cartoonish or hyperbolic.

"Did you find what you were looking for?"

Raisa whirled.

The sheriff stood in the doorway, fingers hooked into her utility belt, watching Raisa. She had the odd urge to take a half step to the right to hide the letters. But if Mason had thought these letters were truly damning, she would have destroyed the messages twenty-five years ago, when there weren't FBI agents swarming around the town.

"Did you ever follow up on these letters?" Raisa asked, waving one of them toward the sheriff.

Mason stepped closer and craned her neck. "Why would I have?"

"This is a written threat," Raisa said. "Believe me, I'm an expert in written threats. This second letter constitutes one, and if my timeline is right, it seems to have been written just before Tim Parker's death."

"It was some disgruntled former student." Mason didn't even sound defensive—she didn't think she'd done anything wrong. "A math student, at that, in case you missed that part. They're not exactly dangerous."

Raisa wasn't going to bother to argue that ridiculous take. "Do you have a name?"

"No."

Well, Raisa recognized a brick wall when she came face-to-face with one. "What do I need to do to take this box?"

Samantha followed Raisa's hand wave to the table behind her, where the diaries were spread out. Raisa would have said Samantha was on alert before, but at the sight of them, she completely stilled. Her face was frozen, not giving anything away, but it was the nothingness that told a story.

There was something in those diaries Samantha Mason didn't want Raisa to see.

Raisa would bet the remains of her tattered reputation on it. "Do you need me to call Agent Sand?"

"That won't be necessary," Samantha said, regaining her composure. "Make sure to log what you take."

"So Amanda told me," Raisa murmured, and then decided to go for it. "Hey. Do you have any doubts that it was Alex Parker who killed his parents?"

"Are you letting that podcaster get to you?" Samantha asked, sounding amused for the first time since she'd interrupted Raisa.

"No, the new killer," Raisa pointed out.

"If I had any doubt that Alex did exactly what it looked like he had, I wouldn't have closed the case, Agent Susanto," Samantha said. "Now some sicko from the internet wants to drag this town through hell once again and I'm supposed to think we're the bad guys here? No, absolutely not."

"No one's calling your department the bad guys."

"Aren't they?" Samantha asked, and it was clear in her voice what she'd been going through the past few days. "How many times have you questioned my abilities in the past two days?"

Because Raisa was a straight shooter, she answered. "Seventeen."

"You didn't even have to think about it."

"Why did you close the case so quickly?" Raisa asked.

Samantha chewed on her lip, but she'd broached the topic, and she seemed to realize she'd brought this on herself. "In the nineties there was this idea of contagion."

"Oh," Raisa breathed because she hadn't thought about that. That's what confirmation bias did to your brain.

"I was young—I'll admit I probably handled it poorly," Samantha continued. "But we had the satanic panics in the eighties, when I was growing up. And then when I was getting trained, everyone warned about suicide clusters. I had to believe the same applied to murder-suicides. I didn't want anyone getting ideas."

And that made sense if you viewed it through the lens of a brand-spanking-new sheriff.

"The only mistake I made that summer that I regret was not listening close enough to Becks about how worried she was over Alex," Samantha said.

Summer of '98 would have been before Columbine and the national reckoning with the violence simmering among the nation's teenage boys. If someone had been called "troubled" back then, it likely would have meant that they talked back to the teacher, showed up late to class, and maybe smoked a little pot.

"Do you know what happened to the sisters?" Raisa asked, since Samantha was sharing for some reason.

"To be honest, I lost track of them," Samantha said, her mouth twisting into a sad grimace. "We got a lot of national reporters buzzing around right after . . ." She paused. "Well, right after. Everything was chaotic, and then the girls were swept off to Seattle. I never heard from them again after that."

"You were close with them," Raisa prompted.

"They called me Aunt Sammy," Samantha said, staring at the floor.

"Did you ever think about taking them in yourself?" Raisa asked.

Samantha glanced up sharply, as if it had been a jab. But Raisa was just curious. She tried to make sure her expression reflected only that.

She must have done a decent job, because Samantha's shoulders relaxed. "A single woman with a dangerous job? Three traumatized kids, one of whom was barely out of diapers? No. It wouldn't have worked, and it hurt too much to watch from afar."

Raisa didn't say anything, didn't want to pass judgment. But if someone like Samantha had cared enough about her after her parents had died to save her from the foster system, she would have wept with joy. All those considerations adults made about jobs and circumstances didn't matter to kids.

Instead of spilling all that out in a messy, emotional heap, Raisa changed the subject. "Can I ask you something?"

Samantha laughed, and Raisa smiled ruefully. She'd already asked plenty.

"Sure, why not?"

"Where would you start? If you were running this investigation." Raisa had the impression that Samantha had yet to be asked that.

"That damned message board," Samantha said. It wasn't a surprise, but it was a bit of a disappointment. They had people looking into the users who posted on "Alex is Innocent" already.

"And here in town?" Raisa pushed.

"This town is full of good people, Agent Susanto."

Raisa wanted to say she hadn't suggested otherwise. Instead, she just nodded. "But . . ."

"Good people do bad things."

That was more than she'd expected for Samantha to admit, and the woman seemed to read that in her expression.

"I think we're all learning that none of our hands are clean when it came to the Parkers," Samantha said. "Some part of me knew that." She stared down at her own hands. "I just didn't realize how dirty they were."

EXCERPTS FROM BECKS PARKER'S DIARY

August 7, 1998

The woman was outside again today. Now I feel as paranoid as Tim. She waited in her car, with big sunglasses and a baseball cap on, as if that did anything but draw my attention to her. If I had been passing her on campus, I would have said she looked like any other coed. She's been parked on our street for four days now. I thought about calling the sheriff, but Samantha wouldn't be able to do anything. The woman isn't breaking any rules. She's on public property.

Maybe I am just paranoid.

August 8, 1998

Her name is Talia. She found me today, thinking I might be easier to reach than Tim, I suppose. I actually took a wrong turn on my way to a faculty meeting. I can't remember the last time I got lost on this campus, this place I know as well as my home. I must be distracted. Can you imagine why? Somehow I ended up on the Language department's stairs and she tapped me on the shoulder.

She thinks Tim stole from her. She showed me the work she'd done.

He lied to me.

August 10, 1998

I told Samantha I was considering a divorce. People always wanted to know what I'd seen in Tim. Our entire marriage we've pretended we didn't hear the question beneath everyone's congratulations. I had never doubted us, though. I loved Tim's mind, the layers of it, the intricacies. I know I'm just letting my emotions speak right now. I can't divorce him, Samantha pointed it out and I agreed. People will think it's because he's losing his sanity, when in reality it's because of what he did when he had it.

Is this how the rest of my life will play out? Having no respect for the man I married, only pity and anger and resentment?

August 11, 1998

Tim denied the allegations, of course. Isn't it funny that I've never once asked him about the rumors I've heard of his lovers? I don't care about his body, who he shares it with. He became so angry with me, though, that he left the house for the night and didn't return until the next morning. Who knows where he spent the night, or who he spent it with.

I'm contacting the journal that published his proof. I haven't told Talia yet.

To think, a few days ago I was worried about Larissa's language struggles. Now, I hope our baby isn't a genius.

It's not worth the pain.

CHAPTER TWENTY-THREE

RAISA

Delaney and Kilkenny were nowhere to be found when Raisa got back to her cabin with her box of goodies. Raisa was glad for it, to have the time and space to read through the diaries. Those would be her main priority.

Twilight had settled into the woods, the trees absorbing any lingering sun from the late afternoon, so she flipped the porch lights on.

It took an hour to read through Becks's journal. Raisa didn't bother with notes yet. She wanted to get a feel for Becks's voice before she deconstructed it. There was a dryness to her tone, a distance, too.

I get all his lovers confused, read one entry, a few days after she'd considered divorcing Tim.

Mark the TA had been mentioned, as if the relationship were real. Had Mark lied? Raisa didn't think so. He hadn't seemed like he was trying to hide anything. His demeanor had been open, friendly, and helpful. Becks even admitted later that she had never confronted Tim about his supposed affairs.

Raisa thought about Kilkenny's gut feeling about these rumors—that there was something malicious at the root of them. There were too many, they were too scintillating. It was like a caricature of a scandal-ridden family rather than a real one.

Did anyone on campus have it out for Tim? Or the Parkers?

Well, there was one young lady, Mark had said.

Talia.

Becks had put a name to the letter writer. The girl who had searched Becks out only two weeks before both Parkers were killed in their bed.

Raisa shot off a quick text to the research assistant—not Topher, but the one actually assigned to their task force. She asked him to try to locate a Talia who had attended Everly and majored in mathematics. She got a thumbs-up emoji from the twenty-three-year-old grad student. For some reason it read different coming from him than from Sand.

There wasn't much else shocking in Becks's diary except that she had considered divorcing Tim and had told Samantha Mason that plan only to be talked out of it.

But what did it really matter? Becks hadn't killed Tim for lying to her, and Tim hadn't killed Becks for planning on leaving him—even though that was a common motive for family annihilators.

Alex had killed them both.

A shadow moved at the edge of her vision, and she glanced up to find Kilkenny leaning on the doorjamb to the porch. Was everyone these days just going to take their turns standing around watching her work in a creepy manner?

Raisa gestured for him to join her, and got the sense that he would have respected her wishes had she shooed him away.

"What are you looking for?" he asked.

"I don't know," Raisa admitted, shoving her fingers through her hair. "Maybe a big sign that says 'Alex really was guilty, stop wondering.'"

"Did you find anything close to that?"

"Of course," Raisa said. "Because everything played out exactly as you would expect. On August 1, Becks wrote about how she was starting to worry Alex was a 'monster.'"

"Hard for a mother to admit," Kilkenny said.

"I'm not sure Becks was that type of mother." Maybe that wasn't fair; Raisa only knew the woman through the diaries. But even so, she got the distinct impression that Becks viewed her children as legacies instead of individuals. "Seemed more afraid for herself." Raisa rubbed her hands over her face. "It's hard to see this case clearly."

Kilkenny worried at his wedding ring. "It's the puppet-master personality. They muddy the waters on purpose."

"That's why you're so interested in the rumors," Raisa said. "Making up lies about the whole family is something a person like that would do."

"It crossed my mind, yes," Kilkenny confirmed. "I just got off the phone with the woman who used to run the newspaper here. Dora Ramirez. She moved to Florida a while ago and is in a senior living facility."

"She wasn't the author of the Everly Ears gossip column, I take it," Raisa said.

"No. And Dora has dementia," Kilkenny said. "In a lucky stroke, her daughter was there when I called, and agreed to let Dora answer a few questions. When I asked who the author of the Everly Ears column was, she told me Eleanor Roosevelt wrote it anonymously."

"Oh dear," Raisa murmured. It was then she noticed the folder he held. "Are those samples of the Everly Ears columns?"

"Yeah, I thought maybe you could work some magic and see if the writing compares to anything you've managed to obtain from anyone involved in the case," he said, and it sounded like a peace offering.

She took the metaphorical olive branch along with the folder, though she wasn't sure she'd soon forget the sting of his casual dismissal of her profession earlier. "I'll read through them tonight."

"They're quite poorly written," he said.

Raisa looked up. "Like 'could have been written by a teenager' poorly written?"

"What are you thinking?"

"Cara James," Raisa said. "She was the girl who was raped by Alex that summer. Bob and Gina Balducci provided Alex the alibi that got her accusations dismissed."

"The columns did stop after Alex died," Kilkenny said. "It would make sense."

"I think she was about the same age as Isabel, the oldest daughter," Raisa said. "That might have given her an in on some of the Parker family drama. Enough to give some credibility to her lies."

"Is it wrong of me to say I wouldn't have blamed her?"

"Please, she should have done worse," Raisa said. "Gone for the jugular. What's a few cheating rumors?"

"Maybe she did eventually go for the jugular," Kilkenny said.

Raisa inclined her head. "Touché."

He glanced at his watch. "You should get some sleep. I'm fairly confident our unsub won't kill someone in Stewart's stead tomorrow. That would take too much work on the fly."

Raisa actually had other plans, but she wasn't going to mention them to Kilkenny, olive branch or no.

"So speaking of Stewart . . ."

Kilkenny sighed. "You're worried about Delaney."

"You know she shouldn't have been able to guess Stewart."

"Some people just have a good sense with those things," he said and truly sounded like he believed it. "Like Sherlock Holmes."

Raisa chewed on her lip. "You know Conan Doyle successfully predicted the use of forensic linguistics with Sherlock Holmes?"

"What?" Kilkenny asked, sounding a bit delighted.

She smiled. "Yeah. Eighty years before the field was officially birthed into the world. Sherlock uses forensic linguistics in several of the cases. I wrote a term paper on it once. Got an A."

"Of course you did," Kilkenny said fondly. "How did he use it?"

"Doyle actually used it fairly frequently," Raisa said. "But there's a notable case when he employed what's known as Native Language Influence Detection long before that mouthful was ever created."

"In what story?"

"'A Scandal in Bohemia.' The king is being blackmailed, and he writes a letter to Sherlock asking for help. Of course, Sherlock can 'deduce' his identity, but partly because of forensic linguistics. Here's the quote." She easily found it on Google. "'And the man who wrote the note is a German. Do you note the peculiar construction of the sentence—"This account of you we have from all quarters received." A Frenchman or Russian could not have written that. It is the German who is so uncourteous to his verbs. It only remains, therefore, to discover what is wanted by this German who writes upon Bohemian paper, and prefers wearing a mask to showing his face.'"

"That must have been a fun assignment."

"Yeah."

A bite must have been lingering in her voice, because Kilkenny's half smile faded. "I do trust you, Raisa."

"It doesn't seem like it," Raisa said, hating the petulant note in her voice.

"It's not my secret to tell," Kilkenny said, gently. "But Delaney Moore isn't our killer."

Raisa forced a smile and then stretched her arms in an exaggerated yawn. "All right. I think I will actually try to grab some sleep." She tapped the folder of Everly Ear columns. "I'll wake up early to tackle these."

He eyed her for a long moment, but he was too polite not to take the hint. "Task force meeting at six a.m. Setting the twenty-four-hour countdown. I'll bring you some good coffee."

"Thanks," she said, and followed him up as he stood. He lingered in the doorway for a moment before he nodded once and disappeared into the night.

She waited until the light flipped on in his cabin. Then she pulled her sweat-stained shirt over her head, yanking on a black tank in its place. With her jeans, it would have to do. Raisa's hair was cut short these days, the curls more manageable that way. She ran a bit of product through the strands, getting more bounce.

Then she shoved her feet into sandals, grabbed her wallet, and took off, heading out from her porch into the woods. There was exactly one bar in Everly, and it was near enough to the sheriff's department that Raisa now knew the way fairly well. Her foot plunged into a blessedly icy stream at one point, but beyond that she only tripped a time or two, and never bad enough to go down. She was getting familiar with the lay of this land.

She pushed through the Old West–style swinging doors ten minutes later. The place was surprisingly crowded, but she supposed that's what happened when you were the only watering hole in town.

It was a mix of a restaurant and bar, but this late at night, most people were crowded toward the back, ordering or nursing drinks.

Raisa found who she was looking for easily. She would have been impressed with herself if the guess of where he'd be tonight hadn't been so obvious.

Shawn Dallinger laughed when he saw her, his hand tightening around his beer. She wondered what number he was on.

"Miss High and Mighty," he crowed as she climbed onto a stool opposite of his. He'd parked himself at a back high-top where the foot traffic was lighter. His eyes were a little bleary, but he didn't seem so gone that she would feel guilty about questioning him. "You got me fired."

"I did not," Raisa said, and turned to smile at the overworked waitress who stopped by her elbow. "Gin and tonic."

"Fancy drinks for a fancy city lady," Shawn drawled out, some of the words sliding together, though that was inevitable for so many y-ending words in a row. Shawn held out his hands. "You gonna interrogate me."

"Nah," Raisa said, shifting so she could take in the room. She recognized two FBI agents in the corner, but neither glanced in her direction. Beyond that, it seemed to be packed full of mostly locals. "Just came for a drink."

Shawn laughed long and hard at that, then took the fresh beer the waitress brought with Raisa's G&T.

"You be good, Shawn," the waitress said, with an uneasy glance at Raisa.

"Girlfriend?" Raisa asked.

He waggled his eyebrows at her. "Wouldn't you like to know."

"I would mostly like to know about Isabel," Raisa said.

The leering grin dropped away at that. "Most people want to talk about Becks."

"Then or now?"

"Always," he said, with a smile. "We weren't fucking. Becks and me, that is."

"Okay," Raisa said, not flinching at the obscenity. She'd heard much worse. "Why did everyone think you were?"

"Don't know—all I know is every time I denied it, it seemed to make it worse," he said, drawing the tip of his finger through the condensation on his glass. "Now Isabel, haven't thought about her in ages."

"What was she like?"

"She's hazy," he said, tapping his temple with his finger. "In my memory."

"Fair enough," Raisa said, having picked up the phrase from Kilkenny, like she did sometimes with people she spent time around. Her vocabulary tended to be spongelike. "How did you two start dating?"

"She was tutoring my brother," Shawn said, smiling down into his drink. "She wasn't, you know, a bombshell. But she was nice. I was a screwed-up kid raised in a trailer by the river and she actually talked to me. Gave me a soda after school one day."

"Ah, true love," Raisa teased.

He laughed. "Yeah. It's stupid. No one had bought me anything before, though."

Raisa didn't want to like him. But she could understand that feeling.

"How long were you dating?"

He scrubbed a hand over his head. "I mean, we were kids. I don't know, three months? Five months? Something like that."

It was a strange thing. Isabel—and Lana and Larissa even—was frozen in Raisa's mind at the age of the murder-suicide. But unless more tragedy had befallen them, they would be around this man's age. Or Isabel and Lana would be. They'd been fifteen and twelve, which put them at forty and thirty-seven now. Larissa would be in her late twenties.

They weren't victims, stuck forever at the age of tragedy. But it sometimes seemed that way.

"What was Isabel like?" Raisa pressed, holding up a hand. "Besides her looks."

"Smart and shy," Shawn said, without missing a beat. "I did cheat on her a couple of times. She was so young we weren't really doing much. So."

Right. "Why were you dating her in the first place, then?"

He rolled the pint glass between his hands, considering. "From the outside, she had this perfect little family. Everything I wanted, you know? Since I was a kid. They had dinners together every Sunday. They had goddamn family trivia nights." Shawn shrugged. "And then you got inside and they were batshit crazy. I'm telling you, so many screws loose in that house."

He was so much calmer now than he had been earlier. It was lucky that alcohol seemed to mellow him instead of pushing him further into rage.

"More than the obvious?" Raisa asked.

"Yeah, course. Becks Parker was an ice queen," he said. "Everyone wanted to be her, and it went to her head. She would cut a bitch over the pettiest shit."

"Anything in particular?"

"There was a teacher who didn't suck up to their family like the rest of the town did," Shawn said after thinking it through. "Gave Lana a C one time. The next day the man was fired. Something about a lapsed certification or something. I don't remember, but it was some peanuts thing. Becks Parker always got what she wanted."

Raisa was getting a clearer picture of the woman, but homicide was homicide no matter how unlikable the victim. "What do you think about the theory that you had something to do with Tim and Becks's murders?"

Shawn laughed, spittle landing on the table. He wiped the back of his hand over his mouth. "Sorry, sorry. I might be dumb as rocks. But do you think I'm such an idiot I'd confess to killing them all just because I've had a few beers?"

"No," Raisa said, honestly, tilting her head. "I don't think you had anything to do with it."

"Yeah, well. It's easy to blame the poor kid, you know?"

"I do," she said softly. "So who do you think our copycat is?"

"Ain't with the department no more," he said, seeming to deliberately emphasize the poor grammar.

"If you were," Raisa prompted, unfazed.

He didn't say anything until he had a fresh beer in front of him, the waitress sending looks Raisa's way once more.

"Greg Balducci is back in town," he finally offered. "To bury his folks."

Raisa tried to figure out why that would be important. "So?"

He shrugged and left it at that.

"You picking up my tab?" he asked, with a careless, charming grin. It was the first time she saw the teenage boy he'd once been. "Don't think I didn't notice the interrogation. You can write it off as a business drink."

"Sure," Raisa said, knowing she'd just pay for it herself. "But one more question if this is official."

"Lay it on me."

"Do you have any reason to doubt that Alex was guilty?" she asked, watching his face closely.

"Nah," he said, but he was looking away. "Kid was a scumbag. And he beat on the girls when the parents weren't looking."

Attic days.

"No one did anything about it, though," Raisa said, even if she wasn't actually surprised by the fact.

Shawn huffed out a breath. "Lady, this is Everly. We were all busy covering our own bruises."

CHAPTER TWENTY-FOUR

DELANEY

Tell me a secret.

Delaney experienced a moment of dissonance as she checked her phone to make sure she was on the right app. That kind of demand usually came from the dark message boards she frequented.

But no. Her first glance had been right. It was from Kylie.

The phone's screen went dark as Delaney left the message on preview. Kylie would be notified that she'd received the request as soon as Delaney opened the app, and Delaney wasn't quite ready for that yet.

Tell me a secret. Not quite the refrain she heard from her apex predators, but it was close enough to send a shiver along her skin. Once again, she was reminded Kylie was a stranger.

Another message popped up.

I'm bored. Come on!

Delaney smiled.

That sounded more like Kylie. They had been talking for two years now, and Delaney had picked up on most of Kylie's patterns. There was a reason she was texting Delaney now—there was always a lull in the salon around this time.

You first, Delaney typed to buy herself a minute. And she wanted to see the level of secret Kylie was talking about.

That was something else Delaney had learned over the years. People had different tiers. There were harmless, tiny, might-as-well-not-even-be-secrets secrets. Those were essentially, *I tell people I'm a natural blonde.*

They got deeper from there until you hit Delaney's level.

Dots appeared and then disappeared, which got Delaney's full attention. She didn't think this was going to be of the bite-size variety.

I broke my sister and her fiancé up because I was in love with him.

The surprised judgment flared bright and hot, but Delaney stamped it out quickly. Who was she to pass criticism on anyone's life? That would be a bit like throwing stones at glass houses, only instead it would be her body that was made of glass. Delaney had thought Kylie above such cruelty, though. She was a bit emotionally careless, but she hadn't seemed to have a malicious bone in her body.

How did you do that? was all Delaney could think to ask.

Got him drunk, pushed him together with a friend he'd always been half in love with. I did my sister a favor if it was that easy to get him to cheat.

But weren't you in love with him? Delaney asked.

Yeah, but I couldn't be the one he was caught with, that would have ruined my relationship with my sis

Delaney chewed on her lip. She doesn't know?

Nope

Then came, Don't tell her with a winky-face emoji.

There was no good response to any of that. Delaney didn't have the skill set to reassure Kylie in a way that showed she clearly didn't condone the behavior. That took a delicacy and nuance Delaney had simply never learned.

So instead, she gave Kylie one of her precious secrets.

I lied to my sister once, too.

Kylie's response came quickly. Only once? Look at you, angel.

Delaney laughed at that. She was many things, but an angel wasn't one of them.

When Delaney didn't say anything, Kylie nudged.

What about?

Of course, Delaney would never hand over specifics. Kylie thought she was talking to Hannah Smith of New York City. But there was one way Delaney could be truthful.

Something important.

CHAPTER
TWENTY-FIVE
Raisa

When Raisa stepped out onto the cabin's little front stoop at 5:45 the next morning, Kilkenny was already waiting, coffee in hand.

"It's the cheap stuff from the lobby, but it will help," he said.

Raisa took it with an embarrassingly troll-like sound. "Bless you."

She had spent the night breaking down idiolects, first by reading through the "Alex is Innocent" thread and then by combing over the Everly Ears columns. She'd walked away with two conclusions. If the killer had posted before on the thread, he'd successfully masked his own voice when he'd written under the Galahad name. That didn't come as a surprise, considering how careful their unsub was, but it would have been nice to walk away with *something*.

Two, the author of the gossip columns was young, female, and from Everly. Raisa hadn't been able to shake the familiar feeling she got from the style they'd been written in. But comparing the samples to her other known idiolects from the case so far had yielded nothing.

"The gossip columns don't share any striking similarities to our known authors," Raisa said, as they headed toward the main building and the war room, where the task force would be gathering. The light was already trying to chase away the dark, the very edges of dawn creeping over the mountains' peaks.

"Thanks for looking at them," Kilkenny said and sounded like he sincerely meant it. He would have known she was going to get little sleep for doing him the favor. "It probably is just a horse race."

Raisa smiled into her cup at the reminder of their conversation about wild-goose chases, liking that they had inside jokes.

They filed into the conference room with the rest of the crew and took seats toward the back. There was a large countdown timer sitting at the head of the table, Agent Sand looming over it. He had the type of face that showed every minute of exhaustion.

"Twenty-four hours," he said, slapping the top of the clock, starting it. "That's how much time we likely have until we have another victim. If we don't stop this guy before then, that person's blood will be on our hands."

As someone who handled kidnapping situations more often than any other crime, Raisa was used to working under tight, high-stakes deadlines. The speech never got old, though. It was always a good reminder that there were real people's lives on the line, especially for Raisa, who could get caught up in statistics and variables.

Neither Kilkenny nor Raisa had anything to add to the meeting. In these types of meetings, agents would often try to BS their way into sounding important, but that would more likely get you kicked off the task force when there was a literal ticking clock counting each precious second.

There weren't many updates. The crime scene liaison confirmed that the Terri Harden homicide scene had been as clean, evidence-wise, as the Balduccis' place. All three victims had sleeping pills in their system, according to the rushed tox report. Beyond that, there were few other developments. None of the neighbors had seen anyone strange hanging around the houses in the past few days. There were no records of the places being serviced recently for internet or power outages. Terri had last been seen at the grocery store the night before and had been in good spirits.

"I'm going to check out the social worker's house," Kilkenny said, when they were all dismissed. "You want to come?"

Raisa thought about Shawn's quiet suggestion last night. *Greg Balducci is in town.*

"No, I'm chasing something else," she said.

"Fair enough."

Despite the coffee and the shared joke, they were tenser with each other now. Raisa wasn't so thin-skinned that a careless remark about her job had her cutting off the man who could be her closest ally here. But it went deeper than that. It was more about the fact that Raisa had liked him *because* he'd never cast doubt on her expertise.

"Okay, well, good luck then," she said, and fought the urge to slap him on the arm like she was his T-ball coach.

His lips twitched. "Back atcha."

Raisa checked the time. It was only 6:30. She didn't think she would have missed Greg. It was worth trying anyway.

If someone was staying in town on short notice—and dealing with their parents' shocking, brutal murders—they would likely need caffeine in the morning.

The coffee shop that was walkable from the hotel was a sunny yellow cottage surrounded by flowers that were wilting in the heat. And like many things in this town, it seemed to serve multiple purposes—as a gift shop, bakery, art gallery, and communal meeting area.

The front was dominated by display cases full of cookies the size of Raisa's head, and cakes of every flavor imaginable. Raisa found a small table in the corner that gave her a good perspective on the rest of the room and settled in to wait. It took about forty-five minutes before the bell above the door jangled and a guy about the right age entered.

He was built, the kind of man whose muscles had muscles, his tight gray tee emphasizing his Mack-Truck biceps. He wore a pristine baseball cap and jeans with holes that had clearly been made in a store. His Ray-Bans were hooked into the vee of his shirt, and he flashed a tasteful but clearly expensive watch when he handed over his card to the cashier.

Raisa first noticed him in the way she did anyone who might be a threat. While much of him was city-slicked, the body beneath his designer clothes was a weapon.

Then she wondered if this was her guy.

His eyes were scanning the people crowded into the space. Raisa wore a simple white tee and jeans, and she knew from experience she wasn't easily made as law enforcement. Probably because of her tiny build and big brown eyes that more than one person had called doe-like.

The man's order came up, but she was too far away to hear the name.

Raisa palmed her phone, and quickly googled Greg Balducci. With the kind of subtle wealth the man was displaying, she was sure he'd be in the top results if this was him.

Sure enough, she got a hit on a profile in *Tech Beats*. The article was mostly glossy photos of a Seattle penthouse with stellar views and furnishings that looked exactly like what you would expect from a dude who had probably thrown money at a minimalist designer.

And there in the top photo was Greg Balducci standing by a wall of windows, looking out at his empire and wearing a broody expression that reminded Raisa of that angsty teen-vampire movie. She skimmed past the anecdotal lede and found his bio. Greg had designed and sold an app in his twenties that had something to do with gambling. After that he'd become the money man in Seattle, funding start-ups that always seemed to go big. He had a passion for weight lifting and football, and stayed grounded by visiting his hometown in rural Washington.

Raisa glanced up one more time to check the man in the coffee shop against the photos, but, really, those muscles were distinctive enough that he would struggle to go incognito if he really wanted to.

She grabbed her badge and crossed over to him. In the time she'd been flash-researching, two older ladies had flanked him and were now clucking over him about his loss.

He looked cornered more than anything, so Raisa didn't feel bad interrupting. "Greg Balducci?"

Both women spun as fast as their arthritic bodies allowed, and glared at her.

Protective of the hometown boy who'd made it big.

"FBI Agent Raisa Susanto," she said as she flashed her badge. That did little to calm Greg's two guard dogs, but his shoulders relaxed. As much as they could.

She wondered if he'd thought her a journalist.

"Sure, yeah, you have questions?" he asked, his voice raspy. He had a large iced coffee and he'd already downed half of it. "Mabel, Olive. Thank you, I'll pass on your kind words to my brother as well."

In that graceful way of the ultrarich and sociable, Greg maneuvered both himself and Raisa away from the older ladies and over to the one free table in the shop. Hers had already been sniped.

He took the seat that put his back to the wall. If she hadn't just read his profile, she would have guessed he was ex-military. "I'm sorry, I'm not sure I'm going to be much more help than the statements I've already given. My parents didn't have any enemies. Everyone loved them."

"Actually, I'm working the investigation from a slightly different angle," she said. "I was wondering if I could ask you about the summer of '98. About your parents' Fourth of July party."

The write-up about the bash had been one of the more notable editions of the Everly Ears gossip column.

Greg's eyes went a little distant, his brows drawing down in confusion, before realization hit. "Oh, Jesus. The fight with Alex?"

"You remember it?" Raisa asked.

"Yeah, of course," he said. "I was pretty good friends with Isabel Parker at the time." He laughed a little. "She was dating Shawn, otherwise I would have tried for something more."

"Were you friends with Shawn, too?"

"Nah, he was a royal dick," Greg said, and then half winced. "Sorry."

"I think my delicate sensibilities might survive intact," she teased, and he laughed.

"Too much time with tech bros."

"So Shawn was not a good guy," Raisa prompted. She . . . could see it. There had been moments where Shawn had come across as charming, but most of the time there was an abrasive layer of sandpaper over his personality. "But you didn't get in a fight with Shawn. You got in a fight with Alex."

Greg nodded, his eyes dropping to his coffee. "The party was right after the charges against him got dropped."

"What charges?"

He looked up, surprised. "You don't know about Cara?"

"No, yeah, sorry," Raisa said, wishing she'd ordered an extra-large coffee instead of the small that she'd nursed. "Of course. I wasn't sure if there was something else."

"No." Greg huffed out a breath. "Well, maybe, but I was talking about Cara."

"So the Fourth happened . . ." Raisa prompted.

"Right, that was, like, three days after my parents gave Alex an alibi," Greg said. "Except I knew what night they had been asked about. They'd been lying—Alex hadn't come over to our house."

"Did you tell Sheriff Mason that?"

"No, I was scared of my dad back then." His lips twisted in what looked like self-loathing. "Not enough not to pick a fight with Alex when he started in on some other girl."

"Started in?"

"Just, you know, keeping her drinking," Greg said. "That's what he did with Cara. Got her drunk and she blacked out."

"You were friends with her, too?" Raisa asked.

"We're such a small town we were all quasi friends," Greg said. "But, yeah, when I was back in the summers, Isabel and Cara were around a lot."

"They were the grade below Alex?"

"Yeah," Greg said. "And then he started pulling the same shit and I lost it. We were all drunk—none of the parents cared about what we did at that particular party, so it was always chaotic. The teenagers were in the playroom downstairs. Alex cornered the new girl. I don't even remember her name."

"You probably saved her, though," Raisa pointed out.

"There's only so much you can ignore, even when you're a knucklehead kid," Greg said, waving to himself. He took the top off his drink and downed it in one impressive swallow. When he put the cup back down, his expression was serious. Meanwhile, Raisa was distracted by the fact that he'd just taken eight ounces of black coffee like a shot. "I didn't really realize it at the time, but I was just wallowing in guilt over Cara. She wouldn't talk to any of us. And then Alex showed his face and . . . yeah."

"You beat the crap out of him?"

Greg laughed in agreement. "Yeah. Someone pulled us apart and then a deputy showed up, tried to take us both in for underage drinking. The sheriff sorted it out. But if I said anything about why it had started . . ."

"You would have been implicating your parents," Raisa finished his thought. "Well, that's a sucky situation."

"You're telling me," Greg said, lifting his empty coffee cup in a toast. "To this day I regret not blowing apart my parents' alibi."

"Why did they cover for him?" Raisa asked, because he didn't seem too beat up about his recent loss, as shocking as it must have been.

"It's not that deep," Greg said. "He was the quarterback that year."

"The team wasn't even good, though." It was just a guess—based on the fact that it was a tiny population to draw on—but Greg tipped his head in acknowledgment.

"Still, the season made my dad Everly royalty, and that's what mattered to him," he said.

Royalty. That was a word that came up over and over again in this case. Status had been important, no matter how small the town was. Or maybe that's why it had been even more crucial to come out on top. She wondered if *royalty* had been used in the Everly Ears columns—after all, it was the people who would have been around during that time that she heard it from the most.

She made a mental note to add it to her miscellaneous column on the spreadsheet.

"Plus, back then, guys covered for each other all the time," Greg added.

It wasn't much different now, but Raisa kept her mouth shut about that. "What about your mom?"

"Not to speak ill," Greg said, "but she didn't exactly have a backbone. What my dad said was the rule of law."

"Did Isabel react to the fight at all?"

"She and Cara were close," Greg said, sidestepping a bit. "And she hated her brother. So. She wasn't exactly angry at me."

"Do you know what happened to Cara?"

"No, I lost touch with everyone from here," Greg said. "After what happened with Alex, and then the girls were snuck out of here like state secrets. I don't know, I just mostly wanted to forget everything I'd ever known about Everly."

"Makes sense," Raisa said, and then hesitated, thinking about the way Delaney had reacted to overhearing Raisa run a background check on her. Defensive people were always braced for an accusation. It could scare Greg off—would probably scare him off, actually. But why not ask and see what happened? Greg had been a friendly witness, and he'd already given his statement to the other agents. She wouldn't be alienating someone they needed if this backfired. "Shawn Dallinger, you know he's a deputy now?"

Or was, she corrected silently.

"Really? That surprises me. I thought he'd be on the other side of the bars." His lips quirked. "Or passed out at one."

"Clever," Raisa drawled. "When I asked who he thought our copycat killer was, he said I should ask you."

More or less, at least.

His eyes narrowed. "I've been in Seattle. There's plenty of ways to verify that. And, like I said, I don't know anything about Everly now."

"Sorry, I'm not asking you if you know who the killer is," Raisa clarified. "I'm asking you why Shawn Dallinger would send me in your direction."

The thing with big muscles was that they gave away reactions you might not have wanted read so easily. Greg's biceps jumped beneath his shirt as his fingers curled into fists. "You would have to ask him."

Then he stood up. "Any more questions?"

So many, including what had made this go from an open, friendly interview to feeling like the tail end of a hostile interrogation.

The obvious conclusion was that Greg knew what Shawn was thinking about, but he wasn't going to tell her.

"No. Thank you for your time," Raisa said. She pulled out a business card from her badge holder. "Here's my cell phone if you think about any reason Shawn—"

"Right," Greg cut her off. He took the card. "Have a good day."

She watched him walk to the door, watched him throw the slip of paper in the trash.

There was no doubt about it—the question had spooked him. He had been perfectly pleasant and helpful before she'd asked. But why? If he knew something that would help catch the person who'd killed his parents, wouldn't he have wanted to offer it up? Even if he had a rocky relationship with them? Even if he didn't seem too distraught that they were gone.

Was he protecting someone?

Or, more likely, was he protecting himself?

He hadn't acted guilty, though, until he had. If he was actually the copycat killer—which she highly doubted, given that he probably could verify his presence in Seattle easily—wouldn't he have been alert the entire interview?

Before she could consider that any further, her phone vibrated with a text from Kilkenny.

Get back, as soon as possible.

She stood even as she typed out, What happened?

Raisa stilled as the response came in and she had to read it twice to understand it.

Our copycat killer turned himself in.

EXCERPT FROM ISABEL PARKER'S DIARY

July 5, 1998

Alex and Greg fought last night. It started over some girl, but I know it was really about Cara. She's not talking to almost anyone—I wouldn't blame her if she never talked to *me* again, either. But she doesn't seem to hold Alex's behavior against me.

Maybe it's because she knows if that's how Alex acts outside our house, he must be worse in it.

If only our parents could make that simple deduction, as well. You'd think two geniuses could figure out that all the rumors about Alex are actually true. Or, you know, just look at the way their daughters are terrified of their son. But then how would they maintain their little fantasy of who we all are? The beautiful and talented and perfect Parkers. Never forget perfect.

I didn't wait around to see what Becks and Tim thought about The Fight. I know Becks is finally starting to worry that Alex is following in Tim's schizophrenic footsteps, but really he's just an asshole who was treated as the heir his whole life and is now acting like the spoiled princeling you'd expect.

Meanwhile, Lana has a new bruise on her arm. When I was her age, I dreamed of some white knight coming to save us. That was about the time Alex started sneaking into my room at night, smelling of mint from our shared toothpaste.

I never thought either Becks or Tim could be that white knight. Isn't that funny? And isn't it strange that I feel safe writing this all down here. Some teenagers might worry that their parents would find this. Neither of them care enough about us to even think to snoop. I was the one who got these diaries for everyone for Christmas. Only Becks has used hers with any frequency—yes, I snooped, my dear diary. But you won't tell anyone, will you?

Of course, Becks uses hers to keep track of Tim's symptoms. They only ever had eyes for each other, never for us.

I used to dream about a white knight coming to take us away from them.

It took me a while to realize that I am the white knight.

CHAPTER TWENTY-SIX

RAISA

It took Raisa half an hour to decide that the man who had confessed to the copycat killings was lying.

Actually, it had taken Raisa three minutes, and she'd spent the next twenty-seven building her case. Kilkenny stood beside her as she handed her tablet over to Sand.

They had commandeered a hotel room for this emergency meeting. Sand and Raisa had taken seats at the little table that held the plastic-wrapped plastic glasses and the tan ice container. Kilkenny leaned on the wall, on her side. The location choice wasn't lost on her.

A little wireless video feed of Professor Brian Walker sitting in the sheriff's department interrogation room played on Sand's computer where they could all see it.

He was a short man with thinning sandy-blond hair and an underbite. He looked exactly like a stereotypical professor, down to the tweed jacket with elbow patches.

He was also staring directly into the camera.

"It's not him," Raisa said, tearing her eyes away. It was a creepy sensation, even though she knew he couldn't see her in return.

When Walker had turned himself in, he'd also handed over a manifesto that was essentially a bunch of ecoterrorism ideas thrown in a blender and regurgitated in a strikingly distinct idiolect. "There are no similarities between his writing and the killer's messages."

"You said a voice could be faked," Sand said, not looking at her spreadsheet.

"It can be. Not by him," Raisa said, pointing to Walker, who was still staring, unblinking, at the camera. "He's an ideological purist. He has delusions of grandeur; he thinks he's far more intelligent than he is. Each paragraph is stuffed full of ten-dollar words, and yet they mean nothing in the order he puts them in. There is no way that man is playing four-dimensional chess with us."

"You can tell all that?" Sand asked, sounding doubtful but interested. "Just from a handful of message board posts and a manifesto?"

Raisa zoomed in on one of her columns. "One strong positive correlation that's been found is between grandiosity and an outsize number of references to the body. You see it in Walker's writing: 'It's in our hands'; 'our sweat is the only thing that can feed this earth.' He uses phrases like that over and over again." Sand opened his mouth, and she cut off the question, knowing what it was. "I don't know why there's a strong link, but I do know the research is sound. You don't see any of that in the killer's messages."

"That seems . . . weak," Sand said. "Again, can't he just fake it?"

"Someone with his personality type, which is backed up by his style of writing, isn't going to fake a voice," she said. "He wants to be heard as himself. That's all part of the grandiosity thing."

Sand's eyes shifted to Kilkenny. "What do you think?"

"In addition to Agent Susanto's take," Kilkenny said, deliberately giving her credit, "I'd have to agree, Walker doesn't fit the profile that

I've been building for our killer. He *does* fit the profile of someone who would turn themselves in with a false confession."

"And what profile is that?" Sand asked.

"Everything Agent Susanto said, with the strongest emphasis on his ideological purity," Kilkenny offered calmly in the face of Sand's bite. "He wants attention for his cause—but ultimately for himself—and he'll do what he must to get it. This is a narcissist we're looking at here, not a puppet master."

"Why would he confess to three premeditated murders if he didn't commit them?" Sand asked. "He might be everything you say, but he's not unhinged."

"Because he doesn't think it will go all the way to court. He knows he's not the killer," Raisa said. "But in the meantime his cause will get tons of media attention. Have you asked him something only the killer would know?"

"This isn't my first rodeo, Susanto," Sand said, his normal brusqueness slipping deeper into irritation. They were taking up valuable time, and he was losing patience. But so was Raisa.

"Then he studied the Parker case." There was no way in hell that man in the interrogation room was their killer.

"He knew there was a tombstone on the walls," Sand countered, brows raised.

That threw Raisa. Only the task force had that detail.

Well. The task force and the unsub.

"Puppet master," Raisa breathed out. "The killer fed Walker the details."

"Why would our unsub get the FBI out here just to make someone else confess?" Sand asked.

Raisa fumbled for an answer. "I don't know. I don't . . ."

She glanced at Kilkenny, whose expression was set to grim-neutral. He didn't have an answer, either.

"It buys them time?" she tried.

"Then why contact us in the first place?" Sand asked. When neither of them answered, he stood. "Look. I appreciate both of your specialties, but there's no need to make this more complicated than it is."

"At least stay until tomorrow," Kilkenny suggested, sounding a bit desperate, which got Sand's attention. Kilkenny didn't do desperate. "If there's another victim, we'll know it wasn't Walker. If there's not, what harm is there in staying an extra"—he glanced at the time—"eighteen hours?"

The question hung for a fraught second, but then Sand shrugged.

"Yeah, all right," he agreed easily. "But we're wrapping up after that. The resources we're spending here are not minimal."

Raisa could have pointed out that most serial killer investigations could last months or often years and that an extra few days wouldn't exactly bankrupt the federal government. But she kept her mouth shut, and Sand left the room.

Kilkenny's eyes were on the door. "I don't think there will be a death tomorrow."

Once he said it, Raisa realized he was right. "Why feed someone enough details for a confession, then take a victim when the FBI is still in town?"

"If the killer has enough control over their urges, they'll wait," Kilkenny said. "And from everything I've seen, they have enough control. With the Balduccis and Terri Harden, it seemed like we might have a spree killer on our hands. But since there wasn't anyone today to replace Stewart Young, I think we can assume there's a plan in place and they're not going to detour from it."

Raisa pushed to her feet and began pacing the small space. The two queen beds took up most of the floor space, a strange reminder they'd co-opted a hotel room for this little meeting. "None of this makes sense."

"We're obviously missing a key component."

"You think?" Raisa said, a touch too sarcastic to be professional. "Walker wouldn't have known about the tombstone in any other way, right? Other than the killer telling him?"

"No," Kilkenny said. "Maybe. But doubtful."

"Well as long as you're certain," Raisa said with a laugh that he almost answered.

"It seems unlikely," Kilkenny said. "The only reason we even know what it means is because of Delaney."

"Who would use that symbol?"

"What?" Kilkenny asked.

"Who would use a semi-obscure—for laymen at least—mathematical symbol?" Raisa asked. "As a signature, when most people wouldn't be able to even figure out what it was. If you walked into a crime scene and saw a box painted on a wall, what would you think?"

"I'd make note of it," Kilkenny said slowly. "But I would never have thought *tombstone*."

"Exactly." She kept coming back to messages. The killer *desperately* wanted to communicate. Who their audience was, though, wasn't quite clear.

In the messages they'd posted to the "Alex is Innocent" board, they'd been talking to Raisa. Or, at least, a forensic linguist. "Who were they talking to with a mathematical symbol?"

"Someone who would understand that the black box on the wall was a tombstone," Kilkenny said.

"Delaney," Raisa pointed out.

Kilkenny looked away and Raisa swallowed a frustrated sound. She didn't understand his loyalty to the woman. What had Delaney Moore done to earn it? What had Raisa failed to do?

"There's a reason we're here," Kilkenny said, shifting the conversation. Raisa decided not to fight it. "Our copycat wouldn't have gone through all this trouble to get our attention and then send us home after two days. It doesn't make any sense."

For some reason, the repetition of her own words shook something free. "What if we're looking at this all wrong?"

"How so?"

"The killer has set up a pattern," Raisa said slowly, feeling out the idea. "You feel it, don't you? You told Sand we should wait until tomorrow to see if there's another victim."

"I hope there's not, of course," Kilkenny said.

"No, I know." Raisa waved that away impatiently. "Think about if we had found Stewart Young today at around six a.m. Think about it. We would have had three days in a row of expecting a homicide at six a.m."

"We would think the next one would take place then, too," Kilkenny said, following her thoughts.

"You bet someone's life on it," she reminded him. "Remember? When Sand asked, you said you were certain that the killer would stick to a schedule."

He lifted his brows, looking slightly put out, but nodded.

"You were right," Raisa rushed to say. "But then the killer fed someone enough reliable information that they believably confessed to all this. Why?"

Kilkenny shook his head, but then after a moment said, "So that we drop our guard."

Raisa snapped her fingers. "Right. So that takes care of both the agents who want to believe this Walker guy is *our* guy, and the ones"— she waved between the two of them—"that are convinced the killer has a set pattern."

"He does have a set pattern, though."

"No, he doesn't," Raisa corrected. "You said it before, he kills like a hired assassin. There's a set pattern not because *he* needs it, but because he wants us to get complacent."

"You're guessing."

"Yeah, join me," Raisa said, with more than a little edge. "How else are we supposed to game out the actions of a puppet-master serial killer? Any other ideas? Because that dude sitting in custody is not him, and you know that as well as I do."

Kilkenny looked like he wanted to argue but then sighed. "You're right."

Raisa didn't waste time gloating. "So, if we think about it in terms of Walker turning himself in with information only the killer knew . . ."

"We can assume it's part of the killer's plans," Kilkenny agreed, though he still sounded reluctant to be making logical leaps. "Walker could be a distraction so the killer can leave town."

"But then why bring us all out here in the first place?"

"To prove they can?" Kilkenny suggested, and Raisa had to acknowledge that was a fair point. "It fits with the psychological profile. They wanted to play with us and now they're bored again."

"But what if I'm right? What if they wanted everyone to become complacent so they could take out their toughest victim without worrying about all the extra scrutiny?" Raisa pressed.

"If that's the case, then they'll strike today." He glanced at his watch. "Tonight, really."

"It's the final victim," Raisa said, everything finally making sense. Or, not everything, but some things. "They didn't want anything to go wrong with this one."

"The sheriff," Kilkenny suggested.

Samantha had hightailed it out of the archives room before Raisa could continue to press her about her "dirty hands." But even while admitting her role in the clusterfuck that was the Parker investigation and the months preceding it, she hadn't seemed worried. Maybe she just accepted her possible fate as the next victim as her penance.

"I don't know," Raisa said, hating that phrase. She thought about Greg. "Maybe the Balduccis' son?"

"What did he do?"

"His parents gave Alex an alibi to get him cleared of a sexual assault accusation," Raisa said. "Greg knew about it and never said anything."

"The parents' deaths would have guaranteed he would come back to town," Kilkenny said, with raised brows. He found this theory intriguing. "The accuser. Cara James. You thought she might have written the gossip columns."

"I don't have anything to compare it to," Raisa admitted. "But she certainly would have been justified in having a grudge against the Parkers. I don't even blame her for spreading nasty rumors about them. If it was her. And if you look at the deaths so far . . ."

She trailed off, not realizing the truth of what she was saying until the words were out. "Huh."

"What?"

"The Balduccis and Stewart Young," Raisa said slowly. "They're not only tied to Alex, but tied to the sexual assault case."

He hummed in question, and she filled him in on what Greg had told her about the fight with Alex.

"Stewart Young could have arrested Alex that night on *some* charges," Raisa said. "He would have at least faced some consequences."

"Then wouldn't the sheriff be at fault, too?" Kilkenny asked. "And what about Terri Harden?"

"She was the social worker for Everly. What if Terri was assigned as Cara's advocate?" Raisa asked. "It's a small town, she probably handled most of the investigations in town."

"Maybe," Kilkenny said. "And she tied it to the anniversary because?"

Raisa huffed out a breath. "Isn't this your bailiwick?"

He almost smiled. "She wants to mark it. In celebration, almost. Karma took care of him where others wouldn't." He paused. "Anything in those diaries you found?"

"Nothing about Cara. That rest is more of what we already know," Raisa said. "Alex was abusive, the parents didn't care. Becks had been thinking about getting a divorce about two weeks before they were killed."

Kilkenny sat forward. "Thought about, as in she was angry and was reacting emotionally? Or thought about seriously?"

"The latter, I think," Raisa said. "The sheriff talked her out of it because of Tim's illness."

"A great reason to stay with someone."

Raisa hummed her agreement. "Honestly, if I didn't know either one of them couldn't have been the original killer, I would say they both had motive for slitting the other's throat."

"What was Tim's?"

"Becks was going to expose him for stealing the proof that got him all that praise that summer," Raisa said. "For an academic? A mathematician of Tim's caliber? That would have been tantamount to a physical threat."

"Didn't Mark the TA say he was becoming paranoid about that proof?" Kilkenny said.

"Right, yeah," Raisa said. "And remember he mentioned that girl? Apparently she confronted Becks about it. That's what made her think about the divorce." She paused, considering. "If it was just Tim who'd died, I'd be more suspicious of her. She seemed pretty enraged in her second letter. And, again, I don't know if you've ever worked on cases with people in these kinds of fields, but the dark-academia trend in media is, uh, true to life. To say the least."

"Was Talia actually dangerous?" Kilkenny asked.

"The threat read as credible," Raisa said. "If it wasn't for Becks and Alex . . ."

"Well," Kilkenny drawled out, "if she's a psychopath—in laymen's terms, of course—"

"Of course," Raisa assured him. God forbid Kilkenny do something as imperfect as refer to someone by a nontechnical diagnosis without clarifying he knew it was the nontechnical diagnosis.

"She might not have blinked at killing Becks and Alex as collateral damage."

Raisa made a frustrated sound.

"Why do we keep doing this?" she asked. "Alex wasn't framed—his story and confession letter match linguistically. Why do we keep trying to solve a case that doesn't need solved?"

He sighed. "The magic of a puppet-master personality type. The killer wants us to focus on Tim and Becks's murders, so we keep getting pulled into a riptide of their making."

Raisa swore softly. "Well, you're not supposed to fight a riptide."

She pulled out her phone and pinged the research assistant. **Any update on Talia?**

Was just about to text.

The next message had an address that looked about twenty miles away, back toward the coast.

Raisa brandished her phone in Kilkenny's face. "So, shall we head to the ocean?"

JENNA SHAW: Hello from Everly, my lovely tin-hatters. It has been all excitement, all the time since I got into town this morning. And I'll let you in on a little secret because I know you guys can keep your lips zipped—the FBI task force investigating the killer consulted with yours truly because of my extensive expertise with the Parker case. I can't say too much, but you should know I played an instrumental role in the current case. Don't worry, darlings, don't worry—I'll be sure to spill everything to you as soon as I get the okay from the men in suits.

Now, I've been sitting on a major interview I conducted for the podcast back before all this blew up. It was with Terri Harden, the social worker who cleared Alex Parker just before he allegedly went on to murder his parents and kill himself. I believe if she were still alive, Terri would like the conversation aired.

TERRI HARDEN: It was one of those cases where you look back and think, What did I miss? But then you realize you didn't miss anything. Monsters like Alex Parker are good at wearing masks.

SHAW: That's Terri in what was likely her last interview before her death by the hands of a serial killer.

SHAW: You wouldn't have done anything differently? Knowing how it all turned out?

HARDEN: No, I wouldn't have. I talked to the teachers, I talked to the family, I talked to his friends. I was young, I was new to the job. But I look at my notes from that case every year on the anniversary and I . . . I didn't miss anything.

SHAW: Did you talk to Cara James?

SHAW: Terri broke out into a well-timed coughing fit that I'll spare you lovely listeners from. Somewhat surprisingly, she did agree to send me a copy of her version of the case notes, with her handwritten thoughts on them.

HARDEN: Hindsight is twenty-twenty. Each time I read that report, I realize there was just no way to have predicted how much of a time bomb Alex Parker was going to be.

SHAW: No way to predict it, you say, but what about the English teacher? The one who did predict it— enough to call you in?

HARDEN: Eric Gonzalez. I talked to him after. Not as part of the report or anything like that. But I wanted to know what he'd thought was going to happen. He said honestly that he believed he was being paranoid, that he might get in trouble for wasting the state's time, even. How do you see something like that coming?

SHAW: Isn't that what you're paid to do?

SHAW: Terri Harden did hang up on me and then refuse to return my calls after that. But I wanted to make sure her side was represented fairly here. You, my eagle-eared listeners, can decide for yourself whether anyone could have predicted it. There will be a link in the episode page to the state's report on Alex Parker. See for yourselves.

CHAPTER TWENTY-SEVEN

RAISA

Talia, the former student, turned out to be Talia Evans. She lived in a one-room cabin at the end of a long dirt road at the end of a stretch of farmland.

She must have heard them coming, because she stood on the porch, a two-hundred-pound mastiff at her side. Raisa generally liked dogs, but she had a solid appreciation of any creature that had nearly a hundred pounds on her.

"He's a marshmallow," Talia called out as Raisa hovered by the SUV's open door. "That is, unless I tell him to attack."

"You know," Raisa said, "on second thought, I'm sure this has nothing to do—"

"Come on," Kilkenny said with a half smile. He had already palmed his badge, the gold catching the sun as he called out introductions for both of them.

Talia wrinkled her nose. "The Parker case."

Then she turned and walked into the cabin. Raisa decided to take the fact that Talia hadn't sicced the mastiff on them as an implicit invitation.

Raisa expected to be hit with a wall of heat since it was obvious that, like most houses in the state, the rustic cabin didn't have air-conditioning. But there was a surprisingly nice through-draft pulling from the front door to the back. Talia was already pouring them tall, sweating glasses of iced lemonade, and Raisa took the opportunity to check out the room. There was a wood-framed bed in the corner with a lightweight summer quilt. Everything in the place was a bit haphazard, the picture frames askew, piles of shoes in the corner along with dog toys. It was a bit like the woman who lived there, her curly hair wild and silver-threaded, the neck of her overlarge T-shirt sliding down her arm to reveal a watercolor tattoo on her shoulder.

"Look, I was young and passionate, and I should never have sent that letter," Talia said, as she curled up in the burnt-orange armchair, the mastiff resting his entire body against the side of it, eyes on Raisa.

It was curious that she'd jumped right in with the written threat. "Did Tim really steal your proof?"

"Oh, yeah, absolutely," she said, laughing. "And the bastard paid. Now, don't take that as a confession—I just found karma that summer and have been following in her guidance ever since."

"Do you still work in mathematics?" Kilkenny asked.

Talia grinned at them. "You're thinking about the cognitive dissonance between the two. But what else do you call it when a man who did you wrong is brutally murdered not two weeks after you swear vengeance on him?"

She was a little bloodthirsty for someone who preached karma, but Raisa guessed if you thought the universe paid back what you sowed, and you kept your own actions clean, you could be as bloodthirsty in your thoughts as you wanted.

When Kilkenny raised his brows in a silent reminder of who they were, Talia laughed again. It was a warm, husky sound, clearly well used. "Right, you don't think karma—you think killer."

A clever way with words, Raisa noted. But not in the way their killer used them.

"I didn't kill the Parkers," Talia said. "You don't have to take my word on it, either. I was out of the country. I'm sure if you really wanted, you could find a copy of the transaction. I flew American Airlines."

"We don't think you killed them," Raisa said, a moment of déjà vu hitting her. How many people had she reassured lately that was the case? Why was everyone so certain that was what the FBI was investigating? Or, not quite certain, but giving away their doubts about what had happened with the question itself.

Did everyone in this town see the copycat killings and think the original murderer was returning to the scene of the crime, so to speak? And if so, why was that the obvious conclusion they'd reached when the professionals had all agreed it was someone else?

"Why do you think we'd ask if you had an alibi for twenty-five years ago and not for two days ago?" Raisa asked.

For the first time since they'd arrived, Talia seemed thrown. She blinked at them a few times, and the mastiff let out a low, rumbling growl. Talia curled her fingers into the extra skin of his neck and he settled.

"I guess . . . I mean, I hadn't really been thinking about it, but now that I am? I never saw Alex Parker as a boy who would snap and kill his parents," Talia said, lifting that one bare shoulder. "I know that it's considered a conspiracy theory that he's innocent—and, yes, you caught me, I follow along to that podcast. But I did know him a little. He'd come to campus with Tim, hang out in his office. He was a skeeze but he wasn't a psycho." She glanced at Kilkenny. "Sorry, Doc, I don't know the correct term."

"That works," Kilkenny said, as if he hadn't just used essentially that phrase an hour ago.

"Who would you put your money on?" Raisa asked.

Talia wiggled her eyebrows. "The babysitter."

Raisa was actually surprised at that one. "What?"

"Amanda something or other," Talia offered, and Raisa pictured the woman. She had the look of a fading prom queen, the bottle-blonde hair brittle on older strands now, the tan emphasizing age spots instead of dewy skin.

"Why her?"

"Oh, she was obsessed with Tim," Talia said. "She would take any excuse to drop by his classes, the baby in tow. I was his TA for the semester before I graduated, and he once hid in a closet to avoid her, had me send her to Becks."

Raisa remembered Amanda's bitter expression at the mention of Becks Parker.

"You think that was enough to kill three people over?"

"Well, she wasn't exactly fond of Alex—none of the girls in his vicinity ever were," Talia said. "She was insanely jealous of Becks, and she probably viewed Tim's avoidance of her as some kind of rejection. I could see it."

"That's all well and good in theory," Raisa said. "But Alex was violent and he did hit his sisters. He had a temper—even if that doesn't necessarily equate to homicide."

"See"—Talia toasted Raisa with her lemonade glass—"I didn't know any of that. This is why I have to stop listening to podcasts."

"Just some of them," Raisa said quietly.

"Well, the only alibi I've got for two nights ago is Bruno here," Talia said with a head tilt to the mastiff. "But he'll report that I had a really exciting night full of streaming *Parks and Rec*, eating my body weight in mac and cheese, and then falling asleep at nine fifteen p.m."

The fact that she thought the murders had happened overnight and not early in the morning was telling in and of itself.

"Becks wrote in her diary that she was sending a letter to the journal Tim had been published in to tell them what he'd done," Raisa said. "Did anything ever come of that?"

Talia's brows shot up in surprise. "That was good of her. But no, must not have actually mailed it."

"Do you know if there were any other rumblings?" Raisa asked. "That he stole from other students?"

"No, that was the wild thing," Talia said. "There weren't even whispers about him doing anything like that before. I guess you always start somewhere."

There was one more question niggling at Raisa, ever since she'd seen the dates on the letters. "You had already graduated when you found out about Tim's work, right?"

"Yeah, a year out," Talia said, looking curious instead of defensive.

"How did you hear about what he was doing, then?" Raisa asked. "Your first letter was dated before he'd even completed the work. You said you'd be happy to help him."

"Ohhhh," Talia breathed. She was on her feet in the next instant. "Oh, you're a smart cookie, aren't you? Tiny thing, but big brain."

Kilkenny made a sound that came too close to a laugh, and Raisa glared at him. Meanwhile, Talia was heading out the back door.

"Don't get your hopes up. I probably don't have it," Talia called over her shoulder, Bruno trotting at her heels. Both Raisa and Kilkenny followed in time to see Talia going into an entirely separate building behind the main cabin. It looked like what people were calling "she-sheds" these days, but Raisa took a wild guess that Talia didn't refer to hers that way. "I am a slightly compulsive hoarder when it comes to paperwork, though, so there's a chance."

Her voice carried from inside the little outbuilding, and Kilkenny hung back so that Raisa could poke her head in. Along one wall ran a neat quartet of tall filing cabinets. Talia had the top half of her body buried in one. She didn't say anything for several long minutes, but Bruno was watching Raisa, so she resisted the urge to snoop.

"Aha," Talia called triumphantly, waving something around as she straightened. Raisa caught sight of an envelope, and her heartbeat kicked up a notch. Envelopes meant letters, which meant writing. "I got this completely out of the blue that . . . May? I think. Here, let me . . ."

She trailed off as she pulled out whatever was inside, and Raisa fought the urge to throw evidence gloves at her.

"May," Talia confirmed. She blew out a breath and held it out to Raisa, who inched toward her enough to take it. Bruno grumbled but didn't lunge. "Honestly, I wouldn't have known otherwise. Or probably not until the proof published. Not that it mattered in the long run. But I thought someone was looking out for me."

The stationery was heavy, the writing feminine. Raisa glanced up. "This has the Everly College mathematics logo on it."

"Yeah, I kind of assumed it was the wife who sent it," Talia said, hand resting on Bruno's head.

"No," Raisa murmured as she went back to reading it. "She didn't know about you until August."

"Really?"

Raisa hummed her confirmation, already distracted. The letter was fairly short and to the point. The anonymous Good Samaritan just wanted Talia to know that Tim Parker was planning on taking credit for Talia's work.

But Raisa kept returning to one sentence in particular.

If he gets away with this, I know that it will become Professor Parker's big accomplishment, the one everyone will remember him for.

She exhaled and looked up.

"I know who sent this."

CHAPTER
TWENTY-EIGHT

Raisa

"You know who wrote that?" Talia asked, jerking her chin toward the anonymous letter Raisa still held.

"Not who exactly," Raisa said, an impatient, annoyed sound escaping. Bruno shifted toward her, and Raisa took a step back. "Sorry, no. I mean, I know who but I don't know their name."

"Uh, you okay, hon?" Talia asked, and Kilkenny took Raisa by the elbow, pulling her fully out of the she-shed.

"What did you notice?" he prompted.

"This is the same person who wrote the Everly Ears gossip column," Raisa said, waving the paper in Kilkenny's face. "I'm sure I can do a better analysis with my spreadsheet, but this phrase here." She tapped on the sentence about Professor Parker's big accomplishment. "The columnist used that exact phrase."

"So?" Talia asked over Raisa's shoulder. "Isn't that kind of a common phrase? I'm sure I called Tim Professor Parker fairly consistently."

"If you did, you didn't use it in conjunction with 'big accomplishment.'"

Talia tilted her head. "Oh. Well, fair enough, I suppose. I don't think I've used that phrase in my entire life, actually."

"I know," Raisa said. This was one of the misconceptions she had to fight against all the time. "Everyone thinks they use common phrases in their own speech all the time, but it's just not true."

There were so many cases Raisa could whip out to prove her point. One involved a police statement given by a man who said, "I asked her if I could carry her bags." *I asked her* came up plenty, as did *if I could carry*. So did *I asked her if I could carry*. No one hearing that full sentence would think it was unique, but at the time, no one on the entire internet had ever uttered those exact words in that exact combination. Her field existed for a reason.

"I have seen writing samples from a dozen people involved in this case, and only two—two exactly—have used that phrase," Raisa continued. "And no one else, no one, called Tim Professor Parker. Even people who frequently used alliteration throughout their writing called him Tim or Tim Parker or the professor."

She scanned the letter again, and she hummed in satisfaction. "And she refers to the Parkers as royalty."

"I hate to say it again, but—"

"No, I know, that's less damning," Raisa hurried to say. It wouldn't hold up in court, the phrase too common in the small town. But the fact that the word was there restored some of her confidence in herself.

And she wasn't ready to say it yet, but . . . *royalty* had stood out to her for a reason. She'd nearly memorized Alex's confession letter by now, and she could all but see the neatly typed *favorite king and queen beheaded*.

Wouldn't that be a twist, if Alex had been the one penning the Everly Ears columns, if he'd had it out for his dad enough to anonymously write Talia this letter?

She shook her head. She was jumping to conclusions.

"Okay, well, how hard could it be to find out who wrote those columns?" Talia asked, interrupting her leaps of logic.

"For such a small paper, apparently quite hard," Kilkenny said. "But it's a place to start."

"Right," Raisa said, her mind already moving to the next steps. She turned back to Talia. "Can we keep this?"

"Go for it," Talia said.

Raisa thought about the filing cabinets. "I'll send it back if I can."

Talia's smile softened. "Thanks."

"Is there anything else you can think of from that summer that might be of interest to us?" Raisa asked, because she always liked giving people one more chance to offer something she hadn't thought of.

"I wasn't super involved in the town gossip," Talia said, shaking her head. "I was gone by then."

"You staked out the Parkers' house, though," Raisa said, remembering the small—but now important—detail from Becks's journal. "Not long before the murders."

"That's right," Talia said, sounding almost amused at her younger self. "I probably hadn't settled on the right dosage of medication back then. Let me think." She leaned against Bruno, eyes trained skyward. "Oh. I'm not sure if it means anything, but I saw a kid sneaking into one of the upper windows maybe three nights in a row. I guess that would have been about two weeks before the murders?"

"Alex?" Raisa asked.

"No, Alex Parker was a string bean," Talia said. "This kid looked 'roided out. I very distinctly remember thinking he would have hate-crimed me in high school."

Raisa pressed her lips together at the too-accurate description and pulled out her phone on a hunch. The profile she'd googled earlier of Greg Balducci was still on there, along with the photos of his distinctive build.

"Does he ring any bells?"

Talia made a surprised tsking sound when she glanced at the screen, and then she took the phone to study it closer. "Girl. That's totally him. I mean, eighty-percent sure. Maybe sixty, but the fact that you had this on hand makes me think sixty percent is enough to convince you."

Kilkenny craned his head.

"The Balduccis' son," Raisa told him, and turned back to Talia. "Thank you for your help."

"Anytime," Talia said. "I like you, not your typical suit."

Bruno's tail thumped in what Raisa took as agreement.

When they got back to the SUV, Kilkenny climbed behind the wheel but didn't start the engine. "You just happened to know she was talking about Greg?"

"I think 'built' was the word I used to myself, but you'd understand how I got Greg from ''roided out' if you met him," Raisa said.

"You've spoken to him," Kilkenny said, with just enough ice—for Kilkenny—that Raisa finally picked up on the fact that he was pissed.

"I told you earlier," Raisa said slowly, trying to remember exactly what she'd said about Greg.

"No, you said you had information about him," Kilkenny said. "You never mentioned you'd met up with him."

She supposed that was true enough.

"We're not partners," Raisa said, stating the obvious. "I don't have to report my every move to you."

"Right," Kilkenny said, his expression too neutral. He jabbed the key in the ignition, no longer looking at her, and Raisa was struck by the fact that he might be hurt.

"You don't tell me everything," she said, not one to let things go.

"Right," he said again. Raisa just stared at him, and he shook his head. "You're right, we're not partners."

Raisa knew she'd misstepped but couldn't figure her way out of it. So, instead, she pulled up the number for the task force's research assistant as Kilkenny navigated the tight two-lane highway back to Everly.

Can you look up Cara James? she wrote.

She got an immediate response. Boss sent me home. No more work on the case. Sorry 😕

Raisa cursed quietly and Kilkenny looked over. His curiosity would trump his annoyance, she was sure of it.

"What?" he asked.

"Sand is starting to send people back to Seattle," she said. "He doesn't believe us."

"How do you know?"

"I asked the research assistant to look up info on Cara James," she said. "No go."

"The girl who accused Alex of sexual assault," Kilkenny said, as if reminding himself.

Raisa hummed absently, already googling her. The name was fairly common, but in the twenty minutes it took to get to the outskirts of Everly, Raisa managed to find someone she thought might be the right woman. She sent her a quick message on Facebook and then looked up as Kilkenny turned onto Main Street.

"Do you know where the offices for the newspaper are?"

"They do a print run over in Sedro-Woolley," Kilkenny said. It was the closest town with anything resembling a chain grocery store, so it got deemed "big." "The current editor, Marigold Stevens, runs the whole production out of her loft." He pulled to a stop and pointed. "Up there."

So maybe they weren't partners, but they tended to think the same, and that had to count for something.

Marigold turned out to be a frenzied, middle-aged woman who'd gone to school with Greg Balducci. She kept glancing over at her computer even as she tried to answer their questions, clearly on a deadline but too much of a people pleaser to kick them out.

When Raisa asked about Everly Ears, she groaned and slapped a hand to her face. "That was so embarrassing. Have you read them all?"

"A sample," Raisa admitted.

"They were like a boring version of TMZ," Marigold said. She leaned forward. "But we all read them, of course."

"Did you have any idea of who it was?"

"No, but that was such a hot topic, let me tell you." Marigold smiled like it was a fond memory. "It gave us something to talk about that year."

"So, no guesses?" Raisa pressed.

"Everyone got a finger pointed in their direction," Marigold said. "There weren't that many of us. We figured it had to be someone in close contact with the Parkers, though. They were the main target of the author."

The babysitter? Maybe. Cara? Also possible. There were certainly plenty of options.

"You don't have any paperwork that would track who it was?"

"Oh. No." Marigold glanced between them. "It was completely anonymous. Dora didn't even know. I was interning that summer. We would get a submission slipped under Dora's door in a plain white envelope. I typed them up for print. We didn't even have someone to pay."

"That's quite a system."

Marigold laughed, and it was as nervy as the rest of her. "Welcome to Everly."

Raisa and Kilkenny thanked her and got up to leave.

"I don't know if it will do any good," she said. "But there's old copies of the whole newspaper over at the library. I know we digitized everything back to 1990, but sometimes it helps to see it in full."

"Thanks," Raisa said, mostly dismissing the idea. Kilkenny had already gotten the samples—those were enough to create her idiolectic profile.

"What now?" she asked when they were back on the street.

Kilkenny started to say something, but then was cut off by his phone. The conversation was short and terse.

When he hung up, she almost asked who'd died, but there was a very real possibility that he would give her a name as an answer, so she just waited.

"That was my guy I have posted at the cabins," Kilkenny said. "Delaney's gone."

CHAPTER TWENTY-NINE

DELANEY

In what was becoming a nervous habit, Delaney tapped her phone screen to wake it up. Kylie had never responded after Delaney had shared her "secret."

At first, Delaney hadn't noticed anything wrong. She'd just kept sending Kylie funny memes and article links and thoughts about her day, assuming Kylie had gotten busy at work. But one day's worth of silence had turned into two, and that had turned into three. Delaney had started asking what was wrong, and then if Kylie was all right. She'd even gone as far as to skim Florida newspapers, looking for a mention of any accident or disaster.

After a week of hearing nothing, Delaney had to admit Kylie was ghosting her. If she wasn't dead.

She got a pang in her chest whenever she thought of it. Two years. Her first real friend. Gone.

On week two, the paranoia started to creep in. What if Kylie hadn't just ghosted her? What if she'd catfished her, too? What if Delaney had let her guard down because she'd wanted it to be true?

But she hadn't told Kylie anything important about herself. Out of all the hundreds of millions of people who used the internet every day, Delaney was on the high end of the spectrum in keeping her digital footprint neat and clean.

There was a whisper of doubt, though.

Had she been careful enough? Two years was a long time to talk to someone. Just as she'd realized things about Kylie without her explicitly saying them—like being able to tell when the salon was busy—Kylie must have been able to suss out some personal information about Delaney.

The maddening thing about that was it would never be obvious what Delaney had let slip because you could never see your own blind spots.

Delaney skimmed back through their messages.

Tell me a secret.

She shook her head, kept scrolling.

By the time she got to the beginning, the knot in between her shoulder blades had loosened.

Nothing. There was nothing there. Certainly nothing that would point to where Delaney lived, which was the crucial secret she had been guarding.

Delaney had saved the chats from when they'd first started talking on the message board because she was neurotic like that. She read through all those as well, and still there was nothing.

She slumped back into her seat, her mind darting off in too many directions.

Her phone dinged, but it wasn't with a message. It was an alarm she'd set weeks ago to remind her to tune in to the seminar she'd found out about through her Google Alerts.

Everything had a virtual component these days, so from the safety of her small apartment in Seattle, Delaney logged in to the Stanford portal that allowed nonstudents to watch events.

The university's logo took up the whole screen as the counter ticked down toward zero. Delaney let her eyes unfocus as she stared at the numbers, unable to hold on to a single coherent thought. She was the one who usually took careless people out at the knees. This wasn't supposed to happen to her.

She was the one who was always in control.

She had to be.

The screen flickered, and a video feed of the stage replaced the static image. A petite woman with dark, curly hair walked out to robust applause. Even though she was small, she commanded the audience's attention with her confident stride. When she spoke, it was with a calm, clear voice, not nervous or timid at all.

"Hello," she said. "I'm FBI forensic linguist Raisa Susanto. Let's talk words."

It took Raisa Susanto twenty minutes to get to the Parker case. She gave a quick introduction of the facts and then delved into Alex's infamous short story and last letter.

Delaney had read the research papers on the comparisons between the two, of course, but it was different hearing someone talk about the murders out loud.

At the end of the section, Raisa Susanto mentioned that the anniversary of the deaths was coming up in a few weeks.

And then she moved on. The case just one of many she used in this presentation.

It must be nice, that. To be able to move on.

Delaney swiveled in her chair to stare at her wall. There was a reason she never let anyone into her apartment anymore. On it hung the crime scene pictures of Tim and Becks Parker, as well as the shot of Alex in the bathtub. She had been looking at them for so many years that she'd grown numb to the brutality the film had captured.

Some distant part of her worried this was becoming a dangerous obsession, that she'd passed the point of no return.

She quieted that worry as she logged in to the "Alex is Innocent" message board.

CHAPTER THIRTY

RAISA

"Is there any chance Delaney left because she thought the case was solved?" Raisa asked, though going by that classic Kilkenny grim-neutral expression, she likely already had her answer.

"I don't know," Kilkenny said, his gaze on Marigold's apartment window, though she knew he wasn't really looking at it. He was caught somewhere else. When his shoulders straightened and he met her eyes, she figured he'd decided on finally telling her what she needed to know.

"It's dangerous now, isn't it?" Raisa murmured, not wanting to rub his face in it but needing to know he realized his error in judgment.

He tipped his head toward the SUV and didn't speak until they were both safely ensconced in its privacy.

"Delaney Moore has been a source of mine for years."

Whatever she'd been braced for, she wouldn't have come up with that. "What?"

"I didn't know it was her," Kilkenny said. "She was anonymous until this case."

Anger flashed through Raisa, a lightning strike in the midst of confusion. "You vouched for her."

"And I still do. She's saved a lot of lives," Kilkenny said.

"This is truly unbelievable." Raisa struggled to wrap her mind around the implications, but of course Kilkenny could guess where her thoughts had gone.

"She's not the killer."

Raisa didn't have anything to say to that. Actually, she did. Something about how he had a weakness, that he'd been played by a puppet-master personality before, and how had that worked out? But she managed to hold it back. It would have severed any relationship they'd been building beyond repair, and even in her annoyance, she could acknowledge she didn't want to torch this bridge.

"Delaney finds predators online and sends me leads on how to hunt them down," Kilkenny continued when she didn't say anything. "Usually I do a preliminary check on the information and then forward it along to the appropriate person."

"How did she first contact you?" That was good—that was an actual question instead of an accusation.

"I have a secure tip number on my bureau profile."

They had the option to add that, Raisa vaguely remembered. It was like journalists who promised a secure place for whistleblowers to dump their damning secrets. Essentially ultra-secure drop boxes that couldn't be traced back to the person.

"You never asked why she picked you?" It was an odd choice, given that Kilkenny was a forensic psychologist who wouldn't have much sway in any one division.

"I work with a lot of different people at different levels in the bureau," Kilkenny said, his fingers flexing on the steering wheel. "It was a smart move. Breadth not depth of relationships." He glanced her way. "Don't get me wrong, I didn't trust her for a long time. But she's never steered us wrong."

"So . . . what? It's just a coincidence that you happen to be working on the case with someone who has been your anonymous source for several years?"

When he didn't say anything, something obvious clicked into place.

"Oh, it's not a coincidence," Raisa said and felt stupid for taking so long to get there.

"She flagged the FBI when the video came in," Kilkenny said, a muscle in his jaw ticking. "I just happen to be the agent she flagged."

Raisa stared at him, able to come up with only, "Does Sand know?"

"Of course."

"There's no 'of course,'" Raisa snapped.

"She contacted me as soon as she pulled the video," Kilkenny said. "She revealed who she was because she couldn't waste the time to hide her identity and how she came to see the video. I was able to bring her in through Sand, who wanted me on the case as her unofficial liaison."

"You're not even here as a forensic psychologist?" Raisa asked.

"I obviously am," he said. "Would I have been brought on to the task force without Delaney? Probably not."

Raisa just stared at him.

"This isn't even unusual, you know that. How many times have you been called into an investigation because you worked with someone before and they trusted you?" Kilkenny continued, and Raisa had to admit he was right. There were plenty of cases out there that she could have helped on but the people either didn't know about or didn't trust forensic linguists. The times she'd been brought in were often because she'd helped the agent in charge in the past.

"And she just happened to have a program that would be invaluable to the case," Raisa said. "That she wouldn't just turn over."

"What tech bro do you know who would just hand over something like that?" Kilkenny asked.

"Wait. Did you just say 'tech bro'?" Raisa asked, laughing. Some of the tension between them broke when Kilkenny rolled his eyes.

"It's a very specific type of person."

"That it is, my friend," Raisa said, and then sighed. "Okay, but how are you not worried right now? She has all the makings of our puppeteer."

"She has all the makings of an informant who has never been wrong about a bad guy," Kilkenny said. "Does that sound like our serial killer to you?"

"She's never been wrong that you know of," Raisa said. "She could be only feeding you certain 'bad guys' so that you trust her. You could be one out of a hundred agents she's been toying with. She could be cultivating a stable. And you're just blithely going along with it. You could get someone—"

Raisa managed to grab hold of the word a millisecond before it could wreck its damage. But it was too late; her meaning wasn't exactly hard to guess.

"I could get someone killed," Kilkenny finished the thought for her, his voice hollow in a way she'd never heard it before. In that moment, Raisa hated herself. All her panicked anger seeped out, and she slumped into the vee created by the seat and the door.

"I'm sorry," she said, unable to offer anything else. Neither of them had to acknowledge the way that she'd dug the knife into scar tissue.

"My trust in Delaney feels dangerously irresponsible to you," Kilkenny said, ever understanding. Just like how he hadn't even flinched when Jenna Shaw had been deliberately careless in that Denny's. Raisa was now no better than that desperate, hungry vulture who'd just wanted a reaction and had been shameless in her attempts to get one. "I haven't been reckless, though. I would never put my colleagues in a position like that. We know she doesn't have a record, and we're doing a more thorough background check now."

"And"—he held up his phone—"I had a junior agent tailing her whenever I couldn't be there to keep watch. She only ever left the cabins on official business, and spent the rest of the time on the grounds of the hotel."

Along with telling the agent in charge, Kilkenny had covered all his bases and brought Delaney in on the investigation in the safest way possible.

"I'm sorry," Raisa said again, a bit helplessly. Her gaze drifted to the window, to the woods in the distance that led to the cabins. "It's not just you who has mistakes in their past."

A beat of silence, and then: "Scottsdale."

She could leave it at that. "No."

When she didn't say anything else, he glanced over.

"I was ten when my parents died in a car crash," Raisa said. "A decent amount of people know that. What they don't know was that my parents were driving to the police station to pick me up. Another car ran a red light three blocks away from them getting to me."

"Damnit." It was only the second time she'd heard him curse—if that could be called one.

Raisa pursed her lips to keep her jaw from wobbling before she continued. "We were at a fair. It was really crowded, and I was in a mood that day. I wanted to play one of the games, and they kept pulling me away from the area to go do boring things. They got distracted for a minute, and I just thought . . . you know, why not?"

"You were ten," Kilkenny said gently. "You didn't have higher reasoning skills."

"I played the game," Raisa said, ignoring him. "I won this stupid stuffed frog. I was so pleased with myself. I went back to find them."

"They weren't there."

"No, of course not," Raisa said. "But I'd been taught well, you know? I went to find police officers. It was so crowded, though, and it took a while. Some girl tried to help me, but we ended up even more lost. It took us hours to find the cops."

"Your parents had left?" Kilkenny asked.

"Well, if they hadn't, they didn't come to the security tent when the cops announced over the loudspeakers where I was," Raisa said. "My parents might not have heard, we'll never know. I went to the station with the police we'd found, and a nice officer there was able to get a hold of my parents at home. They jumped in a car to come get me."

"Oh, Raisa," Kilkenny murmured. "But you know it's not your fault, right?"

Raisa stared out the window and swiped the heel of her palm against her cheekbone. "I was reckless and selfish."

She said it because she was hurting and she wanted this conversation to have a purpose. You didn't have to be completely to blame for bad things to happen because of your decisions. From his silence, she could tell it had resonated.

"It wasn't your fault," he said again. "You were a kid. And even if you weren't, the fault lies with the driver who ran the red light."

Raisa forced a stilted laugh. "You don't have to put me on the couch, Doc."

His gentle almost-smile made an appearance at that, and then he grimaced.

"What?" she asked.

"There's something else you need to know."

At that, Raisa's guilt, the echo that had lasted longer than her grief, got shoved aside once more.

"What?" This time it came out sharp and jagged.

He didn't want to tell her. That much was obvious. But her sob story had cracked his walls.

"It wasn't just me who Delaney brought into this case," Kilkenny said, watching closely to see if she understood.

And of course it didn't make sense at first.

Then, an image of Kilkenny leaning in the doorway.

Do you have any assignments next?

Kilkenny confirmed it. "She's the one who wanted you here, Raisa."

EXCERPT FROM ALEX PARKER'S CONFESSION LETTER

I wanted to watch the life snuff out from one moment to the next, that is the moment that transforms you from a man to a God. But I am not strong enough. Tim would have fought me, Becks might have, too, they would have screamed at the very least and the neighbors would have run, run to see there favorite king and queen beheaded. So they went to sleep instead and the razor blade caught the light from Becks's favorite lamp the one with jewled colors, red to match the blood. The edge of the blade sunk in just as I knew it would, a soft resistince and then a give, a pop almost, an exhalation of relief. And then darkness.

CHAPTER THIRTY-ONE

Raisa

Kilkenny drove Raisa straight to the cabin Delaney Moore had been renting and found it empty, just as the junior agent had reported.

Raisa stared at the bed, which had clearly been made up by house-keeping and then not touched since.

"You still trust her now?" Raisa muttered as she shoved past him back outside.

The junior agent who had been in charge of watching Delaney stood there, all but shuffling his feet like a second grader in the princi-pal's office. "She went in, never came back out. I just assumed she was working on the porch like she did yesterday. When housekeeping came, they said the place was empty."

Raisa whirled on him. "Do you know she was working on the porch yesterday or did you assume?"

He just blinked at her, and she cursed.

"See those woods?" she said. "They're not protected by barbed wire."

"But there's no path," he said.

Raisa walked away from him so that she didn't lose it. She had been riding this knife's edge of her temper all afternoon, and this young agent didn't deserve to take the brunt of it.

"I'll address the mistake," Kilkenny said, from behind her. "With his supervisor."

"That will help us find Delaney."

He studied her. "So you think she's our killer?"

Raisa waved to the empty cabin. "Doesn't look great, my friend."

"Why would she . . . ?" he asked, though it seemed more a rhetorical question to himself rather than directed at her.

Still, it had Raisa digging out her phone.

Topher answered sounding mostly distracted. "I'm not done yet. I'm good, but I'm not that good, honey."

"Do you have anything?"

"Hmm, the most notable find so far is that she was adopted," he said. "Delaney Moore came into existence in 1998. But you know how adoption paperwork is. It's hard to go back from there to find her birth name or parents, and it seems like they did an extra good job at sealing her records up tight."

Raisa closed her eyes, overcome by that feeling of a piece of the puzzle clicking into place. "Anything after that?"

"So that's where it starts to get nebulous but also . . . interesting," Topher said. "Nothing linked to her, mind you. But she attended a community college and then a four-year university, and there were deaths at each of them while she was there."

Put together with their facts, that certainly seemed damning. But Raisa didn't want her own confirmation bias to get in the way when coincidence might suffice. "How unusual would that be, statistically speaking?"

"She was only at the community college for one semester, so that's a fairly narrow window," he said. "And it wasn't a big school. It's the only thing that has me eyeing the university death, otherwise. Because that one was just a girl who drank too much."

"Who was the first?"

"A professor, a suicide overdose," he said. "Apparently he'd been pressuring coeds to have sex with him for better grades."

"Tale as old as time," Raisa murmured. "The girl, was there anything notable about her?"

"Nope," Topher said, popping the word. "Popular sorority girl, alcohol poisoning mixed with prescription pills."

The drugging.

If Alex was a—how did Amanda phrase it?—*psycho-killer stabby man*, why had he bothered drugging his parents? That didn't look like a kid with a conduct disorder snapping and turning a straight razor on his closest targets. It looked like cold, calculated premeditation.

Just like their current killer.

"Are you talking to an FBI researcher?" Kilkenny asked from over her shoulder. Raisa thought about ignoring him but then gave a quick nod. "Ask him to look up Benton Davenport the Third."

"I heard that," Topher said. "Whoever you're with sounds hot, is he hot?"

Raisa rolled her eyes. "No."

"Pity," Topher sighed. "Hmm. Car crash."

"What?"

"Benton Davenport—who does *not* sound hot by the way," Topher clarified. "He sounds very sexual assault–y. Anyway, he died in a car crash about eight months ago. If you need more than that, then I need more time."

"You're going to feel bad if he was a good guy," Raisa said, and raised her brows at Kilkenny, wondering if that was what he'd expected. She couldn't tell if he was surprised, but from the tic in his jaw, she'd say he was displeased.

"High-class pimp and rapist," Kilkenny said, clearly having heard the conversation. He was standing near enough that she might as well have the phone on speaker. "Alleged."

"I can always tell," Topher said, sounding smug. "Okay, I have a meeting, gotta run."

The line went dead before she could say anything else.

"Who is Benton Davenport?" Raisa asked, re-stowing her cell.

"Someone Delaney flagged for me about a year back," Kilkenny said. "Jeffrey Epstein–type character. There wasn't enough to move on him, though. I think she checked in a couple months after sending him my way."

"About three to four months after originally flagging him, would you say?" Raisa asked, crossing her arms. "And you didn't think it was suspicious he died in a car crash soon after?"

"I didn't follow up on it," Kilkenny admitted. "I was shipped off to somewhere else, and Delaney—or the anonymous tipster—never asked again."

"Because she killed him."

"We don't know that," Kilkenny cautioned, and Raisa let out a disbelieving laugh.

"Three deaths, Kilkenny," she said. "That we know about. Most people don't encounter even one suspicious death in their lifetime."

"They might not have been her," Kilkenny argued.

"But it probably was," Raisa said. "Everything fits. You said these kills weren't a newbie serial killer. That they had experience." She waved toward where she'd stowed her phone. "Experience."

"Circumstantial."

Raisa made a frustrated sound. "You *know* it looks bad. Why are you defending her?"

He shifted so that he could look at the now-empty cabin. "She doesn't fit the profile."

"And your profiles are always accurate?" Raisa couldn't help the sharpness in her voice.

Kilkenny turned back to her. The detachment on his face had her stepping away. She hadn't realized how much he'd warmed in her presence over the past two days until she was faced with concrete walls once again. No matter how mad she was, she still mourned the loss.

"When you spoke of atonement, you didn't talk about Scottsdale," he said. "Do you know why?"

"It was a blow to my reputation," she tried, her skin too tight around her bones all of a sudden. Why was he throwing this in her face? "Of course I feel bad about it."

He shook his head. "You feel bad that it was a blow to your reputation. You don't feel bad about the work you did."

Raisa just stared at him, hating that he was so damn good at his job. When he wasn't being hoodwinked by women who used him as their own personal FBI agent, that was.

"You don't feel like you have anything to atone for," Kilkenny said. "You blame yourself as a child for a car crash that was in no way your fault. But two months ago, a little girl died because you identified the wrong suspect and wasted valuable time. And no guilt. That doesn't fit with what I know of you."

"The work was sound," Raisa gritted out. "I don't know what happened. But the work was sound."

"So you think you were right about the note and the daycare teacher?" Kilkenny pushed. "Even with how the case ended?"

Raisa curled her fingers into fists, and the confirmation felt like it was dragged out of her. "Yes."

He breathed in deeply, as if he'd just won a boxing match. "My work is sound," he said quietly, which made it land all the more. "Delaney doesn't match the profile."

It wasn't said with arrogance or ego, but with the quiet confidence that she had come to think of as a foundational stone to Kilkenny's personality. She also realized that not once during his questioning about Scottsdale had he judged her. So she let go of the anger, let go of the hurt, and really let herself consider what he was saying.

What had he actually done to warrant her anger? Raisa was most upset about the fact that he hadn't been honest with her. But that was a personal grievance. He'd informed Sand about the true nature of Delaney's connection to the bureau, and both of them had made the decision not to let the task force in on the secret.

Still, there was something else stopping her from just giving in to Kilkenny's arguments.

"Why did Delaney say I should join the task force?" Raisa asked. Before relenting, she needed this answered.

"She said she'd caught a seminar that you'd given recently," Kilkenny said. "She suggested a forensic linguist and then suggested you as an afterthought. Or so I believed."

A bit of tension loosened in her neck, and she realized that had been her main sticking point. At her core, she was still that kid on the streets who had to watch her back, constantly aware of any threats. But Raisa remembered that lecture. It had been open to the public, and the marketing materials had mentioned the Parker case. It was feasible that someone who was interested in language and patterns like Delaney was would keep an eye out for things like that.

"Okay," she said, with a nod.

"Okay?" he asked.

"Okay, I believe you." It was difficult, and she wasn't sure she truly felt confident in his assessment. But she did trust him. "For now."

"You believe me that Delaney doesn't fit the profile?" Kilkenny clarified.

"Yes."

Pleased surprise flashed in and out of his expression so fast she might not have caught it had she not been watching him closely. Hell, a few days ago, she might not have even been able to identify it.

"We still have to find her, though," Raisa said.

"I know," Kilkenny said, nodding to the pocket where she'd stuffed her phone. "Adopted in 1998."

"Records sealed tight," Raisa said, and she met his eyes and said what they both knew to be true. "Delaney Moore is one of the Parker sisters."

CHAPTER THIRTY-TWO

DELANEY

The twenty-fifth anniversary of Tim and Becks Parker's deaths was fast approaching.

Delaney had long stopped thinking of them as her parents. That title belonged to the elderly couple who had taken her in and shielded her from any talk surrounding the murder-suicide. She hadn't loved them, but she hadn't loved her biological parents, either, so she wasn't using that as a barometer for loyalty. Despite her adoptive parents' push for her to fulfill her potential, she'd ultimately learned to appreciate the Moores for what they'd given her.

A safe haven.

She knew she could have had it much worse in the country's broken foster system.

The Moores had died five years back, four days apart, of some combination of old age and heartbreak. Then Delaney had been alone in the world.

Once upon a time, she'd had a big family. By nineties standards, four kids was a lot. People had cut down to two more often than not in those days.

Baby Larissa had likely been a surprise, but even growing up with two siblings had been chaotic.

She wouldn't have called them a happy family, even before Alex started terrorizing them, but at least there had been other people to help share her burden.

Delaney had thought maybe Kylie could fill that role. But now there was no one.

Although . . . that wasn't exactly true.

The FBI man had been in her life for a while now.

He'd proved mostly useful and seemed to trust her.

She had been worried she'd have to cut off contact with the man after that last predator she'd sent him had died in a car crash. The agents who'd been assigned to "watch and wait" had probably celebrated the accident that had serendipitously saved them quite a bit of work.

But months had passed and her FBI man hadn't even asked her about the accident to test the waters. He wasn't suspicious at all. The years of work she'd put in to get him to trust her had paid off.

Delaney stood up from her chair and crossed to the wall of photos. It wasn't just Tim and Becks and Alex on it. There was the man in the car crash, and the others she'd collected along the way. She had done her best to record as much information about their deaths as possible, as if that would atone for her sins.

If the FBI man ever tracked her location—which she was sure he couldn't do—he'd have quite the bounty on his hands.

She moved back to her desk, clicked over to one of her open internet tabs. The "Alex is Innocent" thread stared back at her. The user AlexFan was busy defending himself against some troll, and she had the halfhearted notion to tell him not to bother. Trolls were trolls for a reason. On psychological tests, they routinely scored high for narcissism and sadistic tendencies—they weren't there in good faith; they were there to feed the darkness in their own souls.

She wanted to tell AlexFan that he just had to wait a little bit longer.

Soon, so soon, he would be able to say he was right all along.

———

Delaney had created a calendar counting down the days until the twenty-fifth anniversary.

She'd lost her appetite two weeks out. Logically, she knew she needed her strength, and so she'd forced down bland chicken and rice at least once a day, but she found no pleasure in eating. She stopped sleeping except for stretches of one or two hours at a time. She took a shower only because she knew she would have to look presentable to the FBI man when she finally made contact.

That wouldn't be the hard part, but it still made her a little nervous to think about. Taking off the mask she'd worn for the past few years would be jarring. When was the last time she'd revealed anything personal about herself to someone voluntarily?

Was this voluntary?

Delaney crossed to her wall and wondered once more what the FBI man would think when he saw it.

Callum Kilkenny. He seemed like a fair, intelligent man, well respected. Would he be distraught that she'd fooled him all these years? Would it affect him? He'd managed to work through a serial killer targeting and murdering his wife. An anonymous source who had been less than truthful would hardly make a ripple, surely.

Hopefully.

She had no interest in ruining his life beyond the empty husk it already was.

Her phone dinged, another alarm she'd set. Jenna Shaw's podcast would be posted now.

Delaney had eagerly followed the conversation about the show on the "Alex is Innocent" thread. The posters seemed split on whether it would be a good thing for their cause.

But if anyone was doing a show on the Parker murder-suicides, Delaney was glad it was Jenna Shaw. She had gone back to listen to the first season once Jenna had announced what the second would be on. She'd been braced to be horrified, but had found that if you stripped away the obnoxious dog-whistling to conspiracy theorists, Jenna actually had some insightful things to say.

Would Jenna travel to Everly once the first homicides were reported? Would she interrupt her posting schedule?

How would she cover a copycat killer if she was trying to convince people Alex really was guilty?

"Hello, tin-hatters, skeptics, and everyone just here for a distraction while you do your dishes," Jenna's cheery voice blared through the tinny iPhone speakers.

Delaney smiled as she uncapped her whiteboard marker.

Then she started writing out her list.

Bob Balducci

Gina Balducci

Terri Harden

Stewart Young

She swallowed hard when the tip of the marker touched the board, her hands trembling. She didn't want to write the last name; she hated that she had to.

But there were things that had to be done, whether you wanted to do them or not.

Delaney forced her hand to move.

Lana Parker

CHAPTER THIRTY-THREE

RAISA

"Is she Lana or Isabel?" Raisa asked, knowing that Kilkenny wouldn't have an answer. Then she realized he might without knowing it.

She held out her hand for his phone. "Let me see your message thread with her."

But he, of course, shot that down. "I delete all of my sources' tips from my phone. It's a good security practice."

"No backups?" Raisa knew what the answer would be but had to ask anyway.

"Attached to the individual cases, I'm sure," Kilkenny said. "But that would require me remembering all of the ones she sent. And, to be honest, more often than not it was just bullet points of the facts. There was no style that you could break down into an idiolect."

"I need a sample of her writing," Raisa said, stubborn. She had plenty to go on from both Isabel and Lana; she just needed something from Delaney to compare them to. "She never happened to tell you her age, did she?"

"No. We can have someone check her apartment for a journal or notes," Kilkenny offered.

"You think we have enough evidence for a judge to go along with that?" Raisa asked.

"As you pointed out, she looks suspicious enough on paper," Kilkenny said. "I think we could build an effective argument. I'll call Sand now."

He paced away from her, not far, but enough that she wouldn't be able to overhear the conversation. Raisa wondered how much he'd divulge to their supervising agent, wondered which way he'd spin things.

Raisa headed in the direction of her cabin, trusting that Kilkenny would come find her when he was done.

She didn't want to tell him what she was thinking.

Delaney had said it herself—the victimology had been rooted in neglect. The people targeted were ones who needed to be punished for their roles in the Parkers' murder-suicide. They had learned about this mindset in training. Kilkenny would of course know more about it, but Raisa knew the basics. These types of serial killers were called mission oriented. They viewed themselves as an agent to rid the world of a certain group of people they viewed as degenerate.

At least two of the victims in Delaney's past were sexual predators.

Raisa touched the pocket of her blazer where she'd tucked the letter from Talia. She couldn't see Delaney writing the Everly Ears column, but they'd never connected the author of that to the messages posted by their killer, either. Maybe someone in town really had just had it out for the Parkers and they, like Talia, had been rewarded by a twist of fate.

It did make Raisa remember what Talia had said right before they'd left the cabin.

I'm not sure if it means anything, but I saw a kid sneaking into one of the upper windows maybe three nights in a row.

Greg Balducci had said he'd been close friends with Isabel Parker, but why would he have needed to go through a window? The two weren't even dating, and Tim and Becks didn't come across as the shot-gun type, anyway.

The Balduccis were so tied into all this—their deaths, their party, their drugs.

Raisa glanced over her shoulder. Kilkenny was still on the phone.

She sent him a text that he would be able to read once he hung up: Town. Be right back.

Then she took off running, through the woods, along the stream that led her like a path onto Main Street.

It was dinnertime, and there was only one restaurant—the one that became a bar later in the night. The one where she'd found Shawn Dallinger the day before.

This time, she had a different target in mind.

The evening hadn't cooled at all, so Raisa was sweating and panting when she pushed through the swinging doors. This errand could be a waste of time. She had plenty to do back at the cabins. But she had a hunch and she couldn't ignore it.

Greg Balducci's muscles were easy to spot, and Raisa thanked God for egos and gym equipment. He had taken a stool at the bar and was picking at a basket of fries, dragging one through his massive pile of ketchup while scrolling on his phone.

Raisa climbed up onto the seat next to him. He spared her only a glance at first but then did a double take when he realized who was joining him.

"I can't give you any more information, Agent Susanto," he said, wiping grease and salt-slicked fingers on his denim jeans, his gaze now determinedly locked on the sports game playing on the old TV hanging above them.

Raisa didn't need to be a linguist to hear the distinction there. "Can't or won't?"

He shook his head. "Can't."

"Why?"

"I don't know what you need to know; I don't even know what I know," he said, a riddle almost. But she parsed through it easily.

"What if someone asks you the right question?"

"Well, someone could try."

And just like that, she was done talking in circles. "Are you the one who took the sleeping pills out of your father's medicine cabinet?"

Greg froze. He wasn't even blinking—she could see the TV's reflection in his eyes.

Finally, he seemed to come back to himself, and he glanced around. The bar wasn't as packed as it had been the other night, but it wasn't empty, either. Sliding off his stool, he pulled out his wallet and dropped a fifty on the bar. Then he walked out, the slight tip of his head the only indication that he wasn't running away from the conversation completely.

When they made it onto the street, he headed toward a Harley-Davidson parked at the end of the row of slots in front of the restaurant.

He straddled the hog but didn't make any move to start it. Finally, he looked at her. "I did my friend a favor."

The answer, though expected, still came like a punch.

Raisa took a few stumbling steps back, until she came up against a wooden beam supporting an overhanging porch. She let it take some of her weight, as her view of the case rearranged itself. "Alex wasn't the one who stole the pills."

"No, he wasn't." His chin lifted into a stubborn line. "Are you arresting me?"

"If I did, you'd throw money at a lawyer to get you off," Raisa said. "Let's save us both the paperwork."

Surprised amusement slipped in and out of his expression before he sobered. "I assume this has something to do with whoever killed my parents."

"Is that why you're finally admitting it?" That reasoning made sense. After twenty-five years of keeping the secret, why not just lie when asked?

"Yes," Greg said. "As much as we might not have always gotten along, my parents didn't deserve to die for something I did when I was a dumbass kid."

Raisa could feel her pulse in her head, in her throat, in the soles of her feet. There were moments in life that a golden string of connection snapped tight into place between you and a stranger. She would never have guessed she'd find that with Greg Balducci, with his motorcycle and his muscles and his depressingly clinical apartment and his slightly misogynistic view on life. But here it was.

"But Alex did go over to your house that day of the murders," Raisa prompted.

His fingers curled around the handlebars. "Because I asked him to."

At that, Raisa's legs gave out. She could have stopped the slow slide to the ground, but after the past few hours, she didn't want to.

She just wanted to sit for a second.

"She covered all her bases," Raisa murmured to herself.

"Isabel?" Greg asked, his mouth set into a grim line.

Delaney, Raisa wanted to say and didn't.

"She's the one who asked you, right?" Raisa confirmed. "To do all that? To get your mother's sleeping pills and then make sure it looked like Alex went to your parents' place before going home to kill Tim and Becks?"

He didn't say anything, just nodded once.

"Why didn't you tell someone?" Raisa asked, knowing exactly what he was going to say. It would be the same reason he hadn't said anything about Alex and the fake alibi.

"I was a kid."

That's what all teenage boys used as their excuse. *I was too young to know better.*

What would it be like to live in a world where teenage boys actually had to take responsibility for their actions, underdeveloped frontal cortex or not? If that had happened just one time in this case, Becks and Tim would still be alive, and they might not have spawned one of the most skilled serial killers Raisa had ever dealt with.

"And then Isabel was gone," Greg continued, unaware of the path her thoughts had taken. "And the whole thing seemed kind of surreal, like I'd imagined it had happened or something. The sheriff was out there telling everyone that it was Alex who killed the Parkers—who was I to question the official report?"

"You think Isabel was the one who killed Becks and Tim?" Raisa asked. "You don't think she got the drugs *for* Alex?"

"She hated Alex," Greg said, shadows sliding across his face as the sun sank lower behind the mountains. "She wanted to kill him."

Isabel's diary had suggested as much. Alex had been assaulting her in more ways than one, and Tim and Becks had done nothing to stop it.

She'd become her own white knight.

Raisa tried to parse through the timeline. Christine Keller had said that the girls had left her house around seven. The phone call to the sheriff went out at 7:13 p.m., and the two houses were about three blocks apart. If you assumed Christine had only a vague sense of the time, the girls might have left as early as 6:45 p.m. If they'd run home, that would have given Isabel about twenty minutes to kill Tim, Becks, and Alex. Plenty of time, especially if the sleeping pills had kicked in on all three of her victims.

"If she killed Tim and Becks, then they deserved it," Greg said, his eyes dark pools of anger in the fading light. "Alex was abusing those girls, and the parents did jack shit about it."

"Doesn't mean they deserved to die," Raisa said, though she wasn't sure why she was arguing with Greg Balducci. "Doesn't mean your parents deserved to die."

He looked away. "If Isabel is the one doing all this now, well, then she's changed since I knew her."

"Murdering your family will do that to you," Raisa murmured. She believed in Kilkenny's confidence—she hadn't been lying. He said Delaney wasn't their guy. But a niggling doubt crept in, one she'd viciously silenced while staring into his eyes. It was harder to ignore when she was here, in the dark, and all the arrows were pointing in one very distinct direction.

She could be wrong.

But what she couldn't ignore was that . . . so could Kilkenny.

He'd been wrong before.

Raisa hated that thought, and hated that it was a good point.

If only she had a picture of Delaney to show Greg. But something told her there wouldn't be a single photo to be found on the internet.

And if whoever had protected them twenty-five years ago had done their job right, there wouldn't be a single picture publicly available of any of the girls.

Raisa's eyes snapped open, and only then did she realize she'd let them close; only then did she realize she'd let herself be vulnerable in front of a stranger, one who could be working with Isabel even now.

She scrambled to her feet, and Greg held his hands up, palms out.

"I'm not an accomplice," Greg said, seeming to read her new alertness for what it was. "Just a guy with a lot of regrets."

"Regrets," she repeated, picturing him throwing her business card in the trash. "But you wouldn't have told me all this had I not come and found you a second time."

"I was sitting in there debating going to the sheriff," Greg said. "I just needed another whiskey in me to actually do it."

And that brought her back to her previous thought. That photo of Samantha Mason and Tim Parker hanging on the sheriff's wall.

There had been someone cut out of the picture.

The choice had seemed so odd at the time, but maybe it made all the sense in the world.

The call to the sheriff had gone out at 7:13 p.m. and the first deputy hadn't reported to the Parkers' house until 7:42 p.m. The sheriff had been at the scene of the crime for more than twenty minutes with just the girls.

They called me Aunt Sammy.

The sheriff hadn't cut Becks Parker out of the picture.

She'd cut Isabel out.

Because otherwise someone might have recognized her as Delaney Moore.

EXCERPT FROM EVERLY EARS GOSSIP COLUMN

August 25, 1998

Trouble in paradise? Word on Main Street is that Tim and Becks Parker are fighting. Tim had to sleep on Bob Balducci's couch three nights in a row and Becks was seen drinking mimosas with the sheriff just yesterday. Were those celebratory beverages? Are there divorce papers waiting to be served? Inquiring minds would love to know. But, never fear, if Professor Parker's new address is the Doghouse, your Everly Ears correspondent will be here with all the details.

Speaking of both the Parkers and the sheriff, they all performed their parts as a big happy family for the 5K family fun run this past Sunday, benefiting the Everly Sheriff Department. (See pictures of the event on page 3.) Maybe they'll actually invest in some new uniforms that don't create an eyesore for the tourists.

CHAPTER THIRTY-FOUR

RAISA

Headlights blinded Raisa. The sun hadn't set yet, but she'd been standing in the shadows, her eyes still adjusted to the darkness of the restaurant.

She blinked the world back into focus and saw Kilkenny parked in front of her, his SUV's window rolled down. "That was smart of you, taking off like that with a killer on the loose."

"I have my pepper spray," Raisa said flippantly, before turning back to Greg, only to find herself staring at his motorcycle's tailpipe. "Shit."

She ran around the back of Kilkenny's vehicle and threw herself into the passenger seat. "Sheriff's department."

"What's going on?" he asked, but he was already heading in the right direction. Trusting her.

"Please believe me that I hate what I'm about to say," Raisa said. "But I think Alex Parker was innocent."

He glanced at her. "But that last letter . . ."

"Yeah, I know," Raisa said, with a grimace. Linguistics was not an infallible science, nor was she an infallible scientist. Alex's letter *had* matched the short story, but there could be another explanation as to why. "I mean, I don't know. But Greg Balducci just admitted he was the one who supplied the sleeping pills from his parents' medicine cabinet. And he gave them to Isabel Parker. Then he made sure Alex came over on the right day to make it look like he had stolen them just before killing Tim and Becks."

"The drugging never made sense," Kilkenny murmured.

"It doesn't fit with a psychopath snapping," Raisa agreed. "They make sense if the original killer was a fifteen-year-old girl. She would want to be able to easily control her victims."

"Are we headed to tell the sheriff?" he asked, though he sounded like he knew that wasn't the reason they were driving toward the squat building. Protocol dictated that they tell Sand first if they found anything.

"No, I think she knows who Delaney really is and has been covering for her," Raisa said. "We need to confront her before Delaney warns her we're closing in."

"Why would she have covered for Isabel?" Kilkenny asked. They pulled to a stop behind the only other car in the sheriff department's lot.

"What's done was done?" Raisa suggested. "She could either let Isabel get away with it and lose three loved ones or charge her and lose four? Or maybe she felt guilty for not hauling Alex in after the fight on the Fourth."

"A combination, probably. How do you want to play this?" he asked. "With the sheriff."

"By ear?" Raisa asked, already half out of the SUV.

"Works for me."

The office was mostly empty, as it always seemed to be, but Raisa didn't pause, just headed toward Samantha Mason's office.

Amanda called over to them from the receptionist's desk. "Sheriff's out, folks."

Raisa didn't think the woman's laissez-faire attitude toward the archives would transfer over to them snooping through the sheriff's office.

No harm in lying, though. "Mason said she left a writing sample on her desk for me."

"Hmm, didn't tell me about that," Amanda said, pushing out of her chair. "You all just wait here, I'll get it for you."

"Good try," Kilkenny murmured as they both watched Amanda disappear into the office. Now they had to wait and pretend to be surprised there was nothing for them there.

Raisa thought about how Talia had offered up Amanda—who had babysat the Parker girls—as a suspect. But Raisa couldn't see it.

She could see Amanda lying for Mason, though.

"Can't seem to find it," Amanda said as she re-emerged a few minutes later. "You want me to give the sheriff a ring?"

"Please." Even if Raisa was caught out, then at least they'd know where Samantha Mason was right now.

They watched Amanda try a few numbers, all of them going to voice mail. Her brow wrinkled in exaggerated confusion. "Don't know where she could be. Said she was running out for dinner not long ago, but she always makes sure to check her phone."

Raisa closed her eyes. There was one place in town to get dinner, and Raisa had just been there grilling Greg Balducci about the Parker murder-suicide. They had been talking outside. Quietly, but if Samantha had been lurking in the shadows, she might have been able to hear them.

What would the endgame be to disappearing right now, though? The sheriff couldn't just leave town without drawing suspicion. Maybe she was destroying evidence?

Or maybe, she was the killer's finale, and they'd all gotten complacent about the danger she was in.

Delaney was missing. The sheriff seemed to be missing.

It didn't take too many leaps in logic to draw a picture of what might be happening.

"Hey, I've been wondering something," Raisa said as casually as she could. "Do you know that picture of Tim Parker on the sheriff's wall?"

Amanda hummed. "Vaguely."

"Was there anyone else in the picture up until recently?" Raisa asked. "Like two days ago recently."

Amanda's mostly friendly expression went blank.

"There's a lot of photos in there," she said.

"That's certainly true," Raisa said carefully. Was this loyalty to the sheriff? Or something else? Talia had guessed Amanda was the killer back then, but Raisa couldn't see it.

"I can't be expected to memorize all of them," Amanda said.

Kilkenny stepped in, all smooth and suave. "Ma'am, it would be extremely helpful to our investigation if you could answer the question."

The fight went out of Amanda. "I don't remember. Truly. She has so many pictures. I sort of know the one you're talking about. It was from a 5K fun run the weekend before . . . Well. It was the last photo she had of Tim, which is why she put it up."

That rang a bell, but Raisa couldn't remember why she would have heard about the race before. Had Becks mentioned it in her journal?

"Is there anyone who's been in the station who reminds you of Isabel Parker?" Kilkenny asked.

The surprise on Amanda's face seemed genuine. "What on earth?"

So that was a no. Raisa tried to remember if Amanda had been at her desk when Delaney had walked through the station the day before, but couldn't recall either way.

"What about Lana Parker?" Raisa tried.

Amanda shook her head slowly. "I haven't seen those girls since I was babysitting for them."

Raisa wasn't sure Amanda would tell them even if she had, but she seemed to be genuinely baffled by the question. "Can you try the sheriff again?"

Amanda patiently redialed, but it was clear she had been sent to voice mail once more. "Sorry, folks, I'll let her know you stopped by?"

Once Raisa and Kilkenny were outside, Raisa asked, "You have Delaney Moore's number saved somewhere, right? Can you message her and pretend nothing's changed? Ask for an update?"

"Already done," Kilkenny said. "Nothing in response."

"Okay, if she's not our killer"—a big *if*, in Raisa's opinion—"then where is she? What is she doing?"

"I don't know. But I'm . . . willing to concede that I may be wrong about her," Kilkenny said, slowly. "Or that I'm not seeing the full picture."

"Okay." Raisa exhaled. That made this conversation easier. "Okay. So if she is our killer, who is her next target?"

"Any suggestion I have would just be a wild guess," he said, and Raisa made a sound in agreement. There were names she could throw out—even Amanda's or Talia's. But none of them seemed quite right. What she needed to do was return to what she knew.

The answer was always in the writing. "I have to get back to my samples."

"I'll drop you at the cabins," Kilkenny said. "Then I'm going to try to find the sheriff."

"No, it would be a waste of time to drive me to the hotel. You stay in town to try to chase down Samantha," Raisa said, eyeing the woods. It was a ten-minute walk, but she could make it in half that time at a jog. "I'll head back this way."

He grabbed her arm, though, before she could take off. "Be careful."

Raisa bit the inside of her cheek. "You too."

She wasn't particularly worried about Kilkenny. She wasn't even sure she was worried about herself. But it still felt nice—to care and to be cared for.

Once she got to her cabin, Raisa headed directly to her porch, only popping into the main room to grab her laptop, tablet, and the Everly Ears columns Kilkenny had brought her the night before.

She couldn't say that the columnist was their killer. But the person was a thread tangled together with the Parker family and what was starting to look like a triple murder. They'd kept their identity secret and had an obvious grudge against *all* the Parkers.

That was part of the reason Raisa thought they could rule out Cara James as the author—though Raisa would love to get a sample of her writing to be sure. Alex hardly made an appearance in the columns, and it all seemed to be things people could tell just from hanging around him. The more scandalous, reputation-staining rumors were centered around Tim and Becks.

Another reason Raisa ruled out Cara was because the columns spanned back months before Alex had assaulted her. If she'd been friends with Isabel, why hold a grudge against the family prior to the rape?

Raisa couldn't ignore her gut on who she thought the author was, but she wanted to build the actual proof.

This time, she read through the columns slower. It was a truth universally acknowledged in the linguistics field that having a known sample was worlds easier than trying to winnow down the entire population of suspects.

She could see the similarities between the letter to Talia and the columns even more clearly now that she had both in front of her. There was alliteration, a conversational tone, the author breaking the fourth wall between themselves and the audience. A lot of that was just how gossip columns were written, but this author had a particular flair for it, even if the overall style was juvenile and immature.

Confirmation bias was the enemy of a good scientist, though, so Raisa diligently went through the samples she had of all the Parker women. Showing the differences with the other samples would be a good way to highlight how it matched the one that it did.

Becks used alliteration, too. But she bent toward a grandiose style that was the antithesis of the Everly Ears column.

I was working with two hands tied behind my back, while he got to stretch and flex that brilliant brain, unencumbered by the demands of domesticity.

I've long ago made peace with the fact that I love a man that is flawed because of a mind that I had thought was perfection itself.

These were complex sentences written by a woman with a confident voice. She had some notable grammatical mistakes, and relied too much on *that*, but Raisa couldn't imagine the woman who'd written these entries disguising her voice to that of a teenager's.

Raisa moved on to Lana, who was clearly advanced, just as all the Parker kids seemed to be. But her voice was too young. Teens could and did write with idiolects more mature than their age, but Lana's still carried the markers of youth.

Today was an attic day. Isabel woke me up with a hand over my mouth. She pulled me out of bed.

I climbed the stairs first. That was my job.

While there was some complexity to the paragraphs—repeating words or thoughts for emphasis—the sentences themselves were short, simple, and straightforward. Even in her diary, her tone was formal. At her most flowery, she'd described her baby sister's curls as soft. This was not the same person who wrote: *If Professor Parker's new address is the Doghouse, your Everly Ears correspondent will be here with all the details.*

Which left Isabel.

The diaries were a completely different tone from the columns. They were serious, manifesto-like. But what struck Raisa, seeing them side-by-side, was that they were both performative in the exact same way. The diary entries weren't Isabel's interior thoughts, as much as she might make passing mention to them. Her writing read like an explanation instead of an outpouring.

These diary entries weren't for her to process her own world—they were for an audience.

It took me a while to realize that I am the white knight.

That sentence was far more chilling now that Raisa was fairly certain it had been Isabel who'd killed her family and framed Alex.

None of what Raisa had was actual evidence, though. If she mapped this all out for Sand, there was a solid chance he would think she'd been taken in by the online conspiracy theories.

Raisa stretched, cracking out her neck. She flipped to the next Everly Ears, skimming it just to remind herself what was there. It was dated two days before the murders.

Speaking of both the Parkers and the sheriff, they all performed their parts as a big happy family for the 5K family fun run this past Sunday, benefiting the Everly Sheriff Department. (See pictures of the event on page 3.) Maybe they'll actually invest in some new uniforms that don't create an eyesore for the tourists.

See pictures of the event on page 3.

"Oh my god." Raisa groped for her phone. She had Kilkenny's contact on the screen in the next heartbeat. He answered after one ring. "Any luck with the sheriff?"

"No." Frustration laced his voice, and the very fact that he was letting her hear it at all told her he was at the end of his patience with this case.

"That picture in Samantha's office," Raisa said. "Was from a 5K fun run right before—"

"Right, yeah," Kilkenny said, in an obvious bid to get her to move it along.

"There are pictures from the fun run in the old Everly newspapers," Raisa said. "On page three, the same day the last Everly Ears column came out. In small, local newspapers, they do big spreads about community events like that. They probably even had a few full pages' worth of just photos from the race. And the whole thing was to benefit the sheriff's department."

"Which means Samantha will be featured in at least one of the main photos. And the Parkers were Everly royalty," Kilkenny said, following her thought process. "What editor wouldn't use a picture of both Tim and Samantha?"

"It would be perfect."

"I'll go sweet-talk my way into the library," Kilkenny said. "Unless you—"

"No," Raisa cut him off. "I'm still holding out hope something in all this writing will help us figure out what Delaney has planned next."

"What Isabel Parker has planned next," Kilkenny corrected.

Raisa stared into the shadows of the woods and thought about white knights. But all she said was, "Right. Of course."

EXCERPT FROM RAISA SUSANTO'S LINGUISTICS SEMINAR

Just as with forced confessions, falsified suicide notes reveal themselves oftentimes in the word choices made by the author. Researchers have found that simulated suicide notes are more likely to have verbs that are linked to a mental state—*to know* and *to think*, for example. The writers utilize abstract concepts such as life and the universe. So, for example, *I don't know my purpose here, but I think I might find it in the darkness.*

Whereas in genuine notes, you see simple action verbs—*tell, do*, and *get*, along with more concrete concepts. The directives look like, *Tell John my bank account number is on the paper in the top drawer.* Or, *I owe five dollars to the library, have Deb pay that fine for me.*

Real letters also often have a high instance of what we call trivia, not as in extra facts but as in trivial—insignificant and common, stemming from the Latin word for *where three crossroads meet*. Genuine suicide notes tend to be full of what look like petty details. Instructions on how to dust a table or mow the lawn, or, as in the above example, what library fines are due. Psychologists studying the issue say it's because many people who are considering suicide have lost the ability to distinguish trivial matters from important ones. Others say that what may seem trivial to you and me, might not be to the author. At the end of the day, paying a library fine is about integrity, after all.

But that's not our lane, is it? What we do is analyze, and this is just one more tool in our kit. Whatever the deeper reasons behind it are, the fact remains that genuine suicide notes contain these types of things with a much higher frequency than simulated ones. You should never decide authenticity on the grounds of one factor, but it will inform your decision down the line.

All this is to say that there are ways to tell if a suicide note has been forged or coerced. There are some people out there who think that's what happened with Alex Parker's suicide letter. But if you refer to my next slide, you'll see examples of all the points I just gave out. Alex Parker's suicide letter was genuine.

CHAPTER THIRTY-FIVE

RAISA

While Raisa was fairly certain Isabel had written the Everly Ears columns and the letter to Talia, that didn't give her much to work on in terms of figuring out who her next victim would likely be.

She was just about to reach for the messages the killer posted—hopeful there might be hints in them like the earlier ones—when someone called her name from the front of the cabin.

It was a male voice, but she still made sure to grab her pepper spray as she approached the door. Their killer had hired a man to install cameras in Stewart Young's bedroom, after all.

But it was just one of the junior agents from the task force. He'd been assigned Terri Harden's crime scene, so she hadn't had much interaction with him yet.

He held out a slim folder. "We found this in Harden's home office. She kept old files there since she worked out of her house most of the time. Sand thought it might be helpful for you."

"Thanks," Raisa said, but he was already heading back into the hotel. Most of the agents seemed ready to pack it up now that they had someone in custody. She wasn't sure she blamed them.

She exhaled shakily when she realized what he'd just handed over. The Alex Parker case file.

Not of the murder-suicide.

This was the write-up from Terri Harden's investigation into the Parker children's welfare. Raisa had gone through the official report the social worker had filed with the state protection service back in grad school, but this one had handwritten notes in the margins.

Raisa started reading as she made her way back to the porch, but she paused when she got there.

Footsteps. In the woods. The distinct scuff of shoes against rock.

She tensed. She had a gun, as most FBI agents did. She knew how to shoot it with some accuracy. But she rarely carried it on her person.

Raisa wondered if she could make the lunge toward the cabin's safe in time to get it out.

The bushes rustled, the limbs of the closest tree bowed, and Raisa relaxed.

Just the wind.

She was on high alert tonight, hearing things that weren't there.

Raisa shook her head, and went back to Terri's file. In her capacity as the social worker investigating the claim, Terri had talked to teachers and Alex's peers, as well as his family.

Alex Parker had been taking summer classes, which was why he'd been at school in August. Because Everly was so small, everyone who had needed the extra lessons got lumped together. One of those other students had been Cara James.

Raisa paused again, a sharp flare of anger catching her off guard. But how could that have happened? It was beyond cruel to put a victim in the same classroom as her attacker.

By the note about the classes, in parentheses, was a cross-reference written in pencil.

(Page 12)

Raisa flipped through the file until she found the right section. It was labeled CARA JAMES.

"Miss James, the investigation is closed," the transcript began. *"We've talked to all relevant parties."*

"I know. I just . . . needed to tell someone," Cara said. *"It was just a stupid prank that went too far."*

"What was?"

"The short story," Cara said. *"I'm the one who wrote it. I switched Alex's out when I turned them in to Mr. Gonzalez that day."*

Raisa blinked and read that again. The words remained the same.

"We wanted everyone to see Alex for who he is," Cara continued. *"But it was just a prank that should never have gone this far."*

"We?"

"It doesn't matter," Cara said.

But, of course, Raisa knew. Everything kept coming back to Isabel.

"Miss James, are you aware of how much time and resources have been spent on this case?"

"I know, I know," Cara had said. *"I'm sorry. I know."*

The transcript ended, as did the file.

But none of it made sense. Why wouldn't this interview have made it into the official report on the Parker murder-suicide?

Raisa couldn't recall any of the details from reading it so long ago, but there had been one mention of Alex vaguely suggesting that he might not have written the short story. But it hadn't come off as an actual denial. No one—including Terri or his teacher—had believed him, and neither had Raisa.

She opened her computer to where she kept old notes and files and dug through it until she found one for the Parker case. Research she'd done for her lectures.

In it was a file labeled Terri Harden Report.

It was only eleven pages long.

"Shit," Raisa breathed out and then glanced at the date on the top of the interview with Cara.

August 26, 1998.

One day before the murder-suicide.

Raisa sat back, hand pressed to her mouth.

This little confession had never made it into the official report that Terri had filed with the state. It had only ever lived in Terri's private files she kept in her home. Maybe because it had come in after she'd "closed" the investigation. Maybe because in the mayhem that came the next day, she had actually forgotten to update the file.

Her eyes tracked back to her old folder. Right there, next to the Harden report, was a document labeled Suicide Note.

She clicked into it, but she knew it nearly word for word now.

It still matched the short story. It always had.

Raisa snatched Isabel's diary and flipped through to the entries around the time that Cara had been assaulted. It took four before she found the right one.

There are things worse than death, that's what most people don't understand. Cara understands it. But after we talked, I think she now understands that there are things better than death, too.

Raisa swore again, trying to make the leaps in logic required to fit this puzzle piece in place.

Cara James must have been planning to kill herself. She'd written the note, even.

But Isabel had talked her out of it.

"Isabel stole Cara's note," Raisa murmured, needing to say it out loud. It was outrageous and cruel and sociopathic. Just like their killer. "To use it to frame Alex.

"What came first?" she asked the files in front of her. "The note or the plan to kill her family?"

They had no answers for her.

Raisa flipped back to the beginning of the folder to refresh her memory of what had made it into Terri's official report.

It was clear from the very early sections of the file that Terri had doubts about the case.

Fiction was fiction, and Terri didn't exist as the thought police for teenagers dealing with a traumatic period of their life through writing.

The first interview had been with Eric Gonzalez, the English teacher who had flagged the story in the first place.

"After you confronted Alex, you told Miss Nora Williams about the story?" Terri had asked, referencing the school's guidance counselor.

"Well, after I read the piece, it got me thinking," Eric said. *"Cara James is in my class, too, and I'd heard all the rumors from earlier in the summer. How she said Alex assaulted her. I tried to help keep them as separated as possible, but she's scared of him. It's obvious. And I also had Isabel Parker the year before. She would come to class with bruises on her arms. I didn't think much of it at the time, kids grow up pretty rough and tumble here. But all together, I couldn't keep quiet anymore."*

Apparently, the English teacher had been dating Nora Williams, which made even more sense about why he'd let his concerns slip. Nora had been the one to convince him to file a formal report with the principal.

The interview with Eric and other staff at the school had been Terri getting her ducks lined up.

In the conversation she'd had with the other teachers and the school psychologist, there didn't seem to be much consensus on Alex Parker. Some considered him the golden heir of the Parker family; others thought he was an egotistical miscreant. It was a marked departure from how universally everyone called him troubled these days.

To Raisa it read like the reputation of a charming kid who was good at sports and bad at life. The former covered a whole host of sins for people who cared about scoreboards on Friday nights. Those who didn't, though, probably saw the worst of a rotten system in Alex Parker.

Terri Harden had walked away from the interviews with an obvious opinion. A handwritten scribble at the bottom of one of the pages read simply, "This is a waste of time."

Except she also acknowledged there were enough concerns about the girls and signs of abuse that she would do the home visit.

How must it have felt to have gone through this process only to wake up with a slaughtered family's blood on your hands? How much could you ever trust yourself again?

Maybe Terri had believed her work to be sound, just like Raisa had in Scottsdale. Raisa had continued on, continued looking at herself in the mirror because she stubbornly thought she was right. Another golden link snapping tight with another stranger. What did that say about Raisa? That she kept finding herself in these people who she didn't want to find herself in.

She exhaled and looked up, trying to let her eyes adjust to the dark at the edges of the porch.

Night had well and truly fallen. Yet hers was the only porch lit up. Instead of providing a safe haven of illumination, though, it felt like she had a spotlight on her. Everyone could see her and yet she couldn't see anything outside the soft glow.

No.

Raisa was being paranoid. The sounds of the woods were rich and complex, layered in with the wind and the various scuttling animals.

If there was a monster out there, the rest of the inhabitants would have gone quiet.

After all, out in the mountains, it wasn't the noise you feared—it was the silence.

CHAPTER
THIRTY-SIX

DELANEY

It was easy following Kilkenny. He thought Delaney had left or had at least gone into hiding.

Everything at the hotel was so chaotic with Walker in custody that Delaney had easily talked one of the young FBI men out of their car for the evening. She'd sat in it and watched as Kilkenny and Raisa had discovered her empty cabin, watched as Kilkenny had made a phone call, and then watched as Raisa had taken off through the woods toward town.

Delaney considered trailing her, but since Raisa had chosen the path through the woods, it would have involved too much slinking around in the shadows. Better to wait for Kilkenny, who would surely go after Raisa once he realized she was missing.

That took about five minutes, his body language going through a range of emotions from shocked to frustrated to angry to worried. When he finally made it to determined and pulled out of the parking lot in his SUV, Delaney followed at a discreet distance.

She was in a dark, nondescript sedan, but she still didn't want Kilkenny to notice her.

He was on high alert, too—both he and Raisa were. There had been a clear sense of urgency humming in the air between them. They were onto something.

What had Talia been able to give them?

Or was it just that Delaney had "disappeared"?

A tiny part of her had hoped that, upon discovering her empty cabin, they would just assume she'd packed up like the rest of the agents. Judging from the tension in Raisa's shoulders, her face, her waving hands, when she'd reemerged, Delaney didn't think that was the case.

Kilkenny turned left at the stop sign into town, and for a moment Delaney stared down the long stretch of two-lane highway heading toward Anacortes and the coast. It would be so easy to turn right.

Her fingers tightened on the wheel, and Delaney thought about the whiteboard of names back in her Seattle apartment.

Lana Parker.

There was still work to be done, still a plan in place.

Delaney took the left.

There were only a couple of other cars out, and none of them were the giant SUVs that the FBI favored. Delaney easily tracked Kilkenny to the restaurant on Main Street.

She killed her headlights and parked down a few blocks. She couldn't see what was happening on the sidewalk, but it wasn't hard to tell who came roaring by her only a minute later on his motorcycle. He hadn't been wearing his helmet.

Greg Balducci.

No going back now.

He had probably always suspected what had really gone down that evening in the Parker household, but as far as Delaney knew, he'd never told anyone.

She still remembered how brave she'd thought him, standing up to Alex because of Cara.

He'd been a white knight when she'd all but stopped believing in them.

But now that his parents had been killed, she couldn't even blame him for finally going to the feds with whatever information he had.

He would have told Raisa about the pills at the very least. What else did he have to hand over? Not much, but she could only really guess.

Delaney kept her distance as Kilkenny and Raisa headed to the sheriff's department. Would Samantha be there? Would she still be pretending not to know anything?

The pair wasn't in the building long enough for them to have uncovered anything important. Delaney decided to stick with Kilkenny when Raisa took off into the woods. Around the hour mark, Delaney decided surveillance work really wasn't for her. The adrenaline dump she'd gotten when Raisa and Kilkenny had found her empty cabin had dissipated long ago, and all that was left was boredom and a low-level anxiety.

Until Kilkenny took a sudden U-turn and there it was again: the dose of fear and excitement that had everything around her going bright and sharp. Instead of following—and alerting him to her presence—she watched him in the rearview until he pulled into the library's parking lot.

Delaney glanced at the dashboard clock. It was after hours, but Mrs. Matthews often stayed late to watch her shows on the library's TV. At least she had when Delaney was growing up.

She carefully pulled into an alley that provided her a view of the front of the building, and sure enough, when Kilkenny knocked on the door, Mrs. Matthews was there to beckon him inside.

The library itself was only one floor, with no other doors. Delaney would have to go in through a window in the back if she wanted to find out what Kilkenny was researching. Her heart told her they'd already crossed the line of no return, but her mind kept pushing for more confirmation.

She hated needless deaths. Especially when the victims were the good guys.

Burs caught at her ankles as she trudged through the untamed underbrush that surely had been a casualty of never having enough of a budget for anything. The window was blessedly waist-height, so she was able to heave herself in and drop to the carpeted floor silently.

Delaney crept through the stacks, staying on the balls of her feet. Surprise was really the only thing she had going for her, and if she was honest with herself, she was still hoping this wouldn't end in a confrontation at all. Maybe he wouldn't discover anything. Maybe he'd walk out with Mrs. Matthews in the front and she'd be able to crawl back out the window, no one the wiser.

She found Kilkenny already bent over a wooden table near the section that held the old newspapers. His back was to Mrs. Matthews, who had PBS blaring, conveniently covering any inadvertent noise Delaney might make.

Kilkenny paged through a yellowed stack of the *Everly Weekly News*.

When he found what he was looking for, he stilled. It was obvious in his body language that it was something big.

Delaney silently cursed. This was the moment she decided who she was.

But that was foolish. She'd made that decision at sixteen and nineteen and twenty-five. She'd made that decision when she turned toward town and away from the coast.

She stepped out of the shadows.

Kilkenny raised his gaze to hers, and then from one blink to the next, she was staring down the barrel of his gun.

CHAPTER THIRTY-SEVEN

RAISA

Raisa tore her eyes from the woods, turning her attention back to Terri Harden's report.

After talking to the school staff, Terri had moved on to the Parkers. Tim and Becks had dismissed the concerns as overblown.

"Are we living in 1984, then?" Tim had asked. *"Where you can't think about something without it being a crime?"*

"Have you read the story, Mr. Parker?"

"He's bored, he shouldn't be having to take summer classes at all," Tim had said.

"Alex is just trying to get a reaction," Becks had added.

"Mr. Gonzalez expressed concern for your daughters."

"Mr. Gonzalez can go—" Tim had started. Raisa tried to imagine the man as he must have been not long before his death. Everyone said he was sliding into schizophrenia by then, with a strong instance of paranoia. How must it have felt to have this conversation? For both parties.

"Talk to the girls," Becks had clearly interrupted. It was a transcript, so it wasn't perfect, it didn't convey the mood of the room, but Raisa could see it all playing out. *"Ask them, if you don't believe us."*

Isabel hadn't been home, though.

The only interview Terri had conducted had been with Lana Parker. Before reading it, Raisa flipped through the file, hoping she'd missed something. But no. Terri had never circled back to talk to Isabel.

The neglect here was staggering.

Raisa had met social workers like Terri Harden before. Most of the ones she'd encountered had been kind; they'd just been overworked and underpaid and burned out of a system that offered them no support. But some didn't even like children—they simply liked control and power.

The adults in Isabel's life had failed her time and time and time again. The Balduccis had lied for Alex, her parents pretended they hadn't seen what was going on, a government worker sent in specifically to protect the girls had rubber-stamped the whole process.

The kind of vengeance Isabel was wreaking was never justified, but Raisa couldn't deny that a small part of her at the very least understood why it was happening.

Meanwhile, Lana's interview was short and to the point.

Terri was surprisingly warm and gentle in her introduction to the child. But then she'd segued directly into questions about Alex.

"Has anyone been hurting you?"

Raisa winced. One of the first things agents were taught in questioning minors about accusations or concerns was not to use *hurting*. Children didn't realize even gentle touch was abuse when it came to these sorts of things.

"No," Lana had said, not surprisingly. Terri noted that Tim and Becks were in the room. While Lana should have had an advocate, asking these questions in front of her parents would inevitably skew the results.

"See," Tim interjected next, proving Raisa's point for her.

"Mr. Parker, I'll need you to let Lana speak, please," Terri said. So at least she wasn't completely incompetent.

"Have you been fighting with your brother?" Terri asked, and Raisa silently rescinded her compliment from a second earlier.

"No," was all Lana said.

"Has he ever scared you?" Terri asked. *"Or hurt you? Maybe even accidentally?"*

"No."

It might be hard to judge what someone's demeanor was through a transcript alone, but it didn't take a genius to figure this one out. Lana had been shy to the point of scared, and Raisa didn't blame her. She was being asked probing questions by a strange adult in front of her parents, parents who had been covering for Alex for god knew how long. Terri Harden should have had her license suspended for this interview alone.

In the interview, Terri got nowhere even though she tried a few more ways in, coming at the core question sideways. But Lana had yet to say anything other than *hello* and *yes* and *no*.

Even as terrible as Terri was as an interviewer, she seemed to sense it, too. Her next question was meant to re-engage Lana.

"Is that your homework?"

"No, it's for fun," Lana said. A whole three extra words. But it was something.

Terri seemed to sense that, too. *"You're doing math for fun? What a bright girl you are."*

"I'm good with patterns. And logic, too. Patterns and logic," Lana said.

Raisa blinked, and read the answer again. It matched Lana's straightforward idiolect from her diary, but it also matched something Raisa had heard more recently.

Someone who's good with patterns.

Raisa grabbed Lana's diary.

She read it again, this time seeing the building blocks of someone's adult vocabulary and syntax.

But it was a waste of time, confirming what she already knew.

Raisa had guessed wrong.

Delaney wasn't Isabel.

Delaney was Lana.

That didn't make her innocent, though. If Delaney was Isabel's accomplice, that would square all the round pegs when it came to her involvement in the case. Kilkenny had been right—she'd never quite fit as the killer.

But Raisa had been right, too. Her behavior had been suspicious from the get-go.

If Delaney was the accomplice, though, did that mean Isabel had watched from a safe distance while Delaney had gathered intel for her?

Raisa stared at the papers spread out over the table—Terri Harden's file, the diaries, the school assignments, even the old notes on her computer. But it was the Everly Ears columns that caught her attention. Slowly, she reached for the print-out versions. They had always sounded familiar to her, but she had chalked it up to reading gossipy articles since she was a teenager, flipping through *US* magazine at the gas station even if she couldn't afford to buy it.

Were those celebratory beverages? Are there divorce papers waiting to be served? Inquiring minds would love to know.

She pulled up her spreadsheet of everyone involved in the case.

The killer's idiolect stared back at her.

It was different from Everly Ears and Isabel's diary. But their killer—presumably Isabel—knew enough about forensic linguistics, even back then, to know how to fake a voice.

Except . . .

Raisa highlighted a line from one of the killer's posts.

Keep up the good work, my friends.

It was so simple, and yet it made everything else fall into place—the final piece of blue to make the entire sky. This person couldn't help but speak to their audience. A puppet master who wanted applause but had never been free to seek it.

Up earlier was another instance.

My lovely people.

It was what Raisa would call a tic. Something even the writer didn't realize they were doing—at least not all the time.

It was also one that Raisa finally recognized.

She pulled up her browser and typed in an address.

Then she started a new column in her spreadsheet and wrote:

- *My lovely tin-hatters*
- *You would think she's talking about the murder-suicide, but, folks, she's not*
- *Go ahead and subscribe, my friends*

There were more examples, but Raisa didn't need them. She stared at the list, damning now in black and white.

Isabel Parker was in Everly, but she wasn't Delaney Moore.

It was then that Raisa noticed the woods had gone silent.

She reached for her pepper spray, but was a second too late.

"Uh, uh, uh, my dear," Jenna Shaw said, stepping out from the trees, a gun pointed at Raisa. "Hands where I can see them."

CHAPTER THIRTY-EIGHT

DELANEY

Delaney had seen more than one gun in her life, but she didn't know if she'd ever been on the business end of one.

"Lana?" Kilkenny asked, voice cautious.

It was strange hearing her name again for the first time in twenty-five years.

"I always thought you were clever," Delaney said softly, her eyes tracking down to the newspaper. And there, in the corner of a full-page collage-spread layout, was a picture of her and Isabel, with Samantha Mason and their father in the background.

The weekend before everything went to shit.

She'd been almost happy that day.

"It wasn't me who figured it out," Kilkenny said. He hadn't lowered the weapon. "We thought you might be Isabel."

Delaney stared at the picture of her sister. At that age, it had been obvious which of them had been the oldest. Neither of them had been pretty, per se; mostly they were just awkward, growing into their bone structure and their frames, with pimply skin and unruly hair.

"Do you know who this is?" Kilkenny asked, tapping Isabel's face. Delaney flinched at the assault on the photo even though it was silly to do so.

"Isabel," she said.

"No, do you know what name she goes by now?" he asked.

She simply stared at him. Of course she didn't know. Delaney had spent the best part of twenty-five years trying to figure that out.

He must have read the answer in her eyes, because the gun lowered by just a fraction, pointing somewhere in the vicinity of her shoulder now instead of her face.

"Lana," he said again, and she hated that name on his lips. "This is Jenna Shaw."

The world narrowed to a pinprick and then blew wide open again. Kilkenny was talking, but his voice was distorted, as if coming from a long distance away.

The next time she opened her eyes, she was on the ground, Kilkenny kneeling in front of her, the gun held loosely at his side now. The other hand hovered near her shoulder, but he didn't touch her.

Good. She didn't like being held during a panic attack, or whatever close cousin this was. She looked around, counting five things she could see, four things she could touch, three things she could hear.

Taste and smell took a back seat to the urgency of the moment.

"You didn't know," Kilkenny said.

"Obviously not," Delaney said, scrubbing her hands over her face. The residual anxiety always left her shaky and thirsty and exhausted. "Jenna Shaw doesn't post any pictures of herself, and all her social media is the logo of the show."

"And you weren't there for her interrogation," Kilkenny realized. "You were in the sheriff's office with Raisa."

"I've been searching for my sister since I was fifteen," Delaney said. "As soon as my parents let me onto a computer."

"Adoptive parents," Kilkenny corrected. Though it seemed absent-minded rather than deliberately hurtful, Delaney shoved him back so that he ended up on his butt on the floor, more out of surprise than because of her strength.

"You don't get to call them that," Delaney said.

Kilkenny seemed startled, flustered even. "Sorry. I'm trying to keep the connections clear."

And that was fair. Her parents were Tim and Becks, her sister was Isabel. Just because Delaney felt certain ways about those familial relationships didn't mean it wasn't easier for all involved to call them what they were.

"Fine," she conceded.

"You've been looking for Isabel?" Kilkenny asked, the gun stowed away now. She was glad he wasn't a rookie or trigger-happy; otherwise it might have gone off when she'd pushed him.

She stared at where he'd stashed the weapon and considered the ways she could spin the truth. But they were in the endgame now. One of Isabel's creating. There was no reason to lie anymore.

"The authorities separated us," Delaney said. "For our own good, they said. It would be less likely for any journalists or whatever to track us down. But, really, it would have been impossible to keep the three of us together with the state of this country's foster system."

"No one here wanted to take you in?" Kilkenny asked.

"Samantha, maybe, under different circumstances," Delaney said, a sweet pang at the memory of the woman. It had been hard seeing her older, worn and weathered. But she'd still protected Delaney, just like she always had. "But she wanted us out of town. Just in case. She even convinced them somehow to change our names so there was a better chance we'd be harder to find in case anyone ever tried."

"In case someone started questioning the official story of what happened to Alex?"

So they'd figured out that the police report was a lie. She'd known, of course. She'd known they had the second she'd recognized Greg Balducci on that motorcycle. "Yes."

"What happened that night, Lana?"

"Delaney," she corrected.

"Sorry," he said. "Delaney, what happened that night?"

"Isabel didn't tell me what she was planning. I thought . . ." Delaney trailed off. Memory was a strange thing. Admitting that you were a bad person, well, the brain didn't like that. It would warp the past into something that didn't hurt and make you think that's what happened all along. But Delaney knew she wasn't a good guy. "I didn't know she was planning on killing everyone. But I thought she might feed Alex too many sleeping pills, and I didn't say anything."

"Why not?"

"I was twelve," Delaney said, with a laugh lacking all humor. "I didn't understand death or consequences. But Alex was a dick and he was raping my sister. At the time, I was pretty sure he deserved whatever she put him through—including a permanent sleep."

"Did he ever hurt you?"

"Why does that matter?" Delaney asked, voice going sharp.

"Just trying to get an accurate picture," Kilkenny said, gentle and soothing, like she was a wild animal.

"He hit me," Delaney admitted. "Nothing more than that. But it was coming, both Isabel and I could tell. That also might have been the trigger."

"What happened that night?" Kilkenny asked again.

"Isabel is a planner," Delaney said, her eyes slipping past him into a memory. "She didn't kill him in a rage, you could probably tell that. No excessive stab wounds. Isabel had everything planned. Greg invited Alex over to his house on the pretense of making nice after the fight. It was time to bury the hatchet. But Isabel had him pick another fight to get Alex in a bad mood. She helped my mother make dinner, putting the sleeping pills she'd gotten from Greg into the food, and then when Alex came home in a temper, she suggested that she would take us to Christine's house to get out of the way."

"She waited a long enough time for the pills to kick in," Kilkenny guessed.

"Yeah, and then we ran home," Delaney said. "I was carrying the baby, so Isabel got there a lot faster than me. Tim and Becks were already on the bed. I don't know if she hesitated, or not, but they were dead by the time I got there. Alex had fallen asleep on the couch and Isabel roused him enough to get him into the bathtub."

"You watched all this play out?" Kilkenny asked, no judgment in his voice.

Delaney shook her head. "She had me go get the suicide letter from her room. Cara had written one a few weeks before, and Isabel used it to forge Alex's. She tweaked it to fit the circumstances, obviously. But the bones were there."

"That still must have been quite scary."

"It wasn't," Delaney said, thinking back to the rush of it. Most of the memory was blurred, the soft edges of it soaked with blood. But the thing that she remembered more than anything was wanting to be good for Isabel, to not mess everything up and get her in trouble. Delaney had always hated the idea of getting anyone in trouble.

It was why she'd lied to Terri Harden the day she'd come to interview them. If only Isabel had been home. If only Terri had come back.

Delaney felt like her life had been built on "if only."

"Was it you who called the sheriff?" Kilkenny asked.

"No, Isabel told me not to speak again until the case was closed," Delaney said. "I didn't even know what that meant. But it didn't matter, Samantha knew what had happened. Isabel wasn't as good at killing as she is now."

He licked his lips. "She's the copycat? You're certain?"

"The tombstone," Delaney said. Any thought that it might not be her sister who was terrorizing Everly had disintegrated as soon as she'd seen that small black box. "I told you, I've been looking for her online since I was fifteen. The reason I thought I might be able to find her was because we used to speak to each other that way. With silly mathematical symbols. They all meant different things to us, but our parents were always so pleased when they found papers full of them. They thought we were prodigies."

"Weren't you?" Kilkenny asked, brows raised.

Delaney blushed. "I'm smart, but not like Tim and Becks were. Or what they expected of us. Isabel is obviously a genius, but I'm sure you can tell that."

"What did the tombstone mean between you two?" Kilkenny asked without agreeing to the idea of Isabel's intelligence. He didn't know how much she'd gotten away with, though. Not yet anyway.

"It's always been her signature," Delaney said on a sigh. "She thought it was funny, that it was called a tombstone. We would pass notes to each other and that's how she would end them."

"You recognized it after twenty-five years?" Kilkenny was fishing for what she still didn't want to tell him.

The only thing she'd considered keeping a lie.

But nothing made sense without her own confession.

"No." She pulled out her phone and found the website that was as familiar to her as her own face. It was supposed to be used as an online journal of sorts to track your exercise habits. What Delaney had liked about it was it was easy to hack.

She closed her eyes, inhaled, exhaled, considered fleeing.

And then she handed her phone over to Kilkenny.

CHAPTER
THIRTY-NINE

RAISA

"Oh man, I liked you," Raisa said, as she stared at Jenna, deliberately not looking at the gun.

"I know," Jenna said, with a smirk. She leaned in to whisper, "You have a soft spot for anyone atoning for their sins. Even if they suck as a person otherwise."

Raisa parsed through that and came to another realization. "You lied during that first conversation in the restaurant. About falling for a conspiracy theory. About getting people hurt."

"Oh, I've hurt people," Jenna said, her smirk spreading into a grin. "I've hurt plenty of people. But they all deserved it, I promise you."

"What about me?" Raisa asked, jerking her chin toward the gun. "I don't deserve it."

Jenna's nostrils flared slightly. "Believe it or not, I have no quarrel with you. But now you know too much."

"I don't know anything," Raisa said and Jenna rolled her eyes.

"Don't be cute," Jenna chastised. "Not to be a creeper—"

Raisa snorted, amused more at the absurdity of a serial killer uttering that phrase than anything else.

"But," Jenna said with an annoyed emphasis. "I was watching you. I heard you talking to yourself. You do that more than you realize, I think. You know plenty, my dear."

There was no point in lying. Even if Raisa hadn't figured it out, Isabel had played her hand now. There would be no disappearing back into the Jenna Shaw persona, no one the wiser, if she let Raisa live.

"You're right, you got me," Raisa said. "I figured out your secret. Isabel."

"I would offer a gold star, but I'm all out of stickers." She cocked her head. "And, darling, you haven't even scratched the surface of my secrets."

"Lay it on me," Raisa goaded, knowing without a doubt Jenna would love to talk about her own brilliance. And waste time doing it.

"Ah, ah, ah." Jenna waggled the gun a little. "I'm not an idiot. Far from it, actually."

"I mean, this doesn't seem very smart. What's the play here?" Raisa asked, trying to calculate whether she could go for the pepper spray still sitting on the table. "You're going to shoot me on the porch?"

"No, darling. Delaney Moore is going to shoot you on your porch." Jenna pursed her lips. "Or in the woods. That's probably better."

"You're a one-trick pony, then," Raisa said, poking at her overinflated ego. Jenna cool and calculated would be a challenge. Her angry and sloppy less so. "Framing people. Is that all you've got?"

Something predatory slid into Jenna's expression. "Why play hard when you can play smart?"

"And the fake podcast was playing smart?" Raisa asked, letting the contempt saturate her voice.

"Who says it's fake? I actually quite like this persona. I think I'll keep it." She fluffed her bright-pink hair a little. "People get distracted by all the metal and ink. Forget to look at your actual features."

Raisa lifted her brows. "You really think you're going to walk away from this?"

"I know I am, darling," she said, and Raisa could hear the echoes of young Isabel's Everly Ears idiolect in her voice. "Now we just have to see if I have to kill one FBI agent or two."

Kilkenny.

Raisa's eyes slipped to his cabin. It was still dark, thank god.

"He doesn't know anything," she said. "I'm not lying this time."

"Please, you would say that no matter what."

"Still true, though," Raisa said, trying not to sound desperate.

"I want to believe you," Jenna said on a sigh. "I'd rather not kill him."

"Then don't?"

"Maybe I will, maybe I won't," Jenna said. "That one's still up in the air."

A distant rumble cut through the silence.

An engine.

"Oh, time to play," Jenna said, with a little skip of excitement.

"That's not Kilkenny." At least she didn't think it was.

"It's someone." Jenna jabbed the gun in Raisa's direction. "All right, my love, up you go. I don't want you trying anything. Believe me, if I have to shoot all of you here, I'll do it without a moment's hesitation."

"Then why get me in the woods at all?"

"Flourish," Jenna said, with a wink. It was a callback to their first conversation at the restaurant. "Some people like a little style with their work. And it'll be more believable if this is a chase through the dark and scary woods. It will look more believable that you were running away from my psycho little sister. Now, let's go."

Raisa had no interest in testing Jenna. And even if the car wasn't Kilkenny, the next one might be. How long did it take to check an old newspaper for a photograph? If he walked into this scene cold, Jenna might shoot him before he even got a chance to realize there was a gun involved.

As she stood, she knocked the pepper spray and her can of soda to the ground with a clumsy sweep of her arm. Jenna didn't even flinch at the clatter, which was a bad sign. She wasn't nervous or jumpy. Raisa wondered how many times she'd been in this moment, the moment before a kill.

Kilkenny had been right that this wasn't her first rodeo.

"Let's go, let's go," Jenna called out, and Raisa started down the steps, heading toward the tree line. Hopefully, when Kilkenny got to the cabin, he'd be able to guess she hadn't left willingly.

Raisa knew the area as well as she could after only a few days in town. There was the idea of a path, overgrown and rock-strewn. Raisa immediately veered in the direction that would take her into Everly, but Jenna nudged her back with the gun.

"Nice try, but no such luck," Jenna said, pointing in the direction that led them deeper into the woods. "Don't worry, princess—we won't go far."

Maybe Raisa should have been scared, but something about Jenna made her want to roll her eyes instead. The excessive endearments might have had something to do with that.

"You know Delaney has disappeared, right?" Raisa asked. "How are you going to frame her if you can't find her?"

"Oh, don't you worry your pretty head about that," Jenna said. "She'll come to us."

Raisa stopped, turned. Of course, she had assumed Delaney was Jenna's accomplice, but she'd dismissed the theory the second Jenna had admitted she was going to frame her sister for Raisa's death. "What?"

Jenna's smile had gone manic, the moonlight catching against sharp canines. "You only need to know one thing about Lana. Her biggest fear in the world is disappointing me."

CHAPTER FORTY

DELANEY

"What am I looking at?" Kilkenny asked, holding Delaney's phone. The website Delaney used to communicate with Isabel was open.

Delaney had found it back when she was a teenager, in the early days of the internet. It was a simple interface and designed to act as an online journal of sorts. There was a social element to it, too, which allowed others to read what you posted—except Delaney hadn't accepted any of the "friend" requests she'd received. She'd thought she'd been speaking into the void.

Only this particular void had a way of answering.

Not with words but with action.

There was that first journal entry about Professor Noah Webb. Delaney had written it sincerely, complaining about the man, guessing at how many girls he had pressured into sex. He'd hit on her when she was sixteen, still a high school student, without any sign of fear. That never boded well for what he'd done in private.

He'd proved her right—blackmailing her with a grade she hadn't deserved in exchange for sexual favors.

She certainly hadn't cried when he'd died. But she had wondered.

Especially since an illegally obtained version of his suicide note had been circulating around campus on the down-low. She'd seen the tombstone.

But the symbol had always been meant to be innocuous if viewed by anyone who didn't already know what it was. Maybe it really had been an ink smudge.

Delaney had continued writing the entries, curious but certainly not convinced. In theory, no one should have been able to read them besides her. Isabel always had been too smart for her own good, though. It wasn't out of the realm of possibility that she'd found a way around the security settings.

When Maura had helped get her drunk and into bed with a frat boy—something that would have certainly given Isabel flashbacks to Cara—Delaney had viewed it as an ultimate test.

Maura had turned up dead, of course, and with that Delaney had been fairly certain Isabel had found a way to read the messages. After all, Isabel had always viewed Delaney's life as hers to protect, whether it was through invasive means or not.

Of course, it hadn't been without consequences. Killing their parents and Alex had irreparably fractured Isabel's mind. Delaney was ashamed to say she hadn't been above taking advantage of that.

"You used her as a weapon." Kilkenny's expression, which had been painfully compassionate only moments earlier, had gone neutral, a sure sign of his judgment. "Instead of handing her over to the authorities. You used her."

The truth, once said aloud, would have knocked Delaney to the ground had she not already been there. "It was her choice to take action or not."

Kilkenny rubbed a hand over his mouth. "Christ. You know that's not how it works. Not with people like her."

Delaney closed her eyes. "I tried to talk her into contacting me. I even tried to trick her into meeting up. But she always saw it coming. I was never smart enough to catch her."

"You just let her kill people you didn't like."

"No." Delaney's eyes flew up. "She only killed people who hurt other people."

"Delaney," Kilkenny said softly. "This is conspiracy to commit murder."

"I know." It was why she hadn't said anything before. But now she had to. He would figure out why soon enough. "I wanted you to know what you're walking into, though. Isabel has killed many, many times. And it wasn't just for me."

"Why didn't you tell me before? I could have helped you."

Delaney jerked her hand toward the phone and parroted back his own words. "Conspiracy to commit murder."

"Right," Kilkenny said softly. "You were in too deep since you were sixteen."

"I wouldn't have anyway," Delaney said, staring at the ground so she didn't have to meet his eyes. "I wanted to get her to stop, but I didn't want her in jail."

Even as she said it, she could see the doubt in Kilkenny's expression. He wasn't wrong to think she was, at the very least, fooling herself.

An old proverb came to mind when Delaney thought of Isabel and her own actions: There are two wolves inside you, always battling. One is full of goodness and light, he lives in harmony with the world around him. The other one is evil, consumed with hatred and vengeance. When asked which one will win, the answer is simple.

It will be the one that you feed.

Delaney wanted the good wolf to win, but even she could admit that she had fed the evil one with every person she'd pointed Isabel toward.

Each time she'd told herself it would be the last. What would one more person hurt in the grand scheme of things? Then she would help her sister stop killing.

As impossible—as hypocritical—as it seemed right now, that was still her goal.

She just couldn't yet see a path forward that didn't end in Kilkenny's death. She hoped one would emerge. But she'd made the decision the moment she'd stepped out of the stacks.

This was a micro version of the trolley test. Bringing Kilkenny into the situation ensured that the most people would walk away alive.

There was still time to figure out how to make sure they all did, though.

Kilkenny shook his head, seemingly at a loss. "Why did she come back here? Why did you?"

That last part, at least, had a simple answer. "I knew she would be here."

"But why—"

"The twenty-fifth anniversary," Delaney said in a rush.

"Why not the twentieth? The fifteenth?"

"I don't know, honestly," she said. "But I've been . . . tracking her movements for the past few months."

"How?"

"Digitally, she leaves a footprint I can find sometimes. Every once in a while." Sometimes she wondered if it was on purpose. Isabel had lived so much of her life as a ghost, it must be nice to feel seen. "Um, I noticed activity around some of the key players in this case.

"Like Greg Balducci made tech news when he was hacked about ten weeks ago," Delaney continued. "Not a big deal for someone else, but Greg Balducci shouldn't be able to get hacked. Then the Child Protective Services reported an outage three days later."

"What was she accomplishing?"

"Nothing," Delaney said. "They were bread crumbs. For me. Just like the Flik video that was posted on a hashtag I monitor when I was on shift."

She exhaled and then admitted what she was worried about. "I think I triggered her. I'm fairly certain now that she catfished me, pretending to be a woman named Kylie. I told her I had lied to my sister about something important. That's all it took for Isabel to go digging."

"When was this?"

"Three months ago," Delaney said softly. It was when the first messages had been posted on that "Alex is Innocent" thread. That wasn't a coincidence. And that's why Delaney had known she'd gotten herself added to Isabel's kill list.

It's also why she'd known that Isabel had been fishing for an excuse for this spree in the first place. Why ask Delaney that so close to the anniversary otherwise? Delaney talked to the FBI; she knew Isabel's secrets. She was one guilt-ridden day away from turning over everything she knew about Isabel to law enforcement. Isabel had to view her as a liability.

And liabilities in Isabel's world were eliminated.

The truth was, Delaney had been living on borrowed time. She was always going to become one of Isabel's victims. She had just hoped to outmaneuver her before that happened.

Kilkenny's hand twitched to his gun, as if he was just realizing all she had told him. And everything she hadn't said.

"Why are you showing me this now?"

"I thought I was going to be the next victim," Delaney said. They had been right about tonight leading up to some kind of finale. It's why Isabel had fed that information to Walker. Everyone was supposed to have dropped their guard. She knew her sister's ways at least that much. "I was so sure. So sure. It would be Bob and Gina, who had covered for Alex after he'd assaulted Cara. Then Terri, who could have stopped this all. I know Stewart seems random, but Isabel was furious with him after that party, and she holds grudges. She was talking about ways to kill him back when she was fifteen. So he was going to go, too. And then me. Of course it was going to be me next. I was sure. It made sense it was going to be me."

Kilkenny breathed out, her name riding along the exhale.

"I was going to try to talk her out of it, of course," Delaney said. "I was hopeful I could. It was worth taking the risk. But I was sure I was going to be next. And it was going to be tonight."

"But you're here," Kilkenny said slowly.

Slowly, she nodded. Isabel would have found her by now. "I know."

She waited for him to catch up, and she could see the moment it clicked. For the first time in their conversation, anger flashed in his eyes. "Raisa."

CHAPTER FORTY-ONE

RAISA

"Delaney is your accomplice?" Raisa asked, wanting Jenna to say it explicitly. Enough with the guesswork.

"In a manner of speaking," Jenna said. "Keep walking, babe."

Raisa eyed the path ahead of them. The moonlight cut through the trees, but there were deep pockets of shadows that might provide shelter. The stream was coming up, too. There must have been a storm not long before they'd arrived, because it was swollen, riding high along the banks.

Walking in the water in the dark would be a risk, one that wouldn't be worth taking. But the stream ran into town. If she crossed to the other side and then followed it back, she might be able to lose Jenna while heading toward help.

"But you're going to frame her for my death?" Raisa asked, not caring much about the answer beyond keeping Jenna talking. If she was talking, that meant her attention was divided.

"I was vaguely hoping to get you all in our old house somehow," Jenna said, sidestepping the question. "Wouldn't it be poetic to have you and Kilkenny play the role of Tim and Becks? And then Delaney could be the one found in the bathtub."

"You certainly would have gotten your flair," Raisa said, and tripped over a rock, stumbling forward a bit, but not enough to get Jenna's attention.

"See, you appreciate style," Jenna said, with a little laugh. "But who would have authenticated the confession letter?"

"How did you know back then?" Raisa asked, genuinely curious now. "That it was important to create an idiolect for him."

"I didn't," Jenna admitted. "Please, I was fifteen. I just knew how terrible my attempt at writing a confession letter was. You should have seen my first draft. It was . . . not good. It sounded too much like me. So did my second and my tenth."

"That's what happens when you're a narcissist."

"Oh, burn," Jenna said, mocking and exaggerated. "Darling, do you know the first thing you can do to tell if someone's a narcissist?"

"I'm sure you'll tell me."

"Exactly. They'll tell you," Jenna said, sounding pleased with her own perceived cleverness. "Anyway, I even tried taking out library books that might have suicide notes in them, but Mrs. Matthews started getting suspicious."

"So you used Cara's trauma for your own gain."

"It was for her gain, too," Jenna said, mildly. Not ruffled or defensive because, in her mind, she was morally justified. "Alex deserved to pay for what he'd done to her."

"And to you." It was hard to remember—especially with the grown-up version behind her with a gun—but at the very heart of this was a victim who'd killed her abuser. "What about the short story?"

"Honestly, that was my one last test," Jenna said, with a shrug in her voice. "To check if anyone would give a shit. To see if anyone would see him for the monster he was. Turns out, they almost passed, but then failed spectacularly with the help of my dear sister."

"She was twelve," Raisa said. "And if we're talking monsters . . ."

Jenna laughed at the implication that she was one, too.

"Monsters come in a variety pack," she said. "Especially when it's families. The blood is tainted, but at least we all have our own special flavor."

"Delaney's a monster?"

"Oh, a far more devious one than me," Jenna said. "At least I know what I am."

"You're really just going to kill your own sister? The one you've been separated from for twenty-five years?" If Jenna's whole shtick was that she'd wanted to protect Lana back then, wouldn't she hesitate to kill her now? Even if she didn't have an emotional attachment to her, she'd still want to preserve the image she carried around of herself.

"I like to think of it as giving her a twenty-five-year reprieve," Jenna said. "And now time's up."

"And you'll sail off into the sunset none the wiser."

"More monsters to slay, don't you know," Jenna said, a little too cheerily. "And who best to slay them than someone who knows what it's like to be one?"

Raisa tried to find a flaw in her plan that wasn't *Kilkenny*.

"They're together now, you know," Jenna said. "Delaney and Kilkenny."

Raisa stumbled for real. "What?"

"Yup," Jenna said. "I put a tracker on both of their cars. They're in the library. Hunting up pictures of me, perhaps?"

Raisa let herself trip again.

"Stop being deliberately clumsy," Jenna snapped. "I will shoot you early if I have to."

"You've already told me you're planning on killing me, why would I not try to escape?"

"Hmm, fair point," Jenna said. "What if I ask nicely?"

Raisa was startled into a laugh. "Yeah, that'll probably do it. What position would you like me in?"

"Smart mouth on you," Jenna said, but she sounded amused. Raisa wasn't sure if that boded well for her or not. The threat was certainly real. She had no doubt Jenna intended to kill her. If she and Delaney had been responsible for all those deaths, she had plenty of practice. And those were the ones they knew about.

But at the same time, Raisa didn't feel scared. The clever banter would end at some point, and Jenna would don the cold mask of an experienced killer.

"It's a bummer you have to die," Jenna said. "I almost liked you."

Raisa lifted her brows. "I feel so special. A raging psychopath serial killer likes me."

"*Almost* likes you," Jenna corrected. "Keep walking, babe."

Raisa debated lunging for her. Jenna was alert, though, and her entire attention was focused on Raisa.

She kept walking.

"You wrote messages to me," Raisa said, just to keep Jenna talking. "Or at least a forensic linguist. Why would you do that if you didn't want me to figure anything out?"

"Use that big brain of yours—I know you can do it," Jenna said.

Raisa wanted to smack her. Not in a self-defense, escape-the-serial-killer way, either. Then she did as she was told because Jenna had a gun right now and she didn't.

"You were planning on framing Delaney," Raisa said. "Which involves seeding. I bet if I went to Delaney's apartment right now, there would be writing samples that match those posts on the 'Alex is Innocent' thread."

"Not just a pretty face," Jenna cooed.

"And you what? Just crossed your fingers they'd send along a forensic linguist?" Raisa asked. "That was risky."

"Hmm, no," Jenna said. "I cover my bases. I've been watching your career for a while. I knew what it took—and who it took—to get you called out on a case. And if worse came to worse, I would have sent in an anonymous letter or something. You were the easy part in all of this."

Raisa eyed a low-fallen tree and wondered if she could use it as a moment of distraction.

"Uh-uh, sweetheart." Jenna was right up against her back now, the barrel of the gun digging into the space between her spine and shoulder blade. "Actually, I can't believe you haven't made the connection yet. With the framing and all."

It was so clearly bait, but their goals were the same. To keep Jenna talking. "What connection?"

"Does Scottsdale ring any bells?" Jenna asked.

Raisa froze. And then she whirled on Jenna, not thinking clearly enough to consider the weapon. "What are you talking about?"

Jenna gave her that same obnoxious smirk she'd been wearing all night. "Did you really think you screwed up that badly all by yourself?"

Raisa didn't even think about it; she simply moved. Her hands were on Jenna's wrist, and then her shoulder, shoving her in a blind rage that gave her speed and strength that surprised both of them.

But the fight didn't last long. Jenna was a practiced serial killer and had no fear. Violence ran in her blood in the way it would never in Raisa's.

She brought the gun back and whipped it across Raisa's face, the metal connecting with bone, a sharp crack slicing through the night.

Waves of pain rippled out from the point of contact, bright sparks dancing in her vision. Raisa bent in half, cupping her cheek, struggling to breathe through the throbbing agony.

Here was the calculating murderer.

"Look what you made me do," Jenna said, her voice soft and friendly again. "That was just silly."

For the first time, Raisa could actually picture Jenna shooting her, could almost feel the way the bullet would rip through flesh. Would Jenna take a head shot? Or would she want to savor her kill, cherishing the fear in Raisa's eyes as she bled out?

"You interfered with the Scottsdale case?" Raisa asked, still panting from the pain. "You got a little girl killed and for what?"

Jenna leaned forward to catch Raisa's eyes. "Fun."

If Raisa thought she could have gotten away with it, she would have swung at Jenna once more. But it wasn't the right time yet.

"I don't believe you," Raisa said instead and had the pleasure of seeing Jenna surprised. "You don't kill for fun. You kill for punishment."

"I'm a psychopath, babe," Jenna said, with a careless shrug that didn't come off as believable anymore.

"Sure, but you're a serial killer, too," Raisa said. "There are rules."

"Rules to serial killing?" Jenna asked, amused once more.

"To the psychology of serial killers, yeah," Raisa said, and repeated, "You kill for punishment."

Jenna looked away, for only a heartbeat, but Raisa could tell she'd gotten to her.

"I didn't kill the girl," Jenna said, almost petulant. "If the other agents had done their jobs, she wouldn't have died. You aren't so important that you alone should make or break a case. It was a good lesson for everyone involved."

Rage flared bright in the corners of her vision, but Raisa grabbed hold of it, yanked it back, put it in a cage. It pounded at the bars, but Raisa wasn't a kid on the streets anymore. It had taken her years to learn how to control her anger, but now it was paying off. She couldn't let emotion dictate her actions right now. She needed to be calm, unruffled.

"You forged the emails the daycare teacher sent the parents."

"No," Jenna said, preening. "I faked the hostage note. Matching the daycare teacher's idiolect was easy."

They should have caught that. The tactic happened frequently enough there was even a name for it—POMIC. Post-Offense Manipulation of Investigation Communication.

Raisa exhaled so that the words came out neutral instead of razor-sharp. "How?"

"My best investment to date was finding my freelance hacker, who cares only that I can pay him on time," Jenna said.

Raisa shook her head, truly at a loss. "Why would you—"

And then she realized.

"It was a test," she said slowly. "Not for me. For yourself."

They'd stumbled into a clearing and Jenna hadn't made Raisa start walking again. This way she could see the expressions as they flitted across Jenna's face. She was trying to decide whether to be honest.

"This whole plan relies on it being believable that Delaney is the real killer," Jenna said.

"You wanted to see if you were good enough to fool a forensic linguist. In faking an idiolect," Raisa realized.

"I didn't get this far in life by being sloppy," Jenna said, smile once again smug.

"You must have planted the fake evidence against her before you even came out here," Raisa said, almost to herself. She was still wrapping her head around how long Jenna had been planning all this.

"Yes, but honestly, it didn't take much," Jenna said. "My sister practically had a creepy murder board right there in the open. But you can never be too careful."

It made sense that Delaney had been tracking Jenna's kills, and then anything to do with her family's case. Raisa guessed Delaney had found that "Alex is Innocent" thread long before Jenna had left bread crumbs back to it with the killer's screen name.

"And then with you, I just had to wait for the perfect case to come along," Jenna continued.

Raisa was left baffled. "You were waiting?"

A beat of silence followed the question. They hadn't started walking again, so Raisa could watch Jenna's face. Jenna knew she'd revealed something she hadn't wanted to.

"Why?" Raisa asked. "You could frame Delaney without me. You didn't need to bring a forensic linguist in."

Jenna was calculating how much to reveal—Raisa could see it in her eyes, even in the darkness. It was strange that she was still lying.

I have no quarrel with you, she had said, and it had sounded so believable.

But Raisa had been right. Jenna didn't kill for no reason.

"Jenna," Raisa said slowly. "Why me?"

The silence of the woods was her only answer.

CHAPTER FORTY-TWO

DELANEY

The text came in as Delaney followed Kilkenny out of the library, but she didn't dare check it until he rounded his SUV. He was out of sight for ten seconds, maybe, but that was all it took.

In the woods. Bring him if he knows too much.

That was it.

Isabel had never texted before, but Delaney didn't wonder if it was her. She knew it.

Delaney slid a glance toward Kilkenny as she climbed in the SUV. Isabel must know she was with him. Trackers in the cars? She'd always been technologically savvy.

Kilkenny gripped the wheel, his knuckles white with anger. The moonlight caught the metal of his wedding band and Delaney pressed her lips together.

She didn't want him to die.

She didn't want him to die simply because she'd made a calculation. A selfish one, at that.

He was a good man. He was a much better human than Delaney or Isabel would ever hope to be.

If she brought him with her—like she had been planning since she'd stepped out of the stacks—Isabel would shoot him on sight. That's what that message had meant. No matter what Isabel had planned for Delaney, she would take Kilkenny's presence there as a threat to both of them.

Delaney had thought she could pull the lever on the trolley track, but staring at Kilkenny's profile now, she finally realized why it was hard for some people to make that choice.

As slowly as she could, so as not to bring attention to herself, she slipped her hand into her bag. Her knuckles brushed against the barrel of her gun and she shivered. But she kept searching. The phone jammer she'd learned to carry was there, at the bottom with pens and paper clips and receipts. She palmed it and then closed her eyes as she pressed the button.

"We're stopping Isabel," Kilkenny said, breaking the silence she hadn't realized had dropped. She startled, the jammer falling back to its place among the detritus of her bag. But that didn't matter—it was working. Or should be.

"Until about five minutes ago, you didn't even know she existed," Delaney pointed out, probably not helpfully. But she'd been hunting her sister for twenty-five years. It wasn't as easy as he was making it seem.

"She kills like a hired assassin. They're the hardest to catch," he said. "And you came to me because you think I can help. Why are you arguing now?"

"I came to you because I want you to save Raisa, not stop Isabel."

"It's not the same?" he asked, because he was perceptive.

"When you say 'stop,' you mean 'shoot or arrest.'"

"Delaney," he said, with a gentle patience that grated on Delaney's skin. "You know those are the only ways this ends."

She didn't say anything.

A few minutes later, Kilkenny reached for his phone, only half his attention on the road. He swore, a harsh, guttural sound of frustration. "No service."

He grabbed for his two-way radio and got nothing but crackle.

The hotel's light cut through the darkness up ahead. Kilkenny could take the time to find backup or he could go barreling into the woods in reckless desperation.

In most situations, Delaney guessed he would do the former. Because Kilkenny had a weak spot, and it was the reason she'd chosen to work with him in the first place. Kilkenny believed he had put Raisa in danger. He was the one who had listened to Delaney, who'd brought Raisa onto the task force. In his mind, he was responsible for her safety. And that would make him careless.

As Delaney predicted, Kilkenny didn't even bother to turn the SUV off, his nice shoes skidding over the gravel when he took off running toward Raisa's cabin. Despite her long legs, Delaney was much slower. By the time she caught up to him, he was standing on Raisa's porch, staring down at the diaries that were splayed open, the pepper spray that had been knocked onto the ground beneath the table, the soda can beside it. When he looked up, she saw a decade's worth of grief in his eyes that had little to do with Raisa and a lot to do with those scars that had been the very reason she'd picked him.

"She got here first."

Delaney laughed without humor. "She always does."

A muscle in Kilkenny's jaw flexed. He turned and studied the woods, and Delaney tempered her voice into her normal tone that she'd been told made her sound detached but curious.

And she made her choice.

"Raisa will lead Isabel toward town," she said. She knew Isabel wouldn't let Raisa get away with that. Kilkenny didn't, though. She needed to buy time by sending him in the wrong direction. "She knows these woods. Better than Isabel."

"Maybe," Kilkenny said. But he wasn't taking off like she wanted him to. In fact, he glanced back toward the SUV like he was regretting not trying the radio again. She hoped he wouldn't. Her gadget only worked at close range.

"You know she's smart like that," Delaney pressed. She didn't want to suggest splitting up because he would get suspicious.

"I'll stay here. There's usually a signal," Delaney continued. "I'll call Sand."

He didn't necessarily believe her, she could see that on his face. But he wanted to save Raisa, so he convinced himself that Delaney was telling the truth.

But she *had* come to him in the library. It had built some kind of tentative trust, apparently. He didn't know the way Isabel could flip the script on a dime.

"Get Sand," Kilkenny said before leaping from the porch to the ground without bothering to take the stairs. He stopped right at the tree line, shifting halfway in her direction once more. She couldn't see his expression at this distance, but she braced for the question he only now seemed to realize he hadn't asked.

It came, demanding and urgent, like she knew it would.

"Why Raisa?"

"People forget," Delaney said softly, though she knew he'd hear. "That there were three sisters."

EXCERPT FROM PIA SUSANTO'S DIARY

We knew you were ours the moment we saw you. You were a little thing with big eyes. And you were so quiet, too. So serious. You didn't speak for the first six months that you were with us. Mama was worried, of course, because she's a worrier. But James and I? We knew you would talk to us when you had something to say.

The first word you said was *Lana*.

And then you cried and I cried and James cried and I was certain that we would all be crying for the rest of our days. How did such a little body hold so much trauma?

I swore that day I would never tell you who you really were.

That wasn't a fair decision. You should know James argued that you had a right to know who your birth parents were. You had a right to know that they wanted you. That they loved you. That you had darkness in your past but you also had light.

The second word you said to us was six weeks later. You called James Papa.

He never brought up telling you again.

I never said we were saints.

Maybe one day we will tell you, when you're older. Maybe one day you'll find Lana. And Isabel, too.

Maybe they'll love you like sisters should or maybe you'll fight like cats and dogs. Maybe they'll feel like family or like strangers or like something in between.

Maybe you'll hate us because we were the reason you didn't find them earlier.

We're not completely selfish. We knew the world is too curious about you, and because of that we needed to protect your identity.

So Lana and Isabel are hidden, too, just like you.

But just like you found us, I have a feeling you'll make your way back to them one day.

Even if you don't know who they are, some part of you will recognize them and think, *Mine*.

CHAPTER FORTY-THREE

RAISA

"You still haven't figured it out," Jenna said. Gone was the smirk. In its place was a strange, almost disappointed smile.

"This has been fun and all, but I'm done playing your games," Raisa said, distributing her weight onto both feet. She was ready. It was time. They were in a small clearing, but Raisa was close to the trees. A few steps and she would be swallowed up by the woods. She just needed the exact right moment to bolt. "Either tell me what you want to or don't. I don't give a shit. But don't expect me to take the bait."

"Aren't you curious how I know atonement is your weakness?" Jenna asked, her voice dangerously compelling. Raisa understood why she'd succeeded on her podcast despite the fact that it had been created for an ulterior motive.

"No," Raisa lied.

"I almost believed that. Once more with feeling, little one."

"You know what? Just shoot me."

Jenna waved to her face. "Are you sure I don't look familiar?"

Raisa's eyes trailed over the bright hair, over the tattoo by her eye, the ring in her nose and the bars in her brows. Jenna had been right. The decorations all caught her attention before the actual features.

Adrenaline still coursed through Raisa's veins from the gun-whipping Jenna had treated her to. Everything was more vibrant than it should be, the neon pink almost too much to look at, the moonlight glinting off the stud in her dimple. But Raisa started stripping each piece of that away. She studied the slope of her nose, the curve of her cheekbone, the divot in her chin.

A shadow slipped across the very edge of her memory. When Raisa went to grab hold of it, though, it shifted into nothingness.

"You're not very memorable," Raisa said.

"Maybe this will help." Anger had crept into Jenna's expression, but when she spoke, it was in a crooning, soft voice, pitched to sound much younger than she was. "Let me help you, sweetheart. Should we find the police?"

Raisa inhaled sharply as the shadow took shape. "No."

The girl from the fair. The day her parents had died, the one who had helped her.

"Yes." Jenna was gleeful.

"What the hell?" Raisa was too shocked to feel anything else. The only thing she knew to be true was that Jenna wasn't lying. Even if it had taken Jenna's prompting for Raisa to remember, she now could see the young woman so clearly, standing in front of the Ferris wheel, holding a gloved hand out. Raisa closed her eyes, saw the gentle swing of a ponytail.

Let me help you, sweetheart. And then an extended palm, a tug in the direction *away* from where Raisa had come. A fleeting thought that her parents were back behind them, but the girl, this girl, was someone she should listen to.

"I wanted to see what you were like," Jenna said, a little dreamily. "No longer a baby."

That got her eyes open once more. "What?"

"I didn't mean for your parents to die," Jenna continued. "You don't have to believe me, but I really didn't. They seemed like good people. I just wanted to see what you were like."

Bells rang in the distance, excited screams from kids on rides that were held together with bubble gum and hope. Bright lights that popped. Games. A few games, not too many. Her parents would be worried about her. But the girl was so nice. She smelled of strawberries and had pretty, long, dark hair, and when she hugged Raisa, it seemed like she meant it.

"You killed my parents?" Raisa asked, even though Jenna had just said she hadn't. Raisa was so confused, though, her mind refusing to acknowledge the burning sensation in her chest.

"I didn't," Jenna snapped, her voice no longer sugary. "I wanted to see what you were like."

It was the third time she'd said it, and it finally sank in. Raisa shook her head. "No."

"You're smarter than you're acting now," Jenna said. "Come on."

"We took so long to find the police," Raisa said, her fingers numb, her lips numb. "We took so long and they left."

It had been nighttime when they'd been coming to get her from the station. It was raining. They shouldn't have been driving then.

That's what the cruel voice in her head had always whispered to her. When she'd been lying awake in the latest foster home, praying no one opened her door in the middle of the night, that voice had whispered that she deserved all of it. Because she was the reason her parents were dead. When her stomach ached from hunger, when her bones ached from being pushed to the ground, when her heart ached from vicious words thrown carelessly in her direction, she'd told herself she'd deserved it.

What would it mean if she hadn't?

"You were sweet," Jenna said. "And a little bit naughty. And I thought maybe you could be my favorite, even over Lana."

Raisa closed her eyes against the truth of it, her world shifting on its axis. Delaney, Lana. Larissa, Raisa. They were close enough for girls who were too young to answer to a whole other name.

"What was your name?" Raisa didn't know why she asked it other than she was desperately trying to find her center. "At that time."

"Bella," Jenna said. "Beautiful."

For some reason, it was that answer that hit her the hardest, as if it were confirmation, more so than Jenna's taunts.

Raisa couldn't breathe. She bent over, hands on her knees, black curling in at the edges.

"It's okay, little one," Jenna said, all of a sudden much closer than she had been. Her palm cupped the nape of Raisa's neck, a protective gesture that felt so at odds with the past half hour that Raisa wondered if she was imagining it. "You were so young. Your foster parents never told you."

Rage fizzled through her bloodstream.

"My parents," Raisa managed to get out, slapping Jenna's arm away. She realized the gun was pointed at the ground, realized this was the moment to run.

And she also realized exactly what Kilkenny had known all along.

Jenna could make them dance. All she needed to do was flick the strings.

Because Raisa wasn't running, even though she could have.

Raisa wasn't a puppet.

She was an FBI agent. She was Raisa fucking Susanto. And Jenna Shaw wasn't going to tell her otherwise.

Raisa straightened. She softened her expression, letting her eyes go big and watery. If Raisa had learned anything from those diaries, it was that Jenna had always wanted to play the white knight. Hell, she'd even used Galahad for the killer's username.

But Jenna didn't remember they always had a weakness.

The damsel in despair.

She thought about her parents, the ones who raised her, let herself picture how scared they must have been when they'd seen those headlights coming toward them. Her eyes filled with real tears.

"Isabel," she murmured, letting her voice crack. Raisa reached up, slowly, like she was going to cup Jenna's cheek.

In a lightning-quick move, she curled her fingers around the barrel of the gun and wrenched it from Jenna's grip, just as she'd practiced hundreds of times in training. She took a step back, holding the sight on Jenna's chest.

The whole thing happened in the span of three heartbeats.

Raisa cherished Jenna's surprised anger, the little huff of breath, the line creasing her forehead. She so clearly and desperately wanted to hide it, to seem in control, as if she had planned on Raisa taking her gun.

But not even Jenna could sell it.

The satisfaction lasted for only another three heartbeats, because the darkness at the edge of the clearing shifted into something real. Something human.

Delaney stepped into the moonlight, her own weapon trained on Raisa.

Jenna started to laugh, an eerie sound that slithered along Raisa's skin.

"Well, isn't this grand?" Jenna said. "One big, happy family reunion."

CHAPTER
FORTY-FOUR

DELANEY

Isabel had left a clear trail through the woods—she had wanted to be followed. Of course she had. She thought Delaney would be on her side.

Why wouldn't she?

Delaney hadn't told the FBI she was a Parker, hadn't disclosed any of the information she knew about Isabel. From the outside, Isabel must be confident in where Delaney's loyalties lay.

And Delaney couldn't say she was wrong. But Isabel wasn't quite right, either.

Delaney wanted what was best for Isabel, but that didn't mean she was on her side.

She heard the voices before she could see either Isabel or Raisa, and she slowed. Delaney had a gun. She'd carried it since she turned eighteen, even though she'd never used it outside a shooting range.

Still, she'd practiced enough that the weight of the weapon was warm and familiar against her palm.

Delaney glanced over her shoulder. If she had been able to find this standoff easily, so would Kilkenny. How long did they have before they'd be interrupted?

She'd done her best to buy him some time. To buy *her* some time to figure out how to talk Isabel off this ledge.

It wouldn't be enough.

The answer here was obvious. She had a gun and the element of surprise on her side. But she couldn't quite give up on the hope that kept her from taking a knee shot from where she stood. Couldn't quite shake the guilt enough to put Isabel down for good like the rabid, feral thing she'd become.

"Your foster parents never told you," Isabel said a few feet away, cupping Raisa's neck.

"My parents," Raisa snapped back, and the déjà vu from Delaney's earlier conversation with Kilkenny slapped her in the face.

Growing up, it had always been her and Isabel against the world. Isabel had made sure of that. At the time, Isabel had become more than a sister—she'd been everything to Delaney. Her best friend, her mother, her priest, her teacher, her white knight. Delaney had lived the rest of her life since then as if she were in debt to her sister, but Isabel had made herself that way on purpose. She had put herself at the center of Delaney's universe and then blocked out anyone else so that Delaney could only care about her.

Now, knowing more about the way narcissists manipulated those around them, Delaney could see the emotional abuse for what it was. It hadn't left bruises on her arms like with Alex. But it had left scars.

Attic days.

She'd always thought it odd that Alex hadn't found them. Delaney hadn't misremembered the abuse—Alex had been a monster. But Isabel had also used Delaney's fear to her advantage. She'd stoked it from a low simmer into a wildfire until Delaney had helped cover up the slaughter of half of her family.

Her finger twitched against the trigger. And then the moonlight slid across Isabel's face, and Delaney softened. It was so easy to soften when she could see the bones of her sister beneath the face of a stranger.

How could you love a monster? But how could you not when they had become one by protecting you?

A flurry of movement happened between one breath and the next. Somehow, Raisa had the gun now.

Delaney's inhale was ragged. She didn't know what to do. All she could picture was her fantasy, the one she'd had before all this had happened. Of her and Isabel escaping to some country that existed outside the reach of the United States' legal system. The updated fantasy of both Raisa and Kilkenny deciding that it was best for everyone if they never found the Parker sisters. Of everything being wrapped up in a nice bow where they all lived happily ever after.

She knew, logically, that was absurd. They'd passed the line of no return so many times, so long ago that they couldn't even see it anymore.

But before she knew what she was planning on doing, Delaney stepped into the clearing, her own weapon pointed at Raisa.

Isabel started laughing.

Raisa's eyes flicked toward Delaney for only a split second before her attention was back on Isabel. Despite the fact that it was Delaney holding the gun, Raisa had assessed the threat. Delaney didn't blame her for identifying the real predator in these woods.

"So glad you decided to join us," Raisa said, ice dripping from her voice. "Lana."

Delaney wasn't like Isabel and Raisa. She didn't have any witty rejoinders, and right now terror and shame and love and guilt and hopelessness had frozen her tongue anyway. She didn't even have any demands. All she could do was neutralize Raisa's threat to Isabel.

When she didn't say anything, Raisa asked, "Did you know who I was?"

"Yes," Delaney managed.

Raisa laughed, but it was a mean, terrible sound. "Is that why you brought me on the case?"

"Yes. You were bait," Delaney admitted.

"What?"

It was Isabel who elaborated. "She knew I wouldn't be able to ignore your presence here. She was hoping she'd be able to see if there was anyone in particular who paid close attention to you. If it would draw me out of whatever disguise I wore."

She glanced at Delaney then, and they locked eyes for the first time in more than two decades. "You can't play a player, darling."

"And yet here we are," Delaney said softly and had the pleasure of watching awareness flicker into Isabel's expression. Now Delaney knew exactly what name Isabel went by. She knew what she looked like as an adult. She knew the ways her sister could hide in plain sight.

All because Isabel had gone after Raisa.

Just like Delaney had predicted she would.

"Do you know what she plans on doing?" Raisa asked, still looking at Isabel. But the question was clearly directed at Delaney.

"She plans on killing us both. I'll have already sent a confession letter to Sand, probably, admitting that I was responsible for all the deaths, including yours," Delaney said, as calmly as she could. She had always known Isabel wanted her to take the fall for the Balduccis and Terri Harden, but it wasn't hard to figure out where Raisa fit into the plan.

Isabel clapped lightly.

"But why deviate from the list?" Delaney asked Isabel. "Raisa hasn't done anything wrong."

"There's exactly one restaurant in town," Isabel said with what sounded like true regret in her voice. "She talked to Greg."

Greg Balducci. One of those lines of no return. Delaney had wanted Raisa to be bait, but she truly hadn't thought Isabel would add her to her list. Isabel had only ever killed those who deserved it before.

This was a deviation.

But that's how feral things survived. A threat was a threat, and it couldn't be allowed to live.

"How were you going to kill us?" Delaney couldn't help but ask.

Isabel didn't look at her. "Quickly."

"Why Delaney? Because she lied when she was a child?" Raisa asked. "That was the social worker's fault. She questioned Delaney in front of your parents. There's no way that—"

"You might not want to speak on things you don't know about, little one," Isabel said, cutting Raisa off.

Raisa took a breath, likely hearing the edge of rage in Isabel's voice now. There was some calculation in her eyes when she glanced at Delaney once more. Whatever she was about to say was her attempt at de-escalating the serial killer.

"How did you know Isabel had found me?" she asked.

Isabel was the one who answered. "Scottsdale."

"Christ, does everyone know about that?"

"You were on my radar anyway because you talked about Alex in your lecture," Delaney said, offering her the longer answer because Raisa deserved to know everything. Even if Delaney decided this was where their stories ended, she still deserved to know. "I've been tracking Isabel's hacker for a while now. Like I said, I'm good with patterns. They left a trail that led to Scottsdale, which in turn led to you."

"Good help is so hard to find," Isabel said.

"They're good," Delaney assured her. "I'm just better."

"I'll still have to kill them."

Delaney ignored her bluster for what it was. "I don't believe in coincidences. I started looking into possible connections. The first thing I stumbled on were rumors that the case had gone south in a way that was unusual for you. I put two and two together and got four."

"Coincidences," Raisa huffed out. "What about me giving lectures on my own goddamn family?"

"It's actually not so strange, is it?" Delaney asked. "Linguistics is math more than anything else. I've heard you say that before."

Isabel hummed, her face alight with curiosity. Delaney guessed that's what she looked like sometimes—and also realized why it was disturbing to some people.

"It's like twins who were separated at birth," Isabel said, with that weirdly guileless enthusiasm. "They gravitate toward the same vacation spots, have the same favorite foods, end up in the same city even if they were raised a country apart. Genes are a powerful thing. They dictate who we are."

"They don't," Raisa snapped.

Isabel made a sweeping gesture to encompass the three of them and vocalized exactly what Delaney had been thinking earlier. "Look at us, little one. How can you even argue?"

"Because both of you are willing to kill people, and I'm not."

"Oh really?" Isabel crooned and then took three steps, until the barrel of Raisa's gun pressed into her chest, just above her heart. "Are you sure about that?"

Raisa took three quick steps back, smartly putting distance between them once more. Isabel's move had likely been a play to get the weapon back.

"Get on your knees."

Isabel sighed. "I don't know why I even bothered with you. You're nothing but a disappointment."

Delaney couldn't swear to it, but she thought she saw Raisa flinch. That was Isabel's power. Even when you knew you shouldn't want her approval, you craved it anyway.

Raisa recovered, though, and shot a look at Delaney. "We can bring her in together, Delaney. This doesn't have to end in bloodshed."

Isabel watched them with narrowed eyes. She didn't like that they knew each other, didn't like that they'd had interactions that she hadn't been involved in.

"Well, look at you two." Isabel's voice took on a silky-smooth coating, one that Delaney instinctually recognized as dangerous. "So chummy."

"I'll be charged with conspiracy to commit murder, at best," Delaney felt compelled to point out. Despite the fact that it wasn't as terrifying as other aspects of this moment, it still was a factor.

"But you haven't actually killed anyone yet," Raisa said. "Just drop your gun. That's all you have to do."

Something shifted in Isabel's expression, in her body language. She almost smiled at Delaney, her shoulders rounding in a soft welcome. "But Delaney's a good girl. You learned your lesson, didn't you, babe? Family sticks together."

"I'm your family, too," Raisa said.

But it was different. They all knew that. Raisa had been a baby. And she'd grown up not even knowing who she was.

Isabel and Delaney had always known.

"Why didn't you tell her?" Isabel asked Delaney. It was quiet, as if Raisa wouldn't hear. "About me."

"I was hoping I could save you," Delaney admitted.

"Aww," Isabel said, hand over her heart. "You were worried for me."

Delaney waggled the gun she still held on an FBI agent all so that Isabel could walk free. "You think?"

Isabel smirked.

"I don't want to hurt Raisa," Delaney told Isabel. "And you don't want to kill her, I know you don't. We can disappear, just the two of us. We're both good at starting over."

"You know that can't happen," Isabel said. And if Delaney didn't know better, she'd say she sounded . . . sad. "You know what I'll do to you."

Isabel didn't let go of grudges, didn't cross a name off her list once it was added on. Death was the only way out. The one exception had been Samantha Mason, and her penance had been steep. Having had to clean up the deaths of her two close friends and then lie about it professionally for years couldn't have been a walk in the park.

"Delaney, we both have weapons and she has nothing," Raisa said. *She has nothing.*

But Isabel didn't look like a woman who had nothing. She was calm, with a slight smile on her face. It was the first time Delaney wondered what her endgame was. Delaney had thought it was to kill Raisa, then fake Delaney's suicide, and escape into the night with none the wiser. Perhaps she'd run into Kilkenny in the woods and kill him too, or maybe she'd just let his grief eat him alive before he could worry about her.

The only other option hit Delaney like a blow to the solar plexus.

Isabel had a backup plan. You didn't live a life like she did without one.

"You have to end it, Lana," Isabel said, reading the shock on Delaney's face. "I don't want to kill you."

But the compulsion—the one that had driven her to take a straight razor to their parents' necks—would make her do it. She was asking to be put down before she stepped over a line she knew she *would* but didn't want to cross.

Raisa was smart. "No, Delaney. She doesn't have to die. Stop listening to her—she's not in control here. If we arrest her, she'll pay for her crimes. But she'll be alive."

"I'm not meant for jail, Lana," Isabel said, and Delaney let herself squeeze her eyes shut for one precious second. The names were throwing her, cutting her ties with reality. She was Delaney Moore. This was Isabel Parker in front of her. Their sister, Larissa . . . No, Raisa. Delaney shook her head as Isabel went on. "I wanted it to end here. Can't you feel how right it is? Take the shot, make it clean."

Something in Delaney snapped, and she found her tongue.

"Christ, always pulling the puppet strings right up to the end, huh, Isabel?" Delaney spit out, resentful and bitter that Isabel always got what she wanted. Because this, right here, was Delaney's punishment.

Just because Isabel was a monster didn't mean it would make it any easier for Delaney to kill her. It would leave Delaney untethered, lost and without the only family she loved.

"I was wrong," Isabel said, her voice going a bit dreamy. "I thought the best way for this to end was to frame you for Raisa's death. But this is so much better. It's perfect, really, don't you see?"

Delaney did see it, of course. The way she would pay the price for her betrayal was to kill her sister, to finally become the murderer that Isabel had turned herself into to protect Delaney.

"Don't make me do this," Delaney said and felt something wet against her cheek, against her chin. Tears. She couldn't remember the last time she'd cried.

"Oh, little Lana, I'm not making you do anything," Isabel said. "You always have a choice."

Raisa shifted, like she was going to take her gun off Isabel and aim it at Delaney.

And in that tiny movement, everything clicked into place.

Isabel always got what she wanted.

There was no backup plan.

"No," Delaney yelled, but she was too late. Raisa had finally taken her full attention off Isabel.

Before Raisa could react, Isabel pulled a gun from the waistband of her pants. She didn't hesitate like Raisa or Delaney would have.

She aimed. She fired.

She hit her target.

CHAPTER FORTY-FIVE

RAISA

The bullet tore into Raisa, shredding flesh, piercing bone.

Raisa's finger pressed against her own trigger.

Delaney screamed again. *"No."*

But the time for talking was over.

She got Isabel in the chest. A head shot would have been cleaner, but with the wound, the distractions, and the darkness, Raisa had played it safe.

Isabel collapsed and Delaney sprinted to her sister, dropping her own gun as she did.

Raisa used the last of her strength to direct her own weakening body toward Delaney's discarded weapon. She landed on top of it, and decided that would have to be good enough.

She stared at the trees swaying above her and wondered if she'd killed her own sister. Raisa felt nothing at the thought—just a deep, welling grief for the people she had called parents, the ones who had actually made her who she was today. Their love, their patience, their strength of will had shaped her life long after they had gone.

And Raisa could rationalize all she wanted—she knew in this moment of clarity and pain that she was the reason they had died. It didn't matter that she had been tricked that day at the fair. Isabel might have been the one to lead her away, but why had Isabel been there in the first place?

Raisa. She really *had* deserved all the misery that followed that fateful day.

Everything came back to Raisa and her family, whose blood was clearly tainted by darkness.

Genes are a powerful thing. They dictate who we are.

They don't, Raisa had said, though she hadn't actually believed her own denial.

She was just a different flavor of monster—one who brought terror into people's lives. One who brought *Isabel* into people's lives.

Her parents.

The girl in Scottsdale.

How many others?

Someone in the distance yelled her name.

Kilkenny. *Kilkenny.* Just one more of her victims. Because he was about to find her, just a bit too late, possibly, and the grief would eat him alive.

Still, it was a relief that he was here. He would take care of the rest of the mess.

She closed her eyes and the world faded to black.

CHAPTER FORTY-SIX

DELANEY

Isabel crumpled like a puppet whose strings had been cut.

A ringing in Delaney's head drowned out every thought other than needing to get to her sister.

Her knees hit the ground right next to Isabel's prone body, her hands scrambling to find the wound.

They came away wet. Like her tears. Except this time it was blood. Too much blood.

She tugged at Isabel's clothes so she could find the bullet hole. *Pressure,* some distant part of her urged. She needed to apply pressure.

"Lana."

It was nothing more than a rasp, but when Delaney looked up, Isabel's eyes were open and alert.

She wore a half smile, revealing a crooked canine tooth that Delaney had forgotten about. She'd thought she remembered her sister in such detail, but she had changed so much. The baby softness of her teenage face maturing into the sharp lines of a fox.

Still, there was the tooth and her eyes and the way she looked at Delaney like she'd tear down the whole world for her.

Something crashed into the clearing behind them, something big and loud and frantic.

Delaney knew it was Kilkenny without looking.

"Help Raisa," she said, not taking her attention off Isabel.

Kilkenny probably hadn't needed the directive. Of course he'd go to his partner first.

Delaney licked dry lips, her skirt now wet from the blood—the life—seeping out of her sister's body.

There was no way they'd make it back to the hotel, not if a medical team wasn't on Kilkenny's heels.

"Anyone else coming?" she called over to Kilkenny, who didn't respond.

She wondered if Raisa was dead and then put the thought out of her mind.

"Let it be, Lana," Isabel managed before coughing. The jarring hacks seemed to sap the energy out of her, though, because her body went limp when the fit was done.

"Why couldn't *you* have just let it be?" Delaney asked.

There was no answer.

EXCERPT FROM DELANEY MOORE'S DIGITAL JOURNAL

I used to tell myself I'd be able to stop you. Even as I watched the news for unexplained deaths.

What does that say about me? Hubris is so often the downfall of Gods, and, me, a mere mortal, believed I could change both of our fates.

Only . . . I remember you, the real you, before vengeance and justice became the bars that locked you in a prison of your own making.

I remember when I fell off my bike and you drew me pink flowers in chalk on the sidewalk to make me feel better; I remember you climbing into my bed to tell me fairytales when I couldn't sleep after a scary movie; I remember you bringing apples into the attic when we were hiding from him.

I remember the way you loved—fully, with actions more so than words. I love the way you love.

I just wish it wouldn't have brought us here.

Do you ever think about what might have happened? If we'd just . . . left Everly? We could have driven all the way across the country to New York City, the place you used to talk about like it was Camelot. We would have gotten meaningless jobs and shared an apartment the size of a broom closet, and yet we might have been happy?

Or were you always destined to become a monster? Are we all? Us Parker girls, our lives defined by circumstance and blood.

You just posted the video I've been dreading.

It was for me. A message? A dare? A test?

I love the way you love, Isabel.

But here's the way I love—I'm going to save you. I'm going to save all three of us.

Maybe that's me flying too close to the sun, but I've also come to accept one truth—if I burn to ash, I promise I'm taking you with me.

CHAPTER FORTY-SEVEN

RAISA

Raisa's shoulder ached from physical therapy, and the slate-gray Seattle sky matched her terrible mood.

She didn't want to be here.

She couldn't be anywhere else.

There was one bright spot in the day—Kilkenny. He was waiting for her on the courthouse steps looking extra dapper and distinguished in his perfectly tailored suit.

Most of that night in the woods with Isabel and Delaney was a blur, but Raisa was pretty sure she would forever remember that moment of knowing Kilkenny was there, that he would take care of everything. Of realizing she could close her eyes.

He later confessed that he'd thought he'd lost her then.

One more thing to feel guilty about.

Aren't you curious how I know atonement is your weakness?

Raisa shook her head to get rid of Isabel's voice, which had haunted her for the past three months. She'd started turning the TV on at home, started blasting the radio while she was in the shower, become addicted to podcasts on her runs—all to avoid silence that could so easily be filled by memories.

I thought maybe you could be my favorite.

She forced a smile for Kilkenny that became real as she got closer to him. She hadn't seen him since she'd woken up in the hospital, but they texted nearly every day now. They were friends, almost, and she was genuinely glad to see him despite the circumstances.

When he noticed her, his eyes immediately dropped to her shoulder. The mess hadn't been pretty that night, and it still looked like something that had been chewed up by a wild animal, the scar tissue thick and pink, a stark reminder. But Isabel had managed to get off a clean shot. If she hadn't, Raisa could be dead now instead of having a bum joint, and a long road of recovery in front of her. That was what she told herself when she was sweating through PT.

Kilkenny made the wise choice and kept silent about it. She'd taken to snapping at him whenever he asked how she was doing. She was no longer on death's door and she didn't need his paternal hovering—even if it was only via text. A part of her knew, though, that Kilkenny felt responsible for her now.

The saving grace was that she felt responsible for him now, too.

At least it was mutual.

"Are they letting you testify?" She hadn't asked before, hadn't been allowed to talk officially about the case. That's what happened when it turned out one of your biological sisters was a serial killer and the other had been her quasi accomplice.

At night, over drinks cities apart, Kilkenny sometimes quibbled over Delaney's role. They always alluded to it vaguely, just in case someone subpoenaed their text messages, but it was obvious who he was talking about.

He was convinced that Delaney had played a smaller part in everything than the prosecutor wanted to make it seem. Then he started talking about psychology and dominant and submissive criminal duos and Raisa would have to shut him up with an absurd GIF that offended his sensibilities.

They both let her get away with it because it was her not-so-subtle signal that she didn't have the mental or emotional capacity to deal with whatever he was saying.

It didn't matter either way. Delaney had gotten a fancy lawyer, who had successfully argued that there was no way to prove that she had known Isabel was reading those journal entries. There was nothing linking Delaney to the deaths themselves—no thank-you messages to Isabel, no hints that she knew what would happen if she mentioned a "bad guy" on the website.

The argument was helped by the fact that Isabel had hacked her way into Delaney's account. Delaney had never actually friended Isabel, which for some reason gave her plausible deniability when it came to the murders.

On the day that Delaney was cleared of any charges, Kilkenny sent Raisa a recommendation for therapists in Tacoma. Raisa had saved the information despite the fact that she wasn't sure she had the words to talk about everything that had happened, even with a trained professional.

There was violence in her blood. There was a family history full of grief and trauma and neglect that she couldn't even begin to grapple with.

Every time Raisa tried to think of starting to *consider* dealing with the fallout from all that, her brain went blank. There would be times she found herself staring at a wall, then looking at the time and realizing she'd been paralyzed for hours, not moving, not thinking.

There were nights she woke up in a sweat-soaked bed, her fingers clutching around a straight razor that only lived in her nightmares.

Raisa forced another easy smile when she noticed Kilkenny holding the door for her. She must have stopped walking, frozen. How much time had she missed?

"You okay?" he asked quietly. There was no judgment in his voice, but she made a mental note to look up some of those therapists he'd sent her.

Because she knew the answer to his question.

And she knew she was lying when she answered, "Yeah, sorry."

They found seats in the back row of the courtroom. The place was packed with spectators and journalists and even people Raisa recognized from her short stint in Everly.

It made her skin feel too tight over her bones. Despite the fact that she'd been shot in the middle of the woods, it was crowds that made her skittish now. Kilkenny gently touched her shoulder in support as he sat on the hard wooden bench that reminded Raisa of a pew.

The door opened to bring in the defendant.

Isabel Parker looked far less chic than she had back when she was playing the role of Jenna Shaw. Her pink hair had faded; the metal had been stripped out of her face. The conservative suit was tailored but didn't fit her, not the way ripped fishnets and Doc Martens had.

She was pale, as if those three pints of blood she'd lost back in the woods before the medics had gotten to her had never been replenished.

But she didn't look small or cowed. Instead, she looked smug.

And she was staring at Kilkenny.

He, in turn, watched Isabel with narrowed eyes, his shoulders tense. "What?" Raisa asked.

"She seems . . ." Kilkenny trailed off. "Happy."

Kilkenny was right. Of course he was.

Isabel might have been playing them that night in the woods— getting Raisa to start to view Delaney as the bigger threat than her. But Raisa didn't think she'd been lying. She wouldn't do well in jail. Masterminds only succeeded in situations like that in TV shows and movies. In real life, Isabel would get her ass beaten on the first day in.

While Raisa didn't know many details from the official case, she had to assume the prosecutors had managed to compile enough evidence for several consecutive life sentences. As long as they weren't completely incompetent.

Yet Isabel still looked happy.

"She's watching me," Kilkenny observed, his thumb toying with his wedding band.

That observation was both true and unsurprising. Out of everyone Isabel could have blamed for that night, she had emerged with a grudge against Kilkenny for saving her. She'd wanted to die out there rather than pay for her crimes, but Kilkenny had thought to call in emergency services once he no longer had to deal with Delaney blocking his cell service.

The forethought hadn't been what had saved Raisa. Nothing serious had been hit—she would have lived even if Kilkenny'd had to carry her out of the woods himself. But it could have, so in theory, she owed him big.

Isabel seemed to feel the same way, if her rant when she'd woken up in the hospital was anything to go by. But when she talked about owing Kilkenny big, it wasn't in quite the same way as Raisa did.

Through the opening of the trial, Isabel kept glancing back at them, wearing that same obnoxious smirk from the woods.

"I don't like this," Kilkenny said quietly.

Raisa didn't, either. The lawyers were talking, but Raisa couldn't pay enough attention to hear what they said, her mind working through the possibilities.

Except she didn't need to wonder long.

Kilkenny's phone pinged, loud enough for the judge to shoot a warning look in their direction. The hunger on Isabel's face was clear and terrifying.

Raisa couldn't help but glance at Kilkenny's screen.

On it was a screenshot of a headline.

Seventy-two hours before execution, serial killer says

FBI agent's wife wasn't one of his victims

Beneath it, the subheadline read:

> While giving an interview for an HBO documentary, the Alphabet Man admits that Shay Kilkenny, the wife of the FBI agent who eventually caught him, didn't die by his hand.

"Kilkenny," Raisa said, though she wasn't sure if it was a warning or a comfort.

It didn't matter, because Kilkenny pushed to his feet and then slammed out of the courtroom, the doors banging against the outside wall.

A hush fell over the spectators and Raisa met Isabel's eyes across the distance that separated them.

And Isabel smiled.

In that moment, Raisa truly understood how much she could hate someone else. In that moment, she looked at Isabel and thought, *Mine.* Not in the way a sister recognized a sister, but how a predator locked onto prey.

Raisa wasn't sure how Isabel had managed to get the Alphabet Man to lie about Shay, but she knew without a doubt that her sister had a hand in it. And she would pay for this latest cruelty. Raisa would make sure of that.

For the first time since the clearing, Raisa felt grounded. She had been untethered the last three months—unsure of how to reconstruct herself out of these new foundational blocks. She had started to view herself as Larissa Parker, with all the baggage that entailed.

But that was not who she was. Her parents were Pia and James Susanto, and they had taught her how to be kind and smart and tough.

Against all odds, she'd become a respected FBI agent and a leader in her field of study.

She'd faced down a psychopath with a gun and emerged the winner.

She was Raisa fucking Susanto.

As she stood to chase Kilkenny down, she vowed that no one—including Isabel Parker, including herself—would ever forget that again.

ACKNOWLEDGMENTS

This book wouldn't have been possible without the work of real-life forensic linguists and their generosity in sharing their knowledge, techniques, and tricks of the trade. Linguist Robert Leonard is a real-life hero who has helped solve multiple cases with the use of language. His lectures and seminars on YouTube were especially helpful. Other experts whose work helped lend authenticity to this story: (legendary) FBI Agent Jim Fitzgerald; Malcolm Coulthard, Alison Johnson, and David Wright, the authors of *An Introduction to Forensic Linguistics: Language in Evidence*; Jan Svartvik, author of *The Evans Statements, a Case for Forensic Linguistics*; Alison May and Rui Sousa-Silva, who authored *The Routledge Handbook of Forensic Linguistics* along with Coulthard; and Jess Jann Shapero, who wrote "The Language of Suicide Notes" as her thesis.

I'd also like to thank the whole team at Thomas & Mercer, including but not limited to Megha Parekh, Charlotte Herscher, Sarah Shaw, Gracie Doyle, and so many others who have made this book sparkle and shine and find its way into the hands of readers.

I'm forever grateful to Abby Saul, my agent and the best first reader an author could ever ask for. Our mojo rocks.

As ever, so many thanks go to my family and friends, whose support I could not do without.

And to my readers: Thank you so much for trusting me with your time and attention. I hope it was a fun ride!

ABOUT THE AUTHOR

Photo © 2019

Brianna Labuskes is the Amazon Charts and *Washington Post* bestsell-ing author of the psychological suspense novels *What Can't Be Seen*, *A Familiar Sight*, *Her Final Words*, *Black Rock Bay*, *Girls of Glass*, and *It Ends with Her*. She was born in Harrisburg, Pennsylvania, and gradu-ated from Penn State University with a degree in journalism. For the past eight years, she has worked as an editor at both small-town papers and national media organizations such as Politico and Kaiser Health News, covering politics and policy. Brianna lives in Washington, DC, and enjoys traveling, hiking, kayaking, and exploring the city's best brunch options. Visit her at www.briannalabuskes.com.